A WORLD APART

'You're talking about Sam, aren't you?' Winnie nodded her head up and down wisely. 'You're remembering that married man from London who talked posh. You've never said a word about him ever since, but you're talking about him now.'

Daisy blushed. 'I thought the world had come to an end when he went back to his wife. But when I married Joshua I knew how silly I'd been. I could hardly believe I was that same woman who had wanted to die for love of a man I hardly knew.'

'And you think that when I marry Leonard I'll forget all about Chuck?'

Daisy put all the conviction she could into her voice. 'There's nothing more sure.'

'You never ever think of Sam? Not even now and again?'

'Never,' said Daisy, lying in her teeth.

A World Apart

MARIE JOSEPH

Gainsborough Press

This edition published in 1996 by Gainsborough Press
An imprint of Leopard
20 Vauxhall Bridge Road, London SW1V 2SA

London Melbourne Sydney Auckland
Johannesburg and agencies throughout the world

First published by Century 1988
Arrow edition 1989
Reprinted 1989 and 1990

Printed and bound in Great Britain by
Cox & Wyman Ltd, Reading, Berkshire

ISBN 0 752 90406 X

For my friend Bunty with grateful thanks

PART ONE

Chapter One

Folks said that the wind was coming straight from Siberia. In Blackpool skaters glided over the frozen lake in Stanley Park, and a six-inch layer of snow turned the Fylde countryside into a living postcard.

In the coldest winter in living memory folks ventured outdoors only when necessary – wearing three of everything, sometimes even in bed.

Snowstorms stopped trains from running, and biting blizzards kept ships in port. In the first week in February, Shinwell told a shocked House of Commons that the power stations were so dangerously low on coal stocks that electricity would be turned off for five hours a day to save fuel.

The war was over and done with, but slowly and surely the country was freezing to a halt.

It was 1947.

Daisy Penny, standing on a snow-packed pavement in her third queue of the morning, accepted that she was going to be late back from the shops. She knew she'd have to look sharp to get the dinner on and ready in time, and the washing-up done afterwards. All before the electricity went off again at two o'clock. Her feet were solid blocks of ice, and she could imagine the gyp her chilblains would give her that night in bed.

She asked herself who in their right mind would be a landlady when it looked as if rationing was going to go on for ever even though the war was over? Then reminded herself that Blackpool had come off lucky.

One solitary bomb on Seed Street and North Station, that was all.

In fact Daisy knew she should be feeling glad and grateful for all kinds of reasons, but that morning she was feeling as nowt as a wasp, so she thrust all positive thoughts firmly aside. She had the reputation of being such a good and imaginative cook that it had been said she could make a meal out of a dishcloth if needs be, but Daisy was fed up to the back teeth of making do. She had jokily promised her boarders a toasted crumpet with a poached egg in every other hole when the war was over, but up to now there was no earthly chance of that coming true!

The rations were hardly worth the bother of queuing up for. One person was allowed a measly one and a half ounces of cheese. Hardly enough to tempt a mouse into a trap. One solitary ounce of cooking fat. Daisy shuffled forward, leaned sideways and calculated that at this rate she could actually have a toe inside the butcher's shop within ten minutes. She moved another step forward and settled herself deeper into the woollen scarf wound three times round her neck. She looked at the woman in front of her, who was wearing a fur coat that the moths had claimed as their own years ago, topped with a man's flat cap tied underneath her chin with a long khaki muffler.

What price glamour? Daisy set quite a store on glamour. Even during the darkest days of the war when she had done her stint as an air-raid warden she had walked the blacked-out streets wearing her tin hat at a rakish angle, thinking it suited her better than straight on. She wasn't vain, she was sure of that. To be vain you had to be pretty and Daisy had never seen herself as that. Not ugly, mind you; not so plain that a man had never been tempted. Not like poor little Miss

Grimshaw, one of her regulars, who had once confided she would die as pure as the day she'd been born.

'But then, no man has ever tempted me,' she'd said, 'so how do I know whether I'd have succumbed or not?'

Poor Miss Grimshaw, not to have had even the most fleeting moments of passion to look back on. Daisy's expression was smug as she faced the butcher at last. She handed over her ration books, and flashed him what she thought of as her Betty Grable smile, all twinkling teeth and fluttering eyelashes. When she whispered that she'd like best mince for now, a piece of topside for the weekend, and was there a chance that he had a rabbit going spare, the butcher sighed and made a great to-do of wiping over the bloodied chopping block with a damp rag.

'And don't go telling me there's a war on,' Daisy said gaily, sliding her flirty eyes away from his stained apron, worn over an ex-army greatcoat to keep out the cold. 'We've won. Remember?'

'Bloody Germans.' A man behind her dressed like a Commando in a black boiler suit, with his face swallowed up in a balaclava helmet, stamped his boots up and down in the sawdust. 'By the left, but they've a lot to answer for. Followed old Hitler like sheep they did, and now not one of them reckons he'd recognize him if he passed him in the street. It'll be the same as after the last war; they'll be living off the fat of the land in no time.'

'The Germans are actually starving, as a matter of fact.' The butcher was in that kind of mood when he would have contradicted the Pope right to His Holiness's face rather than agree. 'Berlin is in ruins, like the rest of their country. They've been reduced to eating dogs and rats. So now you know,' he added, going hastily through into the back for Daisy's mince.

'Who started it, then? That's what I'd like to know.'

The man in black turned round to address the shop at large.

'We've come to something when we've to kow-tow to a bugger like that for half a pound of stewing steak.'

'I'd lick his boots for a nice thick piece of fillet,' a woman said, then went quiet as the butcher reappeared.

'Here you are, Mrs Penny.' He handed over a wrapped parcel, winking at Daisy to indicate, she hoped, that it contained all she'd asked for, as well as a skinned rabbit.

Making sure of keeping quids in, she winked back.

She had the mince in a big pan with carrots, onions and a handful of barley before she got round to taking her coat off. In the steamer a bright yellow sponge made with dried egg and the minimum of fat was rising nicely, pushing up its mobcap of greaseproof paper. And now the dinner was organized and on the go, Daisy could relax for a minute or two.

Out of season the boarding house, with the name of Shangri-La, now a Guest House since the war to give it more tone, was barely half full. In the lounge, little Miss Grimshaw was sitting hunched up to the coal fire, crouching over it to make the most of it, as if the government were just waiting to put it out at two o'clock. Of an indeterminate age, she was all protruding bones and teeth; so thin that once Winnie Whalley had reckoned that the elderly spinster could be posted underneath a door without flattening her perm.

Daisy could hear Winnie now, singing a mournful-sounding song at the top of her voice as she got on with giving the landing and the stairs their weekly bottoming. Daisy blessed the day ten years ago when the scrawny red-haired fifteen-year-old girl had come to work for her. Winnie, for all her apparent lack of muscle, could clean a bedroom in double quick time, flinging wardrobes and dressing tables about as if they were matchboxes.

She came into the lounge now, muffled to the eyebrows in a sailor's pullover, hand-knitted in navy oiled wool, her chin sunk deep into the polo neck.

'You'll singe the hairs off your legs if you don't move back from the fire, Miss Grimshaw,' she said. 'I thought I could smell something burning from upstairs.'

Daisy could tell Miss Grimshaw wasn't in the least put out. It was no good trying to curb Winnie's tongue. She said exactly what she was thinking, straight out, the minute she thought it. She had made herself so much a part of Daisy's family that their troubles were hers, their dramas part and parcel of her own life. If Daisy had asked her to put her hand in the fire, she would have done so; for Joshua, Daisy's husband, she would have laid down her life.

She followed Daisy into the kitchen, closing the door behind her.

'Miss Grimshaw says the Bolshies in this new Labour Government are keeping the middle classes half frozen on starvation rations, to bring them down to the workers' level.'

'It'll be a Socialist plot.' Daisy laughed. 'Poor Miss Grimshaw. I doubt if the world she grew up in will ever be the same.'

'Up the Revolution,' Winnie said, making a start on the potatoes, working in rhythm with Daisy, sidestepping her as neatly as a ballet dancer. 'By the way, the kids are upstairs in their room. Sent home from school on account of a burst boiler. They've been as quiet as mice for over an hour now. God knows what they're up to.'

Immediately, still holding a wooden spoon in her hand, Daisy went to the foot of the stairs.

'Oliver? Sally? What are you doing up there?'

'Nothing! We're not doing nothing!' There was a hint of bravado in Oliver's young hoarse voice. The last thing he wanted was his mother coming upstairs, just when they'd stripped both their beds and up-ended two chairs to make a den on the carpet.

'We're not doing nothing!' Sally's voice was an echo of her brother's.

'Well, stop it then. This minute!'

Daisy almost decided to run up and investigate, but changed her mind. She was fretting a bit because the mince should have been flash-fried first to seal in the flavour, but there hadn't been the time. There never seemed to be the time to do anything properly these days. In a strange way her life had been more organized during the war when the house had been full of airmen billeted on her. The children had been easier too, as babies sleeping in prams. Or even when things got too hectic, in carry-cots in the kitchen.

Making do had made you feel patriotic during the war, as if you were doing your bit and helping us to win. Now that the war was over, the satisfaction of making do was wearing a bit thin. In her present mood she could almost make herself believe that Miss Grimshaw was right. That the Bolshies in the government were trying to wear everyone down to the same drab grey level.

'Well, here goes,' she said, watering down a pint of milk for pouring-custard to go with the jam sponge. Smiling, as if she thought it was all a bit of a lark.

She didn't fool Winnie – not for a minute. What Winnie didn't know about her employer could be stuck underneath an eyelid without making her blink.

Daisy had a calm face, not a wrinkle in sight, even though Winnie knew for a fact that she was thirty-seven if she was a day. Daisy kept all her real feelings tight inside her. She never shouted her head off or howled like a dog when something terrible happened. When Joshua had nearly died in hospital before the last Christmas but one she'd gone serenely around the house just as if he'd gone in for an inflamed bunion, and not to almost cough his stomach up.

Winnie didn't know how she did it. It wasn't because Daisy had no feelings. Sometimes the empty sadness in her eyes made you look away. You knew she was worried sick about Joshua being ill so often and having to take so much time off his teaching job at Preston. She was nearly out of her mind with worry right now, but you'd never know by listening to her moaning about the shortages, when Winnie knew for a fact she could have turned a couple of carrots and an Oxo cube into a banquet.

Feelings were there to be let out. Winnie firmly believed that. How else could she have gone on living, when in the first year of the war the boy she loved with all her heart and soul had been shot down over Belgium? And how could she have faced the truth when the GI who had promised to send for her to follow him to America, had sent her a letter saying he was very sorry but he was marrying a girl called MaryLou?

That time Daisy had come into her room and got into bed with her, to hold her shaking and quivering, and promise her that someone else would come along, and that some day Chuck would be just a memory of a tall, fair, bristle-haired young man who had cycled over from his army camp at Lytham and swept her off her feet.

'It's long past the time Joshua should be back from Preston,' Winnie said, knowing she was speaking out of turn but not caring. 'He's not fit to be out in weather like this. He's no right to be sitting in an unheated train. What if he's collapsed on his way back from the station? What if he's lying out there buried deep in a snowdrift?'

Daisy went on with what she was doing without turning round from the stove. 'This is Blackpool, love, not the North Pole.'

If Winnie did but know it, being buried alive in a snowdrift was a mere nothing, a piece of cake, as the young men billeted on her would have said, compared to the terrible disasters her vivid imagination had been conjuring up all morning.

Winnie was quite right. Joshua hadn't been fit to go out first thing, even to an interview he reckoned was so important it couldn't be missed. He was fifty-two, that was all. Nowhere near the age of retirement, but Daisy knew it in her bones that the powers-that-be were going to suggest to him that when he returned to work it would be on a part-time basis. Until his health improved. His salary had been paid all through the long weeks of his increasingly frequent absences. But there was a new brand of teacher coming up, trained by the government's Emergency Scheme. Daisy had seen two of them at Oliver's and Sally's junior school. One an ex-paratrooper, bursting with ideas, and the other a girl from ENSA, fresh from entertaining the troops in the Far East. Now, after merely one year at college, she was in charge of the nine to ten-year-olds, who hung on her every word, because using her professional experience she made them act out most of their lessons.

Daisy hoped with a great sigh that Joshua wasn't going to be replaced eventually by an eager beaver young enough to be his son. Joshua's work was highly specialized. He had a special rapport with the backward children in the big red-brick school on the outskirts of Preston. Daisy had seen a fourteen-year-old mongol child snuggle herself on to his knee, staring up at him with adoration. She had seen him coax a spastic boy to speak and smile through the laboured contortions of his face muscles. And she had seen him weep when a tiny lad with a wasting disease had died.

Winnie was keeping her mouth shut just for once. She knew the score, and in her opinion Joshua would be lucky to keep his job. She had seen him slowly wither in the past two years, grow more stoop-shouldered and grey-faced. Her heart ached for what dismissal would do to him.

'I think that's Joshua coming in now,' she said, testing a salt cellar for its pouring ability on the back of her hand, tossing a pinch over her left shoulder for the luck she felt was going to be needed.

But it wasn't Joshua. Instead it was two civil servants wearing tightly belted beige gaberdine raincoats and black berets, like lady spies; followed closely by a commercial traveller who was doing a thankless round of restaurants and shops in the sub-zero weather, trying to flog machinery for making ice cream.

Joshua knew he'd feel better the minute he'd told Daisy what had happened. You opened the big front door of the tall old house and there she was, in the kitchen at the end of the long hall. Standing at the cooker more often than not, stirring something in a pan, her cheeks flushed and her eyes bright. She'd once told him that she opened the kitchen door when the time came round for him to come home, and be blowed to the cooking smells seeping into every corner of the house.

As he turned the corner of the familiar street he slipped on the ice and almost fell outside his own front door.

'Whoops-a-daisy!' a woman called out, and he touched the brim of his brown trilby to her, praying she wouldn't stop but knowing full well she would.

'How are you today, Mr Penny?'

Mrs MacDougal from Balmoral next door thought

he looked shocking. She'd only slipped into Daisy's house for long enough to borrow a cup of arrowroot, but she'd realized at once that something serious was going on. There had to be a good reason for anyone as poorly as Mr Penny to venture out in weather like this. Daisy had nearly snapped her head off when she'd mentioned, as nice as ninepence, that she'd just happened to see him leaving the house that morning, even before the streets were aired. After all, she'd known Joshua Penny longer even than Daisy. She'd seen him come to lodge next door when Mrs Wilkinson was in charge, right after burying his first wife who had shrunk to the size of a pullet with the consumption. Now it looked as if he was going the same way.

All right then, if he didn't want to talk to her so be it. It was taking her all her time anyroad to keep her balance on the icy flagstones. Even though Angus, her husband, had shovelled the snow off and sprinkled salt twice that morning.

'Mr Penny's a terrible colour,' she told Angus as soon as she got inside her own front door. 'He'll never make old bones, not by the look of him. Them flamin' Germans have a lot to answer for. Gassing a nice man like Mr Penny in the first war so that his chest's never been the same since, and freezing us to death after the second.'

'You can't blame the weather on the Germans.'

Mrs Mac put the cup of arrowroot down carefully on the table. 'The atomic bomb changed the pattern of the weather all over the world,' she explained. 'It said so in the paper. What would we have been doing mucking about with a thing like that if the Japanese hadn't sided with the Germans in the war? And we all know who started it all off in the first place, don't we? So?'

'So what?'

'Hitler may be dead, but he's got a lot to answer for.'
Angus gave up. It made his life a lot easier.

Joshua opened the door just in time to see Daisy disappearing into the dining room carrying a loaded tray. Avoiding her by a whisker, Winnie rushed past him into the kitchen, narrowly missing bumping into Oliver who was chasing his sister down the hall.

Slowly Joshua unwound the long woollen scarf from his neck, took off his tweed overcoat and hung it with his trilby on the hall-stand. Daisy came out of the dining room and stopped just long enough to kiss his cold cheek and tell him to go through to the fire in the lounge which was empty at the moment. She'd join him as soon as she got a minute to spare.

'How did you get on?' Even as she asked the question she was poised for flight.

This was the trickiest part of the whole day, and if Joshua had looked at his watch he would have known it. Midday dinner was served on the dot of one o'clock. Hot food on heated plates, with no one kept waiting longer than was necessary. Daisy and Winnie were like clockwork dolls, passing each other without speaking, each knowing exactly what to do, the whole performance a miracle of split-second timing.

Joshua stared coldly at his wife. He didn't mean to. He had prepared the little speech he was going to make to her, breaking the news gently, explaining that he was honestly quite philosophical about the whole thing; reassuring her that it wasn't the end of the world, my goodness no. That they would come to see in time that it was all for the best.

'Later,' he said, and instead of going through into the lounge, started upstairs.

'Joshua?' Daisy hesitated, one hand on the banister rail. There were four more plates of mince and carrots

13

to take through. The potatoes were still in the pan, keeping hot. There was an extra pan of gravy ready to pour into a gravy-boat to hand round for those who wanted it. There was the pudding to turn out while the first course was being eaten. There were the children to settle at one end of the kitchen table, with Oliver refusing to touch his dinner if he got the slightest suspicion that an onion had touched his plate, and Sally picking over her mince in case of a speck of lurking fat, just like a mother chimpanzee searching her offspring for lice.

'I'll manage, Daisy. We've got the worst over, anyroad.'

Like a good genie materializing from a lamp Winnie appeared, wild of eye, her red hair standing on end. She jerked her head upwards. 'You go on up and see to him. It won't hurt that lot in there to have to wait a bit for once.'

'Try and keep some back for . . .' Daisy was halfway upstairs. Deserting her post at this stage was the equivalent of an actress walking off the stage in mid-speech, but one look at Joshua's face had shown her something was very wrong. He looked like a man who had been told he had only a month to live. Daisy shuddered, and followed him along the landing, up the shorter flight of stairs, to their room at the top of the house.

He was standing by the window, staring down into the narrow walled yard. She closed the door and went to stand beside him.

'How did it go, love?' She laid a hand gently on his arm.

'How did you expect it to go?' Her hand was shrugged away.

'Joshua . . . please.'

'Go back downstairs. Get on with what you were

14

doing when I came in. Don't let me interrupt you. I never do, after all.'

'Winnie can cope.' Daisy stood her ground. 'Look, love. You have to tell me. Why not tell me now?'

'So you can dash back to get on with your job?'

'So that I can finish serving the meal.' Her voice was very quiet. 'Have they cut your working hours down?' She risked touching him again. 'We half expected that, didn't we?'

'You mean *you* half expected that. Not me.'

Daisy blushed, and found herself blustering. 'Well, it was on the cards, wasn't it, love, considering all the leave you've had.'

When he turned round his cheeks were redder than hers. 'Through my own fault, of course?'

'Well, of *course* not through your own fault! You have a chronic complaint, Joshua. Old Doctor Armitage explained the lung damage you've suffered.' In her distress her voice rose. 'You've coped *marvellously*. You've worked harder than thousands of people who have nothing wrong with them. You've *fought* it, love. You've gone to work time and time again when we've both known you ought to have been in bed. So what does it matter if you work less hours for the time being? It's not the money, Joshua. We're not going to starve.'

'With you as the breadwinner, how *can* we?' He coughed and ran a finger round his collar. 'Even if they've retired me completely, it's of no consequence, is it? Not as long as I've got a clever young wife to keep me.'

He went to lay down on his bed and closed his eyes.

Daisy ignored the sarcasm. She looked stricken. 'But they wouldn't do that.'

'Do what?' He sounded slightly bored.

'Retire you completely.'

'As from today.' He waved a hand. 'Well, to be exact,

15

back-dated from the first of January, if you want it spelt out.'

'That last medical . . .?'

'Exactly. The medical examination, the X-rays, the tests. I thought it was merely routine, but they were quietly assessing me, it seems. Deciding whether to put me out to grass. Like a horse that has outlived its usefulness.'

To Daisy's horror she saw his lower lip begin to tremble.

'Oh, they want me to go back for what they call a "little presentation". In recognition of my years of dedication. It seems there are a lot of grateful parents who will want to show their gratitude. You know the kind of thing. An embarrassing little ceremony in the Headmaster's room. You'll be invited, I'm sure. It's jolly decent of them, on the whole.'

Daisy sat down on the bed. 'But it's so *unfair!* You've had pneumonia and flu, all in the space of six months. *Anyone* can have either of those. You'll perk up when the warmer weather comes, just like you always do. You put hours and hours in more than you're expected to at that school when you're on the better side . . .'

'I'm finished, Daisy.'

The long winter of illness had taken its toll. Nights of coughing the hours away, of sleeping at times in the chair by the fire, of struggling for breath, had seeped his resistance. And, for the moment, his courage.

'I need to work, Daisy,' he whispered. 'My kind of teaching is more than a job. Take that away and what's left? Tell me what's left?'

She took his hand and held it to her cheek. 'I'll tell you what's left. Do you want me to do that obnoxious thing and count your blessings for you, Joshua Penny?'

He turned his head away, but she went on: 'There's me, for one thing, and the children for two more.'

16

'And Uncle Tom Cobley and all.' He sat up and swung his legs over the side of the bed. 'I won't be lonely in this house. So there's another of your blessings to count. There aren't many men who get locked out of their own bathroom, or who pass perfect strangers at every hour of the day on their own landing. Oh, God no, there's no chance of me being lonely.'

Daisy took a deep breath. 'Then we'll sell up.'

'Don't be ridiculous.'

'I'm serious.' She stood up and faced him. 'Our arrangement has worked whilst you've been out teaching, but I can see that it won't when you're in the house all day.'

'Under your feet. In your way. Or would you like to buy me a pinny so I can wait at table with Winnie?'

'Stop it, Joshua! Stop feeling sorry for yourself!' She had thought it was the right thing to say, the *only* thing to say to make him pull himself together. 'There isn't time to talk now, but we'll sort this out between us.'

'With you playing the role of the sacrificial lamb?'

'What do you mean?' She was shouting now.

'Giving up your job just because I've lost mine? That's carrying things a bit far, isn't it?' His face twisted out of shape with the force of his emotion. 'Don't try to emasculate me *too* much, Daisy, because I won't stand for it.'

'I'll go down and help Winnie.' It was the best thing to do. Joshua was taking his hurt out on her, Daisy realized that, but she'd meant what she'd said about selling up and moving out. It had come to her in a flash, in exactly the same way as the day ten years ago when she had stood outside the tall boarding house and known she was going to buy it with the proceeds of her mother's pie shop. 'We'll talk later,' she said, and opened the door.

17

To reveal Oliver, eyes bulging with indignation, a gravy moustache adorning his short upper lip.

'Winnie's given Sally twenty times as much custard as me. And she swore at Mr Livesey.'

'I'm coming down.' Daisy closed the door gently. The last thing Joshua wanted was a domestic crisis.

'Mr Livesey brought his pudding through into the kitchen and said it was stone cold.'

'Oh dear.' Daisy was already halfway down the second flight of stairs.

'She called him a fussy bugger,' Oliver shouted, following on her heels, and shocking little Miss Grimshaw into dropping her knitting bag as she made her way back into the lounge to claim her chair by the dwindling fire.

Nothing was said all that long, cold afternoon. Winnie tried a few feelers, but Daisy wouldn't be drawn. The electricity went off promptly at two o'clock and Joshua did a thing Winnie never remembered him doing before. He joined Miss Grimshaw round the coal fire in the lounge for a game of Ludo with the children.

It was an unspoken law that the family never sat in the lounge with the house guests. Their role was to keep out of the way, but Winnie was no fool. Nor had she been born yesterday. Joshua was in there because he was keeping out of Daisy's way, and not entirely because the upstairs rooms were like little ice-boxes.

Winnie's friend Leonard Smalley came round after tea, and he too went straight into the lounge and stood on the rug by the fire, jingling the coins in his pocket, telling Miss Grimshaw all about his mother's arthritis. He was such a good son, Winnie reminded herself, watching from the door with a tea towel draped over her shoulder. And as everyone said, good sons made good husbands. Winnie narrowed her eyes, trying to see him in a different light.

It wasn't in every man to be a hero. Chuck had been a hero, with so many medals to his credit at the end of the war his knees would have buckled under him if he'd worn them all at once. Chuck had been all the things Leonard was not. Coolly Winnie enumerated them one by one. Better looking. Brave. Jokey. Lively. Rich – or at least he'd *said* his father owned a ranch in Texas the size of Lancashire. Leonard kept a firm hand on his money. Perhaps that was why he jiggled it about in his pocket so much.

Leonard was telling Miss Grimshaw now that he was quite prepared for his mother's fingernails and toenails to drop off eventually. Rotted by the excess acid in her bloodstream, he explained.

'Did Leonard always have a beard?' Daisy asked Winnie, when she went back into the kitchen. 'It's funny I've never noticed it before.'

Winnie wiped a plate and slotted it into the long rack above the sink, then reached for another. It wasn't really surprising that Daisy hadn't noticed Leonard's straggly little apology for a beard. Leonard could walk into a room with horns sprouting out of each neat little earhole, and no one would turn a hair.

When Chuck had walked into a room in his mustard-coloured uniform, with his yellow hair cropped close to his scalp like the pile on a length of velvet, Winnie's heart had turned right over. She picked up another plate. Yet Chuck had promised to send for her when he was settled back on his ranch in Texas, and all the time he must have been writing to a girl called MaryLou. Winnie conjured her up for a moment, looking just like Jeanne Crain in *State Fair*, all sweetness and light, with her hair fussed out in little tiddly curls, and her skirts sticking out like lampshades.

19

'Leonard has asked me to get engaged to him,' she said suddenly.

Daisy's hands in the soapy water were still for a moment. Winnie had known Leonard for a long time. Held back from joining up during the war because of his work on munitions, Leonard had come and gone from the house like a shadow. One minute there and the next one vanished. The thought of Winnie with her bright face and brighter hair married to the colourless Leonard with the anonymous features appalled Daisy. He was so highly nervous that once she had seen him flinch and twitch when a Brussels sprout had rolled from the kitchen table to plop on the oilcloth.

'He's joined the St John's Ambulance Brigade,' Winnie said, as if that explained a lot. 'Looking after his mother means he needs all the medical knowledge he can get. She's in bed all the time now, apart from the hour or so she's helped out to sit in her wheelchair by the window.'

'So you'd be taking her on as well as Leonard?'

'That *would* be a bit of a bind, I admit.' Winnie still used quite a bit of wartime slang. 'But a woman who used to work in Squire's Gate factory goes in of a morning to see to her; then Leonard's home by dinner time. A postman's job fits in nicely with his routine.' Winnie picked up and wiped a vegetable dish she'd dried and put down not a minute before. 'I wouldn't want to stop working here in any case, though my room would give you another let when you're busy during the season.'

'Suppose – just for the sake of supposing – that Joshua and I decided to sell this place?' Daisy chose her words with care. 'There'd be no guarantee that the people we sold to would want to keep you on. There's a house down the end of the street gone to a couple from

Rochdale with a daughter who worked in the mill. They're going to run it as a family.'

'Good idea.' Winnie's tone was brisk. 'But you and Joshua would never sell this place. You'd never sell Shangri-La. You're like me, Daisy. You have to keep working. I can't see you sitting down with your feet up reading a book in the middle of the morning.'

'Try me,' Daisy said.

As it was Winnie's afternoon off, and Leonard's mother was having a bit of company for the afternoon, they went to the pictures to see *Brief Encounter*. Winnie didn't think much of it, but Leonard thought it was inspiring.

'It made it all the more poignant because they never ... because nothing came of it,' he said on the way home, walking beside Winnie, his small head jutting forward like a pecking bird.

'That spoiled it for me,' Winnie said firmly. 'They would have had something to remember. Or it would have made a lot more sense if she'd left her husband and gone off with Trevor Howard. It was a lot about nowt, if you ask me.'

She was in a mood because Daisy hadn't let a single word slip about how Joshua had gone on that morning at his interview. And she was deliberately trying to blot from her mind Daisy's remark about selling up and moving on.

Joshua and Daisy were her family. Shangri-La was her home. Even marrying Leonard wouldn't alter that. She squeezed his arm. He really was quite sweet, and kind with it too. Winnie happened to believe that kindness mattered above all else. Yes, she could do a lot worse for herself than Leonard. Even if he'd never make the short list for Mr Universe.

Snuggling closer to him, she whispered that she'd been thinking about them getting engaged.

'And?'

'What would you say if I told you the answer was yes?'

Leonard skidded on the frozen pavement, but righted himself in time. 'I would consider myself to be most blessed amongst men,' he said with such feeling that Winnie's eyes flew wide.

'Trevor Howard's got nowt you haven't got in abundance,' she said, kissing him on his little frozen beard.

Winnie was very proud of the fact that a doctor came to the house regularly as a friend. It showed that Daisy and Joshua were a cultured family, she felt.

Daisy too often reminded herself of how pleased her mother would have been when young Doctor Armitage breezed into the house, coming straight through into the kitchen, with no side on him at all. When he had first asked her to call him David she'd blushed every time she said it for a while. He was *Joshua's* friend after all. But he was so pleased when she managed at last to say it naturally, she felt she had to explain that in her childhood the doctor was as important as a priest; that nobody liked to trouble him until their cough began to resemble the death rattle, and that houses were cleaned from top to bottom before he was allowed to set foot inside.

She was glad when he called round that evening, even though it meant another chance to talk to Joshua was lost.

'Mind if I go up?' he asked, as he always did when he first arrived, putting his head round the kitchen door and smiling at Daisy and Winnie as they finished clearing away. 'The kids in bed?'

'For which small blessing may the Lord be praised,' Daisy said. 'Yes, go on up, David. I think Joshua will have something to tell you.'

Winnie's expression set grim. 'About how he went on at the interview this morning? Oh, don't bother to tell me. I'm only a servant after all.' With that she flounced out of the kitchen, wagging her bottom the way she always did when she was angry or upset. And this time she was both.

The commercial traveller had checked out after tea, so she went into his room and started to strip the bed . . .

Joshua had been given the sack. Well, not the sack, because teachers and doctors and the like were asked to take an early retirement, never sacked. That would be why Daisy came out with the remark about the possibility of them selling up.

Yet Daisy was always saying what a good team she and Winnie were. Daisy was a superb cook and a born organizer, but Winnie could best anybody at cleaning and polishing and waiting at table. It was a life she loved; she would have no other.

And it was coming to an end. She could feel it in her bones.

'Aw, Holy Cow!' as Chuck would have said.

Her sudden acceptance of the inevitability of what was to be brought a lump to her throat. She flipped a clean sheet over the mattress, tucked it in viciously then snatched up a pillow and clutched it to her flat chest.

Why couldn't Chuck have loved her as much as she loved him? She'd told him her entire life story, wanting him to accept her for what she was, and to make her feel better he'd confessed that he came from a long line of horse thieves. There was Red Indian blood coursing through his veins, he'd said, his blue eyes laughing. Was he serious? And did it matter? Winnie wouldn't have batted an eyelid if his grandma had turned up at their wedding looking like a wrinkled Minnie-Ha-Ha. She wouldn't have cared if his grandpa was coal black, rolling the whites of his eyes and saying things like 'Hush yo mouth, honeychild'. Everyone knew that Americans were very often of mixed blood. It made them all the more fascinating.

One night she had walked slowly along the promenade with Chuck's arm round her, from the north to the south pier. Two little red lights shone from the top of the Tower. 'Like bloodshot eyes,' she had said, feeling poetical.

That was the night Chuck had said he would send for her when he'd got the business of his father's ranch in Texas sorted out. That was the night she had given him her all.

Winnie had quite enjoyed the war. Blackpool had been like an animated League of Nations. Shangri-La had bulged with airmen. Three of them had slept in this very room ... Winnie stood for a while with a mauve candlewick bedspread cradled in her arms. All those uniforms! She remembered trying to teach a Polish boy how to speak English in Stanley Park. She remembered being on the prom one night during the Liverpool blitz, holding on to a sailor's arm as they watched the bomb flashes and the dock fires lighting the sky.

She took a crumpled packet from her skirt pocket and lit a cigarette, first putting out her tongue at the NO SMOKING IN THE BEDROOMS, PLEASE notice pinned to the door.

Daisy could smell the smoke on her way up to the top landing. She had accepted the fact a long time ago that Winnie preferred to be a furtive smoker, lighting a cigarette when alone then stubbing it out with exaggerated guilt when anyone caught her at it. There were times, like today, when Daisy wished she too was a smoker, but she'd tried once or twice and never got the hang of it.

David Armitage stood up as soon as she went into

the room. 'I'm going now, Daisy. I only dropped by on my way back from a call.'

'Sit down, man.' Joshua's voice had a cutting edge to it. 'Daisy is only paying a flying visit.'

Daisy could hardly bear to look at him. His face was sunk into deep lines of exhaustion, while two red flags flamed on his cheekbones. David's father, old Doctor Armitage, was Joshua's doctor, but surely David could see how ill Joshua looked? Surely he ought to be ordering him to bed instead of keeping him talking?

David didn't behave as Daisy had been conditioned to think doctors should behave. He didn't even *look* like a doctor in his shapeless tweed jacket with his fairish hair straggling slightly over his collar at the back.

She sat down on the edge of her bed and smiled at David, just to show him that Joshua hadn't meant to be curt with her; hadn't intended to sound as if he was dismissing her. She wanted to know if they had been discussing Joshua's interview at Preston when she came in, and if their sudden silence confirmed her suspicions.

'Would you like me to get you both a hot drink? I'll ask Winnie. She's determined to be a martyr, so she'll welcome an extra job when she should be finished for the day. She's so sorry for herself this evening she can make the same sigh last for ten minutes.'

David laughed, but Joshua looked at her with a strangely cold expression.

'I expect you've got plenty to do downstairs,' he said.

Daisy got up at once and left the room, closing the door with such careful deliberation that the effect was the same as if she had slammed it hard.

She was no rusher-out-into-the-night kind of woman. Not now her fortieth birthday was within sighting distance. Daisy left that kind of carry-on to Bette Davis and Joan Crawford. But she needed air. Even frozen air would do.

25

She snatched her coat down from the hallstand, wound a long woollen scarf once round her head and twice round her throat, and pulled on her rubber overshoes. Even in her distress she was well aware that neither Bette Davis nor Joan Crawford would have stopped to wrap themselves up warmly before making their grand gesture. More like flinging themselves out into a thunderstorm in their nighties.

She opened the door and stepped out into a cold so intense it whisked her breath away. The street was deserted, the frozen snow piled high, leaving a channel free for pedestrians to walk along. A biting wind sent flurries of snow into her face, half blinding her, and she slithered along, her footing as uncertain as if she walked on a moving carpet of ping-pong balls.

'Do you normally choose a night like this to go for a walk?'

Coming up behind her David Armitage startled her so much she cried out and had to grab his arm to stop herself from falling over. As she stared up at him a large icicle let go from the roof of a house to fall silently into a drift of snow.

'Over there.' He nodded at the pub on the corner. 'I'll buy you a drink. If you're daft enough to come out in weather like this when you don't have to, you must need one.'

The saloon bar was empty. The landlord sat behind the bar on a stool, remembering the glorious days during the war when you couldn't have put a pin between the airmen using it as their local night after night. The Americans had been the best once they realized that their comments about the lukewarm and watery beer were making them unpopular. Many a bag of doughnuts or oranges had made their way over the counter and into the back for the missus, not to mention the boxes of candy and tins of corned beef, and once an unforgettable banana. The couple who'd just walked in looked frozen to the marrows. He stood up as the man came towards him.

'Nasty neet, sir.'

During the war his Lancashire accent had gone down a treat. He'd broadened his vowels so much that there were times when even his missus couldn't tell what he was saying. But the tall man wearing an officer's great-coat merely nodded and ordered two double brandies.

'Coming up, sir.' Disgruntled, the landlord went back to his stool and the evening paper.

'I only drink brandy for medicinal purposes, actually.' Daisy sipped her drink and pulled a face. 'It's horrible!' She took another sip. 'Best thing to do with this is to set it alight on a Christmas pudding.' Another sip. 'Though I suppose you could get used to it.'

'Force yourself.'

Daisy felt a warm glow going all the way down to her stomach. 'I must say it grows on you, but it's a bit strong, isn't it?'

'Where on earth do you think you were going?' David leaned forward, holding the balloon glass in cupped hands. 'Joshua would be worried stiff if he knew you were out in this.'

'Did he hear me go out?' At once Daisy stood up and pushed her chair back. 'I must go back now -- straight away.'

'He didn't hear you. When I left him he'd turned the wireless up. I doubt if he even heard *me* go. Sit down and I'll get you another drink.'

'My goodness, no thank you.' Daisy sat down again and unwrapped the scarf from her head. It was too late to stop him now. David was already at the bar. She stared at his back. It looked as if the landlord was trying to keep him talking, and knowing David, he'd be too polite to walk away. How thin he was – unnaturally thin. But then any man who'd been a prisoner of the Japanese in Burma for the last two years of the war was bound to be thin. She unbuttoned her coat and fanned her hot face with her hand. She should have made her drink last, it had really taken hold of her. She caught herself smiling and wondered what at? The day had been so long, so awful, so depressing. For Joshua in particular.

'I'm thinking of selling Shangri-La and buying a cottage in the country with roses round the door,' she said, when David came back. 'It's always been a secret dream of mine – to live in a thatched cottage with roses round the door, and a black cat sunning itself on the window sill.' She half closed her eyes. 'With a garden for Joshua to potter about in, and a rocking chair for him by the fire.' She lifted her glass. 'It's not much of a life for him being married to a landlady. He hasn't known a real home for a long, long time.'

'And now he won't be teaching . . .'

'You know, then?'

He nodded. 'That's why I think your dream of buying a cottage in the country could be just what the doctor ordered.'

Daisy looked at him carefully. There was an underlying meaning here. David had latched on far too quickly to what was, after all, hardly a germ of an idea as yet. 'Did Joshua mention any of this to you?'

'No, not a word.'

She wished he would stop smiling, so to cover her growing distress she drank her brandy too quickly again, spluttered and coughed. 'It was your father's report that helped Joshua on his way to enforced retirement, wasn't it?'

'Not helped, *advised* that to continue working might endanger his health.'

'But he's not *that* bad.' Daisy picked up her glass,

28

bringing a round cardboard mat with it. 'Joshua has *always* had trouble with his chest. You're his friend. You know that. But lots of people suffer from bronchitis in the winter, then they pick up as soon as the warmer weather sets in. Ever since the first war he's had bouts of bronchitis. Men who were gassed in the trenches and lived never really get over it. But they *survive*.' She began to feel sick. 'You're not hiding anything from me, are you, David?' Her voice wobbled on the verge of lost control. 'Because if you are . . .' The table in front of her seemed to be undulating like a turbulent sea. 'I am more than capable of hearing the truth.'

'Joshua isn't my patient. It would be quite . . .'

'Unethical,' Daisy finished for him. 'I want the truth, David. I'm calm, as you see, and I want you to speak frankly to me.'

She could hardly credit that she was talking so freely to the man sitting opposite to her. He might be Joshua's friend, but he was still a doctor, worthy of respect and even awe. Why, not all that many years ago, a person could be dying but the doctor wouldn't be allowed upstairs until the sheets on the bed were changed, even borrowed from a neighbour if their whiteness wasn't up to standard.

To her astonishment David reached across the table and took her hand in his own. 'Will you stop anticipating trouble, Daisy? You're putting thoughts into my head that weren't there to begin with.' He took a deep breath. 'The reason I said that buying a cottage in the country might be a good idea was because I agree with you. When Joshua's not teaching he spends far too much time sitting alone in that upstairs room. I noticed at Christmas that the children were beginning to irritate him . . .'

'Because they can't have the run of the house. Because

I kept sending them upstairs to Joshua to keep them quiet.'

'Exactly.' He got up and pushed his chair back. 'And now I'm going to get you another drink.'

Daisy meant to refuse, but the relief was so great she could only sit there, nodding and smiling foolishly. She was too much like that, always jumping in feet first, *anticipating* trouble. David must have felt acutely embarrassed. Of course Joshua would be all right. *If*, as David hinted, he was taken more care of, given a house of his own without having to talk to complete strangers on the landing, and find his own bathroom locked against him. She would force Joshua to listen to her. Now that she knew David was on her side she'd ask him to talk to Joshua. Between them they'd win Joshua over.

David was only half listening to the man behind the bar.

'Stuck upstairs in that poky attic,' his father had said. 'Coughing his heart up. Keeping out of his wife's way.'

'Daisy's not like that,' David had said quickly. 'She works so hard with only that flame-haired girl to help her. Most women make the bringing up of two children a full-time job. God knows how Daisy manages.'

'She manages because she knows no other way. *Her* mother worked all through her pregnancy, I bet, and brought up Daisy while running a business at the same time. It's a repeating pattern. Good God, you've seen it often enough yourself.'

'And you feel environmental reasons are impeding Joshua's recovery?'

'Environmental, psychological, circumstantial – use whatever word you like. But if he isn't out of that room, and out of that house . . .' The old man had shaken his head sadly. 'I give him twelve months, that's all.'

Daisy grew sentimental over her third brandy.

'Joshua didn't mean to be short with me,' she confided. 'He's lovely, really.'

'He's had a bad day.'

'I've never had much of a head for strong drink,' Daisy said, tipping her glass up and sipping the brandy slowly. 'I must say this grows on you.'

'You're all right, Daisy. In fact, you're a lot more than all right.'

She frowned and bit her lip. Someone else had once said that to her. Another man. A long, long time ago. She drank again and stared at David through half-closed eyes. His looks were improving by the minute. What an attractive mouth he had, curvy, even when he wasn't smiling.

I'm drinking on virtually an empty stomach, she told herself, remembering she'd hardly eaten a thing all day. In the dim light of the saloon bar David Armitage looked quite a lot like Leslie Howard. Very English with his fair hair and blue eyes. Definitely Leslie Howard – dead for four years now, a casualty of war.

'We are all casualties of war in some ways,' she said, accepting that the brandy was setting her tongue wagging, quite enjoying the feeling. She was relaxed for the first time that day, *warm* for the first time that day. Strong drink always had the same effect on her, she admitted. It didn't make her irritable, noisy, depressed, belligerent, or any of the things it was supposed to do. Instead it made her love the entire world; gave the company she was with an aura so that she wanted to tell them how much she admired them and how lovely they were.

'I'm *so* glad you're Joshua's friend,' she enthused, brandy-induced affection for him softening her expression. 'I'm so glad you're *my* friend. But then,' she giggled, 'any friend of Joshua's is bound to be a friend of mine.'

31

She smiled gently at him. 'Dear David. You never talk about how it was for you in Burma, but there's no need to say anything. Not to me.' She leaned forward. 'I've never mentioned this before, David, but I want you to know how sorry I am that your marriage didn't last the war out. Was she *very* young? Joshua said something, but not much.'

'Peggy never forgave me for joining the army when because of my age and my job it wasn't strictly necessary. By the time I went to the Far East she was already serious with the man she's going to marry.'

The brandy had done its work on Daisy with a vengeance. She reached across the table and covered David's hand with her own. 'Oh, poor David. But you'll meet someone else, and marry, and have children. You're not the kind of man to live his life alone.'

David couldn't take his eyes off her. With her hair mussed and her cheeks brandy-flushed, she looked about twenty years old. Her voice was low and filled with warmth, and she had the kindest eyes he'd ever seen in a woman.

He wished his father hadn't told him that for a long time now Joshua had been impotent, that pride prevented him from going to see one of the newfangled specialists in Manchester. That after that initial embarrassed confession Joshua had refused to discuss it further.

If ever a woman was made for passion it was this bonny lass holding his hand and looking on him with melting compassion.

Suddenly David wanted to make love to her so badly that he snatched his hand away from hers and stood up.

'I think I ought to take you home. Before Joshua misses you,' he said.

Chapter Two

For a while Joshua tried to listen to a Schubert concert on the wireless. But for once the music failed to comfort him.

Why, in God's name, had he spoken so sharply to Daisy? *Why*, when she was his love, his friend, his one bright star? She'd flinched as if he'd hit her, before dashing downstairs. David hadn't wasted any time in leaving either.

Joshua stared at the fire without blinking until his eyes felt dry. David had come round to sympathize, that much was evident. David might not be Joshua's doctor, but his father was. They shared a practice and there wouldn't be much they didn't know about each other's patients.

Joshua buried his face in his hands. The wind had got up and was rattling the sash window. It felt strangely as if it was blowing in his head. He felt so restless, so uneasy, it was as though his skin crawled, and out of the corner of his eye he could see the long brocade curtains billowing slightly into the room. He switched off the wireless and walked towards the door.

The house teemed with people, most of them, he guessed, in the lounge sitting round the coal fire. But for how long before the grate was empty? Only weeks into nationalization, and the country was in the middle of a severe fuel crisis. Already Daisy was regretting her switch from gas to the electric cooker in her kitchen. She must have had one hell of a day ... Joshua stood for a moment on the landing. Yes, indeed, the house might be teeming with people but Daisy was downstairs dispensing warmth and food and her own brand of serenity. Being all things to all men, as usual. How did she do it? Joshua started to cough and leaned for a moment against the wall.

He was achingly tired. The long cold day was almost over, but before it ended he had to talk to Daisy to put things right between them. He hesitated at the top of the short flight of steep stairs, wracked again by a spell of coughing. When it was over his body sagged as he fought for breath, then making a determined effort he moved forward and his foot caught in the frayed piece of carpet on the top stair. With his left hand he reached for the banister, but grasped at nothing but air. As he fell he twisted sideways, rolling neatly like a stunt man down to the main landing. To lie shocked and stunned with a leg crumpled beneath him.

'What was that?'

For the space of a second, down in the kitchen, Winnie held her head to one side in a listening position.

'I didn't hear nothing, Winnie.'

Leonard knew he wouldn't have let on even if he *had* heard something suspicious. Winnie would send him upstairs to investigate, and he could be there on the landing startled by someone popping their head out of a bedroom and wanting a chat with him. People were always appearing suddenly in this house. Perfect strangers smiling at him and saying what a dreadful day for the time of the year, or asking him did he know the time as their watch seemed to have stopped. Leonard had no small talk. He could never flash out with a flip remark like Winnie.

'Probably the chap in number three fell out of bed,' Winnie said. 'You know the one I mean. He walks like somebody's starched his underpants.'

Little Miss Grimshaw looked up at the ceiling. The wind was making the old house creak and groan like a house in a horror film. She shivered and went back to her library book. She'd read Charlotte Brontë's *Villette* twice before, but it never failed to enthral her. All that emotion locked away behind such a decently covered bosom. Miss Grimshaw remembered once being in love with a young man who went to live in Australia. They met one day by chance in the street and he talked to her for almost ten minutes. She could see him now swaying up and down on his heels by the kerb, swinging his hat in one hand and laughing, with his head thrown back showing the masculine curve of his throat. When he sailed away she disguised her handwriting and wrote a letter to herself as though it came from him, declaring his sadness at having to leave her when their friendship had only just begun. She wrote it to show to her mother to prove that she wasn't one of nature's old maids. His name was Geoffrey, and she had never forgotten him.

Three commercial travellers were playing pontoon at a card table over by the window. The banker was waving his arms about, arguing the toss with a dough-faced man who had twisted when he should have stuck.

Joshua moaned and opened his eyes. He tried to sit up, or at least kneel to pull himself upright, but the pain in his foot was so agonizing it seemed to burst through the top of his head. He was very cold, and when he gingerly touched the crown of his head his fingers came away covered in blood. When he shouted for help something seemed to have happened to his voice.

Where was Daisy? The long window at the far end of the landing rattled in its frame. 'Daisy!' The effort of trying to shout brought a spell of coughing on again. He clutched his chest. 'Daisy!' Oh, dear God, there were enough people in the house. Couldn't a single one of them hear him?

'Daisy!' He fell back, exhausted. Why didn't she come? Down all the years of their marriage she had always heard him and come running when he called her name. If he closed his eyes it was as if he were being pulled against his will down a long dark tunnel with just a pinpoint of light at the end. He struggled to keep his eyes open. He was dying. This was how it felt. No one could possibly have told him, but he knew. A trickle of blood from the deep cut on his head was meandering down one side of his face, but it didn't matter. Nothing seemed to matter any more.

Little Miss Grimshaw closed her book, first keeping her place with a thonged leather marker which told her in bright gold lettering that *Books Are Silent Friends.*

Winnie Whalley was saying goodnight to her man friend in the hall. In a way he reminded Miss Grimshaw of Geoffrey who had gone to Australia so long ago. Mr Smalley was shy, you could tell that, and he had the same trick of jiggling the coins in his pockets. Privately Miss Grimshaw thought that Winnie wasn't really his type, but perhaps if she married Mr Smalley she would calm down and not be quite so ebullient and overly familiar. A wise woman would always lift herself up to her husband's level.

'Goodnight, Winnie. Goodnight, Mr Smalley.'

'Goodnight, Miss Grimshaw. Sleep tight.'

As Winnie watched the neat little woman walk upstairs, her back as rigid as a rolling pin, she knew a sudden comforting moment of truth. By marrying Leonard she would never have to become a Miss Grimshaw in her old age, wearing her glasses on a gold beaded chain round her neck and swallowing so many vitamin pills it was a wonder she didn't sound like a pair of maracas every time she moved.

When Miss Grimshaw almost tripped over Joshua unconscious on the landing, lying all twisted like a bent paper-clip, she thought her own end had come. The shock sent waves of panic straight to her stomach, so that she felt it squeeze itself into a tight knot.

'Winnie!' The terror in her voice made it come out in a croak, but Winnie heard her first time.

'Oh, flippin' 'eck!' Winnie knelt down and lifted Joshua's head up. His eyes were closed and his face the colour of wet concrete. She accepted the handkerchief Miss Grimshaw was holding out to her and gently wiped away the blood from his right cheek. 'I think he's had his chips,' she said, in a terrible voice of doom, making room for Leonard who was by now kneeling down beside her.

'Mr Penny?' Leonard's normally quiet voice had such an authoritative ring to it that Winnie immediately moved aside to make room for him. 'Mr Penny? Open your eyes. You're quite safe now. Open your eyes please. Can you hear me, Mr Penny?'

Slowly Joshua opened his eyes and saw a small pinched face with a threadbare goatee beard a few inches away. He tried to sit up.

'Lie quite still, now.'

Joshua felt a hand move gently but firmly down first one leg then another.

'You can straighten your leg, can't you, Mr Penny?'

Joshua proved that he could.

'Now, this may hurt a little, but it won't take a minute.'

The probing fingers were touching his ankle joint. Joshua winced with pain.

The sparse little beard quivered with importance.

'There doesn't seem to be anything broken, but there's some swelling round the joint and quite extensive damage to the tissues. In all doubtful cases we must treat the injury as a fracture. You've also got a tiny surface cut on the crown of your head, but there's no sign of concussion. A bit of blood goes a long way, you know.' He nodded his head in a satisfied way. Not for nothing had he learned his first-aid manual off by heart.

He turned to Winnie. 'A pillow for Mr Penny's head and a blanket to cover him, please.' He resumed his examination of Joshua's ankle. 'I would swear you've merely sprained your ankle, but there is tenderness at the fracture site, though there's no deformity of the bony arch.' Suddenly he took off his coat and, rolling it up, made a support for Joshua's foot. 'I'm going to ease your slipper off, Mr Penny, then after I've telephoned for the doctor I'll splint and pad your foot on the sole with a figure-of-eight bandage.'

Winnie was back with the pillow and blanket, anxious for further instructions.

'Bring me the first-aid box, dear, then telephone the doctor.' He smiled on Joshua with reassurance. 'You're going to be fine, Mr Penny. We'll have you sorted out in no time.'

Winnie couldn't get over it. She'd seen Lew Ayres in all the Doctor Kildare pictures: *Young Doctor Kildare, Calling Doctor Kildare, The Secret of Doctor Kildare, Doctor Kildare's Strange Case, Doctor Kildare Goes Home, Doctor Kildare's Crisis, The People versus Doctor Kildare, Doctor Kildare's Wedding Day*, and *Doctor Kildare's Victory*. She'd seen them all, and in not one of those pictures had Lew Ayres looked half as noble as Leonard did ministering to a casualty. Besides, Lew Ayres had been a conscientious objector in the war, while Leonard was working a twelve-hour shift on munitions, bravely putting up with having his skin turn bright yellow.

As she hurried to do his bidding, the front door opened and Daisy and young Doctor Armitage walked in.

Daisy's hair was any old how. Winnie could smell drink on her breath.

Supported by David on one side and Leonard on the other, Joshua managed to get back into the bedroom. David had made quite a good job of the figure-of-eight bandage, Leonard thought, but felt at a pinch he could have done better himself.

'You'd have made a lovely doctor,' Winnie told him. 'I bet you'd have ended up in Harley Street wearing striped trousers and a bow tie, and whipping rich women's wombs out so you could spend your holidays in Monte Carlo.'

They were saying goodnight down in the hall, standing with their feet in the draught coming from beneath the big front door.

'Oh, I don't know, Winnie. I think my line would have been research.' Leonard kissed her absent-mindedly. 'Trying to find a cure for my mother's arthritis.'

'God bless her,' said Winnie, with deep insincerity.

Joshua said what a lot of fuss about nothing. He lay in bed with the blankets draped over the top of an old fireguard to keep their weight off his feet.

He looked quite perky, more like his normal self, Daisy thought, the brandy still singing in her veins and keeping her wide awake. Brandy being a stimulant, she supposed.

She put her hand out across the narrow divide between their beds and tried to touch Joshua. To feel that he was close. From the landing below she heard the click of a door and wondered which of her guests was making a last trip to the bathroom. She tried deep breathing; tried to make her whirling mind a blank, willing a sleep that wouldn't come. For a moment she considered getting into Joshua's bed, curling herself up against him, never mind being squashed. Sleeping with Joshua had been so lovely . . .

The decision to exchange their double bed for singles hadn't been taken lightly.

'The beginning of the end,' Daisy's Auntie Edna from Blackburn had said when she'd heard about it. 'And it's nothing to do with "that there". Your Uncle Arnold never bothered me much in that direction.'

Daisy and Joshua had been very sensible about the decision to sleep separately after Joshua came out of a longish spell in hospital. They agreed it was impossible for Daisy to get the rest she needed so badly when Joshua lay propped up on four pillows by her side. It was utterly ridiculous for both of them to lie awake, and it wasn't as though they were planning on separate rooms.

'Royalty have separate bedrooms,' Daisy's Auntie Edna had told her. Nothing to do with her and Joshua, Daisy had thought, but Edna obviously considered it to be a valid point.

She tried a method she had read about in *Woman's Own*. First she stretched then relaxed her toes before working her way determinedly up the length of her body, tightening and relaxing, tightening and relaxing. She had got as far as her shoulders when for no reason at all she remembered running along the deserted beach in the year before the war began.

It was winter, an afternoon when they had stolen a few precious hours away together from the boarding house, leaving Winnie in charge of a handful of guests, and enjoying a session of secret smoking, Daisy suspected. It was one of those rare moments when every-thing sparkles, and you are suddenly aware of a total undiluted happiness. The sea was a vivid green, the long stretch of clean rippled sand bleached as if by a summer sun; the lawns emerald green and velvet smooth, the hotels beyond them as clearly etched against the blue sky as drawings in a child's painting book.

The war was less than a year away, but for now there was joy and *passion*. Daisy had always set a great store on passion, right from the time when at twenty-six she was sure she was cut out to be an old maid, one of life's unclaimed blessings, as she'd described herself.

That day on the beach she had spread her arms wide and started to run. Fast, then faster still. The wind had tangled her hair, brightened her eyes, and brought a glow to her cheeks. She ran on, running because she was happy, and because that morning Joshua had wakened early and made love to her.

'Joshua?' She whispered his name. 'Are you awake?'

Before they bought the twin beds they had talked in a civilized way about what they called 'that' side of their marriage. After Joshua's lengthy hospital stay two years ago, he had made five or six abortive attempts to make love to her, failed and from then on lost interest altogether. Daisy understood it was because he'd been so very ill, and told him so, but obviously embarrassed he had refused to discuss it.

Daisy stared up into the darkness and across the divide between their beds at the rounded dome protect-ing Joshua's legs. Knowing it was impossible, perversely she wanted to be held – to be much more than held. She needed to comfort Joshua, to tell him that losing his job was going to be the best thing that could have happened to them. That some things were meant to be, and that David had thought a cottage in the country was a marvellous idea.

41

She would sell this place where he woke in the night knowing the house was filled with sleeping strangers. They would find a cottage far out in the country, a thatched cottage in the middle of a bluebell wood, beside a waterfall with tumbling water cascading down into rocky depths. Her imagination soared. A cottage set in a fragrance of roses and honeysuckle. The harvest in the nearby meadow being gathered in, pale spring sunlight washing across the cottage walls, dappling them to a soft apricot. Daisy smiled to herself. Harvest and bluebells? Roses and honeysuckle? Not all at once, of course. How wonderful it would be to live in a house with a garden. Once, during the war in a fit of patriotism, she had tried to plant a row of runner beans in the minute strip of sandy soil against the back-yard wall. It had been quite difficult to decide what to do with the resultant crop. Two long stringy beans lying sadly side by side on the kitchen table.

'You should have let them mature on the plant,' Winnie had advised, 'then you could have shelled them and dried the inside beans to tide us over the winter.' She was perfectly straight-faced. 'I hope you didn't give yourself a hernia carrying them in from the yard.'

What would happen to Winnie when they moved to the country? Daisy's sigh fluttered the ribbon tie at the neck of her nightdress. She flopped over on to her back and wondered if counting sheep really worked? If she wasn't asleep soon she'd get up, go downstairs and make herself a pot of tea.

'Dear God,' she prayed. 'Give me a sign that selling this house is the right thing to do.' She squeezed her eyes tight shut. 'If it's going to help Joshua to feel better, then there really isn't any choice. But a sign would be welcome all the same.'

As her eyelids drooped, she remembered that Winnie

and Leonard were now engaged. So taking Winnie with them wouldn't be necessary.

Which was perhaps just as well, was her last coherent thought before she slept at last. She couldn't see Winnie and Mother Nature making much of a team somehow.

Winnie was no eavesdropper. She wasn't averse to listening in to other people's conversations if they insisted on talking so loud she couldn't help but hear, though she would never stoop so low as to press a tumbler against a wall or press her eye against a keyhole.

But Daisy was in there laughing and joking with Joshua, as if losing his job the day before and falling down and spraining his ankle was funny enough to make a strip in *Comic Cuts*.

'If we're lucky enough to find a cottage quickly we can be out of this place by the summer.' Daisy almost sang the words. 'A country cottage with a big garden, and a swing hanging from an apple tree for the children.'

Silly beggar, Winnie thought, creeping closer and inclining her head towards the half-open door. Why, Daisy hardly knew the difference between a rhododendron bush and a clump of pansies.

'A house with a bathroom that no one else but us uses.'

More likely an enamel washing-up bowl in a stone slopstone with one cold tap, and a jug and basin up in the bedroom. Winnie bit her lip to stop it trembling.

'It's been no life for you, darling . . .'

So far Joshua hadn't said a flamin' word. Winnie held her breath. Maybe he'd refuse to go. He could be stubborn as a mule when he'd a mind.

'We can begin to *live* again,' Daisy was saying in what Winnie had always thought of as her put-on

43

poetry voice. 'I'll be looking after you, not other people. Don't you see?'

In her own room Winnie closed the door carefully and leaned against it. Knowing she'd been right all along that Joshua wasn't going to catch the early train to Preston any more – that Daisy was going to sell up and move away.

She examined her face in her dressing-table mirror: Winnie Whalley, twenty-five years old. Looking far older, for the simple reason that she had looked twenty-five for as long as anyone could remember. Freckles so close together they could be mistaken for a nice light tan till you got near. Bosoms no bigger than walnuts, and a bottom like two hard-boiled eggs in a handkerchief. Winnie knew her limitations, always had done.

When she was young she had got away with looking like Minnie Mouse. She had what everyone called 'personality'. She could say the most outrageous things and get away with it. Some of the boarders had come back the minute the forces had left. They swore they couldn't make up their minds whether it was Daisy's cooking or Winnie's wisecracks which drew them back. In the street she was a stick-thin young woman who didn't warrant a second glance. In the dining room of Shangri-La she was a star!

'You want to watch 'im,' she could say to a wife whose husband patted Winnie's non-existent behind as she moved between tables. She could land a disruptive child a fond clout without its mother taking umbrage. And she could bottom a room so thoroughly that if she hung a cord across the doorway you could be forgiven for thinking it was a window dressing in Lewis's in Manchester.

To her amazement, because Winnie had never been an easy crier, she watched flabbergasted as two perfectly formed tears rolled slowly down her cheeks. Impatiently, almost angrily, she dashed them away. She took the lid off a glass powder bowl and fluffed Rose Rachel tinted powder firmly into her cheeks. Being an old misery-guts wouldn't get her anywhere, and besides, there was nothing definite. Daisy was like that. She was always making stories up about how it would be when her ship came in. She went to the pictures far too often in the winter when things were slack and came back all of a glow, *living* what she'd seen. After her third visit to see *Mrs Miniver*, she was Greer Garson, having a stiff upper lip for weeks. Though that was preferable to the time when she saw Bette Davis in *The Little Foxes*, and walked about the house swaying from the hips, snapping all her words out and popping her eyes at you.

Winnie turned from the mirror. Oh, dear God, why didn't she face the truth? Daisy was all Winnie wished she herself could be. Wise and kind and tolerant. What you could write down on paper about Daisy's nasty ways wouldn't be enough to make a butterfly a pair of knickers.

Daisy was in the kitchen mixing the ingredients for two syrup loaves to have for pudding. She was low on points, but the recipe called for nothing more than self-raising flour, bicarbonate of soda, milk, or milk and water, and warmed golden syrup. It was more than a bit of all right eaten straight from the oven, and to pour over it she would make mock cream with arrowroot, milk, a knob of margarine and a shake of sugar. She wouldn't even think about real dairy cream poured thick and yellow from the milkman's special skip, and she would try not to remember the Victorian sponges she used to make with butter and proper shell eggs, sandwiching two layers together with raspberry jam.

She looked up as Winnie came in. 'Why have you

got your coat on? It's snowing again. Do you *have* to go out?'

'Needs must when you feel like *I* do. Me nerves are twanging like a catapult.' Winnie's tinny little voice was strident with despair. She looked as if she was coming down with a cold. Or as if she'd been crying.

'It's going dark,' Daisy said.

'I *know* it's flamin' going dark.' Winnie tightened her lips. If Daisy didn't stop whipping up that flamin' pudding with those neat little expert flicks of her wrist she would snatch the wooden spoon from her and clock her one over the head with it. 'I heard what you were saying to Joshua about going to live in the country, and I'll tell you something for nothing. It's shaken me to the nellies.' Reaching deep into the pocket of her tweed coat she took out a plastic hood and shook it out of its concertina folds. 'You never gave me a thought, did you?' She pulled the hood on and tied the tapes underneath her chin. 'No mention of me. Nothing!'

Daisy sat down at the kitchen table and pushed the mixing bowl away from her. 'I would have told you the minute it looked as if it might be happening, but there's honestly nothing to tell yet. I'm not even sure if Joshua wants to move.' She looked Winnie straight in the eye. 'I only know it wouldn't work, him living here when he hasn't a job to go to during the day. *You* know that too.'

'Too much up top,' Winnie said at once. 'Not cut out to be no more than a landlady's husband. He's never really mixed up with the boarders.'

'So you *see*, then?'

'I see I'm not wanted.' Winnie blinked the tears back. She'd be damned if she'd break down, but she'd come downstairs determined to have her say and say it she would. Even if Daisy *was* talking sense.

'Who kept this place going for you when you had

46

Oliver? And the same when you had Sally, even though your Auntie Edna came over from Blackburn to rule the roost. And who carried on regardless all those afternoons when you were up at the hospital with Joshua?'

Daisy opened her mouth to say how truly grateful she'd been and always would be, but like a policeman stopping the traffic Winnie raised her right hand, palm outwards.

'I knew I counted for nothing when Chuck wrote me that letter from America telling me he was getting married. Chucked by Chuck. That's funny, isn't it? Go on, you can laugh.'

Daisy did what she did in every emergency. She stood up and put the kettle on for a cup of tea. 'I'm not laughing. And you're wrong, you know. You count for a good deal.' She set two cups down on the table. 'Take that thing off your head and sit down. I can't talk to you when you look like a caramel waiting to be unwrapped.'

For a moment Winnie's lip quivered as if she might smile. The sight of Daisy calmly going about the familiar task of making a pot of tea made her want to lay her head down on the well-scrubbed table and howl.

'I really loved Chuck,' she whispered. 'I gave him my all the night he went away, and what did he do? He threw it right back in my face.' She tugged at the tapes underneath her chin, pulled off the hood and snapped it back into its folds. 'Now I've shocked you, haven't I?'

'Sit down, Winnie.'

The kettle was coming speedily to the boil. Winnie abandoned the idea of rushing round to Leonard's house to persuade him to marry her quickly to show Daisy that you couldn't treat people like they counted for nothing and get away with it. She began to unbutton her coat. Nobody could make a pot of tea in such a comfortable way as Daisy. First warming the pot, holding it with her hands cupped round it to make sure it was heated properly before rinsing it round and tipping the water out. Dipping the special spoon into the caddy and always remembering the extra spoonful for the pot. Stirring it briskly then letting it stand for three minutes before pouring it into the cups, milk last, after the sugar from the glass bowl. One spoonful for Daisy and two for Winnie. Handing the cup over strong and sweet, just the way she liked it. So strong a fly could skate across it without sinking.

'Leonard's mother likes her tea like gnat's piss,' she said suddenly, sitting down and making the strange tinny sound that passed for crying.

Daisy hesitated. Miss Grimshaw had the children with her again in the lounge playing Ludo or Snakes and Ladders, completely oblivious to Oliver's cheating methods. Joshua would be reading or listening to the wireless and the civil servants wouldn't be in until a quarter to six, with the commercial traveller following on at six. The syrup loaves took no more than half an hour to cook in a hot oven, and the rabbit pie was already cooked, needing no more than heating before serving. She could afford to catch her breath for a few minutes.

'The way you felt about Chuck wouldn't have lasted,' she said slowly. 'That floating on air sensation isn't real. Nor is the thinking of him before you go to sleep at night and opening your eyes to see his face again when you wake in a morning. That's not love, Winnie. It's *romance*, it's obsession, it's a disease gripping you so that you can't see or think straight. It blinds you to his faults; you live only for the times you can be together, and when you're apart you're merely existing.' Her eyes stared at Winnie without seeing her. 'You build him up into something he isn't. You turn him into an *object* to give you an excuse to experience all the feelings you didn't know you possessed. You want to touch him when he's near; you ache in your stomach for him when he isn't.'

'You're talking about Sam, aren't you?' Winnie nodded her head up and down wisely. 'You're remembering that married man from London who talked posh. You've never said a word about him ever since, but you're talking about him now.'

Daisy blushed. 'I thought the world had come to an end when he went back to his wife. But when I married Joshua I knew how silly I'd been. I could hardly believe I was that same woman who had wanted to die for love of a man I hardly knew.'

'And you think that when I marry Leonard I'll forget all about Chuck?'

Daisy put all the conviction she could into her voice. 'There's nothing more sure.'

'You never ever think of Sam? Not even now and again?'

'Never,' said Daisy, lying in her teeth.

Daisy got into Joshua's bed that night. The fireguard protecting his ankle had been discarded as Joshua said it had let a draught in under the bedclothes. She lay straight as a ruler by his side, careful not to touch the bandaged ankle. Then in whispers, because the walls separating the attic rooms were very thin, she told him about her talk with Winnie. Omitting, of course, any mention of Sam.

'I like Leonard.' Joshua moved obligingly so that Daisy could snuggle her head on to his chest. 'He'll never set the Thames on fire, but he'll not play ducks and drakes with her either. He could be just the calming influence Winnie needs.'

'I think she was really in love with her GI.' For some

reason she couldn't fathom, Daisy felt a need to talk about Chuck. 'He brought colour into her life.' She opened the top of Joshua's pyjamas so that she could kiss his smooth chest. 'She'd had it rough before she came to me, and now her mother's married again and gone to live in Scotland she needs us more than we know.'

'I liked Chuck too,' Joshua said, surprising her. 'Especially the tins of corned beef he brought with him, and the boxes of candy.'

'And the cigarettes and chewing gum for Winnie. I liked his dimples,' Daisy said.

Closing her eyes, she could see Chuck in his uniform with its metal buttons gleaming, snatching off his funny little cap and running his hand over the pale stubble of his close-cropped hair. He was all of a tone – barley pale, with eyes that flashed and teeth that sparkled. Once he'd called for Winnie riding a tandem and Daisy had waved them off at the door, laughing at the sight of Winnie's stick-thin legs going like pistons.

She pressed herself closer to Joshua, snaking a hand inside his jacket, making patterns with her fingers, kissing him with a slow lingering at the corners of his mouth.

'What's brought this on?'

The room behind the close-drawn curtains was so dark she couldn't see Joshua's expression, but she could feel him smiling.

'It's not funny.' She raised herself up on an elbow, trying to make him look at her. 'I know you don't like talking about it, but we have to *try* to discuss it.'

'Not tonight, love.' He coughed, turning his head away. 'Do you realize how late it is?'

'I realize that since we got these twin beds we hardly have any physical contact at all.'

'I'd rather you . . . I don't think this is the time . . .'

'It's got to be said, Joshua.' Daisy lowered her voice to the barest of whispers. 'I don't mean what you think I mean.' She fought to find the right words. 'Because we don't share the same bed we never even *hold* each other. And because we live as we do, in a house full of strangers, most of the time bed is the only place we can *talk* intimately.' She sighed. 'We don't *cuddle* any more, Joshua. We are practically living as brother and sister.'

'You don't feel like my sister.'

As Joshua's arms came round her she began to kiss him gently, slowly, lingering, parting her lips to his response.

'Go back to your own bed, love.' There was nothing rough in the way he pushed her from him, but his rejection was like a slap.

Immediately she did as she was told, curling herself up into the foetal position in her own bed and pulling the blankets over her head. *Dismissed.* The word came to her instinctively. She shivered, turned on to her back and thrust her feet down into the cold far reaches of the single bed. She stared up into the inky darkness, telling herself she *understood* Joshua's reluctance to talk about it. It was his *pride.* He'd been so mortified the last time he'd tried to make love to her and failed, even though she had told him over and over that it didn't matter.

And of course it didn't matter. Their lovemaking had never been the kind you read about in books, all groans and muffled cries and sweat-drenched bodies lying limp with satisfied desire. But Joshua had been a caring, tender lover. All she wanted was to be *held.* Just held close – and caressed.

'Goodnight, love.' There was a hesitancy in his voice, an *insecurity* that almost broke Daisy's heart.

The worst thing a woman could do was to emasculate her man. Who had said that? Where had she read it?

51

Good God, if Joshua never touched her again, never came within three feet of her, if they did no more than shake hands when they went to their separate beds – she'd still love him more than life itself.

'Goodnight, sweetheart.' She used the old-fashioned endearment with feeling. No more would she embarrass him by bringing up a subject that was bound to humiliate and wound him. It wasn't a subject for a decent woman to be discussing anyway. Good heavens, her mother would be revolving in her grave if she knew the way her daughter's mind had been working.

'Them's mucky thoughts, our Daisy.'

Daisy could hear her saying it as clearly as if she stood at the foot of the bed with her arms folded over her one-piece bosom.

'I made your father sign the pledge the day I turned forty.' Her mother's voice echoed down the years.

'He never bothered me much in that direction.' Was that her Auntie Edna?

'Me husband's had his raincoat castrated at the cleaners,' the pregnant girl sitting behind Daisy on the Cleveleys tram had said.

'A pity he weren't in it,' the girl's mother had said. With feeling.

Daisy crossed her hands across her chest and composed herself for sleep. Not for the first time her sense of humour had come to her rescue, putting things into proper perspective, showing her what really mattered. She fell asleep like a stone with a sensation of sinking through the mattress. She dreamt that she was standing on the Boulevard at Blackburn with Sam in the pouring rain, looking up into his handsome face and never mind that her hair had come out of curl.

'I will always love you,' he was saying. 'Because of the children I must stay with my wife, but you are my heart's desire.' His brown trilby had slipped to the back of his head as his kiss had deepened. 'Oh, God, you're all woman. How can I ever leave you?' Then he'd swung her up against him so that she felt his hardness . . .

She came awake with a jerk, feeling a shaming pain low down in her stomach. And slept again, to dream that she was swimming starkers in the sea with an equally bare David Armitage . . .

'It's funny.' The following night David sat with his father round the fire enjoying a nightcap of whisky and water before turning in for the night. 'That wife of Joshua's is a complete enigma.' He stared into the fire for a long moment. 'I could have sworn that I really got through to her when I took her out and softened her up with brandy the other night. She talked to me as if I was a normal human being instead of a doctor and therefore sacrosanct.'

'And this evening?'

'She blushed to the roots of her hair every time I spoke to her. Couldn't look me in the eyes at all.'

David Armitage senior chuckled. 'You've been away so long you've forgotten the drill.'

'What drill?'

'To the working classes a doctor is a thing apart. On a par with a priest. Only a step or two down from God.'

'*Working classes*? You're showing your age, Dad. The class system was buried once and for all in the rubble of the war.' David sat forward. 'If you're forced to stand in the sun bare-headed for twelve hours and decapitated if you fall down, the man standing next to you is your *brother*. From that moment and for the rest of time. Anyway, if you want to go down *that* road, Daisy's lower middle class, surely?'

The older man shook his head. 'Class is ordained by politics, traditions and accident of birth. There will always be some more equal than others. Come on, lad,

53

face the truth. Wealth brings power, and war or no war over sixty per cent of the population are still doing manual work of some kind or another.'

David didn't seem to be listening. 'Daisy Penny intrigues me. She's as feminine as the Mona Lisa, yet beneath all that softness there's a domineering woman.' He hesitated. 'I don't mean domineering in an aggressive way. I'm sure she never shouts the odds, but she's the boss all right.'

'You don't like her very much?'

'Oh, I wouldn't say that. But without him knowing it, she has Joshua where he belongs.'

'Under her thumb?'

David laughed. 'He'd think we were talking about two other people if he could hear us.'

'Does Daisy realize just how ill he is?'

'That would be your job to tell her, wouldn't it?'

Doctor Armitage leaned forward to knock his pipe out against the bars of the grate. 'But you know as well as I do that Joshua's lung-heart condition could deteriorate quickly, or stay in a state of remission for months, possibly for years. He's only fifty-two.'

'And you really believed that travelling and teaching on a day to day basis was killing him?'

'I said so in my report.'

'And sitting cooped up in that attic room, or forcing himself into the role of a landlady's husband could kill him off just as quickly?'

'That's about it.'

'Then I think I'm about to play God,' said David, standing up and draining his glass.

With the thaw came the burst pipes and the floods. The streets ran with slush, and after the twenty-four degrees of frost experienced during the coldest week, the weather seemed almost spring-like.

Joshua's chest trouble improved. He drove Winnie mad by 'helping' her do out the bedrooms, choosing only the jobs he felt were less of an affront to his masculinity. He would trundle the vacuum cleaner around, but he would not dust. He would sweep the stairs down as long as all the guests were well out of the way. In the kitchen he would peel the vegetables, but he wouldn't mix a cake, even under instruction. He set off to do the shopping with a paper carrier-bag because a basket was apparently sissy, and he came back almost at once because on principle, as he said, he had never lowered himself to tag on to the end of a queue.

Winnie planned a May wedding, surprising everyone by announcing that she intended to be a white bride. With all the trimmings.

'Perhaps *off-white*, with me not being exactly a virgin,' she whispered to Daisy, with Leonard standing not all that far away.

'You should be the one blushing, not me,' Daisy whispered back. 'You're terrible.'

'But fascinating with it,' Winnie said. 'Do you think you can manage the coupons for Sally's bridesmaid's dress? Are you sure Oliver couldn't be persuaded to be a pageboy in a white satin suit?'

'Yes to both questions,' Daisy said.

Joshua was to give the bride away, and Daisy was to be chief bridesmaid. Or dame of honour, to be quite correct. She had never owned or worn a long dress in her life, and wasn't too sure about the candy-pink Winnie had set her heart on.

'I'll be mutton dressed as lamb,' she complained.

'Have a perm,' Winnie told her. 'That waved style went out twenty years ago.'

Joshua said he'd never speak to her again if she had her softly waved brown hair frizzed up in rows of sausage curls. He was going to have his own thinning hair trimmed at the barber's instead of Daisy cutting it for him as usual with her nail scissors.

'The barber'll need a search warrant,' Winnie told him, laughing her tinny little laugh. 'If I were you I'd knot those few hairs at the front before they escape.'

David brought up the subject of a country cottage again, and in his present mood of optimism Joshua agreed it might not be a bad idea.

'But let's get Winnie's wedding over first. I'm sure the planning of the D-Day landings wasn't half as complicated.'

Daisy's Auntie Edna and Uncle Arnold came to stay for Easter, travelling from Blackburn on a coach, which came out cheaper than the train, Edna explained. Daisy gazed on them both with fondness. Edna had snapping eyes that never missed a trick. They darted all round the bedroom missing nothing, taking everything in. She withdrew a lethal-looking hat pin from a felt hat shaped like a boiler shovel, and took off her navy-blue single-breasted coat to reveal a paisley-patterned dress pouched up over a length of knicker elastic. To avoid the shame of it showing beneath her coat, Daisy knew, remembering her own mother doing exactly the same. Edna had overdone the pouching so that Daisy caught a glimpse of a pair of rheumaticky knees, like swollen spring buds on thin twigs. Come to think about it, her auntie did look a lot like a twig – brittle and ready to snap in two as though all the sap in her had dried up long ago.

When Daisy embraced her Uncle Arnold it was as if she hugged an empty suit of clothes. His bones were bird bones, light and fragile, and the jacket of his shiny dark-brown suit seemed to be held together by the shoulder padding.

'He's lost weight,' Edna said, as if he wasn't there.

'You could drop me down a drainpipe and I wouldn't even bark me shins,' Arnold winked at Daisy.

'When you get to our age you either widen or wizen. All his family are whippet breed. If a door opened and shut in our house when his mother was alive and nobody came in, you'd know it was her. And his father could have gone to a fancy-dress dance as a length of fuse wire without dressing up.'

'How's your Betty?' Daisy tweaked a corner of the green candlewick bedspread into place.

'Nicely, thank you. But that husband of hers has got too big for his boots since he come back from the war.' Edna lowered the circle of elastic and stepped neatly out of it. 'He's talking about changing his job and moving down south.'

'Edwin's ten, going on eleven now. Taking his scholarship for the grammar school,' Arnold said quickly, trying to keep the conversation running on pleasant lines.

'He's every chance of passing.' Edna opened the wardrobe door and put her hat away on the shelf. 'There's one thing certain: he doesn't get his brains from Cyril's side. Cyril's mother was as thick as two short planks.'

'And his father?' Daisy could never resist egging her auntie on when she was in this mood.

'Well, *his* brains are in his trousers, always have been.'

Edna thought that Joshua looked shocking, even though he was supposed to be on the better side. She said she'd always known, right from first setting eyes on him, that he would never make old bones.

'The last war was bad enough, but the fourteen-eighteen one was worst. The men who survived the trenches were never the same. You think how many we know who have popped off in their fifties. It sapped their spirits, that terrible war.'

'I'm living on borrowed time then, love.' Arnold went to the door and opened it. 'Look what I've found on the landing!'

Oliver was always pleased to see his Auntie Edna and his Uncle Arnold from Blackburn. His uncle could make a sixpence come out of an ear, and although Oliver knew the sixpence was in his uncle's fist already, he was quite willing to go along with the pretence as long as the money was forthcoming.

Sally thought they were *very* old, but her Auntie Edna kept sweets in her knitting bag and always saved the black ones for her. She wasn't keen on her uncle's bald head, and lived in fear in case he asked her to touch it; she had a dread that it would be soft, leaving dents where her fingers had been.

'Have you broken up for Easter yet?'

Oliver nodded. 'For a week and a day and a half,' he said proudly.

Winnie could never quite understand Daisy letting her aunt and uncle have the best front bedroom free for a week at Easter when she could have let it ten times over. She'd even managed to squash them in during the war years, doubling and trebling up the airmen till it was a wonder they didn't have to sleep with their legs sticking out of the window. She dithered about asking them to the wedding, but decided against. She wondered about writing to her mother up in Scotland with her new husband and the two youngest children, but decided against that too. It was funny how you could feel nothing for your own flesh and blood.

Daisy said she had no need to feel shame on account of Winnie's mother never showing her real love. Winnie wondered sometimes if she could be a changeling – rather liking the idea.

David Armitage came that Thursday afternoon, the day before Good Friday. Edna and Arnold had taken the children out for the afternoon, even though the weather wasn't really fit, and Winnie had gone with Leonard to see the vicar about the wedding ceremony.

David thought Daisy looked tired almost to the point of utter exhaustion. She was in the kitchen as usual doing three things at once. A large round simnel cake on the kitchen table waited for the mock marzipan Daisy was rolling out with deft little flurries of a rolling pin. David watched her. Fascinated.

'Soya flour and ratafia instead of ground almonds.' She pushed a stray lock of hair behind her ear, leaving a streak of flour. 'But Easter wouldn't be Easter without simnel cake. Not to me, anyway.'

She took the tin the cake had been baked in and laid it on the rolled-out marzipan, cutting round it with a knife.

'I know of a cottage you might like,' David said.

Carefully, Daisy lowered the circle of marzipan on to the top of the cake, over a coating of plum jam.

'Joshua's not really improving, is he?' She sat down suddenly, as if, he thought, she had suddenly realized the extent of her exhaustion. 'It's not working out, him being at home all day.' She paused, frowning. 'He's not, well, he's not *domesticated*, not in the least.' She smiled. 'He made me an omelette the first time we met. I'd come to view this house after the previous landlady died, and Joshua was living upstairs, fending for himself.' She began to cut perfectly-formed 'leaves' from the left-over scraps of marzipan. 'When the omelette was cooked I told him I could be forgiven for thinking it was a corn plaster!'

'And his domestic skills haven't improved?'

'Worsened, I'm afraid.' She traced authentic-looking veins along the length of a leaf. 'Sit down, David.'

He did as he was told. 'You're nobody's fool, are you, Daisy Penny?'

She looked down at the knife in her hands. 'I know that Joshua is living on borrowed time, if that's what you mean.'

He drew a sharp breath, opened his mouth to speak then closed it again.

'It's all right. I know I should be saying all this to your father, with him being Joshua's doctor. But he wouldn't be as honest with me as you are.'

'He thinks, as I do, that if Joshua was more settled in his mind . . .'

'With me there to look after him instead of spending all my energy looking after other people.'

'He didn't say that.'

'But it's true, David! I see it clearly and accept it completely. He needs my *company* as much as anything. He needs this precious time to sit with me in the sun, to *talk* to me, without me having to run away to satisfy strangers' wants. He needs a garden to potter in.' Her face lit up. 'I've never lived in a house with a garden. A square of back yard is all I've managed up to now.'

David stood up as he heard voices in the hall. Daisy looked so vulnerable, he had an irresistible urge to stretch out a hand to her and pull her close, to promise to protect her, to stand by her, whatever the future might hold. Joshua had been in a strange, optimistic mood that afternoon, thanking David for his friendship, enthusiastic about the cottage, wanting details, wondering when they might go to see it.

'If Daisy doesn't stop pushing herself so hard she's the one who'll need a doctor, not me. I'll be glad to get her out of here,' he'd said.

David spoke quickly. 'We'll have to go and see the cottage soon. I know the owner's son, and he's said he'll let us view it before it goes on the market.'

'The sooner the better,' Daisy said.

'Sally's been sick.' Edna handed over a green-faced child, with the front of her tweed coat stiff with vomit. 'But she's all right now. She was all right the minute she got it up.'

'On the tram,' Oliver explained. 'She kneeled up on her seat and sicked on a lady sitting behind us.'

'On her shoes,' Sally verified.

'There were bits of nuts in it.' Oliver turned to his sister for confirmation.

'And carrots.'

'From her dinner.' Oliver opened his mouth wide. 'I wasn't sick, but I've got black spit from treacle toffee.'

Edna removed Oliver's cap from his head and stuffed it in his pocket. 'Remember Miss Manners next time, Oliver.'

'We went on the horses twice.' Oliver had decided to ignore his aunt.

Edna watched Daisy peel her small daughter out of the sour-smelling coat. 'That child's got acidosis. Our Betty, bless her, had regular attacks once a month till Doctor Marsden whipped her tonsils out on our dining-room table for half a crown. I expect you'd have to take her to the hospital nowadays.'

'I'm not going to the hospital. I'm not, am I not, Mummy?' Sally began to cry in a high-pitched wail.

As Daisy picked her up she saw Oliver stuffing a piece of the mock marzipan into his mouth. On the stove a pan boiled over, spluttering and hissing on to the hot plate.

'You're a naughty boy!' Daisy rescued the pan, pushing it to the back of the cooker. 'Can't you behave yourself, just for once?'

The gentle smack she gave Oliver was no more than the reflex action of overstretched nerves, but he yelped as loudly as if he'd been given a vicious swipe with a cat-o'-nine-tails.

'You're a cheeky monkey!' he yelled, marzipan and black saliva running down his chin.

Controlling herself with difficulty Daisy lifted a strand of Sally's sticky hair. 'I'll take her upstairs and give her a bath and wash this.' She turned at the door. 'You can stop that noise, Oliver, and when I come down again you can say you're sorry for speaking to me like that.'

'You'll kill yourself,' Edna said in a voice of doom, following her into the hall. 'Having the house overflowing for Easter, with all you have to do on top.' She went with Daisy to the foot of the stairs. 'I noticed a funny smell in the kitchen just now. You don't think it's the Good Friday fish going off?'

From the third stair Daisy looked down at her auntie. Not one word of apology for stuffing Sally full of chocolate, rock, candy floss, ice cream and God alone knew what else. No wonder her mother had once said that her sister only needed to walk past a cow in a field for its milk to curdle.

Edna hadn't finished – not quite. 'You'll have to master that lad. Before he masters *you*,' she predicted. 'Our Betty, bless her, would never have spoken to me like that.'

'If I'd had a knife on me I'd've plunged it into her chest. Till it came out the other side,' Daisy told Joshua that night as, too tired to wet the front of her hair into a wave, she got into her bed.

'Did David tell you about the cottage he thinks we'll

like?' Joshua sounded enthusiastic, bright with hope, the ring of optimism deepening his husky voice.

'You sound more like Robert Donat every day,' Daisy whispered, asleep almost before her head touched the pillow. 'You have a lovely voice just like his.'

'I love you too,' Joshua said, knowing even as he spoke that she was already dropping into sleep.

Chapter Three

On the day David drove them in his old Wolseley out to see the cottage the air was warm with the promise of summer. Puffball clouds skidded across a bright blue sky, and not far out of Blackpool they passed a man walking down a road in a short-sleeved shirt.

Daisy, to tone in with the countryside, was wearing a red and white checked gingham dress in the new length, which David thought suited her perfectly and said so.

'Because it covers my legs,' Daisy said.

'There's nothing wrong with your legs,' David had said, then wondered why Daisy had blushed to the roots of her hair. 'Not that I've seen much of them,' he'd added, making it worse.

Winnie and Leonard had waved them off from *Shangri-La*, promising to see to everything, including the children on their return from school. Daisy had made it easy for Winnie by organizing a ham salad, with new potatoes to go with it to make it seem a bit more substantial.

She wondered how David had managed to find the petrol for such a comparatively long drive, but she wasn't going to ask. He drove casually, with one hand on the wheel and the other held loosely on the gears. She thought he looked more like Leslie Howard than ever that day.

She found him most attractive, and why not? She wasn't doing anyone any harm admiring the way his fair hair grew into an endearing peak at the back of his head, and if she would have liked to reach out and stroke it, then so what? She wasn't exactly a *young* woman, but she was a long, long way from being old, and it was such a *change* to be sitting still, with her hands idle in her lap, bowling along country lanes with the hedges growing greenly on either side. It beat working for a living any old day, she told herself; it beat slaving over a hot stove and running up and down stairs like a yo-yo on elastic. And she had to admit, it did make her feel deliciously abandoned to be admiring the way another man's hair grew, as he sat beside her unsuspecting husband.

'All right there, in the back?' David glanced up at her through the driving mirror and thought she looked a trifle hot. 'Wind the window down if you like. Joshua will say if he feels a draught, won't you, old chap?'

By the way Joshua moved his shoulders impatiently Daisy knew he resented being asked.

'Mrs MacDougal next door looks at me these days as if she thinks I'm a coffin dodger,' he'd said that morning, and Daisy had said what a dreadful expression but she knew what he meant. Mrs MacDougal flirted with her own death every single day.

'Even her goosepimples turn septic,' Daisy had said, causing Joshua to laugh out loud.

She settled back in her seat. The cottage was a long way from Blackpool, almost twenty-five miles, David had said, but closer to Blackburn, Daisy's home town.

'It's a cottage with a lot of character,' he told them, as they drove through the outskirts of Preston. 'It has the triple windows of the period, and one of the original window openings of the loomshop has been enlarged to make a separate doorway.'

'A handloom weaver's cottage?' At once Daisy substituted the thatched roof she'd been imagining for the grey slate of a hundred and fifty years ago. 'My father once took me to see a house like that at a place called Copy Nook, not far from where we had our pie shop. But in that case the loomshop had been made into a separate house. My father was an amateur historian, cum botanist, cum architect, David, as well as being an unqualified engineer. He would have pointed out that row of almshouses we've just passed and told you the exact year they were built. I wish I'd known him better,' she added wistfully. 'I'm always telling Joshua how much *he* reminds me of my father.'

So *that* was the initial attraction? Smoothly David changed gear. He'd wondered lately. It was a happy marriage, he was sure of that. Joshua *adored* his wife, but lately, since that freezing cold evening in the pub, David had found himself watching Daisy – and wondering. Was she as contented as she appeared to be, or was she, unknown to herself, playing a part? Were her feet as firmly on the ground as he believed them to be, leaving her head up in the clouds? She was a Gemini, he knew that – a real two-headed woman.

'Stick to what you know about,' his father always said, when he tried to equate his patient's symptoms with their attitude of mind. 'Leave all that Freudian guesswork to the headshrinkers.'

David half-turned round, keeping his eye on the road. 'There are times when I wish I didn't know my own father half as well as I do,' he said aloud, and they laughed.

Daisy thought she knew exactly what he meant. Old Doctor Armitage was a product of the old school, the doctor of Victorian drawings. He had worn a top hat right up to the war starting, and even now he carried a black bag, the kind her mother had explained was the right shape for bringing babies in – rounded, without corners, so the baby could lie comfortably.

'If you specialized, what would it be in, David?' By

the way Joshua's head was lolling forward it looked as if he had gone to sleep.

There was no hesitation. 'Nutrition,' David said at once. 'For well over a year I thought about little else but food. The Japs were diabolically clever at doling out just enough to keep a man half alive and well enough to do the work of a navvy. I found the constant grumbling about rationing hard to take when I came home at first.'

Daisy felt a pang of shame.

'There's talk of the government reducing the daily intake of calories to over two and a half thousand, and the Conservatives are bleating about malnutrition!' David stepped on the accelerator, surging forward to overtake a red Ribble bus. 'Good God! I wonder how far they'd have got on a spoonful of rice a day?' He slowed down. 'Sorry. I didn't mean to get on my soap-box. I don't often. Can you see the two green domes over there? That's Stoneyhurst College. Do you know what colour they would be if they were cleaned?'

'A bright copper. The green is verdigris,' Daisy said promptly, glad that he had changed the subject and disgusted with herself for feeling like that.

'Her father told her that,' Joshua said, proving he was wide awake after all.

Daisy lowered the window a bit more to have a good sniff at the country smells. They were so different from the seaside smells of salt, shrimps and fish and chips. She imagined a picture postcard cottage, with honey-suckle and roses climbing up the grey walls, and a bluebell wood at the bottom of the garden.

Her knowledge of the countryside could have been written on a postage stamp and still left wide margins. Her eyes were town eyes, but from now on things were going to be very different. This time next year she would be an apple-cheeked sturdy countrywoman, leaning over a gate in a poke sunbonnet. But not *too* sturdy, she amended, admiring the way the belt on her new dress clinched in her waist.

'You mean this is it?'

Daisy couldn't hide her disappointment. This was no isolated cottage of her imaginings, sweetly buried in a meadow of wild flowers, with pepper-pot chimneys sending dear little puffs of smoke up into a blue sky. This cottage was in the middle of a longish terrace of handloom weavers' dwellings, with the long tripled windows in uniform rows. Just as David had said.

Joshua shaded his eyes against the sun. 'Pendle Hill looks as close as if it was within walking distance.' He pointed to the hump-backed hill. 'Yet it's miles away. It's strange how such a vast area always seems to be in the shadow of Pendle. It broods over the whole landscape.'

Daisy ignored Pendle. She was looking down the road trying to see if there was a school within walking distance, but as the road curved round all she could see was a horse-trough across the road, a garage with two petrol pumps in the forecourt, and further on than that a church with a spire and a pub with a swinging sign.

Each cottage was set back behind a tiny front garden fronted by a low stone wall. David walked up a path and lifted the knocker on a front door.

'You need to see it from the back. You're in for a surprise when you see the view from there.'

'Thanks be to goodness,' Daisy whispered to Joshua. 'I get more of the feeling of the countryside from my two plants on the kitchen windowsill.' She raised her eyebrows at the two petrol pumps. 'Can't you hear the ring of the hammer on the anvil? Can't you smell the hot aroma of horses on such a summer's day, and the Sunday dinners cooking on open hearths?'

A man wearing an army beret was standing watching them from the forecourt of the garage. To Joshua's embarrassment Daisy gave him a cheery wave.

Mrs Rothwell opened the door and stared anxiously at her visitors. She never let anyone over her doorstep if she could help it, but her son had persuaded her that the time had definitely come to move. The garden was too big for her to manage, and since Mr Rothwell had suffered a seizure he was of no more use than a chocolate fireguard. If he couldn't decide which day it was, how could he help her to make up her mind about something as important as this?

'You'd best come in,' she said reluctantly.

She had known young David Armitage since the days when his mother and father had a weekend cottage in the village. He'd been a real tinker, forever riding on the flags on his bicycle and scrumping apples. Though the way he was looking now she bet he could be dropped through a flute without setting it playing.

She led them through a room so overcrowded with furniture and knick-knacks they had to pick their way carefully. Daisy looked up and saw cobwebs dangling from the oak beams and thought how picturesque. The furniture was so dusty her fingers itched to get a cloth to it.

'That's what's worrying me,' Mrs Rothwell said, as if continuing a conversation. 'How am I going to fit everything into the bungalow at St Anne's my son picked out for us? And how can I ever get used to going to bed downstairs?'

In the back room an old man slept in a rocking chair by the fire, parchment hands clasped over his stomach. His hair was so thin and white and lay so loosely on his scalp, it looked as if a sudden draught from the door would blow it away. A large chesterfield covered in horse-hair was set at right angles to the fireplace, and an oak dresser dripping with willow-patterned crockery stood against the far wall.

Daisy walked over to the window.

On that spring day, with the air as light and fresh as a glass of sparkling wine, Pendle's graceful outline was as clearly etched as if it lay just across the meadows. Not another house in sight.

There it was. The *real* countryside. Daisy clasped her hands together. She stared in awe at the fringe of far-away trees, leaning into a non-existent wind. The long garden was full of blossom and birdsong. Quite carried away, she imagined she heard a cuckoo calling from a distant wood.

If they bought the cottage – and oh, dear God, they just *had* to buy the cottage – she would have a *view* to look at instead of a brick wall. She leaned forward and rubbed a clear patch on the none too clean window pane. Surely that was a hare lolloping across the grass? She almost wished she was wearing her glasses.

'It was once two cottages,' Mrs Rothwell was saying. 'Two up and two down, but with sculleries built on at the back. I've heard tell that two brothers lived in them with their young wives.'

Reluctantly Daisy turned her back on the view.

Joshua's face was rapt. 'Can you tell us any more about them?'

Mrs Rothwell nodded. 'Oh aye. Mr Rothwell could write a book on the history of the village. He reckons the brothers were farmhands, paid nobbut a pittance, so to make ends meet they put their wives to weaving at looms set up in the two front rooms. They worked as long as the light held, poor souls, and if you look underneath the oilcloth on the floor you can see the outline of the holes they dug beneath their loom tread-les.'

'To fill with water.' Joshua's expression was alight with interest. 'So that evaporation would help to keep the warp in the right condition for weaving.'

'The Hindu weavers used to do the same.'

Everyone turned to stare at the old man. His voice was surprisingly strong and booming. 'The Hindus dug trenches in the shade of trees, and where the water flowed they put their looms.'

Mrs Rothwell's round head bobbed up and down again. 'He could write a book on cotton. He was a weaver himself before they shut the mill down.'

'That Gandhi has a lot to answer for. Coming over here cracking on to be humble.'

'He never liked Gandhi,' Mrs Rothwell explained, as her husband went back to sleep. 'He doesn't trust foreigners. Our Walter married a girl from Ireland, and he found it very hard to take to her at first.'

She was looking more anxious than ever. Young David's letter had asked if he could bring a couple of friends along with him to see the cottage, nothing serious at all. But the girl in the red checked dress meant business. She was staring through the window again and any minute now she'd be whipping the money out of her handbag and throwing it down on the table. The sharply scored wrinkles on her crab-apple face deepened. Their Walter was in it somewhere, she'd stake her life on it. In the letter David had mentioned a cash sale as his friends had property to sell in Blackpool. She bowed her head. Couldn't they see she hadn't made her mind up yet?

'We'll have a cup of tea,' she said, thinking to delay any dangerous talk about buying and selling. 'It's all ready on a tray.'

Daisy followed her through into the scullery with its stone slopstone and rusting water geyser.

Mrs Rothwell could tell what this determined young

woman was thinking. 'The water heats up from the living-room fire,' she said, as huffed as if Daisy had insulted the geyser. 'There's no call to bother with that. Walter paid for us to have a bath and a toilet put in upstairs, but we haven't really taken to the bath. We mostly have a wash-down in here. With it being what we're used to. Mr Rothwell was in the Boer War, and he got accustomed to washing himself in a saucerful of water. It was needs must out there.'

Daisy picked up the tray. 'Your son must be very relieved to know you're going to live quite close to him at St Annes.'

'But not *with* him! Mr Rothwell could write a book about the trouble we've seen in this village with old folks moving in with their children. The young ones have their own lives to lead and their lives aren't like their parents'. How can they be when you think of all the years between?'

'How old is your son?'

'Sixty-one come August.'

'A mere strip of a lad,' said Daisy.

'Well, what did you think, Daisy?'

David stopped the car a mile or so down the road.

'What did *you* think, Joshua?'

David could feel Daisy treading with caution, letting Joshua have his say first, not rushing him. He could almost hear her holding her breath.

Joshua took his time about answering. He had been very quiet back there in the cottage. A totally impractical man, he could see the whole place needed a lick of paint, but that shouldn't create much of a problem. The garden, though – that was another matter. David hadn't told him about the greenhouse; it needed seeing to but it could soon be made usable.

'I had a greenhouse for a time,' he said at last. 'I grew

tomatoes in the summer and chrysanthemums in the winter. Mop-head. This big.' He cupped his hands into a circle. 'Disbudding is the secret if you want giant blooms.'

It was the first time Daisy had heard about a greenhouse. Joshua had said that the house he lived in with his first wife had a garden of sorts, but he'd never mentioned the greenhouse. Was it just one of the things he'd pushed to the back of his mind after she'd died? Along with all the other memories he hadn't wanted to share? Mrs Mac from Balmoral next door had said that Joshua's wife had ended her life choked up with consumption, a bag of skin and bone.

But all that was before he'd moved into one of the attic bedrooms at Shangri-La, where Daisy had first seen him smiling down at her from the landing, his pipe in one hand and a book in the other. Reminding her of Herbert Marshall.

'Joshua?' Daisy touched him. 'What did you think? I'd rather hear your opinion first.'

He smiled on her with love. 'That cottage has been waiting for you. Living there is where you're meant to be,' he said.

As David drove on Joshua closed his eyes, seeing the garden as he knew it would look once the worst of the trailing weeds had been cleared away. He would fill in the small spaces between the perennials in the border with annuals and white alyssum planted in clumps. He might risk fuchsias as the garden was fairly sheltered by the stone wall at the bottom. He settled lower in the passenger seat. He might have to replace that rusty old relic of a stove, because the greenhouse must be kept warm to overwinter his houseplants and his chrysanthemums. It was too late now for tomatoes, but next year – oh, *next* year. What a glory of a garden it would be. He had spotted wisteria growing up a side wall, and half hidden in the long grass a magnolia tree. He smiled to himself . . .

As happy as a sandboy, Daisy thought, leaning over to look at him. 'I think we've found another Shangri-La,' she whispered, and David said he thought so too. 'And we have you to thank for finding it for us. Thank you for being our true good friend.'

'I wouldn't count too many chickens. Mrs Rothwell hasn't made her mind up. She's lived in that village all her life, you know.'

David put his foot down hard on the accelerator. Why had he said a thing like that so quickly? Why had he put a damper on things? What was wrong with him? During that terrible time in the war, when to survive was all that mattered, he had been forced to acknowledge his gift for self-analysis. So that now he could ask himself why Daisy's enthusiasm for the cottage had strangely irritated him.

He'd noticed her expression when Mrs Rothwell had taken them through into the adjoining cottage and explained that before her husband's stroke she had run a small shop from the front room, selling sweets and confectionery.

'*Home-made* confectionery?' Daisy's question was loaded. David had known that at once.

Mrs Rothwell had explained that it had never been more than a little hobby, and that during the war she had only opened up when she felt like it. The points system for the sweets and all the form-filling had upset her, what with the Food Office being a bus ride away and filled with snappy spinsters when you got there.

'Old age is a *bore*!' she'd said fiercely, showing David a fleeting glimpse of the bright young woman she had once been.

Oh yes, he was in no doubt at all about what Daisy's plans would be for the neglected little shop with its dusty shelves and mahogany counter covered by a tattered bedspread. In spite of all her protestations and avowed intention of being no more than a devoted wife and besotted mother, he knew Daisy for what she was: a product of a mother who had worked till she dropped, whose mother in her turn had left her looms in a weaving shed for barely long enough to have her babies, enduring the enforced lying-in period impatiently till she could get back to work.

He drove on, wondering just how long it would be before Joshua's wife would be back in business again. Not that it mattered, it wasn't his concern one way or the other.

Joshua and Daisy were talking to each other, happiness singing in their voices.

'Mrs Rothwell says it's a church school, so that's good, and there's a butcher's shop, a small grocer's, and a greengrocer's cart that comes round twice a week.'

David could see Daisy's animated face through the driving mirror. She was in her element. Joshua had been right when he'd said Daisy was always looking for some new challenge. David frowned and changed gear. He hoped she wasn't going to tire Joshua out with her wild enthusiasms.

'There is actually a dress shop, run from the front parlour of one of the cottages, though they probably sell things I personally wouldn't be seen dead in.'

'Such as?'

David could always tell when Joshua was teasing his wife, but she explained quite seriously: 'Magyar nightgowns, slips with built-up shoulders, pink and green directoire knickers and elastic stockings.' She leaned forward, resting her arms on the back of Joshua's seat. 'I didn't see a bakehouse, though there could have been one at the back of the grocer's shop. There must be one somewhere to buy morning fresh bread.'

'The crocuses should have been dealt with before now,' Joshua said, managing to get a word in at last. 'And the dead heads on those daffodils should have gone weeks ago. The hyacinths ought to have been beheaded and their bulbs buried if they are to come up next year.'

'The whole place needs a good airing, though the living room is cosy with its open fire,' Daisy said.

'The cottage has obviously been neglected.'

David drove on, wondering if he'd become invisible. When Joshua began talking about felling a couple of trees to make room for a hen cote at the bottom of the garden, he gave up. Was this the man both he and his father had envisaged spending the few remaining years left to him nodding in the sunshine as the serenity of country life flowed sweetly round him? More importantly, was this the escape Joshua had secretly yearned for, shut away at the top of the boarding house, hating the bustle and noisiness of Daisy's chosen job of work?

Already Joshua seemed to have shed years. His pale face was flushed, his eyes bright. And he hadn't coughed once for at least an hour.

No, he wouldn't come inside, David told them, shaking hands with Joshua on the pavement outside Shangri-La. He kissed Daisy's cheek.

'I'll write this evening and make the Rothwells a definite offer. Thanks again, David.' Joshua's smile was rueful. 'I know I've been a bit depressed lately. I must have been a real old misery at times.'

'You can't be anything but lovely.' Daisy took him by the arm and together they climbed the three steps to the front door.

They went inside, still talking, forgetting to turn round and wave.

The house David shared with his father was built of

smooth red Accrington brick and had a surgery built on to the side. It was empty when he let himself in, and there were no messages on the telephone pad. For a moment he felt almost let down.

When he went into the kitchen he saw a tin of Spam placed pointedly in the middle of the scrubbed table, with a tin opener beside it. That, he knew, was his father's way of showing and telling him what to eat on the day when Mrs Platts their housekeeper went to Fleetwood to visit her widowed sister who was having a bad time with her nerves.

The kitchen was very tidy. Mrs Platts prided herself on never leaving anything 'out', so that it gleamed and shone, as bare and unlived in as a hospital theatre. Mrs Platts washed everything with unyielding blocks of hard yellow soap: their shirts, the floor, even her hands and face – which contradicted all the beauty manuals by remaining as smooth as if they went to bed every night under a layer of Ponds cold cream. The soap had a distinctive carbolicy nutty smell, overriding any cooking smells which might have lingered in the kitchen. David stood by the table, holding the rectangular tin of pink and rubbery meat. Daisy's kitchen smelled of hot crusty loaves, roasting lamb spiked with rosemary, and bubbling raspberry jam.

Throwing the tin back on the table David walked quickly into the hall, picked up the telephone and dialled a familiar number almost without volition; almost as a reflex action, in fact.

Nora Jolly answered the telephone quickly, but not *too* quickly. She knew it was David's day off and had been expecting him to ring, but her simulated surprise would, she prided herself, have guaranteed her a place at RADA.

'Hallo? Who? Oh, *David*! How are you? You sound a bit fraught.'

'I'm okay. I've just got back from showing a cottage off to some friends of mine. Joshua Penny? You know, the bloke I play chess with, when I get the opportunity.'

Nora wasn't interested in Joshua Penny. 'Have you eaten, David?' In a flash she sacrificed the tin of salmon bought with sixteen carefully saved points, and hoarded against the possibility of her having to eat alone on her fortieth birthday six weeks away. 'I can rustle up a salmon and cucumber salad in no time at all.'

'Did you say *salmon*?'

'Right then. I'll expect you.'

'When?'

'An hour? That suit you?'

In the time it took Nora Jolly to change into a beige linen dress which exactly matched her beige hair, and make up her face with beige face powder and a touch of coral lipstick, Daisy had given Joshua his meal on a tray, told Winnie and Leonard to go for a walk, made Miss Grimshaw a fresh pot of tea because she complained that the one Winnie had made her was stewed, tidied up the kitchen, eaten her own meal standing up and chivvied the children in and out of the bath.

Rosy and tired, but determined not to admit to it, they sat on Joshua's knees while he told them about the cottage.

'Where will the sea go to?' Sally found the idea of moving house hard to come to terms with. 'Will they lift this house on to a big lorry?'

'The sea will stop *here*,' Oliver explained, exchanging a manly look of tolerant exasperation with his father. 'You stupid clot.'

At once Joshua opened his knees so that Oliver slid

off. 'That's not a very nice thing to call your sister. Is it?'

'Well, she is.' Oliver was unrepentant. 'Winnie says stupid clot all the time, and it's not a swear word because I asked her.'

'Bugger's a swear word,' explained Sally, gazing up into Joshua's face with wide and innocent eyes.

'And fart is rude,' Oliver said, eager not to be outdone.

'And bosom,' said Sally, with a triumphant glance at her brother. 'That's the worst swear word of all.'

'That will do!' Joshua was having difficulty keeping his face straight. He made room for Oliver on his left knee again, even though their combined weight was giving him pins and needles. 'You'll *love* living in the country.' He lowered his voice dramatically. 'There won't be anyone else sharing the house with us. There'll be just the four of us, and maybe – just maybe a little dog.'

Entering into the conspiracy both children hunched their shoulders and compressed their lips together.

'And a cat?' Sally's big eyes were as round as chocolate drops. 'A weeny teeny lickle kitten?'

'And a horse?' Oliver asked, with the air of someone who knows he hasn't a chance but might as well ask.

'Maybe not of your very own, but there were horses in the field. And cows. I bet the farmer lets you watch him milk the cows.'

Oliver pretended to spit from the side of his mouth. 'Catch me doing a horrible thing like that.'

Sally's thumb was in her mouth. She leaned into Joshua's chest. Her eyelids were drooping, but when Joshua whispered it was time she was in bed she sat bolt upright at once.

'Are we going to live in the country tomorrow?' she wanted to know.

Within a few minutes of Daisy tucking her into bed she was asleep, the fiercely sucked thumb at the ready an inch from her mouth. Oliver, flat on his back in his own narrow bed, looked anxious and worried.

'Will I be able to take all my things? My cricket bat and football? My Bagatelle and my books?' He began to read out the titles of the books on the shelf underneath the window. '*The Water Babies, The Magic Day at the* . . .'

'All your books,' Daisy said firmly, tucking him in, knowing Oliver's delaying tactics far too well to let him get away with it. Bending down, she kissed him on his forehead, surprised when Oliver's arms came up round her neck, pulling her down to whisper in her ear.

'Will the country make Daddy better?'

Daisy held her breath. They'd tried so hard to keep the seriousness of Joshua's illnesses from the children; told themselves that kids were notoriously selfish and probably hadn't understood. Now all the pent-up anxiety was there in Oliver's hoarse little voice.

'He's better already, just for seeing it,' she said. 'By the time we've been there a few months he'll be as strong as . . .'

'Tarzan?'

'He'll make that old Tarzan look like a pale stick of celery,' she promised, walking softly to the door and switching off the light.

'Mummy? Can I have . . .?'

'A drink of water? There's one on your locker.'

'Mummy? I've got a pain in my stomach.'

'I'll come back in ten minutes and if it hasn't gone then I'll give you a dose of syrup of figs, okay?'

'Mummy? Can I have . . .?'

Firmly, with a decisive click, Daisy closed the bedroom door.

'Have you told Miss Grimshaw you're leaving?'

Winnie, back from her walk with Leonard, was in one of her truculent moods. She stood by the kitchen table, threading a rayon headscarf through her fingers. 'She's bound to take it badly.'

Daisy moved quickly to close the door.

'The reason I haven't told Miss Grimshaw yet, or the other regulars, is because nothing's settled.' Daisy was busy stretching ten rashers of bacon to give twenty-two people a hearty breakfast. Rolling out pastry made with the congealed fat from the streaky bacon. It was time-consuming and fiddly, but she needed the rest of her visitors' weekly bacon ration to go with the liver the butcher had promised her for Wednesday. 'It's not even certain that the couple who own the cottage will accept our offer.'

'Oh, so you've offered then?' Winnie took off her coat and looped it over her arm. 'The very first cottage you saw? You must be in an almighty hurry to get shut of this place.'

'Joshua's writing to the owners tonight.' Using a small pudding basin, Daisy began to cut the pastry into rounds. She took one look at Winnie's mutinous face and sighed. 'He really *took* to the place, Winnie. Can't you see why?' Gathering up the off-cuts she began to roll them out again. 'It could be the making of him.'

'There's plenty of fresh air going begging at Blackpool. If I hadn't grabbed on to Leonard he'd have landed up in the Isle of Man, it was that windy on the prom tonight.'

'You *know* what I mean.' A note of exasperation crept into Daisy's voice. 'For one thing it's too bracing for Joshua here.' She thumped another circle out of the pastry. 'He stopped going for his nightly constitutionals ages ago.' She gathered up the remnants for the last rolling. 'So where does that leave him?'

'You'll never get four more circles out of that.'

'Want a bet?' Daisy sprinkled flour on to the table. 'It leaves him sitting upstairs on his own now he's stopped working. It leaves *him* up there, and *me* down here, too busy to talk to him.'

'Mr MacDougal next door does the shopping and the washing-up for *his* missus.'

The look Daisy gave Winnie made her blink in surprise.

'Joshua isn't Angus MacDougal. Now, come on, Winnie, admit it!'

Winnie had to agree. 'Angus MacDougal is a lazy tyke with a beer belly as big as a gasworks who would sit on his backside all day if his wife would let him.'

'Exactly!' Daisy picked up the last pastry circle rolled to the thickness of thin tissue paper. 'Now pass me that bowl of chopped potatoes and leeks if you're looking for something to do. There's a sprig or two of parsley on the dresser. I think this lot needs a bit of colour.'

'It's me what needs a bit of colour,' Winnie said, bursting into tears. 'With me being nearly three months up the spout.'

'I'll come up as soon as I can, love.'

Joshua was sitting in his chair reading when Daisy ran upstairs. The finished letter to the Rothwells was on the table by his side, but Daisy said she would look at it when she came up later, that at the moment there was a bit of a crisis going on downstairs. He looked tired, so she suggested that he got into bed and she would bring him a hot drink up in a little while.

'You spoil me,' he said, his eyes twinkling.

'You're worth it,' she answered back.

Winnie had stopped crying when Daisy went back into the kitchen. She was sipping the cup of tea Daisy had automatically produced, her pointed features sharpened with anguish.

'I'm ready to talk now,' she said. 'I've got to tell somebody. I've got to unburden meself.'

Daisy poured herself a cup of tea and sat down. 'What does Leonard think about it?' She stretched a hand out across the table as Winnie burst into noisy tears once again. 'He *knows*, doesn't he?'

'He's as chuffed as if I'd made him a present of the Town Hall clock.'

'Well, then. It's not the end of the world, love. You won't be the first girl to anticipate her wedding night.'

'You mean to get caught.' Winnie's face twisted out of shape with the force of her emotions. 'Why don't you call a spade a flippin' spade?'

'All right then. Get caught. But you're getting married in less than a month's time. Oh, love, I wish you'd told me before instead of keeping it all to yourself. I'd have understood and tried to help.'

'You mean gin in a hot bath? Or castor oil? Or would you have taken me to that old witch by the bus station who charges thirty pounds to get rid?'

'Winnie!' Daisy was startled at the way Winnie spat out the words. 'Why on earth should you want to get rid of it when Leonard's so pleased?'

She was at a loss for words, that was all. She wasn't *shocked*. If Winnie was trying to say that she wanted the baby aborted then she would try to make her see how dangerous that could be. A memory flashed into Daisy's mind of her mother and her Auntie Edna talking in whispers about a weaver from the mill who had done something unspeakable with a knitting needle and died four days later septic to her bone marrow. And another woman with six children who, rather than have a seventh, had persuaded her husband to help her. Only to die with her life's blood running down the ambulance steps as they took her away, too late to save her.

Winnie wished she didn't have to tell Daisy the next

bit. She wished she had a mother she could tell; she wished she was religious and could make a confession to a priest in a kiosk like she'd seen on the pictures, with Bing Crosby sitting in it dressed up as Father O'Reilly. It would be such a comfort to light a few candles and say a few Hail Marys, and go away cleansed and forgiven.

But all she had was Daisy, and even if what she was going to tell her would shake her to the nellies, Daisy would understand. Winnie couldn't go on, not a day longer with the knowledge and the guilt gnawing away at her, like a rat shoved down the front of her blouse.

She started to cry in earnest again. 'It's not Leonard's baby,' she sobbed.

'Oh, my God!' The blasphemy slipped out before Daisy could bite it back. 'Then whose?'

Winnie rolled a sodden handkerchief into a ball. 'You remember the fella in number five when the cold snap was on? The one with the rude tattoos all down his arms?'

'The Desert Rat?' Daisy remembered him at once. Corn-gold hair and a dimple in his chin. Big and brawny, with a laugh like the bath water going down, and a habit of coming out on the landing in his vest and an old pair of army trousers. 'But how? When? He was only here for two nights.'

'It was when I went to put a hot-water bottle in his bed. You remember we were short of the rubber ones and we had to use that ancient copper thing? He made a joke about it having come out of the Ark and keeping Noah's feet warm and I laughed – and he laughed – and that was it.'

Daisy passed her a dry handkerchief. As in any crisis, a deadly calm had come over her. 'Look, love, don't upset yourself by telling me any more. What we've got to decide now is how to do the best for everybody.'

Winnie's head came up with a jerk. 'It's got nothing to do with *everybody*. What I'm telling you must never go beyond these four walls. I'm only telling *you* because the not telling nobody is killing me.' She looked suddenly very affronted. 'I'm not a sex maniac, that's the funny part. There were two men, and near as dammit *three* during the war. Then Leonard on the times we could get his mother to bed and hide her sticks.' She raised a tear-stained face. 'But this one I can't explain. When he kissed me I went to jelly, and when he went to turn the key in the door and I knew what was going to happen I couldn't help meself.' She closed her eyes. 'It wasn't romantic, Daisy. He never told me he loved me or nothing. And I had that many clothes on he almost needed a search warrant to find what he was looking for.'

'Winnie!'

'Well, it's true! But oh, Daisy, it was like all the dreams I'd ever had about lovemaking come true. It was the best loving I've ever had; he was so . . .'

Daisy felt it was time to interrupt, or goodness knows what details Winnie would reveal. 'And you think this baby is his and not Leonard's?'

It was almost a rhetorical question. For a brief hysterical moment Daisy saw, in her mind's eye, a vision of the two contenders for fatherhood standing side by side. On the left the Desert Rat, torso rippling with tattooed muscles, an Adonis-like head rising from a strong tanned neck, and on the right Leonard Smalley, thin, with brushed-back black hair, a quivering goatee beard and a tendency to flinch if anyone coughed or raised their voice above a whisper.

'Are you going to tell the father?' We've got his address in the book. He *ought* to be told if you're sure.'

'And his wife and his three kids? Ought *they* to know too?' Winnie's eyes were no more than swollen slits.

'No. It's *got* to be Leonard's, and if it's a boy with fair hair and shoulders on him like an ox, I'll say I have a weight-lifting uncle who was once a runner-up to Mr Universe.' Like a child, she knuckled her eyes, leaving a circle of white from the flour-dredged table. 'What do *you* think I should do, Daisy? It really matters to me what you say I ought to do.'

A couple of visitors were going upstairs to bed. They called their goodnights and Daisy answered back. She frowned. Joshua would be waiting to talk to her; the circles of pastry still waited for their fillings. If she was going to bake them tonight, leaving them to be merely heated through in the morning, it was going to be going on for midnight before she went to bed.

But Winnie was waiting here and now. She was peering at Daisy through those puffy eyes with their sandy eyelashes as if Daisy were God and her idol Vera Lynne rolled into one. It was a terrible responsibility, because whatever Daisy said Winnie would accept as gospel and act upon. Daisy knew that for the truth it was. She took a deep breath.

'There's that terrible word "principles", Winnie. Things we are supposed to try to live up to, for the good of our souls. There's honesty too, and the sadness of living a lie and deceiving a good man into believing that a child is his own flesh and blood.'

'So you think I should tell Leonard?' Winnie's face was peaked and terrified, like that of a small mouse driven into a corner, waiting for the cat to pounce.

'No!' Daisy's voice was firm and strong. 'Principles are all right as long as they're kept in their place. But the way I see it is this: if you write and tell what was his name – the Desert Rat – then you hurt his wife and his children, and maybe wreck his marriage. You know his circumstances better than me.'

'I didn't really *know* him,' Winnie whispered, hope dawning in her eyes.

'If you tell Leonard, do you think he'd tell you it didn't matter whose child you were carrying, and bring it up as his own?'

'Never! I kidded him into thinking it was the first time with him, which wasn't easy with him being in the Red Cross and knowing about such things.'

Daisy interrupted before any more intimate details were forthcoming. 'So to tell Leonard would make him unhappy and possibly end any hopes of him marrying you?'

Winnie nodded. 'That's for sure. He's funny about faithfulness and things like that.'

'So that would be at least six or seven people with their whole lives ruined on account of *your* principles.'

'You mean I should keep it a secret?'

'Between you, me and these four walls,' Daisy said with firm conviction. 'And if that makes *me* a woman without principles, then it's God help us both.'

'Amen,' Winnie said, smiling properly for the first time in days.

'Let's have another cup of tea,' said Daisy.

Nora Jolly served David coffee in exquisite gold fluted china cups that had belonged to her grandmother. He settled back into the corner of her well-upholstered sofa, feeling relaxed and tired and yet wanting to talk.

'She's a real puzzle to me, that wife of Joshua Penny's. You get the impression she's so controlled an earthquake wouldn't shake her composure, and yet today I saw her transformed from a hard-working drudge into a young girl about to realize her wildest dreams.'

'I thought you said her husband was terminally ill?'

'Not in so many words I didn't.' David put his coffee cup down on the small sofa-table by his side. 'It's a case that could go one way or the other. Doctors can be wrong, and when they're proved wrong it's a time to welcome and accept their own fallibility.'

'You'll always do that, David. Your experiences during the war must have taught you humility. Extreme privation must be totally destructive of arrogance.'

Now what had she said wrong? Nora moved quickly to refill his cup. The sudden flash of coldness in David's blue eyes made her realize that not for the first time she had overstepped the mark by mentioning his time as a prisoner of war. She added a spoonful of lovingly cherished brown sugar.

'And you think they'll buy the cottage?'

'No doubt about it. Daisy has made up her mind, and my guess is that when Daisy Penny's mind is made up it's a *fait accompli*. Joshua once told me that a couple of years before the war she walked into the boarding house, had a quick look round, inspected the contents, including Joshua himself, and decided. Wham! Just like that.' He accepted a second cup of coffee. 'You see, the way I look at it is this. The running of a boarding house ought ideally to incorporate a partnership, a husband and wife, a mother and daughter, two sisters. What I'm trying to say is that there ought not to be one member of that partnership working like stink, while the other remains almost disconnected from the whole venture.'

'But I thought you said Joshua isn't well enough . . .'

'Not now, he isn't. But if he *had* been he wouldn't have been interested. He's an academic in some respects. A quiet sensitive man who got his lungs filled with poison gas during the first war, settled for teaching backward children.' David corrected himself quickly. 'No, not *settled* for teaching them. Threw himself heart and soul into teaching them, nursed his wife through galloping consumption, sold his house and garden lock stock and barrel and moved into the boarding house.'

'Where Daisy came in.'

'Exactly.'

'And caught him on the rebound?'

'I never said that.'

Nora knew at once she had said the wrong thing again. She made swift amends. 'I didn't mean it in the literal sense, David. What I was thinking was that Joshua met Daisy at just the right time, when he *needed* someone badly.' She poured herself another cup. 'He was *vulnerable*.' She crossed her long legs without bothering to adjust the flowing skirt of her beige woollen dress. 'As we are all vulnerable at some point in our lives, David. Don't you agree?'

She could have screamed when he answered her: 'Vulnerable? Yes. That's exactly the right word for Daisy Penny just now. She's so strung up she bursts into sudden laughter when you know she's screaming inside. And she has the kind of laugh you can't ignore. It's like a child's – uninhibited, infectious, but all the time you know what she's thinking.'

'And what *is* she thinking?' Nora said through gritted teeth.

'That if she doesn't get Joshua away from that room at the top of the boarding house, it's going to be too late. She's blaming herself for neglecting him.'

'And has she?'

'Of course not!'

Nora had never seen David so seriously intense. Peggy, his ex-wife, had been one of her friends, and one of Peggy's complaints had been that her husband never did more than skim the surface of his emotions.

'He is a doctor first and a man last,' she had said. 'Feelings embarrass him. All he knows about are symptoms. When he's holding your hand he's more than likely taking your pulse.'

He was actually glancing surreptitiously at his watch

now. Nora looked at him sitting there, thin, handsome, worried, frowning and biting his lip. She wondered why she wanted him so much. Was it because she could feel herself turning into a typical old maid, neat of person, elegant rather than attractive, becoming set in her ways if she wasn't careful?

Or was it because from the moment she'd met him long before the war she had made up her mind to have him in spite of the fact that he was newly married to Peggy, her best friend? All she knew was that even if he wasn't her last chance, she would never have a better. They got on well together and were good friends. She had all the qualities for a doctor's wife. Discretion, loyalty, a nice manner on the telephone, with an ability to take down messages correctly. In triplicate, if necessary. Her job as a civil servant had taught her that.

And if David couldn't see the sign that said 'available' on her forehead, then he must be blind.

Chapter Four

When Daisy went upstairs Joshua was still sitting in his chair, so still he might have been growing from it, she thought, marvelling at his serenity. The letter was on the table beside him.

Daisy picked it up, glanced quickly through the closely written lines and said she would read it properly when there was more time.

'But there never *is* enough time, is there, my love?'

He said it so gently she knew at once it was in no way a complaint, merely a statement of fact.

'There'll be all the time in the world soon.' Leaning over the back of his chair she dropped a kiss on the incipient bald patch on the top of his head. 'I wish you'd go to bed, or at least get undressed. I've to finish the preparations for the breakfast, then I'll be up.' She came round to face him. 'Joshua Penny! You're still wearing your outdoor shoes.' She knelt down in front of him.

'I quite like you doing that,' Joshua said, as she untied the laces and slid the shoes from his feet. 'It makes me feel important. I've always liked subservient women.'

'All Lancashire men do.' Daisy sat back on her heels. 'My mother used to put the sugar in my father's tea, and got in real bother if she forgot to stir it.'

'In India, of course, with a wife coming up to forty, I'd have thrown you away and started again.'

'Oh . . . love.' Daisy could only guess at the depth of Joshua's exhaustion by the way he joked instead of trying to stop her helping him. It was as though the now familiar weakness had sapped his normally fierce independence. She glanced at the clock on the mantelpiece's tiny ledge. 'The two lads in number three said they'd be in by half-past eleven. If we were staying on here I'd definitely have a set of keys made to hand to the late stoppers-out. Mrs Mac locks the door on her lot if they're out after midnight. It's no wonder they call her Gestapo Gertie.' At the sound of a foot on the stairs, she nodded. 'That's one of the lads.' She held up a finger. 'Hold on a minute . . . there goes the other one. I can bolt the front door now and finish off in the kitchen. *Please* be in bed and asleep by then, sweetheart. It's been a long day for you.'

'Come here, Daisy . . .' Joshua's voice was so low Daisy wondered at first if she'd heard him properly. 'Stay with me for a while.' He inclined his head towards the letter on the small table by his side. 'Until I wrote that I had no idea just how much I wanted to leave this place. For your sake just as much as mine.' He drew a sheet of paper towards him. 'I've done some sums as well, and we'll manage financially. You were wise to *buy* this place with the money from your mother's shop. That means that with the difference between what we get for this and the cost of the cottage, plus our savings, plus my war pension – both my pensions . . .' He closed his eyes. 'I think I will go to bed now. I'm a bit whacked.'

Daisy knelt down by the side of his chair. His face was grey with a paleness that was almost transparent. She spoke quickly to hide her anxiety.

'I wish we were going to the country next week. Tomorrow. But I warn you, you'll have to tell me the difference between a buttercup and a primrose. I've never had much truck with Mother Nature. Joshua? Are you all right?'

At once he opened his eyes and smiled at her.

She gabbled on, trying to make him lose that frightening look of utter fatigue. 'There was no green in the street where I lived. If a blade of grass dared to poke through the nicks in the flagstones, the soot in the air did for it straight away. My mother never bought cut flowers off the market because she said they didn't last and were half dead when she bought them anyway.' She laid her head against his arm. 'We're going to be so happy. We'll have breakfast in the kitchen, just the four of us; I won't be rushing around plating twenty-two breakfasts up first. We'll have our own hens, and I'll go out with a basket and collect the eggs, and the white will be all pearly like it is when an egg is new laid. There'll be marigolds in a blue jug, and birds twittering in the trees outside, not seagulls swooping about the sky screaming blue murder.'

She felt his hand on her hair and sighed with relief. He was all right. Of *course* he was all right. Just tired, that was all.

'I feel quite philosophical tonight somehow. I've been advising Winnie what to do with her life. I'm in one of my moods for putting the world to rights . . .'

'The gas was terrible when it came,' Joshua whispered.

'*What* did you say?' Daisy looked up at him. 'Did you say the *gas*?'

He spoke quite clearly but in a hesitant way, holding his head high and staring straight in front of him.

'The Germans put it in shells, you see, and if the soil was dry, or if it was in a wood, it evaporated slowly. They said it was a humane weapon.' His voice trembled. 'Oh, dear, dear God. One of my men had his eyes eaten away by the gas, and I saw a lad of eighteen die screaming in agony for his mother. Men who had denied God all their lives shouted and yelled at Him to help them, but He wasn't there. They poured oil all over that young lad, the medicos, you see, because they daren't touch him. He was raw – like a peeled tomato.'

93

A tear rolled down his cheek. 'I saw them all in the hospital, in the clearing station at Bailleul. I wrote to you from there.'

Daisy knew he was talking about his first wife, talking *to* his first wife. There was such a fear growing in her that only a part of her was taking in his words. She couldn't for the life of her move from where she knelt.

'It was hell on earth, you see. There can be no real hell any worse than that.'

Another tear rolled down his face, then another, slow tears, no sobbing, just a dreadful silent weeping.

'Joshua?' Daisy didn't know what to do. She took both his hands in her own, and was startled by the cold clammy feel of him. She glanced at the door as if willing it to open and someone walk in bringing help. A part of her wanted to run downstairs and telephone for the doctor, but another part of her knew that she must not leave him, that to leave him would be to abandon him to – to what? She shivered, joining his hands, rubbing them together.

'Joshua?' There was desperation in her voice. There was no way of knowing if he had even heard her. His eyes were wide open and filled with an unhappiness as empty and bleak as a bottomless pit. It terrified her.

'There was a dog.'

'A dog, lovey?' She took a handkerchief from her apron pocket, wiped his face and left a streak of flour on his chin.

'A dog found me and wouldn't leave my side. It was a mongrel, bedraggled, come from God knows where, but battle trained.' He was fighting for breath. His hands lifted as if he would claw breath from the air.

'Don't try to speak...' Daisy turned her head and shouted for Winnie; shouted for anyone who might hear.

'That old dog could dive for shelter quicker than any

of my men. He would lie there quivering with his head between his paws till he thought it was safe to stand up again.'

To Daisy's horror the tears began again.

'The men fed him. They fed him and helped to hide him when it seemed he might be discovered ... I'm very tired, Daisy.'

'I know you are, love. Finish telling me about the dog tomorrow.'

'I want to ... tell you *now* ...' His long-drawn-out cry was the wail of a child. 'I *have* to tell you now.' He said something she couldn't catch before his voice strengthened again. 'The French came slowly back to their homes when it all ended, walking across the fields to ruined shells of houses. Cursing as they tried to patch them up. The French never stopped being angry, and who could blame them?' Two small flags of colour flared on his cheekbones.

'I'm going down to telephone David,' she said. 'He'll give you something to help you sleep. There's been too much excitement for one day. Deciding to buy a cottage just like that. It's been a big decision to make.'

'I had to leave the dog. It wasn't possible to bring him home ...'

'I'll only be one minute, love.' Daisy backed away from him, but as if he had stretched out a hand his voice stayed her.

'We were marching to the coast ... two months after it was all over ... and we passed a house ... a French family round the table, happy to be back where they belonged ... they gave us bread ... the sun was out, though it was so cold we shivered in our greatcoats. I asked them if they'd keep the dog ... It's gone very dark ...'

The standard lamp by Joshua's chair shone full down on his face. Daisy moved a hand in front of his eyes.

When his unblinking stare never wavered, she turned in a panic to run across the room to the door, bumping into a bedpost, tripping over the edge of the carpet.

His voice followed her. 'I left the dog with them. There was nothing else I could do, you see. I told him to *sit*, and I told him to *stay*, and I told him he would be happy. When I turned round at the end of the lane he was obeying me . . . but his tail was wagging . . . I've always believed that his tail was wagging . . .'

Daisy had never been to the red-brick house where David lived with his father. But as she dialled the number she could 'see' the telephone on a table, with an extension in the surgery. She could 'hear' it ringing and see David picking it up and answering it.

'Oh, God, please let him answer quickly! Let him *be* there. *Please!*'

Holding the receiver to her left ear she groped with her right hand for the list of emergency numbers, written down by Joshua a long time ago. Where was it? Oh, dear God, suppose she couldn't find it? Her fingers scrabbled through a sheaf of papers, old receipts, a forgotten letter, even one of Oliver's drawings showing two men with bows, aiming arrows at each other's foreheads. A couple of cards advertising plumbers and window cleaners looking for work dropped to the floor.

Her hands shook as she replaced the receiver, then as she stood irresolute, her heart beating with loud uneven thumps, she remembered. Joshua had put the all-important list in the glove drawer of the old-fashioned coat-stand with its antler pegs.

'You might be the best cook in the world,' he had teased, 'but even I who love you would never employ you as a secretary. See, here it is. Do you think you can remember?'

Even in her acute distress she recalled thinking that

Joshua treated her at times like one of his mentally retarded pupils.

'Every man to his own job,' she'd said.

Oh, God, she thought as she dialled the new number, I wish I'd never said that. I wish I'd never said one unkind word to him.

'Doctor Anderson?' She read the name from the slip of paper. 'Can you come at once?' She tried to modulate her voice but it was no good. She could hear herself almost screaming at the unknown doctor on the other end of the line. 'Something bad is happening to my husband. No, he hasn't collapsed. No, he doesn't seem to be in pain. Yes, he can talk. He won't stop talking. No!' Her voice rose to a shout. 'He hasn't been drinking!' She glanced wildly down the long hall to the kitchen door, open and showing the bacon patties still waiting to be baked. She fought for control. 'It's Mrs Penny. Shangri-La . . .' She gave the name of the road and even found herself explaining in a reasonable way that both the Doctors Armitage were taking their day off, otherwise she would have . . . 'Please come! Right away! I *demand* that you come,' she yelled. And slammed down the receiver.

When she went upstairs and into the room on the top floor she saw that Joshua had slipped sideways in his chair. Before she reached him she knew that he was dead.

Dry-eyed, she told David not to feel bad about it when he protested that he should have been there to help his friend.

There was nothing he could have done, she explained. Doctor Anderson, the relief doctor, and David's father, who had come round early that morning, had said the strain on Joshua's heart through his constant coughing had weakened the valves.

97

'His heart just stopped beating, letting him go gently, without a struggle. Instead of condemning him to more years of strain, of only being half alive,' she told David.

Totally composed, she rang her Auntie Edna and Uncle Arnold in Blackburn to tell them the news – at least, she rang her cousin Betty who lived a few doors up the street.

'Now just keep calm. For the childrens' sake,' Betty said, bursting into instant tears. She said she had known for a long time that Joshua was a sick man, but it still came as a shock, didn't it?

She ran down the street to bring her mother and father to the telephone and Edna told Daisy to keep a tight grip on herself and bear up, because that's what Joshua would have wanted her to do. She said Arnold would come on the next train and fetch the children back with him, to keep them out of the way while all the funeral arrangements were going on.

'It's what your mother would have done, and at a time like this I'm standing in for her,' she said. 'It's no use you saying you can manage because I won't take no notice. You always were an obstinate little beggar. I can remember you going off to the second-house pictures many a time when anybody with half an eye could see you were knackered.'

Daisy wished she could react more. Instead she felt charged with adrenaline, ready to organize the funeral, well able to keep the house in working order. She held Winnie close and assured her that it was better this way than that Joshua went on suffering, ending up a bent old man scarcely able to walk more than a few yards.

So on that Monday morning after Joshua had been taken away by the undertakers, to lie in the Chapel of Rest in a cubicle behind blue curtains, she stood with David in the upstairs room and showed him the letter.

'I wish you'd sit down.' David had come over straight

after morning surgery, wanting to help, prepared to take over and do the things he knew his friend would have wanted him to do. Instead he was faced with this calm, but far from serene woman, channelling emotion into anything but her grief.

Daisy glanced at the chair he was indicating and shook her head. Joshua had died in that chair, alone, while she was downstairs making that futile telephone call. Now she would never know whether he felt pain in those last few minutes, or if it had been just like going to sleep. She would never know if he had spoken her name, or just sighed . . .

She pulled herself together. 'Read it,' she said, holding out the letter. 'I'd like you to.'

Dear Mr and Mrs Rothwell,
Thank you for allowing us to look round your home this afternoon. I am wasting no time in making you an offer, with a down payment of fifty pounds, but I must stress that in no way must you feel that I am putting any kind of pressure on you.

My wife and I must sell this place as a going concern before we can think of moving, and I realize that you too need a little time to adjust to the idea of living near to your son at St Annes.

This is merely a preliminary letter, asking for first refusal on your cottage. I know that I would be very happy to bring my family to live in your village . . .

David read to the end.

'So that's one letter you don't need to bother with.' He put it back on the table. 'In a way it's as well this happened before you'd committed yourselves about the cottage. I'll write to the Rothwells for you and explain.' He seemed not to notice Daisy's expression. 'There isn't much anyone can do at a time like this, but I *can* take over all the correspondence for you if you'll allow me. Joshua took me completely into his confidence.'

He was very polite, very *shy* in his politeness. Daisy was able to observe him quite dispassionately. He didn't seem to realize that she could manage on her own, that if she stopped to think about it she had been managing on her own for a long time.

'I will be moving to the cottage with the children,' she told him. 'Just as Joshua wanted. This letter is his dying wish. It is what he wanted for us. You heard him say yesterday that as soon as he walked into the cottage he knew it had been waiting for me.'

'But that's unthinkable!'

'Why do you say that?'

David had had quite a bit of experience in talking to the bereaved. You spoke quietly, holding their hands maybe, giving assurances, helping them to bear their own helplessness. But this was different. This one wasn't playing the game according to the rules.

'You're in a state of shock,' he told her gently. 'Quite the wrong time to make decisions.' He combed back his thick fair hair with his fingers. 'You need this boarding house more than ever now. You've worked it up into a success. You're going to need something to keep you going – and I don't mean financially.' His voice rose. 'Look, Daisy. I'm talking to you as a friend as well as a doctor. To cut yourself off from the life you know just now would be *mad*. I can't stand by and let you do it.'

'Joshua said the cottage was just waiting for me,' Daisy repeated.

'I *know* he did. I *heard* him. But he meant for you all to be together, not for you to be left to struggle in a strange place on your own, with two children to bring up.' His face was working in disbelief. 'You saw that cottage at its best yesterday. With the sun shining, and the surrounding countryside looking like something out of a picture book. But I've seen it with the rain lashing down. I've seen it up there snowing as late as April and May, with that view you were so taken with obliterated by a curtain of damp grey mist. When the winter winds blow I've seen the very walls of those moorland farms falling in. Besides which, they're *clannish*, the people who live out there. You've got to live there at least twenty years before you're reckoned not to be a foreigner. And that cottage is in urgent need of repair. It's been neglected for years and years.'

He knew he was exceeding his brief. He accepted there was something almost obscene in arguing with anyone so recently bereaved. But, God dammit, she wasn't *acting* like someone recently bereaved. She was smiling at him gently as if forgiving him for his outburst.

'I know you're trying to be kind.' She was walking past him to the door, the letter in her hand. 'But my mind is quite made up.' She turned at the door. 'I neglected Joshua, but I'm not going to neglect the children! They're going to have a mother who has time to read them a story when they go to bed, and time to play with them and *listen* when they tell me things. But thank you for being such a good friend, David. Joshua once told me you were the best friend he'd ever had.'

Surely she would break down now? David followed her out on to the landing. She ran on ahead of him when the telephone in the hall started to ring. He motioned to her that he would let himself out of the house, leaving her giving clear and precise instructions to someone at the other end of the line. About the funeral arrangements, he supposed.

'Definitely no flowers,' Daisy was saying. 'Donations to the British Legion would be welcomed. I know that's what my husband would have wanted.'

Old Doctor Armitage said he was going to do his

level best to persuade the powers-that-be an inquest wouldn't be necessary. Joshua had been an invalid and his patient for years, though no one had suspected his heart would give out as suddenly as it had.

'Joshua's wife is so controlled she frightens me.' David met his father briefly after morning surgery. Glared at him as if it was his fault. 'She's talking about going on with their plans for moving to the country. Selling the boarding house and burying herself alive with those two young children. Joshua had written a letter to the Rothwells almost with his dying breath, and she's taking it as some sort of sign from above.'

'That's Daisy Penny all right.' His father smiled. 'She's a mixture of sound common sense and naivety. But there's a shrewd business sense there as well. The value of those boarding houses is falling rapidly. Up to thirty per cent in some of the older type. They're even talking about mounting a two-year advertising campaign in four American newspapers to try to bring in visitors from overseas, but those Yanks had a taste of our weather during the war – they're not going to come all this way to get rained on to no good purpose.'

'For Pete's sake, Daisy isn't taking anything like that into consideration! She's probably never *heard* of any two-year advertising campaign. She's using her heart instead of her head, and for Joshua's sake I'm finding it impossible to stand by and watch her make one hell of a mistake!'

Doctor Armitage watched his son slam from the room. Then he shrugged his shoulders and went to tell Mrs Platts that he would be in for lunch. But that cold would do.

Uncle Arnold came as promised to pick up the children and Sally told him that her father had gone to live with Jesus.

Oliver said that he didn't like Jesus and never had, and when Sally began to cry he told her to shut her big fat gob. When his mother failed to tick him off for being so rude, he said it again, bewildered and scared by her lack of reaction.

Arnold took one look at Daisy's white face and decided to catch the train before the one he'd intended to. He picked up the children's case and watched as she kissed them goodbye on the doorstep.

'Your Auntie Edna thinks it's more important keeping them with us than bringing them back for the funeral. But she says to tell you that Betty and Cyril will be coming and *we'll* draw the curtains back and front and take the children to feed the ducks in Corporation Park. Your auntie was fond of Joshua.' He stood on the pavement wearing his flat cap over his shiny bald head, obviously feeling he ought to say something to this favourite niece of his, but unable, for the life of him, to think what. 'You had the best part of ten years' happiness,' he managed at last. 'That's more than what a lot of people are granted.'

'I know,' Daisy said. She waited until they'd turned the corner, watching Sally clinging to Arnold's hand and Oliver stumping along with his hands in his pockets, his socks falling down and the belt of his raincoat trailing down at one side. They didn't turn to wave.

As soon as she closed the door she picked up the phone to make yet another call. It seemed important that she didn't stop for as much as a single minute. She worked against the clock, rushing from one job to another. It occurred to her once or twice that perhaps her behaviour wasn't 'seemly' for one so recently bereaved. David's father had offered her tablets which he said would help her through the next few days, but she'd refused them. Joshua would have been ashamed of her if she'd collapsed and had to be put to bed with a damp cloth on her forehead, leaving Winnie and Leonard to do their inadequate bests in the kitchen.

She shut herself away with her pots and pans and casserole dishes and got on with reconstituting eggs from the dried powder, pouring the mixture into small greased cups, then standing them in a pan of boiling water till they set well enough to have sliced with the sausage-meat loaf they were having with salad on account of the weather being so unusually hot.

She didn't want to go through into the dining room in case she embarrassed the visitors, so she plated the meals in the kitchen and sent them through with a red-eyed Winnie, and a Leonard who winced if he happened to catch Daisy's eye. He was avoiding her, she told herself, as if she was a carrier of one of the diseases he'd swotted up from his Red Cross manual.

She never stopped working. When everything was finished she began to prepare the meals for the following day. Everyone in the house had been very kind, very tactful, tiptoeing about and not making too much noise, just as if Joshua was lying upstairs in his coffin.

Friends called, neighbouring landladies, expressing sympathy, offering help, telling her that if there was anything they could do she only had to ask. A tin of shortbread biscuits, hoarded since rationing began, was left on the dresser; a slab cake on the table with a note attached: 'It won't keep with not having the fat it should have in it, and cross yourself in awe if you come across a currant, but it'll do to cut at when folks drop in with their condolences.'

Mrs Mac from Balmoral next door came in and prophesied that Daisy would be bound to have a reaction when the truth hit her. 'I saw a film once,' she said, accepting a cup of tea, 'where this actress was told her husband had been killed in the war just as she was about to go on the stage.' She accepted a biscuit. 'Anyroad, where was I? Oh yes. She played her part right through without missing a single cue, then she took five curtain calls, held out her arms to the audience and fell stone dead into the orchestra pit. Reaction had caught up with her, you see.'

Somebody called Nora Jolly rang up about eight o'clock in the evening. She said she was a friend of David Armitage's, and she expected Daisy had heard him mention her name. She said how sorry she was to hear about Joshua, and was there anything she could do? She said David had told her about the cottage and she thought how right and how brave of Daisy to want to keep to the plan of moving into it. She said that two of the girls in her section at the office boarded with Daisy and that they could stay with her for one night if Daisy needed their room for visiting relatives.

'For the funeral?'

'Well, yes.' Nora was a bit taken aback at the brisk way she was answered.

'Joshua's only relative is in an old folk's home, and mine can get here and back in the day. But it's very kind of you to make the offer. People are being so exceptionally kind.'

'Your friend rang up,' Daisy told David, when he called round on his way to a patient who had gone into an early labour. 'You're a dark horse. Keeping her so quiet.'

She was actually *teasing* him. David wanted to shake her and make her cry. He wanted to hit her to wipe the frozen look from her face. He left her standing at the door looking small and lonely, and he turned back to advise her to have a tot of Joshua's whisky to help her sleep.

Daisy said she would, but when she climbed the stairs and opened the door of the room at the top of the house and saw the two beds standing side by side, she closed it quickly and went back downstairs.

She sat in the kitchen for the best part of an hour. She thought about the future and how she was determined it would be. A great believer in things that were meant to be, she was convinced that Joshua's delight in the cottage was his way of showing her that the next chapter of her life should be spent sunning herself on a doorstep shelling peas into a basin, walking across the fields from the farm carrying milk in a big blue jug, tending the garden, even if she had to look up how to do it in a gardening manual. Spending time with the children, sitting by their beds when they were ill, not leaving them alone for hours on end because the visitors' needs must have priority.

The cottage had been *waiting for her*. Joshua had said so.

When her head ached with weariness and her eyelids drooped, she walked slowly upstairs. For a while longer she sat on the edge of her bed staring at Joshua's winged armchair. She closed her eyes and told herself that when she opened them he would be there with an open book on his knee. With the wireless turned low so as not to disturb the visitors, and his reading glasses on the little table beside him, the resigned patience of the chronic invalid lying like a shadow on his thin face.

But Joshua hadn't been patient all the time. There had been days when he had raged against the pain and frustration; when he had sent the children from his room because their presence irritated him. There had been days when he had looked at Daisy as if silently daring her to show him pity.

And so she wouldn't show him pity now. He deserved better than that. The last thing Joshua would have wanted was a showy funeral with mourners wearing black and crying into white handkerchiefs.

Daisy dropped to her knees by the arm of the high winged chair, laying her head on the padded arm. Suddenly she knew it was always going to be like that, the loneliness, the empty chair. A raucous sob broke from her throat, an ugly sound releasing the pent-up emotion of the long, long day.

At last the tears came . . .

Chapter Five

Winnie went round to Leonard's house the day before the funeral. She was going to be kind to the old bat, she'd decided, even if it killed her. She wished she could like her, but that was taking things just a bit too far. Winnie was glad Leonard took after his father in looks, because if he'd resembled his mother she could never have fancied him in the first place.

Winnie had more than a sneaking suspicion that Mrs Smalley cracked on her arthritis was far worse than it was. The old lady had to be helped to the toilet, yet she managed to walk on her own into the kitchen for a biscuit or a nice piece of cake if there was any in the tin. She played on Leonard for all she was worth, having him fetching and carrying for her like a slave.

In Winnie's opinion he had already made a rod for his own back by waiting on her hand and foot. 'She ought to try to do things for herself. You have to be cruel to be kind,' she'd told Leonard, but it was a waste of time.

'I'm the only one who knows how much she suffers,' he'd said.

Winnie stared at Mrs Smalley's big square face, trying hard to think of something to say to make it smile.

'From the day my son was born,' Mrs Smalley was saying, 'he has never given me a single moment's anxiety. And there aren't many mothers who can say that.'

'I was a big trouble to *my* mother. She was glad to be

shut of me when I went to work for Daisy,' Winnie said, wanting to shock, thinking to get a bit of a laugh.

'Where is your mother now?'

Mrs Smalley took everything Winnie said at face value; never even stopped for a moment to realize that beneath the flippancy there was a desperate longing to be liked. She'd never liked sandy-haired people, and this sharp-nosed young woman had a look about her as if she'd been left out in the rain to rust. Besides which she was common. And forward. She must have egged Leonard on for all she was worth. Seduced him without him really knowing what was going on. Still, what could you expect from a girl who came from a family like the Whalleys? The husband had fathered dozens of children on his sluttish wife, then gone and died. One of the welfare ladies, who should have known better, had told Mrs Smalley that she'd seen with her own eyes Winnie's many sisters and brothers sitting round a newspaper-covered table dipping bread into a tin of condensed milk, and drinking fizzy pop out of jam jars. And now they were all grown up and doing God alone knew what.

'My mother?' Winnie stared up at the ceiling. Better to tell the truth than lie and be found out afterwards. Besides, the only way to get on with Leonard's mother was to be open and frank with her. As far as she could . . .

'The last I heard of her she was living up in Scotland. Her bloke must have thought a lot about her to take the kids on, but I never hear from them now.' She stared down at her small work-roughened hands. 'One of my brothers got killed in the war, and another got in with a bad lot and scarpered God knows where.' She finished the last bit in a rush. 'And one of my sisters married a soldier from Nigeria.'

'Black?'

109

'As the ace of spades,' said Winnie.

'I don't suppose any of them will be coming to the wedding?' Mrs Smalley's eyes were closed in horror.

'No fear! They crossed me off years ago. Daisy and Joshua were my family.' Winnie lifted her chin. 'And now I've got Leonard.'

She wanted to say 'and you', but she couldn't. If Mrs Smalley had held out a hand she would have taken it; if the old woman had even smiled, Winnie would have burst out laughing and come out with something barmy, and everything would have been all right. But there was nothing, not a flicker.

'I'll look after you, Mrs Smalley,' she said, her very heart swelling with noble thoughts. 'We'll get along all right. You'll see.'

'I wish you were getting off to a better start.'

Mrs Smalley had a lip, Winnie noticed, that curled of its own volition. She tried not to look at it.

'I'm not narrow-minded about such things, but in my young days a girl kept herself pure for her wedding night. But then I suppose the war changed all that with the town being filled with foreigners. *They* wouldn't have stood by you the way my son is standing by you.'

'He was there at the time, Mrs Smalley.'

The old woman closed her eyes as if to shut out the sight of her future daughter-in-law. Winnie stared round the room with its dark-plum carpet and matching curtains, at the heavy mahogany furniture and the fireplace with its inset of bottle-green tiles. There was a pungent smell of decay as if the squat little figure in the high-seated chair had been sitting there for years, slowly rotting inch by inch, beginning at her yellowed toes.

How could she even think of living here after living with Daisy in the boarding house teeming with guests, laughing and joking because they were on their holidays? Thinking Winnie was a right card because she said such awful things?

'Would you like me to help you up the stairs, Mrs Smalley?' She was trying to help, hoping to please.

'I don't go to bed till nine o'clock, Winnie. Leonard and I like to spend an hour either with the wireless or reading a book before he takes me up. It relaxes me.'

'I don't expect you sleep all that well?'

'Not a wink. If Leonard senses I'm awake he goes down and makes me a cup of tea. I'd like one now, Winnie, but with more sugar than you put in last time. I know it's rationed, but I have to keep my energy up. "You must keep your energy up, Mother." Leonard's always telling me that.'

For what, Winnie wondered, having a bit of a cry in the kitchen as she waited for the kettle to boil.

'The way to get those quarry tiles on the kitchen floor clean is to scrub them with a hard brush and plenty of marela soap, then finish them off with a cloth dipped in a saucer of sour milk. That's the only way you'll bring up the shine,' Mrs Smalley told her when she took the tea through into the living room. 'The woman who comes in to do the rough only gives them a lick and a promise, but then she won't be coming that much longer. Not when you and Leonard are married.'

A warning bell rang in Winnie's head, but she took no notice of it. Leonard was coming through the door smiling at the sight of his mother and his bride-to-be chatting together over a cup of tea. Getting on with each other like a house on fire.

Mr and Mrs Rothwell's son Walter came over on the bus to see them the day Daisy's letter arrived.

'I think we ought to respect Mr Penny's last wish,' his mother told him. 'In a way it's like a command from beyond the grave.' She was very relieved now her mind had been made up for her. It put an end to all that dithering, and now the letter penned with Mr Penny's dying breath meant she felt duty bound to let him have the last word. 'He must have been taken very sudden,' she said. 'He walked round the cottage and down the garden as nice as ninepence. It just shows we never know what's round the next corner.'

'In the midst of life . . .' Mr Rothwell boomed, raising his head from his chest, his eyes skinning over with sleep even as he spoke.

Mother and son took no notice of him.

Walter Rothwell tapped the letter. 'Let *me* answer this, Mother. I'll take over from here for you.' He nodded towards the old man sleeping away what was left of his life in the chair by the fire. 'You've enough on your plate looking after Dad. In fact, if you like, I'll go along and see this Mrs Penny. You won't be able to fit all your bits and pieces in the bungalow, you know, and Mrs Penny might be interested. She won't be able to bring much stuff with her, and the utility muck's not up to much.'

'She's got to sell first.' Things were moving just a fraction too quickly for Mrs Rothwell. It was all right making her mind up, but nobody, not even her son, was going to whip her into a bungalow till she was good and ready. 'Mrs Penny's acted hasty, in my opinion. She hasn't given herself time to get over the shock. There's not enough going on here for a young lass. She was telling me she liked to go to the pictures when she got the chance.'

Walter Rothwell took no notice. The letter was in his pocket and his acceptance of Daisy Penny's offer would be in the next post. He'd have his mother and father winkled out of this damp decaying mausoleum of a cottage before the summer was out. And never ever again, please God, would he have the worry of the last winter when the village had been cut off for weeks on end; when it had looked as if supplies of flour weren't going to get through, and he had worried himself sick in case the old folks' supply of coal ran out.

'Don't you worry about a thing,' he told his mother, as he kissed her goodbye on the doorstep. 'There might be one or two papers for you to sign, but that's all, and when it comes to the actual move me and Theresa will see to everything.' He glanced at his watch to check he wasn't going to miss his bus.

'You're a good lad, Walter.'

His mother watched him walk down the road. She had watched him in exactly the same way when as a small boy he attended the church school in the village. And again when home on leave from France in the first war he had marched away from her with his soldier's slog. It was ridiculous to think he was retiring next year.

'Our Walter's grown into a nice lad,' she told her husband, when she went back into the cottage.

'Considering he married an RC,' Mr Rothwell wakened up for long enough to say.

Joshua's funeral was held on the Friday morning with a handful of mourners going back to Shangri-La for ham and tongue sandwiches, the bread sliced thin by Winnie with the crusts cut off.

Daisy had organized the timing so that she could count on the house being empty for the time it would take, blessing the fact that the day dawned bright and sunny with a paint-box blue sky.

'I thought he looked lovely.' Mrs Mac from Balmoral next door had insisted on going to the Chapel of Rest to view the remains. 'They'd touched him up nicely. He'd been a shocking colour for a long time,' she whispered to a distant half-cousin from Rochdale seated on her left.

'Chests ran in Joshua's family,' she was told. 'With some it's rheumatism, and with others it's chests.'

'Our family seem to have got the lot.' Mrs Mac was obviously proud of her relatives. 'Diabetes, arthritis, dropsy, goitre, varicose veins – you name it, we've had it.' She nodded her chin at the big table in the dining room set with Daisy's best plates and lace-edged cloth. 'Joshua would feel proud if he knew how brave Daisy's being.'

'He *will* know, dear.' The Rochdale cousin reached over and took another ham sandwich from the plate with the little flag marked 'without mustard'. 'He's not gone far – only through that door.'

Leonard Smalley looked nervously over his shoulder.

'When you're dead you're dead,' Winnie said loudly. 'There's nobody come back to prove otherwise, has there?'

'Except our Lord.'

Everyone stared at Daisy's cousin Betty from Blackburn, who blushed bright pink at having been so bold.

Leonard smiled at Winnie. Since hearing he was going to be a father he appeared to have grown in stature. Even his beard looked fuller, his nose less pointed. Daisy just wished she could stop remembering what Winnie had told her every time she looked at him. She had never got the chance to tell Joshua about it, she thought, blinking hard to stop the tears forming in her eyes.

Immediately David's hand covered her own. 'It's almost over,' he whispered. 'They'll be gone soon.'

David had been marvellous. But then so many, many people had been marvellous. Daisy had thought she hadn't had the time to make friends, always too frantically busy to chat on the telephone, or have people round for cups of tea. But they'd been there all the time, just waiting to declare their affection, offering help. That very morning she'd had a letter from Mrs Rothwell's son saying he would like to come and talk to her once the sad formalities were over. She wondered now why everyone used euphemisms rather than say or write the word *funeral*? Joshua would have smiled at that.

Cousin Betty's husband Cyril knew a couple in Blackburn who were looking around for a little business to buy with his gratuity and an unexpected windfall for her. The bloke, Cyril had explained, had been a chef in the Catering Corps, which meant surely that running a boarding house would be a doddle for him.

Daisy looked across the table at Cyril. The war had done marvels for him. He was hardly recognizable as the pale young man, dominated by his wife and mother-in-law, going off each morning to his job as a clerk, with a pension to come when he was sixty-five. Now, after six years in the army, his thin frame had filled out, and he was talking about moving south with his wife and young son to start up in the second-hand car business with a sergeant he'd been with right through the desert campaign.

Catching her eye, Cyril winked at her, then looked down at his plate, horrified at forgetting momentarily where he was and what for. But, as he might have known she would, Daisy winked back. Cyril relaxed. He had always liked his wife's cousin, even though once long ago she had blotted her copybook by supposedly having an affair with a married man. Cyril stole another glance at her, sitting there wearing a navy-blue dress with a single strand of pearls. Why had he never realized before what an attractive woman she was? She had the kind of face that expressed her every emotion, with a smile that knocked you for six. He'd always thought old

115

Joshua was a bit dull for her. It had struck him that Daisy was holding herself aloof somehow, acting a part of never stepping out of line ... He took an egg and cress sandwich and bit into it thoughtfully. Once in Cairo he had seen a beautiful girl do the dance of the seven veils. Her body had writhed and twisted itself into suggestive positions, her skin had been as smooth as liquid toffee, but her face with its waiting watching expression, its languorous longing had, to his astonishment, reminded him of Daisy.

Why was Cyril looking so guilty all of a sudden, his wife Betty wondered. She mee-mawed to tell him there was a piece of cress dangling from the corner of his mouth.

'This apple chutney is lovely, Daisy.' The Rochdale cousin spoke into a silence. 'It's got a flavour I can't quite place.' She made little smacking noises with her lips. 'It has a sort of sharp tang. You wouldn't be averse to giving me the recipe, would you, love?'

'Now?'

Daisy could hardly credit it. Surely this was hardly the time or the place? But a pencil and paper were being fished out from the depths of an enormous handbag. A pair of eyes fixed on her expectantly.

'Well,' she said faintly, 'there are the apples of course, and brown sugar and vinegar. Two heads of garlic, if you can get them, plus onions and crystallised ginger. And a pinch of cayenne. That's all.'

'But the *quantities*, love? We're not all cordon blues, you know.'

Cyril wondered if it would upset anyone if he lit a cigarette ...

Most of them went away soon after that. Cyril managed a few minutes alone with Daisy to tell her that they were definitely moving down south, and that Betty's mother was barely on speaking terms with him.

'She's bound to miss Betty.' Daisy had a clear memory of her Auntie Edna treating her daughter's house as if it were an extension of her own, going in without knocking, sitting in Cyril's chair, advising Betty on the best way to bring up her baby, and behaving as though Cyril were expendable. 'Especially young Edwin. She practically brought him up during the war.'

'Whose side are you on?' Cyril's nice kind eyes twinkled at her. 'We're not going to the moon, you know.' Suddenly he put his arm round Daisy and pulled her to him. 'Is it true you're thinking of leaving this place?'

'It's true. I'm going to take the children away from this madhouse.' She nodded at Winnie and Mrs Mac frantically clearing the dining room, while Leonard stood at the sink in the kitchen making a good job of the washing-up. 'I'm going to close the door of the cottage at nights, and there's just going to be the three of us.' Her eyes filled. 'I might not have had enough time to spend with Joshua, but the kids are going to have a better deal.' She leaned against Cyril's comfortable shoulder. 'Why did he have to *die* before I realized just how lonely he was?'

'Joshua lonely?' Cyril lifted her chin with his finger so that she was forced to look up at him. 'I never got to know Joshua all that well, but every time I saw him he struck me as being one of the happiest blokes I'd ever met.' He gave her a little shake. 'It's *normal* to feel guilt when somebody dies. When my mother died I blamed myself for not going to see her more often, for not writing to her more often during the war, for disappointing her by calling Edwin after Betty's grand-father instead of after mine. And when my best pal got

117

killed in the war I suffered the tortures of the damned because I hadn't given him my last cigarette.'

A Preston cousin said her goodbyes, actually thanking Daisy for a lovely meal and giving her the pleasure of meeting people she hadn't seen in years.

'Time's the great healer, chuck,' she trilled, walking backwards down the steps. 'And we've all of us got us cross to bear in some form or another.'

Nora Jolly rang David as he returned from his afternoon visiting. She told him she'd got two tickets for an amateur production of *The Merry Widow*, and that the friend she was going with had developed a summer cold and wanted to go to bed with a Beecham's Powder.

Joshua's funeral had upset David more than he cared to admit. He had thought that his profession and his time in the Far East had immunised him against dwelling too long on the inevitability of death. He ached to go back to Shangri-La, to see Daisy, to try to take that shut-away bewildered look from her face. But he wasn't *family*, and he had no right. He had been Joshua's friend, not Daisy's, and yet could anything have been more horrible, more ghoulish than that dreadful funeral spread with Daisy dictating that bloody recipe to the insensitive cousin from Rochdale? Daisy had sat there reeling off the ingredients, and he'd badly wanted to ask her if she always kept her chin up, even when she was crying inside.

So he went with Nora, and they sat too near the stage so that he could see the black lines drawn round the merry widow's eyes, and a glimpse, he vowed, of her tonsils when she hit the high notes. They had a night cap at Nora's flat, then another, and after the third she was somehow in his arms, and he was kissing her with a kind of desperation.

'I love you too,' she whispered, though he couldn't remember having said it first.

At midnight Daisy sat alone in the kitchen willing herself to walk down the hall and shoot the bolts on the big front door now that everyone was accounted for. Winnie had been down twice, worried at seeing Daisy sitting there stone-still, but Leonard had explained that Daisy was in shock, and the kindest thing she could do was to leave her alone. To come to of her own accord. It was a period of grieving Daisy had to go through, he'd explained, and the more she cried the better it would be.

Daisy went into the lounge and sat down on the piano stool, swivelling it round and seeing the room the way it had been when she'd first moved in over ten years ago. A threadbare carpet, flanked by boards stained a strange mahogany shade, springless chairs with frayed covers, and a crêpe-paper fan in the fireplace. She trailed through into the dining room and looked at the wall where a flight of plaster birds had soared on outspread wings, and the carpet had shouted at the flocked wallpaper, both so hectically patterned that if you stared at them too long your eyes went out of focus.

Soon someone else would be taking over and maybe *her* taste in colours and furnishings wouldn't please, and the whole cycle would repeat itself. Another page turned, another chapter to write itself.

A great wodge of sentimentality settled round her heart, like a sticky suet pudding. She felt that Joshua's gentle ghost came into the room, took her by the hand, and walked with her up the stairs. Now that he was dead everyone was praising him, his bravery in the first war, his stoicism during his long struggle against ill health. They said he had been a giant amongst men, that the purity of his character had stood him apart.

She stopped on the top landing and opened the door of the room they had shared together. The first thing she saw was his empty chair. And knew she *had* to get out of the house.

She felt no fear when she stepped outside, closed the big door softly behind her and began to walk down the familiar street. As if to make up for the harsh freezing winter, the air was soft, and lifted her hair away from her neck as she walked in the direction of the sea front. The weather man on the wireless had promised a long hot summer after what was now being called The Big Freeze, and it looked as if he was going to be right.

Couples still strolled along the promenade, lingering to stare at a sea so calm and silver-blue they could have been forgiven for thinking it was the Mediterranean.

Daisy stopped in the dark shadow of the North Pier and leaned on the railings.

The long day was over. The children would be coming back on Sunday, and for their sakes she had to go on. She was glad they were old enough to keep the memory of their father with them for the rest of their lives. She would talk to them about him so that they would grow up believing all the wonderful things that were being said about him.

She shivered and pulled the collar of her linen jacket further up round her neck. She would remember Joshua too, but the man she remembered would be *real*, not the superhuman being the vicar and all his many friends had spoken of all that week.

The Joshua she would always remember had on occasions drunk too much when he was upset or weary. There had been a great and roaring rage inside him at the injustices of the world. He had deplored the deprivations of the underprivileged; he had wept unmanly tears when moved by the plight of his backward pupils. Joshua's occasional frustration with his restricted way of life had been a terrible thing to witness. Once, when the hospital had advised him to walk with a stick, he had left the house with it, then suddenly hurled it from him over the railings into the sea.

The tears ran down Daisy's face. She tasted the sad saltiness of them as they ran past her open mouth. But she had found the Joshua she wanted to remember.

A youngish man came up to her and asked her was she looking for company? She turned her tear-wet face to him, shaking her head, and muttering apologies he walked away.

Chapter Six

The couple from Blackburn, with the gratuity and the unexpected windfall burning a hole in their pockets, came on Cyril's recommendation to view Shangri-La.

Percy Bulcock had a thick thatch of black hair which looked as if it had been trimmed round a pudding basin, and Winnie was sure that his wife Ruby had been intended by nature to be a fine figure of a man.

I wouldn't like to meet *her* down an alleyway on a dark night, Winnie thought, eyeing her malevolently, standing her ground, though she knew that Daisy would have preferred to talk to the couple alone.

Every time Daisy tried to explain the routine of catering for and looking after up to twenty-two visitors Ruby gave a sarcastic laugh and Percy's mouth curved into a knowing snigger. They reckoned they could double that number with a bit of organization.

'Such as?' Daisy's tone was deceptively casual.

'The bigger rooms could easily take a plywood partition, dividing them into two, and there's a heck of a lot of wasted space on the landing . . .'

'You could always put a board across the bath to make an extra bed,' Winnie suggested, dead-pan.

Daisy had heard enough. 'The more visitors you crowd in, the less able you'll be to keep up standards. Folks are canny. They come prepared to spend their hard-earned money, but they won't *waste* it. I've kept this place full for three-quarters of the year by giving value for money. Short-change your visitors and you won't see them back the following year.'

Percy waved away Daisy's little speech. 'If anyone knows all the dodges for making a bit of meat go a long way it's Percy Bulcock.' He winked at Daisy. 'Well in with the local shopkeepers, are we?'

They moved into the lounge.

'We'll kip down in here at nights,' Percy told his wife. 'Swap this settee for a put-u-up, and Bob's your uncle. We'll be as snug as a couple of bugs in here.'

At the thought of them snuggled up together in bed Daisy felt quite sick.

Back in the kitchen Percy took a small black notebook from his pocket and began jotting figures down in it. He asked Daisy how much she paid for a hundredweight of potatoes, and when she said she didn't buy in such quantities, preferring to have everything as fresh as possible even if it meant going to the shops every day, he exchanged a look of disbelief with Ruby. As if to say they'd got a right one *there* and no mistake.

'*She's* a fella,' Winnie said when they'd gone.

'I swear I saw his hair move.' Daisy sat down and covered her eyes with her hands. 'But they're genuinely interested, no doubt about that.'

'You wouldn't sell to *them*?' Winnie rubbed her back. 'They'd close this place up in three years.'

'If theirs turns out to be the best offer, then I'll sell. I won't lose that cottage.' Daisy thumped the table with a fist. 'I won't let the kids down, and I won't let Joshua down. He *meant* for us to go. He wrote that letter . . .'

'With his dying breath,' Winnie finished for her. 'But he didn't *know* he was going to die!' She sat down facing Daisy across the table. 'He wouldn't want you to bury yourself alive with those two kids somewhere in the back of beyond. My God, Daisy, I went into the country once and it was horrible. No pictures to go to, nowhere to go dancing, nowt but views for miles around, and in my book when you've seen one view you've seen the lot. Fields full of flamin' cows, and stinkin' cowpats, and sheep staring at you over walls with their potty faces. There's nothing *glamorous* about the country, Daisy. It's not like in the pictures, with everybody sitting in a haycart and singing as they jog along the lane after a day's work in the hot sun. You ought to go and see that new picture – the one I went to with Leonard that made us laugh our socks off. Claudette Colbert in *The Egg and I. She* went to live in the country and boy, did she live to regret it!'

'The countryside in America is bigger and more vast than the countryside over here,' Daisy said firmly. 'You get on with your life, Winnie, and leave me to get on with mine.' She got up and walked to the door, opened it, stepped out into the hall, closing the door behind her with a decisive click.

'You're making a big mistake!' Winnie dashed to the door and wrenched it open. 'Leonard says you're not in a fit state to decide anything.' At the foot of the stairs she opened her mouth and yelled: 'Leonard can remember a woman who got married again three weeks after she'd buried her husband!'

Daisy's face appeared briefly round the bend in the stairs.

'Good for her!' she shouted.

For his mother's sake, Walter Rothwell soon had things sorted out. If he didn't finalize the agreement she could easily change her mind, and he was sick and tired of struggling on and off buses every time he visited them.

At first he felt awkward talking business to Mrs Penny so soon after she'd lost her husband. The newly bereaved had always embarrassed him. You never knew whether to say how sorry you were. Or say nothing.

But Daisy Penny turned out to be as pleasant as his mother had said she was, though Walter felt a curly perm would have suited her better than that straightish style with her hair falling forward a lot so that she was continually pushing it behind her ear.

'A boarding house must be very *trying*,' he told Daisy, sitting in the kitchen with her over a cup of tea and a warm-from-the-oven sultana scone. A red-haired girl scrubbing potatoes at the sink kept giving him filthy looks, making him feel most uncomfortable. It was pouring with rain outside, and the house seemed to be teeming with people. He could hear them charging up and down the stairs calling out to each other. One of them was playing a piano badly, and a little woman with her glasses on a cord round her neck bobbed her head round the door and said there were three little lads using the settee as a trampoline.

Daisy went to deal with that small crisis, leaving Walter with the girl at the sink.

'Mrs Penny's bearing up very well, considering,' he said.

Winnie considered telling him what she thought about Mrs Penny's determination to leave Shangri-La; she even considered confiding that the erstwhile buyer of his mother's cottage was temporarily of unsound mind and not fit to sign a Christmas card never mind any kind of contract.

'*Considering*,' she agreed, with such emphasis that Walter turned round in relief as Daisy came back. He went soon after that, telling Daisy that she was welcome to visit the cottage any time at all; that there could be some bits and pieces his mother wouldn't have the room for in the bungalow at St Annes.

'Antiques, Mrs Penny, and probably worth a fortune, but we don't want the dealers calling offering a pittance, then selling them for twenty times as much to gullible Americans.' He replaced his bowler hat on his head. 'Or to us British, weary of utility rubbish.'

He held out his hand and gave Daisy a spongy handshake.

'God bless you,' he told her, feeling that some token to her tragic situation should be made.

The Bulcocks put their offer in before the week was out, and Daisy accepted it. David Armitage came round and offered to drive her out to the village again the following week, and she accepted that offer too. Winnie said that as the children would be at school, and as Daisy had promised to be back in time to serve the evening meal, which would be a high tea for that day, she thought she could just about cope.

'The Bulcocks have said they'll stand in for me any time,' Daisy reminded her. 'I think they're keen to put some of their ideas into practice.'

Winnie whipped round on her. 'You don't *care*, do you? You don't give a sausage if they poison your visitors. You *saw* them planning to sleep folks on the clothes-line in the back yard; you *know* that terrible man will frighten the life out of little Miss Grimshaw, who likes everything served dainty. Do you think he'll cut the crusts off her sandwiches the way we do? Do you think he'll give a monkey's that she likes the milk poured in her tea last, and that too much lettuce gives her wind?'

Winnie was feeling sick that morning and needed to take her discomfort out on someone. Her face had grown thin over the past weeks and her nose had a pregnant peaky look about it. There was too much happening all at once, and she didn't feel up to dealing with it. What she had really wanted was for everything to stay just the same.

'I'm getting married soon,' she whimpered. 'If I wasn't up the spout I would cancel the wedding to show respect to Joshua's memory, but I can't, can I?' She stood sideways on to Daisy. 'It's no use you telling me I don't show because people have started looking at me funny in the street. I've had to unpick two of the bust darts in me wedding dress already, and I bet I pop me buttons off at the back in the middle of the ceremony.' She began to cry. 'I'm a rotten cow talking to you like this, Daisy. But I don't know what to do! You've always told me what to do, you've *helped* me.' She raised an anguished face. 'I've looked on you as me mother, Daisy, and that's daft because you'd have had me when you were eleven, but all you're wanting to do is to run away from this place as fast as you can. You've forgotten I exist.'

'Winnie!' Daisy held out her arms, but Winnie wasn't to be comforted.

'I'd have topped meself when Chuck's letter came if you hadn't talked me out of it, and you're helping me to keep me terrible secret from Leonard.'

'I think you're wrong about that. I think the baby is his.'

'But you don't *know*, do you?'

Daisy shook her head. 'No, I don't know, but if the other one was only the one time, then it's more likely that . . .'

'I read a true story in a magazine where a husband found out he wasn't able to make babies, and he didn't tell his wife, then she got pregnant and swore it was his, but he knew different so he went for her with the bread knife and she lost the baby. Then the hospital found they'd mixed up his records so he could make babies after all, but by then his wife was barren from the shock of the miscarriage he'd brought on . . .'

Daisy dropped to her knees on the oilcloth by Winnie's chair, pulling her into her arms, stroking her hot forehead, promising her that everything would be all right.

'Leonard won't be like the man in the story. People make those stories up for magazines. You'll go on and have more babies with him, you'll see.'

It was absolutely true that she had pushed the thought of Winnie's wedding right out of her mind. She could only cope with one thing at a time; it was the only way she could go on, by concentrating her mind totally on getting away from the house in the quickest time possible. Could no one see that guilt was almost destroying her? Every time she opened the door of the room at the top of the house she saw Joshua's chair reproaching her. Reminding her of the hours he had sat there alone, listening for her step on the stair – when she could find time to spend a few minutes with him, that was.

Her mind ran riot. The down-to-earth sensible part of her stood aside watching her torture herself, reminding her that over and over again Joshua had accused her of trying too hard to be all things to all men. One night she had dragged the chair out on to the landing, then got out of bed at two o'clock in the morning to bring it back in.

'Tomorrow,' she told Winnie, 'we'll talk about the wedding and make sure everything's sorted out. You can try your dress on for me and we'll see that it's right. You're going to look a picture in it, a proper picture.'

'Oh, Daisy . . .' Winnie's tears started afresh. 'You're so good and I'm so foul. Why don't you shout at me and tell me just how foul I am, expecting you to care a monkey's backside whether I get married or not? Why don't you remind me what a selfish cow I am?' She jumped up, almost knocking Daisy over. 'Why does everything have to be so bloody? Why can't we just go on, you and me, a good team like we always were?'

She flung herself out of the kitchen, slamming the door behind her.

Leaving Daisy exhausted before the morning was halfway over.

'We're picking a friend of mine up from the office where she works,' David said, as Daisy got into the car. 'She had half a day's leave to come, so she thought the chance of a trip out to the country was too good to be missed.' He leaned across Daisy to slam the door so hard it made her jump. 'We'll go for a walk while you're looking round the cottage. Naturally.'

Daisy thought he looked cross, and wished she'd insisted on going by train and bus. Being a widow turned you into a *burden*, making men promise to help out when the shock of the death was on them, then causing them to regret their impulsiveness. That would all be resolved when she moved to the cottage. There, a stranger, she'd be able to stand on her own two feet and not have to ask favours from anyone. She blinked hard to cover the unexpected prick of tears behind her eyes. She'd be damned if she'd be beholden to anyone!

David pulled up outside a red-brick building, and immediately, as if she'd been waiting just behind the imposing front door, Nora Jolly came out. She had given quite a lot of thought to her outfit for that day. Clothes were her passion, and she prayed that the rumour that clothes rationing would end in just over a year's time was true. Bartering for coupons had turned her into a common spiv, she'd admitted to herself on more than one occasion.

Daisy watched her walk towards the car and felt her very soul swell with envy. That was how *she* had always wanted to look. All of a tone, with leather accessories – shoes, bag and belt, just how the fashion magazines advocated in articles entitled 'Getting It All Together' or 'It's the Little Things that Count'. Dior's New Look with its long full skirts and nipped-in waists suited

David's friend to perfection. Who would have thought of putting grey and beige together? Without even the addition of as much as a coloured neck scarf to brighten it up?

'So *this* is Daisy?' Nora held Daisy's hand for a long, telling moment. 'I'm glad we've met at last.'

Her eyebrows were like Joan Crawford's, Daisy marvelled. Perfect dark wings, with little extra ones drawn in where her own went thin at the outside edges. Come to think about it, she was the same type as Joan Crawford, not pretty pretty, but elegant and smart, with a kind of repressed emotion emanating from her.

'I think you know how sorry I was to hear about Joshua.' Her voice was husky with feeling. 'But I'm glad that David is around to help. He thought the world of Joshua, you know.'

No, she wouldn't dream of allowing Daisy to move into the back seat of the car. Daisy must sit right where she was. Her smile was brilliant as she climbed into the back. Like the Cheshire cat's it seemed to linger as David drove the car on to the Preston road. Looking crosser than ever, for some reason.

They didn't talk much on the journey because David was worried about what he thought was a problem with the engine. Twice he got out, opened up the bonnet and peered inside.

When they arrived at the village he drove into the forecourt of the garage in the main street, wound his window down and called out to a pair of feet sticking out from underneath an ancient Ford.

'Yes, sir!'

The man looking up at them with an impudent grin had the twinkliest eyes Daisy had ever seen.

'Yes, *sir*!' he said again, and subdued a salute.

Bill Tattersall usually recognized officer material

when he came across it. After six years in the army – France, Italy, Tobruk, he'd repaired more officers' cars than this bloke had had hot dinners. And talking of hot dinners, this one looked as if he'd missed a few in the past years. Probably a prisoner of war. With the Japs, Bill told himself, listening with apparent intensity to what David was saying.

'Every man to his job,' Nora said, as the trouble was diagnosed after no more than a cursory glance at the engine.

'Give me an hour, sir.' Bill wiped his fingers on an oily rag. 'I'm afraid there's nowhere roundabouts where you can get a cup of tea, and the pub's closed . . .'

But he needn't have worried. It was all sorted out apparently. The tall thin man and the woman dressed up like a dog's dinner were going for a walk, while the lass with the sad eyes was going down the road for her second look at Mrs Rothwell's cottage, with a view to moving into it from her lodging house at Blackpool.

Daisy had no idea that the man with the crumpled forehead and the laugh in his eyes could have told her the day on which Joshua had died; knew that the man driving the car was her late husband's friend, the son of the doctor who many years ago had spent his holiday weeks and his weekends in Orchard House just through the village.

But then Daisy hadn't met Bertha Tomlinson. Not yet. She would, in the fullness of time. Bill knew there was nothing more sure than that. He grinned as he saw a woman come out of her front door, wielding a sweeping brush at the exact time Daisy walked past. He saw her call out, and the way Daisy stopped politely to hear what she had to say.

'Atta girl, Bertha!' Bill turned and walked with his jaunty springing walk through the garage towards his little office. By tomorrow the entire village would know how much the little widow was selling her lodging house for; how much she was paying for the Rothwells' place; who the smart woman turning up the fell road with young David Armitage was, and quite likely what she'd had for breakfast and whether she ever suffered from constipation.

'Stop mucking about and get on with it, Keith,' he called out to a young man wearing oil-spattered overalls. 'You've to clean and polish that Austin 10 before four o'clock. I think it's time for another brew-up. It's hot enough to crack the flags today.'

*

Mrs Rothwell was feeling the heat. Her husband was upstairs having a lie-down and Daisy saw right away that the old woman wasn't up to talking business. 'My son will see to everything,' she kept saying, and though Daisy could see a tray set out in the scullery with cups and a plate neatly arranged with a circle of biscuits, Mrs Rothwell had obviously forgotten all about it.

'Why don't I just wander round with my tape measure?' Daisy said. 'As for the furniture and the bits and pieces, your son can tell me what you're leaving, and we can sort it all out together.'

'I'm a bit mixed up today, love.' Mrs Rothwell sat down gratefully in a rocking chair by a grate with yesterday's ashes in it. 'Do you ever get flummoxed?'

'I am in a permanent flummox.' Daisy put her tape measure aside. 'Would you like me to make you a nice cup of tea? It won't take a minute.'

'I was spittin' feathers for that,' Mrs Rothwell said after her first sip of the hot strong tea. 'Did you manage to find everything, love? I thought Dad and me had finished those biscuits yesterday.'

Daisy let herself out of the cottage and walked slowly

back up the road. While Mrs Rothwell dozed she had washed the tea things, tidied up in the kitchen, covered the butter dish and the sugar bowl, and almost wept at the meagre amount of food in the cupboard.

It was high time the old couple moved to be nearer their son. No wonder Walter Rothwell had been determined not to let Joshua's death delay the transaction. No wonder he had choked back his embarrassment and come round to see her that day.

At least Joshua hadn't had to suffer the indignity of growing old and confused, normal one day then forgetful the next. He would have hated that. Joshua had been such a dignified man.

The sun was warm on her head as Daisy walked past the garage, on down the curving road to a grey stone inn with a swinging sign motionless in the shimmering heat. It was as closed and shuttered as only an English inn could be on a thirsty summer afternoon. Daisy turned into a narrow lane banked high on either side with wild flowers, masses of cow parsley, some over six-foot high.

She climbed a stile and stood on top of it, drinking in and sniffing up the view. Over on the far hills a mustard field bound itself round a hillside like a yellow ribbon. Across the meadow she could see the glint of the river, and on her way down to it she felt cuckoo spit cold and sticky against her legs. This was the *real* country. This was what her mother had meant when she used to pine for a 'bit o' green'. Feeling pleasantly countrified, she bent down to pick a dandelion clock, pursing her lips to blow away the fluff and count away the hours.

The river bank was dotted with groups of people having a nice day out. Couples sat on spread raincoats. Daisy knew that no boy worth his salt would take a girl for a walk without his raincoat looped conspicuously over his arm. She reminded herself that one day soon she would be able to walk from the cottage to this idyllic place in less than five minutes. She smiled at the sight of two small boys wrist-flicking stones into the water, and two more busily pummelling each other into the ground.

'You don't know where we can find a cup of tea, do you, love?'

A middle-aged woman with a face that looked as if it had been boiled in a shoe-bag panted up the grassy slope towards Daisy.

'We fetched a flask with us, but we drank that dry two hours ago.'

'I could sup a reservoir,' the man behind her said.

Bill Tattersall saw her walking slowly along the road before Daisy saw him.

'They've not come back yet,' he said, startling her by appearing suddenly from behind David's car parked in the forecourt. 'I hope they've not got lost. It can get a bit parky up there even on a day like this.' His eyes narrowed into impudent slits. 'Perhaps the lady's got her feet tangled in her high heels and sprained her ankle.'

'Well, she's with a doctor so she won't be left up there to die of exposure.'

Daisy had the garage man weighed up to a T. She'd been dealing with his sort in one way or another since leaving school at fourteen. Flash-tongued but charming with it. Built to a pattern too, broad shouldered and strong. This man had arms tanned by the sun, and laughing eyes that looked her up and down, missing nothing.

'Fancy a cup of tea? If you don't mind drinking it sitting on an oil barrel.' Bill led the way into his office, a tiny room leading off from the garage, furnished with a table piled with papers, an old metal cabinet, a rickety chair, parts of car engines spaced out on the floor, and a rude calendar pinned to the wall with rusty drawing pins. 'Keith? An extra cup, laddy.' Bill nodded at a slightly built young man taking his time about polishing a windscreen. 'We've got company.'

With a flourish he snatched off his beret and dusted the chair seat with it. Thanking him, Daisy sat down trying not to look at the outrageous chest of the calendar girl.

'Is the car repaired?'

'Ready and waiting, madam.' Bill touched his forehead with the rolled-up cap. 'Ah, here comes the boy with the tea.' He turned and took the tray, which Daisy could see had once been the lid of a biscuit tin, from his apprentice. 'May I help you to sugar, madam?'

Daisy looked at him properly for the first time. He knew about Joshua dying, she guessed. He was trying to make her smile, trying to make her feel at home in his terrible little apology for an office.

'The lady with the sweeping brush?' she asked. 'I think she found out everything there is to know about me in three minutes flat.'

Bill nodded and sat down on the edge of the table, stirring his tea round with a dark green Reeve's pencil. 'Mrs Tomlinson. What she doesn't manage to find out she makes up. Would you like me to tell you why the woman across the road hasn't spoken to her husband since a week last Tuesday? And why the vicar calls in on Miss Nuttall every Monday afternoon and stops for long enough to blot his copybook?'

'Oh, yes, please!'

When Daisy smiled Bill changed his mind about her looks. It transformed her into a bonny young woman.

'Bill Tattersall,' he said, wiping a hand down his overalls before holding it out. 'And you are Mrs Penny,

135

a landlady with a reputation for keeping the best table in Blackpool, coming to live in the Rothwells' cottage with your two children, a boy and a girl.' He held Daisy's hand in his warm clasp. 'Your mother was a Martha Bell who ran a potatoe-pie shop in Blackburn, and died on the sands at Blackpool just before the war.' He paused for breath. 'And the driver of the car out there? Well, Mrs T had no trouble with that one because she remembers the time when young Doctor Armitage terrorized the village on his three-wheel bike. It's the lady gone walking with him that will be puzzling her and setting her curtains all of a twitch.' He walked to the open door, shading his eyes against the sun. 'Not to worry. Mrs T has caught them coming back down the road. And has accosted them by her garden gate.'

'So all will be revealed,' Daisy said.

Bill tapped the side of his nose. 'In the fullness of time,' he agreed.

On the way home Daisy sat in the back of the car, and this time Nora made no protest. She looked flushed with sun and wind, and her eyes burned at you when she spoke. She was determined to tell them the history of the hand-loom weavers, and quoted from Mrs Gaskell's *Mary Barton*.

'Who throw the shuttle with unceasing sound,' she intoned. 'That's from the book,' she explained over her shoulder to Daisy.

She thinks I'm an illiterate moron. Daisy would have retaliated if she could have been bothered, but time was getting on and Winnie would be panicking about the meal. The children would be home from school, and there were two new couples booking in late and no doubt wanting something to eat when everything had been cleared away.

'I suppose you've heard of the Pendle Witches, Daisy?' Nora turned round and beamed a smile.

'I am directly descended from one,' said Daisy, beaming back.

David shared a late whisky with his father that night.

'The country's a bit bleak once you get away from the village,' he said, draining his glass and getting up immediately to refill it.

Old Doctor Armitage was no fool. From the day his son had been reported missing, believed killed, to the day he had arrived home by way of Ceylon and India three years later, the doctor had accepted that the man who came back could never be the same man who went away.

Gradually the sweating nightmares had ceased; the bouts of malaria spaced out, but however much David's memories faded he could not come to terms with the fact that *he* had come home while so many had suffered and died. What seemed to be hurting him the most was the fact that by now the vastness of the jungle would have completely obliterated their graves.

'*Their* only memorial,' he had said sadly on his return from Joshua's funeral, 'a name on a casualty list.'

Doctor Armitage watched his son's legs, restless, ever twitching, moving, as if he were remembering the night the Japanese had left him to die with mosquitos droning in his ears and crawling into his mouth, biting at his parched lips. The bleakness of the Pendle countryside should surely have struck him as a haven of peace after the stifling sticky heat of that far-away jungle. The older man knew he would have to tread carefully.

'So you regret playing God to little Mrs Penny? Is that it?'

David shrugged. 'I suppose so. It was a different situation when Joshua was alive. When I took them both out to see the Rothwells' cottage on that last day I could see them spending maybe a good few years together.' He half drained his glass. 'Joshua *needed* to be prised from that room of his, from that *chair*. Daisy would have given him the tranquillity he craved away from the bustling clamour of that boarding house. Now the way things have turned out, the *last* thing she needs is tranquillity. She's so stubborn she makes me want to hit her! The stupid woman doesn't know the difference between a bull and a cow, yet she sees herself as a shiny-cheeked milkmaid skipping through a field of buttercups. We stopped briefly on the way back for Nora to admire a view, and what did Daisy do? She sat down on the grass and made herself a daisy chain! One minute you think she's old and wise far beyond her years, then she's a child, and a pretty naive one at that!' David drained his glass and slammed it down on the round wine table by the side of his chair. 'She won't even listen to reason. One minute she's arguing with you, then the next minute she's asking a favour.'

'To do what?'

'To give that sharp-nosed lass who works for her away at her wedding. As a stand-in in place of Joshua.' He gloomed at the pyramid of coal in the grate, interlaid with sticks of firewood. 'Does Mrs Platts have to be so bloody *symmetrical* in everything she does? She lays a fire as neatly as if she's practising for her Girl Guide badge.'

'Well, going to Winnie's wedding won't hurt you.' Doctor Armitage took off his glasses and rubbed his eyes. 'Why don't you say what's really on your mind, son? Why don't you admit that you're restless? That you've done your level best to settle down since you came home, but that it isn't working out?' He put the glasses back on again, then snatched them off when he saw to his astonishment that his son's eyes were misted with unshed tears.

'Joshua dying brought it all back,' David blurted out. 'Because he was a casualty of war, just like the men I left out there, crawling like ants through long grass, and dying like ants do when a gardener puts his foot down on them. I can't shake them out of my mind, though God knows I've tried.' He got up and walked over to the sideboard again, turning round with the glass in his hand. 'It's all right. It's mostly soda.'

'You're trying to tell me that you're going away again.' Doctor Armitage glanced at his empty glass. 'If I wasn't on call tonight I'd have another one with you. Do you want to tell me just what you have in mind?'

David shook his head. 'Not tonight. I'm not sure enough about anything at the moment.'

The telephone rang, and he sat back in the leather armchair, holding the glass up and staring through the amber liquid as if he saw the answer he was looking for. In the hall he heard his father mouthing soothing words, promising someone at the other end of the line that he would be with them as quickly as he could get there. A familiar scene played out to him since his childhood, except that then his mother had been there to help her husband on with his coat, and run after him with his scarf when the wind blew cold.

That night the worst of the nightmares came back again. Starvation gnawed at his guts; he saw his own small band of men slipping into raving delirium, one after another. He saw the Japanese take his meagre supply of quinine for their own use, and he saw them laugh at him as they took it.

He woke shaking and weeping, his tears mingling with the rivulets of sweat running down his face. He forced himself to lie quietly, breathing deeply to send the terror away. He brought back to his mind the shifting sunlight of the afternoon, colouring the distant mound of Pendle as if it moved in an ever-changing light.

And remembered Joshua's wife sitting on the grass weaving a daisy chain through her soft brown hair.

Chapter Seven

Leonard fainted at the altar, but as he came to almost at once it didn't make that much difference. David stepped forward to hold him upright and tell him to take deep breaths. The minister never batted an eyelid.

Daisy's Auntie Edna, sitting next to Uncle Arnold in a pew on the bride's side, gave a sideways sniff. Winnie Whalley was at least four months gone; you didn't need a dirty mind to have worked that one out. Edna stretched her neck, jerking it like a chicken swallowing. She adjusted a felt hat shaped like a boiler shovel over her eyes.

Her niece Daisy was looking very well, considering, though what she was thinking about giving up her livelihood and burying herself and those two children in the back of beyond, Edna couldn't think. Still, she'd always been like that. Impulsive, not taking advice from nobody.

Standing next to her, Arnold tried in vain to cough away a sudden tickle in his throat. Edna rooted in her handbag and passed him a Fisherman's Friend.

Narrowing her eyes to focus better – she never wore her glasses if she thought she could manage without – Daisy glanced across the aisle at Leonard's mother sitting squarely in her wheelchair, her hippopotamus face set into a fierce scowl. Auntie Edna had said she'd seen nicer expressions on the faces of fish set out on slabs in the fish market, and that if anyone had been on the

141

back row when looks were being given out it was definitely Leonard's mother.

Sally, as pretty as a rosebud in the pink taffetta dress, made without coupons on account of the material being classed as coat lining, was behaving beautifully, holding Winnie's bouquet as well as her own small posy. Oliver, having refused point blank to be a pageboy, glowered into his hymn book by Daisy's side, chewing on a humbug passed to him by Auntie Edna, who was always a soft touch as far as Oliver was concerned. Daisy watched a trickle of black saliva snake from the corner of his mouth. She turned her head away.

It had been a right picnic back at the house, with Winnie trying on her short veil in different ways and at one stage threatening to jump on it. She didn't love Leonard, she yelled, and worse than that she didn't even *like* him. Besides which, his mother was an evil sod.

Used to Winnie's outrageous behaviour, Daisy ignored her, but when she saw her in the off-white dress with her bright red hair gleaming through the net veil and Winnie's little rounded belly pushing the gathers out slightly at the front of her dress, she felt a sudden foreboding.

'It's not too late to call it off,' she whispered.

Winnie stared at her with swimming eyes. 'And what about my fatherless child? Growing up despised and spat upon?'

'I hardly think . . .' Daisy began, but already Winnie was gazing enraptured at herself in the mirror, parting her lips and widening her eyes.

'All brides have nerves on their wedding day,' Edna said. 'I remember our Betty, bless her, wept buckets all the way to the church. Winnie Whalley will walk down that aisle laughing her head off.'

'That red hat might just about get by on Marlene Dietrich, but it does nothing for Daisy,' she told her husband as they left the house together. In a voice loud enough for Daisy to hear every syllable.

Now, in the church, Daisy had to admit that the hat wouldn't come as a surprise to anyone. A dark red pill-box with a tiny veil, it had emerged from a box on top of the wardrobe for special occasions for the past ten years. She had gone to Joshua's funeral hatless because he much preferred her that way, and never mind what anyone thought or said.

When the prick of tears threatened behind her eyelids she squeezed her eyes tight shut. As if she were praying.

Arnold thought his favourite niece looked ravishingly pretty in the little round red hat. He wished his wife would sometimes *praise* someone instead of always doing them down. He wished she would stop staring round her now, smiling at folks with her mouth while sneering at them in her head. Daisy would survive. In his book, his niece Daisy was *special*.

Edna saw him smiling to himself and hoped he wasn't going into an early senility like his father before him. Walking about with his flies unbuttoned, and laughing at nowt.

'Therefore,' intoned the minister in a properly solemn voice, 'if any man can show just cause why they may not lawfully be joined together . . .'

Leonard's mother suddenly sat herself bolt upright in her chair, jutting her chin forward.

For one heart-stopping moment Daisy thought she was going to shout something out, but the moment passed and she breathed freely again.

'Who giveth this woman to be married to this man?'

David stepped forward, serious and achingly hand-some in his dark suit. Daisy lowered her head. If it couldn't be Joshua, then there was no one more fitted

143

to give the bride away than David. What a dear good friend he was proving to be.

Daisy had catered for a small reception back at Shangri-La. She'd made a wedding cake with two mock tiers in cardboard, and the real one miserably short on dried fruit. But the sandwiches had tinned salmon in them, and the sponge fancies were feather-light with fresh eggs brought from Blackburn by Percy Bulcock, who thought that rationing, after we'd gone and won the war, was an inconvenience not to be tolerated.

The Bulcocks were moving into Winnie's room that very day. What was the point, as Ruby said, in paying rent when they could be living on the job at Shangri-La, giving Daisy a hand now that Winnie was leaving?

Ruby sat in the kitchen, splaying her knees wide to accommodate a basin in which she was whipping up a batter for the evening meal. Daisy had advised her not to buy the fishmonger's freshly salted cod, but at ninepence a pound Ruby decided it would have been a crying shame to miss it. Percy was peeling a pile of potatoes so fast it was a wonder they didn't burst into flames, and the individual puddings, small dishes of semolina with a Victoria plum floating on the top, had been ready for ages. Ruby was well-satisfied. Daisy Penny had made a stick for her own back the way she'd fussed about her menus. As far as Ruby could see, the visitors in the house that week had been brought up on cocoa and tomato sandwiches, so why upset their stomachs when they were on their holidays?

'I'll be glad when we see the back of her,' she told Percy, when Daisy left the reception for the second time to come nosy-parkering around to see what they were doing. 'She thinks she's the only one who can serve up a decent meal.'

'I reckon there's something going on between her and

144

that doctor fella.' Percy gathered the peelings together ready to take them down the yard.

'Well, they do say her husband was only half wick for a long time before he died.'

'And the doctor was lost in the jungle without the sight of a white woman for years before he was found.'

'So nature's merely taking its course,' said Ruby, with a leer.

David stood with Daisy on the pavement outside Shangri-La, waving Winnie and Leonard off on their honeymoon. The newlyweds were walking to the station as it wasn't all that far, and though Daisy scattered a handful of confetti over them, she felt her action was forced, silly and uncalled for.

Leonard's mother had gone into a nursing home for two weeks with an expression on her face that said she would see to it that her son and his new wife would pay dearly for their desertion when they got back.

'That woman will break Winnie's heart,' Daisy told David, then turned to him, smiling. 'D'you know, I feel superfluous for the first time in my life. Auntie Edna and Uncle Arnold have taken the children on to the sands, and I'm not wanted in my own kitchen.' She sighed. 'I'm actually feeling a bit jealous, not to mention neglected and unwanted.'

'Then come with me,' David said, barely glancing at his watch. 'I've got an evening surgery, but not yet.' He took her hand. 'Come on! Just for an hour or so.' He tugged at her hand. 'Daisy! Just for *once* let the rest of them go hang. You've said everything's taken care of. The world won't stop turning because you take an hour off.'

It wasn't until they had reached the turn-off to the front that she realized they were still linked together.

Immediately, without breaking her stride, she let go of David's hand.

As soon as they reached the promenade, the wind took her full skirt and blew it up round her legs. It loosened her hair from its special wedding set; it tossed her words away. Across the road on the wide stretch of promenade holiday-makers with brick-red faces strolled arm in arm. The sea sparkled and glittered in the sun. White-frothed foam rose and fell against the black pier-head.

It was as though the war had never been. It was as though already Blackpool was back in its stride, with the Tower rising majestically up to the bright blue sky, the ice-cream vendors crying their wares, and the bustling crowds out to spend the money they'd saved so carefully through the terrible winter when it seemed the sun would never shine again.

It was a day just like the one ten years before when Daisy had walked along the promenade with Sam, the married man she had believed would leave his wife to marry her. It was a day just like the one when her mother had died down there on the beach, sitting in a deckchair with her hand trailing in the sand, her eyes wide open in a terrifying fixed stare.

On a sudden impulse she ran away from David along the crowded pavement to where a Victorian landau, with a patient horse in the shafts, waited at the kerb.

'Let's go for a ride.' She took David's arm, laughing up at him. 'Let's go all the way to the South Pier. Let's be *barmy*, David. Absolutely barmy!'

The small step wobbled as she climbed inside the landau. The worn leather seat was covered by a tartan rug, warmed by the sun. After a snort and a shaking of his brass-trimmed harness, the horse responded to the light touch of the driver's whip and began to clip-clop its way along.

'If you close your eyes,' Daisy said, 'you can pretend we're Lord and Lady Muck.'

But if he closed his eyes he couldn't see her sitting beside him, smiling. With her chin up, which told him that tears weren't far away.

'I'm going abroad,' he said abruptly.

Immediately she turned to him, her eyes alight with interest. 'To somewhere nice, I hope, David.'

A crowd of women crossed the road in front of the landau, chattering nineteen to the dozen, hurrying to get down on the beach to get a bit of colour in their town-white faces. The horse started forward again.

'To America,' David said.

'To *Hollywood*?' Daisy wanted to know, because to her America *was* Hollywood. Teasing him.

'To Washington. Washington DC. To work in a hospital on a kind of exchange scheme cooked up in the last year of the war. To study nutrition. To tell the Americans about the revolutionary eating patterns forced on the British public during the war, and the way community rationing gave the hard-up their first fill of proteins and vitamins. And the better-off a lesson in sensible eating.' He looked away from her. 'And for me, personally, to find out why starvation got to some men before others in the outfit I was with. If malaria hadn't finished them off first,' he muttered, almost to himself.

The afternoon sun was warm on the back of his head and neck. The horse's hooves and their clip-clop rhythm had a mesmeric effect on him. He had told Daisy he was going away, and she didn't care. She was *glad* for him, that was all.

The driver's hair was over-long beneath his tweed cap; it straggled over the collar of his jacket, reminding him of those terrible years in the Far East.

All his men – those that were left of them – had their hair straggling over their tattered shirt collars by the time they had been lost in the Malayan jungle for three and a half months. They had come across a rotting shack buried beneath stinking vegetation and overhanging foliage. They were all swaying on their feet with malaria; they would have died but for the *ubi kayu* brought to them at intervals by a Chinese man who never once spoke to them. Within a week all but four of them were dead, lying in their own filth, with massive black ants crawling over them. In their ears, their mouths, and even their eyes.

'David?'

He turned, his eyes glazed, to see Daisy staring at him anxiously.

'What is it, David?' Her voice was gentle. 'A goose walk over your grave?'

For a minute he couldn't come back ... They had been too weak to dig graves for the dead. They had merely covered them with leaves and left them to the ants, the huge centipedes and the scorpions ...

'David?' Her arms around him were warm and strong, her hair soft and fragrant against his face. 'You're *back*, David,' she was saying. 'Safe and sound. There's no need for you to be afraid any more.'

Instinctively his mouth found hers, seeking the comfort he craved.

'David!'

She was pushing him away, patting her hair, laughing at him.

'David! How many glasses of champagne did you drink? If I didn't know you better I'd say you were more than a bit squiffy!'

Across the road from the South Pier they climbed down from the landau. David paid the driver, and Daisy told him she would catch the tram back along the promenade. She reminded him that he would have to look sharp if he wanted to get back in time for his evening surgery. When she boarded the tram she looked through the window and saw him standing there, tall and straight in his dark suit, with the wedding carnation still in his buttonhole. When the conductor rang the bell she saw him hold a hand up in farewell, still not moving, as if he was saying goodbye to someone he never thought to see again.

Nora Jolly rang David that night and wondered if he would like to go round for a drink? Something had happened at the office and she would like his advice. She sounded tense and unhappy, and because David felt that made two of them, he said he would go.

When she replaced the receiver Nora began to cry. When she lit a cigarette her hands trembled so much she dropped the first two matches and had to scrabble round on the floor for them because, in spite of her distress, it would have been beyond her to leave them there.

'I *really* love him,' she muttered, then looked round startled as if someone else had come into the room and spoken.

'I'm too old to feel like this,' she whispered, going over to the mirror and seeing a face not softened by tears but ugly with weeping. She was more than a little mad, she told herself; she despised women who behaved like this. She would lose her job if she made any more mistakes. No longer was it true that to be sacked, a civil servant either had to strike a superior officer or steal from the safe. During the war girls had been taken on as temporary clerks, fresh from school, without sitting the civil service exam. If she went tomorrow there were half a dozen in her department who could take her place.

She went into the tiny bathroom and splashed cold water over her eyes, instinctively patting round them carefully with the towel, because to stretch the delicate skin was the surest way to get wrinkles.

'If he doesn't marry me I'll die,' she told her reflection, and the sound of her own voice shocked her so much that she began to cry again.

When David came her face was blotchy and a mess, but she was so glad he was there that nothing mattered any more.

It had been so awful that David knew he couldn't go home, not yet. He had told Nora he was going to America and she had ... oh God! He quickened his step. She had cried out that she loved him, that if he went without her she would follow him. That she had loved him even when he was married to his first wife, and that she knew he was going away because of her. But if only he would stay she wouldn't be a nuisance. She *promised*. On her *life*.

Coughing and snivelling through her tears, she had said she wasn't one of those silly misguided women who fancy themselves in love with their doctors, saying they've been made passes at when they were being examined. Far from wanting to get David struck off the medical register she wanted to help him in his career. She was *right* for him, because hadn't her own father been a doctor, so she knew all there was to know about answering the telephone and taking messages down correctly.

He had felt so sorry for her, so embarrassed at seeing her devoid of her usual elegance and poise, he had stayed talking to her until she calmed down, assuring her of his eternal *friendship*, and thanking her for all her many kindnesses to him. And left her knowing that he never wanted to see her again.

There was a pounding in his head. It had begun to rain, a heavy summer shower that reminded him of how quickly the jungle rain turned even small streams into raging torrents, and the ground into acres of treacherous mud. His stomach hurt, still weak from the years of semi-starvation, and he regretted the champagne of the afternoon.

He could have sworn that he had no idea where he was walking to, but when he turned into the street of tall houses where Daisy lived his footsteps quickened. He began to swing his arms, like the soldier he had been, not all that long ago.

'There is something going on between those two,' Edna said, when Daisy had taken the doctor through into the kitchen and closed the door. 'Poor Joshua will revolve in his grave.'

'You mean turn in his urn,' Arnold said, hoping to lighten the conversation. 'Joshua was cremated, wasn't he?'

'I always say,' Edna went on, ignoring him, 'that if this sort of carrying-on happens within months of the funeral, then there's been carrying-on going on *before*.'

'You have a mucky mind,' Arnold told her.

'Well, even that's better than having nowt between the ears, like some I could mention.'

They were stopping with Daisy and eating with Daisy but sleeping next door at Balmoral with Mrs MacDougal on account of Daisy being full up. Before David had arrived they were all ready to be off to their beds, but now Edna had sensed an atmosphere, Arnold knew there would be no budging her till she found out what it was.

Little Miss Grimshaw, sitting quietly in her corner, rolled up her knitting and walked towards the door. 'I'll love you and leave you,' she said, trying hard to be matey with Daisy's relatives.

Trying because Daisy had told her that you had to

go more than halfway if you wanted to be liked, and with Daisy gone there would be nothing for it but to make an effort with Mr and Mrs Bulcock. But oh, she wished they were more Daisy's type, kind and compassionate, but never prying into a person's private life. And, oh dear, it was surely an illusion? A trick of the light maybe? But she could swear that one morning she had seen Mr Bulcock's hair *move*!

'What *she*'s short of is a man,' Edna said, not caring whether she was overheard or not.

As soon as Daisy saw David's face she went to put the kettle on.

'Did I ever tell you that you're the living spit-image of Leslie Howard?' she asked, thinking to cheer him up. 'I bet you thought he was the typical Englishman, didn't you?' She got out cups and saucers and set them on the table. 'Well, he was Hungarian! How about that?'

'*Was*? Is he dead, whoever he was?' David stared morosely at the draining-board.

'*Whoever he was*!' Daisy pretended to faint. 'Don't tell me you've never seen *Pygmalion* or *Gone With The Wind*? You'd be chuffed to little mint-balls at being like him if you knew how handsome he was!'

She was doing her best, but David wasn't responding. Joshua had once told her that his friend still had fearful dreams about the time he was lost in the jungle, struggling alone to survive at the end, before the Japanese captured him and dragged him away to a life of hell in one of the camps. Joshua had said that David was still a sick man – sick in his mind as well as his body. As she poured boiling water into the old familiar brown teapot Daisy felt her heart ache with an almost overwhelming compassion. She closed her eyes for a moment. Two men, two friends, Joshua and David, both of them casualties of world wars, lucky to have come back alive, but broken men all the same.

David was absurdly handsome with his sensitive face and his azure blue eyes. For a moment Daisy forgot he was a doctor, and therefore not as other men. He was unhappy, and to stretch out a hand to comfort came as naturally as breathing.

'Dear David . . .' Her hand was on his head, gently stroking back the thick fair hair. 'I wish I could chase the bad dreams away for you.'

He leaned against her, hearing her voice like liquid silk.

'I too am sleeping badly, and I know I won't rest until I've taken the children away from this house. This house is my conscience, David. I can't go into that room upstairs without seeing Joshua sitting alone there, *neglected*. By *me*.'

She had never noticed before how badly he bit his fingernails. Poor David . . . poor, poor David . . .

'I was never,' said Edna, purple with indignation, 'so flabbergasted in the whole of me natural. I opened the kitchen door, and there they were!'

Arnold tried to ease her towards the front door, but she wasn't having any.

'Would you credit it? Still not out of her black – at least she shouldn't be – and canoodling with the doctor. Bold as brass and twice as brazen.'

'It has nothing to do . . .'

Whatever Arnold was going to say was interrupted by the sudden ringing of the telephone.

Edna jumped a mile. 'Oh flamin' 'eck.' She laid a hand over her heart. 'All me past flashed before me eyes then. Best answer it, Arnold. Them two in there wouldn't hear a bomb drop.'

Arnold picked up the receiver and held it away from

his ear, only to hand it over with relief to Daisy as she came quickly into the hall. For someone caught cuddling the doctor, he couldn't help thinking she looked peculiarly unruffled.

She smiled at Arnold, an *innocent* smile, he would stake his life on it.

'Time we was going.' He held open the front door so pointedly that his wife had no choice but to walk through it.

She wouldn't speak to Arnold all the time he was getting undressed in one of Balmorals' back bedrooms next door. But when they lay side by side in the three-quarter bed, close together of necessity, she did perk up a bit.

'Our Martha would have been over the moon at the chance of a doctor coming into the family. She'd have been one up on all them who were sure Daisy would never get a man. First a teacher, then a doctor, and she's not a patch on our Betty, bless her, when it comes to looks.'

'I'm sure that Daisy and that young man are just good friends.' Arnold held fast to the bedclothes as Edna turned over.

'There's no such thing as a man and a woman being *good friends*. A man has only one thing on his mind.' She yanked the blankets with her. 'And it's not what he's going to have for his dinner!'

'If you don't come round right now I swear I'll swallow the lot!' Nora's voice had cracked with hysteria. 'I've drunk half a bottle of whisky, but there's enough left to swallow these down. I'm warning you, David. I mean it!'

'Nora?' David saw with relief that Daisy was disappearing into the kitchen, closing the door behind her. 'Nora? Are you still there?'

The click in his ear as she banged the receiver down galvanized him into action. Telling Daisy merely that it was an emergency, he left the house, running down the street in the direction of Nora Jolly's flat, feeling his knees buckle beneath him as he turned the corner on to the promenade, but running on, praying that he would be in time.

'You know it's moral blackmail?'

Doctor Armitage pointed the stem of his pipe at his son. 'All right then, if it wasn't moral blackmail, what was it? Do you honestly believe she would have gone through with it if you hadn't rushed round to her flat? She hadn't taken a single tablet, you say?'

'But she was going to.'

To his father David looked as ill as the day he had arrived back in England; almost as bewildered.

'She won't be the first neurotic spinster to fall madly in love with her doctor, you know.'

David shifted uncomfortably in his chair. The pain in his back was as bad as it had ever been. 'I have to take some of the blame. I've enjoyed her company lately. She's intelligent, and we share a lot of the same tastes. For music and books and the theatre.' He shook his head. 'God help me, but I thought we were just good friends.' He frowned and bit his lip. 'With a few friendly kisses thrown in.'

'And tonight has finished all that?'

'When she calmed down she asked me to write to her when I go away. To keep in touch, she said.'

'And will you?'

'Anything rather than risk a repetition of what happened tonight.' He shuddered. 'I'm not proud of what I did.'

'What was that?'

David sighed and stroked his chin. 'She had the

blasted capsules spread out on the coffee table when I got there. She'd drunk almost half a bottle of whisky; she was maudlin and oh, yes, she meant to take them. There was a grim determination about her. I suppose that determination, that total disregard for her life . . . well, it made me almost want to help her on her way.'

'I don't believe that for one minute.'

'It's true.'

David leaned back in his chair and closed his eyes. 'Dear God, I spent months and years with men who clung to life when they were rotting with malaria and gangrene and dysentery and brain fever. They fought for their right to life when there was nothing to eat or drink, when death would have released them from that stinking hell.'

He stood up and began pacing backwards and forwards.

'And that silly misguided woman, with a roof over her head and a pantry full of food, with *everything* to live for, was going to throw it all away.' He began to shout. 'My men drank filthy water!' He swung round to face his father. 'Do you blame me that I yanked her to her feet and shook her till her blasted head was ready to drop off?'

*

Doctor Armitage sat alone, smoking his pipe out, long after his son had gone to bed. He looked at his wife's photograph in the silver frame on the mantelpiece, and he wished that she was still with him. She would have known what to say to this only son of theirs who had endured so much and been hurt so much, and was even now, two years afterwards, finding it impossible to come to terms with his freedom.

On an impulse he leaned forward, knocked out his pipe against the bars of the grate, and walked out of the

156

room, across the wide hall, and into the surgery where he could use the telephone without being overheard.

Here in England it was after midnight, but three thousand miles away in Washington DC businessmen would still be driving home from their offices across the Potomac Bridge. His old friend Ben Coogan would be home from the hospital by now. Taking life nice and easy now he was past seventy, as he'd say himself. Doctor Armitage could see him sitting there in his chintz-covered chair, waiting for his wife Kitty to call him in to dinner . . . By the time the call came through Doctor Armitage could almost smell and taste the roast turkey, the pumpkin pie, the food he always associated with his last visit to his friend's house.

When at last he went upstairs to bed he glanced at the slit of light still showing beneath his son's door. He hesitated for a moment then walked by. It was going to be hard seeing David go away again, and sooner by far than he had anticipated, but what were friends for if not to step in in times of urgent need? David wasn't the only one who could play God.

'Daisy is not God!' Leonard felt his wife needed reminding of that. 'In my humble opinion you spend far too much time talking about her, especially to Mother. She doesn't care for Daisy at all; thinks she's a classic case of still waters running deep.'

'Is that a fact?' said Winnie in a coarse Glaswegian accent just to annoy him. 'I know one thing. Daisy would have had your mother winkled out of that chair by now. Running for a bus, I shouldn't wonder.'

'What a thing to say!' Leonard was getting undressed for bed, turning his back on Winnie as he stepped out of his trousers.

She lay on her side of the double bed watching him closely through her sandy eyelashes, needing to pick a quarrel with him because her day had been so unspeakably awful.

'Why do you keep your vest on in bed?' She had asked him this before but she felt she would like to hear it again.

'Because wool absorbs perspiration and is healthy for the skin.' Leonard buttoned his pyjama jacket over the high-necked vest with its linen-covered buttons. 'Wool allows the skin to breathe.' Taking a clean handkerchief from the top drawer in his tallboy, he folded it neatly into his top pocket.

'I've never seen you sweat, Leonard.' Winnie moved over to make room for him. 'I thought men always sweated when they made love.'

'Now how would a little innocent like you know a thing like that?' Leonard began to tickle her, but in the mood she was in Winnie steeled herself against laughing.

'I sometimes blame myself for stealing your virtue.' Leonard's face was suspended above hers, a small blur in the darkness. Winnie closed her eyes.

'Though one good thing did come of it. I was able to tell Mother that the wedding couldn't be put off any longer.'

Winnie sat straight up, pushing him aside. 'Are you telling me that you were waiting for permission from your mother? That all the while I was deciding whether to get engaged to you, it was really *her* calling the tune?' Her voice rose. 'That if I hadn't gone and got pregnant you'd have gone on waiting till she gave the word?'

'Keep your voice down!'

Winnie knew that her mother-in-law's head was only inches from their own on the other side of the dividing wall, but her blood was up. She'd had her fill of the old woman that day, moaning and complaining, criticizing every blessed thing Winnie tried to do. And sitting, always sitting in the high throne-like chair.

158

'You're married to *her*, Leonard. Not to *me*!' Winnie was beside herself, beyond caring whether she was overheard or not. 'You've got to choose, else there's no marriage.' She flung herself back on her pillow. 'I'm knocking meself out trying to make her like me. Can't you see? But I said *like* me, not dominate me. I won't be dominated, Leonard. I'm a person, not a *thing*!'

'*Be quiet!*'

'No, I won't be quiet. She doesn't frighten *me*. Not like she . . .'

When Leonard's hand clamped itself over her mouth, Winnie's eyes flew wide.

'I said stop shouting. Do you *want* to upset Mother? Can't you see that she's old and ill? Do you want to make her worse?'

His body covered her own. His fingers dug into her cheek, his knee pressed hard into her groin. 'Are you going to *shut up*?'

The Winnie who had married him, not all that long ago, would have bitten his hand, even kicked him out of bed, but shock and surprise and the fear that Leonard's probing bony knee could be hurting the baby made her jerk her head fiercely up and down in acquiescence.

'I didn't want to do that, Winnie. I'm sorry.' Leonard tried to put his arms around her, but she immediately stiffened, jerking away.

'I'm sorry,' he said again, and wearily Winnie told him it didn't matter.

What *did* matter was the discovery that Leonard would have hurt her physically, even risked hurting the baby rather than have his mother upset in even the slightest way. Leonard was a coward in most things, but where his mother was concerned he was a *tiger*. Winnie saw no humour in her thinking. His eyes had glittered at her in the darkness, her mouth still ached from the pressure of his fingers. Put his wife and his mother up against a wall, give him a gun and order him to shoot one of them, and he wouldn't hesitate. Winnie saw herself drop dead, blood pouring from the hole in her chest. Saw Leonard's mother walk away. Triumphant.

Half an hour later they were still lying like that, rigid as pokers, side by side, each busy with their own thoughts.

Leonard spoke first: 'Try and understand, Winnie.' There was a quiver in his voice. 'I hadn't even started school when my father was killed in France in the first war. I can't remember him. I often pretend to Mother that I can, but it isn't true. I don't think our memory can go back that far. I don't believe people who write books saying they can remember being pushed out in a pram.'

'I can remember my mother breast-feeding me,' Winnie lied. 'I can remember the taste of it.'

Leonard gave a long sigh of relief. He could tell by his wife's voice that she had forgiven him. He reached for her hand. In this mood she might perhaps be more prepared to understand. 'Life wasn't easy for Mother, though money wasn't the big problem. She has never got over losing my father. I don't believe she has lifted her head up properly since the terrible day when the telegram came. She's never looked at another man. Never wanted to marry again.'

Chance would be a fine thing, said Winnie in her mind.

'So she made you her life,' she said aloud. 'And you've been so close you'd make Siamese twins appear to live next door but one to each other.'

Leonard squeezed her hand to show he was getting used to the things she said. 'We went everywhere together. We were pals.'

160

'Beautiful,' Winnie whispered, on the very edge of sleep.

Leonard's voice was choked. 'Then arthritis struck her down. Right through her system. I couldn't bear to see her in pain, and one day I made a vow. As far as it was possible I would see that she never struggled again. If the day came when she couldn't walk then I would be her legs. If she couldn't lift a spoon then I would feed her. I would pay her back for all she has done for me. Don't you see?'

Winnie's answer was a soft put-put of a snore.

In the middle of the night she woke up, frantic for a beetroot butty. She could actually feel her taste buds twanging for the taste of the vinegar she had soaked the sliced beetroot in before she went to bed.

Already the big old-fashioned kitchen with its ancient gas oven, its wooden draining board, dark oak cupboards and claw-legged wash-boiler was wearing her down. Set in one corner was a never used tiny fireplace with an iron canopy which Mrs Smalley said must be black-leaded with Zebo every other day. Winnie glanced from it up to the clothes rack draped with her afternoon's ironing, the good things at the front and the towels and underwear decently out of sight at the back.

'Who did all this ironing before I lived here?' she had asked Leonard, and he'd explained that the woman who used to do the cleaning usually fitted it in as best she could.

Now the cleaning lady, the neighbour who did the shopping, even the window cleaner had all disappeared. The laundry man had been told not to call any more, and Leonard explained that his mother preferred home-baked bread.

Winnie bit thoughtfully into a beetroot sandwich . . . And where was the friend who used to sit with her mother-in-law on the rare evenings Leonard had been allowed out to do his courting?

All gone. Like leaves blown away by the wind. Like snow melted by the sun, Winnie thought, munching away morosely.

Leaving *her* to do the flamin' lot. As well as waiting on her upstairs hand and foot.

Winnie took a slice of beetroot out of the dish and ate it with her eyes closed to savour it better. Then crept back upstairs to lie by her sleeping husband and to suffer with heartburn for what was left of the night.

Less than a month later in the hall of Shangri-La David said a lingering goodbye to Daisy. He made her promise to take good care of herself, and told her that he would write often. He assured her of his everlasting friendship.

He looked ill. There was a slightly lemon tinge to his skin, and Daisy wondered idly if he was anaemic. The war had taken a dreadful toll on his health. And his nerves. She could see tiny beads of perspiration on his upper lip, and wondered if he was coming down with another bout of malaria.

She was wishing he would hurry up and *go*. Not because she was wanting to be rid of him, but because goodbyes always demoralized her.

'Goodbye, David.' She held out her hand, then changed her mind and kissed him on his cheek. 'Thank you for all you've done for me since Joshua died.' The emotion of the moment was getting at her already. Another minute and she'd be sunk. There was a deep huskiness in her voice when she spoke. 'Be happy . . . dear David . . . that's the main thing.'

When he saw the tears in her eyes he folded her in his arms, holding her close. 'Will you miss me, Daisy? Will you really miss me *that* much?'

Daisy closed her eyes against his chest. She could feel

him trembling, and knew she'd been right about the malaria. She *wished* she could explain to him that the tears in her eyes weren't *personal*, that once she had disgraced herself by sobbing on the milkman's shoulder when he'd called to say goodbye on his retirement. That in the film *To Each His Own*, with Joshua holding her hand, she had disgraced herself by sobbing her heart out when Olivia de Haviland had been forced to say goodbye to her baby son, leaving him in another woman's arms.

'Of course I'll miss you, David.' She pushed him gently away. 'I wish you could have seen the children, but they're having a lovely time with Auntie Edna and Uncle Arnold. It is really best they're out of the way just now.'

She was being brisk; she was being motherly. Although she knew by now that she wouldn't care if she never saw the Bulcocks again, she wished they would emerge from the kitchen, unlovely as they were, unscrupulous as she was finding them out to be. She wished little Miss Grimshaw would come twittering from the lounge carrying her knitting and her back cushion. She wished the family of three boisterous boys would come in from the beach, bursting through the front door, bringing half the sands with them on their shoes.

David's face was working with emotion. 'I can't go without telling you how fond of you I am.'

Like an answer to a prayer, the couple from number five came round the bend in the stairs, a ferocious-looking couple with identical smoker's coughs, wearing identical manure-coloured jumpers.

'Nice to know it's not going to rain,' they said, wrenching the door open and puffing furiously on their cigarettes. Leaving a trail of smoke behind them.

David tried to close the door again, but Daisy was

too quick for him. '*Please* don't say anything you might regret, David.' She stood aside to let him pass. 'You've been through a lot. And *I've* been through a lot.' She smiled up at him, raising her voice for the benefit of Mrs Mac from Balmoral next door, out there sweeping the flags, with both ears wagging fit to drop off.

'I'll look forward to hearing how you're going on,' she said.

David looked from the big fat face of the woman leaning on her sweeping brush to Daisy, flushed and distressed, her eyes pleading with him not to say words he would regret. He couldn't bear it. He was shaking inside. He wanted to weep, and knew he dare not. He stepped backwards and almost lost his footing. Oh, God! Trust him to make a mess of things.

'I wouldn't upset you, not for the world.' He willed Daisy to look into his eyes, and to stop smiling at nothing for the benefit of her neighbour, who was listening unashamedly, inclining her head to catch every word.

'I know that, David.'

He knew that the false laugh was for the benefit of Balmoral next door. He accepted that for Daisy respectability was all. He had already accepted the gap between the contours of their thinking, their very reasoning.

He muttered something about writing as soon as possible, turned and walked away, in control of himself enough to wish Balmoral good-day.

Mrs Mac wasted no time in joining Daisy. 'Is young Doctor Armitage going away, then? I couldn't help overhearing what he was saying about letters.'

'Yes. He's going away.'

'Far?'

From long experience Daisy knew that to state the

164

facts, which would become known anyway, was the only way to satisfy Mrs Mac's insistent curiosity.

'To America. To work in a Washington hospital on research. Into nutrition.' She smiled into the large fat face. 'You must excuse me, Mrs Mac. I've a lot to do.'

'He looked upset.'

'Yes. He was a very good friend of Joshua's. He misses him very much.'

'And what he went through with them Japs won't have helped.' Mrs Mac folded her arms underneath the flowered pinafore. 'Some of the prisoners of them Japs have no stomach linings left. I read all about it in the paper. If the stomach has nothing in it to digest, it starts to digest itself. If you follow my meaning.' She lowered her voice a fraction. 'He could end up having to be fed through a tube in his side.'

Daisy closed the door and left her standing there. But instead of going straight back into the kitchen, where Percy Bulcock was making her feel superfluous anyway, she went upstairs, along the landing and up the shorter flight to her room at the top of the house.

David was imagining he was falling in love with her. Unbelievable as it sounded, it was true. He was transferring his deep affection for Joshua to her. He badly needed someone to love and she just happened to be there.

Daisy sat down in Joshua's chair. Once she had considered getting rid of it, but she could sit there now without dwelling on the fact that Joshua had leaned his head back against its upholstery and died. She stroked the padded arms.

So he wasn't going to end up with Nora Jolly after all. A good thing in Daisy's opinion, because that one could best Joan Crawford any old day at acting dramatic. David hadn't said much, but Daisy could read behind the lines. Nora was the type who could swallow a man like poor mixed-up David before breakfast. Daisy could just see her swooping up and down in a trailing housecoat, looking anguished and glamorous at one and the same time. David was well rid of her. She looked like the type who would hurl herself off the top of the Tower. Just to get her own back.

Oh, yes. David would be well away from Nora when he began his work all those miles away in an American hospital. Daisy knew exactly what they looked like from the films. All wide shining corridors, with doors leading off them into private rooms for patients. With doctors being matey with the nurses in the lifts, and the nurses plumping up the patients' pillows so positively that even the worst cases died cheerfully.

American nurses wore white coat-dresses, nipped in at the waist, darted at the front to show off their busts. They wore white caps for their hair to curl round, and white stockings and shoes, and they had time to thread baby-ribbon through their patients' hair and tell them they looked 'real cute, honey' before they were round properly from the anaesthetic. In the theatre they fluttered their eyelashes at handsome surgeons, in between wiping perspiration from his brow.

When they saw David with his English gentleman looks and his Leslie Howard tip-tilted eyes, he'd be snapped up faster than a bargain at the sales.

Daisy was beginning to forget the embarrassment of less than ten minutes ago. David was a sad mixed-up man, still suffering the after-effects of his terrible time in the jungle. A change of environment would be the best thing that could happen to him.

She was glad she hadn't confided in David about the problems she was having with the sale of the house. He could go away believing that everything was going ahead without a hitch. He had tried to tell her how foolish she was in allowing the Bulcocks to move in before every single i was dotted and every document signed.

'Winnie can't come back to help me out,' she'd explained. 'Not with Leonard's mother taking a turn for the worse on the very day they came back from their honeymoon. And the Bulcocks are learning the ropes,' she'd added miserably. 'I think Percy's finding that catering for twenty to thirty people takes a bit more finesse than canteen cooking for up to two hundred.'

David had looked at her and said nothing.

Winnie was sure there was something going on between them, but for once she wasn't going to say anything. She had troubles of her own, what with Leonard's mother staring down at everything on her plate with a face as long as Wigan Pier.

'I would never have put Daisy down as a Jezebel,' she remarked to Leonard, who said it was the ones you least suspected who were always the worst.

Daisy settled comfortably in Joshua's chair. To indulge in a good half an hour's worry . . .

According to the surveyor's report it was a wonder the house hadn't fallen down years ago. What with dry rot crumbling the staircase away and deathwatch beetles multiplying merrily in the roof. Not to mention damp patches on the walls, and brickwork almost bald for want of pointing. The cost of all this would leave her with far less money than she had planned. She was in the mood for a good cry, but a fat lot of good that would do. It was just that with David going away and Joshua dying there was nobody she could turn to.

Wasn't that what Joshua had once said? That when it came to the crunch we were all on our own, paddling our own little canoes.

A sudden knock brought her swiftly to her feet. In spite of her bulk Ruby Bulcock crept round the house on fairy feet.

167

Daisy opened the door to see her standing squarely on the landing, puffing with importance. Looking very manly.

'You're wanted downstairs,' she said in her gruff voice. 'That chap we told you about has just finished giving the electrics the once-over.' At the foot of the first flight of stairs she turned to Daisy in triumph. 'I don't like being the bearer of bad news, but he says that unless the whole house is rewired next week, we're all likely to go up in flames.'

Down in the hall, by the little table bearing the telephone and the Visitors' Book, Daisy squared up to a pock-nosed little man. His sharp features were set in mean and furtive lines, and she had the bleak thought that she had seen him before. And not long ago either. There was something very familiar about the narrow rat face and the greased-back thinning hair.

'On what authority do you say the whole house needs rewiring?' She felt suddenly threatened, as if the walls were closing in on her.

'On me own authority, missus.' The shifty eyes mocked her. 'I know a fire hazard when I see one.'

He spoke out of the side of his mouth, like a gangster in a second-feature film, and in that instant Daisy remembered she had seen his double playing the part of a conniving trickster in a one-horse town in the mid-western dustbowl of America during the Depression. In the film the rotten no-good horse-thief swindled a help-less widder woman out of the only thing she held dear – a music box that played a jingled version of 'What are the Wild Waves Saying?' He did this, of course, after wheedling his evil way into her affections, and creeping stealthily into her unsuspecting heart.

Daisy stared straight into the shifty eyes, feeling calmness and reasonableness floating away from her. In that same moment Percy Bulcock materialized from the kitchen, fresh, she guessed, from peeling a sack of potatoes. To go with the small package of pig's liver she had seen bleeding profusely onto her scrubbed kitchen table.

'I can see it's a bit of a blow about the wiring,' he said. 'And of course you do realize that under the circumstances there will have to be some revision of the . . .'

'Stop it!'

Anger rose in Daisy, hot as a scald. She had read about nostrils flaring with anger, but had never experienced it herself. At that moment she was sure that her own nostrils were in such a state of dilation that puffs of smoke coming from them wouldn't have surprised her. All the frustration of the past weeks, her genuine sadness in saying goodbye to David – for ever, she was sure – her pent-up grief for Joshua, culminated in a great rush of overwhelming emotion. She could take no more.

They seemed to be advancing on her, the three of them. Big-boned Ruby, loose-haired Percy, and the conniving trickster. They were trapping her, taking advantage of her widowhood and her trusting nature.

'You think you can do me out of every penny I possess, because I am a woman alone!' she cried. 'If my husband was alive you wouldn't get away with it. My husband would have had you weighed up right from the beginning.' She swung round on a visibly astonished Ruby. 'You waited until my friend the doctor left the house, knowing he was going three thousand miles away. Across the sea.' Her voice throbbed with the injustice of it all. 'You knew he would never have stood for you trying yet another trick on me.'

She ran wildly up the stairs, turning to look down on them from the bend leading to the first landing. Breathless and choked with emotion, she shouted down at them.

'This house had been rewired just before I bought it! I have that on the highest authority, so it can't need rewiring now.' She was so overcome she could feel her heart beating in a coupled rhythm. She gulped on the tears thickening in her throat. 'The contract was drawn up fair and square. My doctor friend checked it over for me. I've complied with every flamin' item on the surveyor's report, and more besides, and I'm telling you now, not one more brass farthing will you get out of me!'

On the landing she leaned dangerously far out over the banisters, shouting down into the upturned faces. In her total despair it was as though the pock-nosed little man actually became as one with the actor she so clearly remembered from the gangster film.

'You're not wheedling your way into *my* feelings,' she told his astonished weasly face. 'Not a chance!'

'She's going a bit funny.' Ruby led the way back into the kitchen with manly strides. 'Going on about her doctor friend. She's upset because he's skedaddled.' She struck a match on the sole of her shoe and lit a cigarette. 'Her *husband's* friend indeed. Who does she think *I* am? Betty Grable?'

Percy coughed on a laugh.

'She's not *that* short-sighted, pet.'

Daisy closed the door of her room and threw herself on her bed. She cried like a child, stuffing a corner of her pillowcase into her mouth to muffle her sobs. Her eyes ran, her nose ran, she shuddered and gasped for five long minutes, then when it was over she got up and splashed cold water on her face and ran a comb through her tousled hair.

Numbed into a state of utter calm, she sat in Joshua's chair and whispered a quiet goodbye to him. She could

170

feel herself being dramatic; she could almost hear him laughing gently at her, but there was a great comfort in what she was doing. In that moment, all alone at the top of the house, she accepted properly for the first time that she would never see him again. And she accepted that soon she would be moving on without him.

Her reflection in the mirror of her dressing table brought her to her senses. Crying never got anyone anywhere. Her mother had taught her that long ago. And it certainly did nothing for her looks. Carefully she dabbed powder on to her puffed and red mottled face.

And went downstairs into the familiar kitchen. In which she was now a stranger.

PART TWO

Chapter One

The sky was as grey and dingy as a horse blanket the day Daisy left Shangri-La to live in a country cottage.

Percy Bulcock was in the kitchen stirring away at a watery stew.

'Little cubes of carrot, leeks and 'taters too,
Simmered with some Bovril,
Make a beefy stew.'

'I don't think,' Winnie said. 'We never had anything as awful as that muck even when there was a war on.'

She had arrived at the last moment to say a surly goodbye, looking pale and distressed in a turquoise woollen maternity dress with an accommodating box-pleat at the front. She had refused to believe that Daisy would stick to her plans and go. Leonard had said the bereaved should never make any decisions for at least two years after their loved ones had passed on.

She kissed Sally goodbye and shook Oliver's hand. She gave in and clung to Daisy, then rushed from the house showing two inches of Celanese underskirt below the thick woollen dress.

Daisy had held back her own tears all morning, though there'd been a tricky moment when the regulars presented her with a leather-bound address book, the first page signed by each one of them with love and affection.

Little Miss Grimshaw had signed it of course, but she had gone completely over to the enemy. She admitted that the Bulcocks were not her style at all, but it was imperative she kept on the right side of them. They had hinted that they were sure she wouldn't mind moving to a smaller room on the top landing, but the important thing was they hadn't suggested putting up her weekly payments as yet. If they charged her more she would have to leave. And where would she go? Miss Grimshaw lay awake at nights with the worry of it. Shangri-La was her home.

It was all very well Daisy saying she had made the Bulcocks promise to keep her on, but out of sight out of mind. No, the only way she could hope to survive the new regime was to force herself to be extra nice and friendly at all times. Even though her dear mother would have paled at the sight of Percy Bulcock, who had already made the dining room seem more like a canteen with his habit of serving the food up on the plates. Right down to the last slosh of gravy.

She sighed. Daisy had always had a gravy-boat on each table, and served the vegetables in tureens. Even during the war she had kept her standards up as much as possible.

'I'll keep in touch with you, Miss Grimshaw.'

Daisy couldn't have felt more guilty if she'd been the captain leaving a sinking ship. She was deserting Winnie. She was deserting poor old Miss Grimshaw. She was trying as usual to be all things to all men. And she knew it wasn't possible.

'As soon as we're settled in you must come and stay with us,' she said, wondering what she'd done now when Miss Grimshaw's mouth set in a grim line.

Daisy was genuine all right, but Miss Grimshaw would never dare to leave her room untenanted. People were taking up holidays in earnest now that the war was over, determined to have the good times they'd missed, and who could blame them? But the very thought of coming back to find her room, her *home*, occupied by strangers, filled her mind with horror, her sleepless nights with dread.

Far better to accept that she would never see Daisy again.

'I'll keep in touch with you, Mrs Mac,' Daisy assured Balmoral next door. 'I promise.'

She lifted Sally up into the front of the van parked at the kerb and told Oliver to climb in. When she looked round Mrs Mac was wiping streaming eyes on the corner of her flowered pinafore.

'Drive away *now*,' Daisy told the man at the wheel, 'before I'm completely undone.'

She was almost undone again when, on arriving at the cottage, she walked through into the back living room and saw a fire burning in the grate, flowers arranged in a blue vase, and the furniture Mrs Rothwell had left behind gleaming with wax polish.

David ... Daisy picked up the envelope propped against the vase, opened it and recognized his illegible scrawl at once. 'Sorry I can't be with you today. Be happy. My love to the three of you.'

She touched the pink and purple star petals of the Michaelmas daisies, then looked through the window across the long garden, bright and glistening now the rain had stopped. A floating drift of thistle heads spilled into the wind.

'Yes, of course you can play in the garden,' she told the children, 'but keep your wellingtons on.'

'I've got a fairy godmother,' she told the van driver as he staggered in under the weight of Joshua's glass-fronted bookcase.

'You're right there, missus. She's coming up the path. I nearly knocked her for six with this lot. Where d'you want me to put it?'

Daisy pointed to a niche in the far wall and turned

177

to see her next-door neighbour watching from the doorway.

Bertha Tomlinson was like a dog with two tails. She hadn't been able to believe her luck when the letter with the card and the postal order had arrived from old Doctor Armitage, sent on from his son in America, with full instructions to make a proper welcome for Mrs Penny and her two children. Now she had a legitimate excuse to ask Mrs Rothwell for a key. Now she could have a good root round the place while she got it ready for poor little Ma Penny and her fatherless children. Now she could gloat over finding newspaper drawer-linings going back to the Abdication. And she could tell her friend Mrs Smith at the post office about the black fungus growing up some of the walls, and the smell of God alone knew what in the front bedroom.

Daisy looked at her fairy godmother. Bertha Tomlinson's iron-grey hair was contained in a wide-meshed net. Her eyes had a baldness about them which puzzled Daisy, until she saw that not a single eyelash grew from lids as smooth as ball bearings.

'We've met before, love. You'd come to view the cottage. You remember? I was sweeping me front.' She nodded at a cardboard carton overflowing with books. 'I see you're a reader, then?'

'My husband was.'

'God rest his soul.' The bald eyes swivelled round. 'What took him off?'

The vicar's wife called with an unrisen cake in a tin, but the *thought* was there. She hoped to see Daisy in church and also at the Bright Hour in the church hall on alternate Thursday afternoons. And if there was anything she could do to help?

'You please yourself about that Bright Hour, love.' Bertha was insisting on helping Daisy to make up the beds. 'That woman's the wrath of God come down in human form. Always praying about something. Though much good that did her in the war when their only son got killed at Dunkirk.'

'Oh, how awful . . .' Daisy wished she could think of some way of getting rid of her neighbour. She had already learned that a girl two doors up had borne a GI twin sons, and that he'd been shot down over Germany before he could do the decent thing and marry her; that Mrs Tomlinson did the washing and the ironing for Bill Tattersall at the garage, who changed his vest and underpants regular as clockwork and never wore the same shirt two days running.

'Me and my friend, Mrs Smith at the post office, call him the mystery man,' Bertha went on. 'He bought that place from old Mr Bolton with his gratuity. He lives by himself round the back.' She examined a flannelette sheet closely. 'He goes off into Blackburn most weekends. Dressed up to the nines. I reckon he's got a woman there, though why he can't fetch her back here and let us have a look at her, I don't know.'

She seemed to have found what she was looking for.

'I *thought* that was a laundry mark. Still, I suppose you had no choice but to send your washing out, with having so many beds to change. You'll soon get them a proper white again when you hang them out in the garden. I put mine out in all weathers, and fetch them in stiff as planks in the winter. You'll have a pink fit when you see the washing the other side of you. I reckon her husband's lucky if he gets a clean vest more than once a month.'

'*Why* don't you think it would be a good idea for me to go to the Bright Hour?' Daisy asked in sudden desperation.

'Because they're a lot of gossips,' Bertha explained.

The children were out in the garden, running around with arms outstretched. Daisy kept her eye on them, wincing only slightly when she saw Oliver shinning up the lower branches of a tree which she vaguely thought might be an oak. Sally was squatting on her haunches, prodding something with a stick.

'It's next door's pig,' Mrs Tomlinson told her. 'The right sort of animal for that lot to keep, pig ignorant as they are.'

She was more than a bit disappointed in young Mrs Penny, if the truth were told. She'd not got anything out of her except that her mother had once kept a potato-pie shop in Blackburn, and that she went to church when she had the time. So she decided to walk down to the post office to see her friend, Mrs Smith.

'That Mrs Penny works that fast it's a wonder sparks don't fly off her. She can do three jobs at once while most folk would be stood standing still looking at them. But I'm sure I was right when I said there's something going on between her and young Doctor Armitage. Terrible when you think her husband's hardly had time to stiffen.'

'He *could* be just a friend, Bertha.'

'And I could be flamin' Greta Garbo.'

'Well, why would he go away to America?'

'To make it look better. To set her up in a love-nest, away from prying eyes.'

'That's a big laugh for a start off,' said Mrs Smith, who could be as out with it as the next when she'd a mind. Proper sarcastic some would have said.

Daisy rushed from one job to another. She gave the children their tea with the food she'd brought with her, and told them not to get too dirty as they wouldn't be having a bath that night. She looked at them and told herself that soil was *clean* dirt anyway, then she sent

180

them out to play again and got on with filling a deep cupboard by the side of the fireplace with odds and ends, and Joshua's pile of records.

All the time as she worked she was composing a letter to David, in her mind:

Dear David,
How can I begin to thank you for the warm and unexpected welcome you so thoughtfully planned for us?

She opened the back door to shake a mat and saw Oliver lying face downwards in a bed of straggled mint. Sally had found her doll and was showing it to the pig in the next garden. Daisy looked through the window ten minutes after that, and found the garden empty and deserted, a rope swinging from a tree, and Oliver's coat draped over a spreading bush.

She had no intention of panicking. In fact, they were probably hiding somewhere, so she ran out into the garden to reassure herself that the wooden fence was intact. It had been put there, Mrs Tomlinson told her, to stop the pig people's dog doing its business in Mrs Rothwell's garden. One glance showed her that the stakes were so close together there was no possible chance of Oliver squeezing himself through, and the bolt on the back gate leading to the ginnel was too high for him to reach.

Tramps and gypsies. Daisy's imagination ran riot. The flow of fields and hedges seemed to stretch out into infinity, up to a wood of tall dark trees. And over all, the black bulk of Pendle brooded, silent and menacing, shrouded in cloud.

She ran back inside, calling their names. 'Oliver? Sally?'

There was no reply when she hammered on Mrs

Tomlinson's door, not a sound from inside or even a twitch of the net curtains. She stood irresolute. The horse-trough across the road was just long enough and wide enough to conceal two little bodies, drowned dead in a foot of green and stagnant water.

She turned into a narrow lane leading to the river, a lane hedged in by beech trees with bushes beneath them heavy with blackberries and another dark red berry Daisy didn't recognise.

Poisonous? The children wouldn't know one berry from another. Toadstools? Daisy stepped on a clump growing lethally by the side of the path. Or were they mushrooms? She had no idea, and oh, dear God, neither would the children. They knew next to nothing about the countryside. They wouldn't be able to tell the difference between a cow and a bull, and Sally was wearing her red coat, with her hair tied up in bunches with two scarlet ribbons.

Daisy almost threw herself over a stile, and just stopped herself in time from stepping down into a herd of young bullocks.

For obvious reasons she could tell they weren't cows and she knew they weren't fully grown bulls, but they had short fiery horns and rolling eyes, and they were definitely pawing the ground and snorting through nostrils as wide as saucers.

She climbed down into the lane and ran for home, praying she would find the children there, playing a game of hide-and-seek.

Bill Tattersall was working on a Rover saloon parked outside his garage. He straightened up from under the bonnet and saw the children walking down the road hand in hand. He had seen the van arrive outside the Rothwells' cottage, and was not surprised; he had also seen Bertha Tomlinson make her flat-footed way up the path minutes later. Instinctively he knew these were the Penny children.

Now that the afternoon sun had gone in, the air was chill with a wind blowing from the fells. The boy looked cold in his short trousers and fawn jersey. The girl was dragging her feet and knuckling her eyes with a fist. Bill stepped out in front of them, crouching down so as not to startle them.

'Hallo, you two! I'm Bill, and that's my garage. You've come to live here, haven't you?'

The little girl lowered her eyes, but the boy pointed to the car on the forecourt.

'Is that yours?'

Bill grinned and shook his head. 'No, worse luck, I wish it was.'

'Whose is it, then?'

'That car belongs to a very rich man. It's been kept in his garage for a long time, and now I'm getting it ready for him to use again.'

'Your face is very dirty.'

'You ought to wash your face,' Sally added.

'I will later.' Bill stood up. 'Where's your mother?'

Oliver put on a hangdog look. 'She's very busy. We have to keep out of the way when she's busy, or else she gets cross.'

A lorry thundered past, exceeding the speed limit. Bill held out both hands. 'I think we'll go home, shall we?'

Daisy searched the cottage, upstairs and down, finding nothing but cobwebs, dust and the almond-sweet smell of mice. When she ran outside again, calling their names, looking like a wild woman with her jumper covered in dust, her face as black as a chimney sweep's, they were coming down the road holding the hands of the garage man who made so much washing for Mrs Tomlinson.

Bill didn't pull any punches, though he could see that from the look of her, young Mrs Penny had just had the scare of her life.

'I found them walking down the road. On the other side.' He followed Daisy into the cottage. As if he had the right, she thought. 'They told me where they were heading for.'

'And where was that?' Daisy got down on her knees to wipe Sally's tears away with the corner of her apron. 'It's not like them to run off.'

'They were going to find someone called Winnie. A Winnie who looks after them when you're too busy to bother with them.'

Daisy swung round in amazement. '*What* did you say?'

'That's what *they* said, love.'

'And I suppose they told you that when I have a chimney needing sweeping I hand them little brushes and shove them up?'

'No, but I expect they'd have got round to it in time.'

Oliver was refusing to meet his mother's eyes. Ever since Joshua's sudden death he had played a game of playing one person off against another. Winnie, Miss Grimshaw, David, and even Ruby Bulcock. Anyone in fact who would listen to a hard-luck story. She gave him a little push. 'Take Sally through into the back kitchen and pour two cups of milk from the bottle on the table. Then it's bed for both of you.'

Bill looked uncomfortable. 'Look here. I didn't take no notice of what the young nipper said. It's just that, well, the road outside may not be choked with traffic but we do get a fair amount, and sometimes it belts round the corner as if the driver thinks he's on the last lap of a race track. But I ought not to have repeated what your little lad said – not with you having all this lot on your plate.'

He stared round at the debris of Daisy's feverish unpacking. He was appalled at the condition of the walls, the end result of years and years of neglect. For once Bertha Tomlinson hadn't been exaggerating when she'd told him that the decorations were turn of the century.

'And I don't mean *this* century,' she'd said, witty for once.

'Thank you for bringing them back.' Daisy sat down suddenly as though her legs had given out on her. 'It's true, you know, what they said. The children have had to get used to amusing themselves. Living in a boarding house meant they had to be kept out of the way of the visitors, especially round mealtimes when me and the Winnie they mentioned were dashing about with hot food. But there was always someone to keep an eye on them. My husband for one, when he came home from work . . .'

As though a hearse had just gone by, Bill snatched his beret off and looked at her with troubled eyes.

'Has some of this stuff to go upstairs?' He jerked his head towards a roll of carpet standing upright in a corner. 'I'll have it up for you in a jiff if you tell me where it goes.'

'The trouble is I'm not sure.' Daisy had no idea how stricken she was looking. 'It was supposed to go in one of the bedrooms, but I may have to use it in here.' She stared down at the Rothwell carpet, so threadbare it showed the nicks of the flag floor through its faded worn pattern. She lifted her head. 'The sun was shining when we came that first time, and the second time as well.' She got up and forced a smile. 'Though to be fair, you should have seen the state of the boarding house when I bought it. You wouldn't have given tuppence for the

185

decorations, and the kitchen was like the Black Hole of Calcutta till we slapped some white paint on it.'

The air was so filled with a sense of doom, Bill felt he must say something cheerful.

'This is a little palace compared to the place I live in. It's so small I can cook my breakfast without getting out of bed *and* answer the telephone at the same time. When a friend comes to visit we have to breathe in and out together so as not to use up the air too quickly. By the way, if ever you want to use the phone . . .'

'Thank you. I'll know where to come.'

Bill knew when he was being dismissed, so he went, walking away down the road with a jaunty stride, whistling underneath his breath, giving no sign of the anger burning inside him.

Good God in heaven! Old Ma Rothwell's cottage needed *stoving* out, not decorating. No wonder the old bat hadn't let anyone through her door for years. He turned into the garage and to relieve his feelings shouted at his apprentice. What on earth had the *husband* been thinking about to make an offer for a rundown place like that? If he hadn't died he would surely have had second thoughts when he'd seen it again. And the doctor chap? The chinless wonder who'd taken the snooty woman for a walk that day while little Mrs Penny looked over the cottage on her own. Bill slammed the Rover's bonnet down with a crash. He'd be the David who had signed the card and arranged with Mrs T to do the necessary. Some pal he was turning out to be, telling that bonny lass to 'be happy', then not being there when he was needed.

Bill climbed into the driving seat of a dilapidated van and started the engine. He felt none of his usual elation when it started straight away, as sweet as a humming bird. He could swear that as he'd picked his way out through old Ma Rothwell's front room, past furniture that wouldn't have fetched a penny at a sale room, he could swear he'd seen bugs crawling up the filthy flower-patterned wallpaper. He could swear he'd seen it move.

The vicar's wife came again the next week, bearing a batch of scones risen to the thickness of a digestive biscuit, tasting of not much else but bicarbonate of soda.

'I know you're up to your eyes in it, Mrs Penny, but now the children are at school you can't work all day and every day. Please say you'll come to the Bright Hour on Thursday. We've got a speaker this time. She's going to show us how to make Christmas decorations out of next to nothing.'

'Christmas?' Daisy fanned her hot face with a flapping hand. 'I haven't got my mind on tomorrow yet, never mind Christmas. I'm trying to make the children's room fit for them to sleep in. There's moss growing in the corners.'

'You need to get out and meet people,' the vicar's wife said. 'And please call me Minnie. I know I'm thought of as a bit of a caution, but I can't stand formality. I think the GIs who came over during the war taught us a lot about the advantages of informality.'

Daisy hesitated. The cottage was slowly but surely defeating her. It needed more work doing to it than she'd ever bargained for. Like razing to the ground and building again from scratch. Green slime still crawled out of the bath taps when she turned them on, and opening windows wide even when it rained hadn't got rid of the smell of mildew and rotting dead cats.

'The plumber is coming on Thursday,' she said. 'So I'm sorry, I won't be able to come to the meeting. But thank you for asking me, and for the scones.' She hesitated. 'Minnie.'

'You mean Mr Osbaldeston?'

'Yes, that's right.'

'Then you can come along without the queasiest of qualms. If Mr Osbaldeston says Thursday, there's not the slightest point in you expecting him until at least the following Wednesday. He's so slow he'll turn up late for his own funeral. You'll never meet people if you don't make the effort.'

Considering she hadn't had a proper bath for over three weeks, or bothered to sleep in curlers, Daisy felt she looked the part of a member of the church's Bright Hour. Washing all over at the back kitchen sink, then drying off in front of the living-room fire, wasn't much of a punishment. The hard part was going up to bed to the mouldy damp of the upstairs rooms, pulling sheets as clammy and chilled as tripe over her. She kept telling herself that soon she'd be as tough and hardened as a mountain goat, but every day she found muscles she didn't know she had.

'Season of mists and flamin' fruitfulness,' she muttered, setting off down the road in her best coat and hat into a dampness as dense as a cloud.

'Going to a wedding?' Bill Tattersall's battledress top was beaded with a drizzle that came, not from the sky, but from the air itself. 'You off to brighten up the hour?'

Daisy stopped. Beneath the leather rim of the inevitable beret, Bill's dark eyes mocked and teased. 'I've been wondering all week what you would do. Take the advice of the vicar's good lady and go, or agree with Mrs T and decide you'd be better staying at home.'

Daisy had to laugh. Of all the smart Alecs she'd met in her time, this one took the biscuit. He obviously hadn't a care in the world, one of the take-each-day-as-it-comes brigade. Already Oliver thought he was wonderful because Bill had allowed him to sit in the driving seat of a car, turning the wheel and making revving noises.

'I must say I like your hat,' Bill was saying now. 'It tones in beautifully with the tip of your nose.'

'And a merry Christmas to *you* as well.' Daisy walked on, knowing he was standing there with a spanner in his hand, watching her, grinning all over his impudent face no doubt. She made a conscious effort not to wobble her bottom.

Further down the road she turned in at a path leading to the church hall, a small building with a corrugated iron roof, looking as if it would sink at any minute into the sea of nettles and the mini-orchard of stunted apple trees surrounding it.

Everyone turned round when she went in and to add to her embarrassment Minnie Rostron, standing behind a table at the front, rang a little brass bell for attention.

'Come along in, my dear. Stand up here with me where we can all see you.' She looked as pleased as if the sight of Daisy coming through the door had given her a new lease of life. 'Ladies! May I crave your attention for just one moment, please? Thank you. This is Mrs Penny, who has come to live amongst us with her two children.' She laid a hand on Daisy's arm. 'I know she's going to be a very useful member of our little circle, and I know we will each and every one of us extend to her the hand of friendship. So shall we welcome her in the usual way?'

For a single terrible moment Daisy wondered if she was expected to make a speech. So, smiling her thanks, she moved quickly to a vacant chair on the back row between an elderly woman who was already fast asleep and a girl with a peek-a-boo hairdo which cancelled out one side of her face completely.

'Let us pray,' said Minnie Rostron.

Praying anywhere else but in bed or in church always made Daisy feel acutely uncomfortable. She stared down at the floorboards ridged and pitted with the erosion of years, decorated by what looked like a discarded piece of chewing gum so ancient it was almost a fossil, made slippery by what she guessed was decades of Cubs and Brownies running wild.

'Oh, Lord,' intoned Minnie, in a properly solemn praying voice. 'Let Thy blessing shine down on us this day. Keep us from the sins of the soul and the temptations of the flesh.'

'She'd be lucky . . .' a voice whispered on Daisy's right. 'Aaaamen.' As they sat down, the same voice said: 'Shirley Hindle. Nice to meet you, Mrs Penny.'

Daisy smiled into the eye she could see. 'Daisy, if you don't mind. Nice to meet *you*, Shirley.'

'Shirl to my friends.'

'Shirl.' Daisy was beginning to wonder if the long fall of white-blonde hair hid an empty eye socket – some tragic legacy from the war years. The lashes on the visible eye were so stiff with spit mascara they looked in danger of snapping off, and on Shirley's engagement finger she wore a ring with a stone like a car headlamp plus a wedding ring as thick as a tap washer.

'And now,' said Minnie from the front, 'we have as our speaker this afternoon Mrs Little from the Clitheroe Guild. She is going to show us how to make our own Christmas presents from bits and bobs we might have discarded.' She held up an empty cocoa tin. 'So that when the festive season is upon us we will be able to give our friends little gifts that will delight and surprise them.'

'Bloody amaze them, she means,' Shirley said, without moving her mouth. 'Does she know that she's come out with the tea cosy on her head?'

Over a cup of tea and a tiny fairy cake so heavy its name was a joke, Daisy learned that Shirley was not, as she'd imagined, the barmaid from the local pub but a farmer's wife.

'I married my husband when he looked gorgeous in his flying officer's uniform,' she confided. 'Now he's wedded to "the soil". He starts his day at four o'clock, before dawn has even *thought* of cracking, and when he ends it at eight he's so tired it's like going to bed with me Auntie Nellie. In the winter when the frosts were on us I swear he never took his gumboots off for three weeks. What did your husband do? You're a widow, aren't you?'

'He was a teacher. He taught handicapped children.'

'And you're managing okay?'

'I'm managing okay.' Daisy passed her cup and saucer along the row to the lady whose turn it was to do the washing up that week. She hoped, no, more than that, she *prayed* that Shirley Hindle was going to turn out to be a friend. There was an honesty about her, a directness that Daisy identified with. But she couldn't help wondering, as the meeting ended and Shirley snuggled her way back into a short squirrel coat, whether she knew that her nipples showed clearly through the purple jumper clinging to her like a second skin.

'I'd ask you to come and have a cup of tea with me.' Daisy watched Shirley pick her way along the rutted unmade path outside the hall, in shoes consisting of a web of leather straps. 'But I'm sure you've got to get back to the farm.'

'What for?' Shirley's visible eye was twinkling. 'To milk fourteen cows before stirring the oxtail stew? Sure I'll come with you. I've been wanting to have a peep inside old Ma Rothwell's cottage for years.'

'Where is the farm?'

Shirley waved an arm in the direction of Pendle Hill.

191

'Don't worry, I'm not going home, not yet awhile anyway.' She lifted a strand of hair to peer into Daisy's face. 'I'm going out to tea and to the pictures. I've got a date. With a fella.'

Daisy's face was a study. 'Don't you mind me knowing?'

'I trust you.' Shirley thrust a hand through Daisy's arm. 'You have an honest open face.'

'That's what they used to say about Wallace Beery.'

Shirley laughed out loud. 'You're a funny girl, Daisy Penny.'

'Ha ha – or peculiar?'

Bill was in his office as they passed, but he watched them go by: Shirley in her short fur coat and tight skirt, and Daisy in her camel hair with the little red pillbox hat worn straight on her head. They seemed to be giggling. Thoughtfully Bill started to rifle through a pile of invoices. He glanced at his watch.

'Oliver and Sally have gone out to tea with Mrs Smith at the post office. She told me she had evacuees during the war and misses having children around.' Daisy opened the front door, giving it a hefty push because the damp had got at the wood. 'Come on through. The water heats from the fire in the back room, so that's where we live.'

As she was talking Daisy was setting aside the fire-guard to give the banked-up fire a poke, getting her best flower-sprigged cups from the cupboard in the alcove, rushing into the back kitchen to put the kettle on. Shirley took off her coat and had a good look round.

Daisy had put her own stamp on the room, she knew that instinctively. The brass fender and fireside tidy gleamed like molten gold. The carpet was faded in parts, two even rectangles, as if at one time it had been covered by beds. *Twin* beds. Shirley twisted round in her chair. The sideboard was backed by a huge mahogany-framed mirror, so old that blisters had formed in the glass, and the table in the middle of the room was covered by a maroon plush cloth with half the bobbles missing from round its edges.

'I bought a lot of stuff from Mrs Rothwell.' Daisy kept appearing at the door, then bobbing back like Mrs Noah in a weather vane. 'Now I've examined it properly I can see that a lot of it is dropping to bits, but it'll have to do for a while. My last home was a boarding house at Blackpool, so most of the fittings and furniture had to be sold with it.' She set the teapot down on its round brass stand in the hearth for the tea to brew the required four minutes. 'Mrs Rothwell's son Walter told me most of the things he let me have are genuine antiques. For instance, that table goes back to Oliver Cromwell.'

'Pity he ever parted with it,' said Shirley, lifting the plush cloth and having a look. 'Give me a decently polished bit of reproduction any old day.'

Daisy was finding the urge to unburden herself irresistible.

'I'm sure I wasn't thinking straight when all this was going on. The first time we came here the sun was shining and the view from that window had me bowled over. Joshua had been pensioned off through being so ill. He couldn't get over the garden. He was full of what he was going to do with it all the way back home. Seeing that garden made his last day on earth happy, and so for that reason alone I'm going to try to lick it into shape.' She poured milk into two cups. 'And as I can't tell a buttercup from a dandelion, it's going to be quite a job.' She passed a cup to Shirley. 'I wake in the night and wonder if I've made a dreadful mistake.'

'I know *I* made one when I married Farmer Giles.'

193

Shirley discarded her saucer to hold her cup with both hands. She kicked off her shoes and put her feet on the padded seat round the fender. To keep them out of the howling draught she could feel coming at her from underneath the ill-fitting door.

Before Shirley went off for what she called her assignation, she listened with fascinated interest to Daisy's plans for the shop she was determined to open as soon as possible.

'I've got to earn some money.' Daisy felt she'd burst if she didn't tell somebody. 'Have you any idea how long it takes solicitors to work out property deals, and what they call conveyancing? I'm beginning to suspect that Joshua did his sums wrong when he said there would be enough capital for us to live comfortably for the rest of our lives. He didn't know about the dry rot in the Blackpool house then, and he certainly had no idea how much this place was going to cost to make it halfway decent.' She pulled up a chair and joined Shirley on the fender. 'David said I was mad for going ahead with things after Joshua died. I think he had doubts about this place right from the beginning. He was the friend who first drove us out here.'

'The David who wished he could be with you?' Shirley looked up at the card on the mantelpiece. 'I read it when you were making the tea. A secret admirer?'

Daisy looked into the fire for a full minute. She compared her work-roughened hands with Shirley's perfectly manicured fingers with their red polish. She thought about the white-blonde hair, bleached so fair it glistened as if it were powdered with moondust. The fire was bringing out the scent of her new friend's body, sweetly cloying April Violets, she guessed, while *she*

194

smelt of a combination of carbolic mixed with Lysol, tinged with mothballs.

'A secret admirer?' she said at last. 'David?' She allowed a smile to play about her lips. 'Yes, I suppose you could say he was that. You see, I'm trusting you as much as you are trusting me.'

'My lips are sealed,' said Shirley, getting up to go.

That evening, after the children were in bed, Daisy took David's card down from the mantelpiece. She wished she hadn't said that about him being a secret admirer. It cheapened their friendship somehow. David was such a *dignified* kind of man. Very much like Joshua, now she stopped to think about it. It was right that he had gone away. Meant to be in fact. Because of what the war had done to him and because Joshua had died, David had been in danger of imagining himself just a little in love with her. He *needed* to be loved.

'Don't we all?' Daisy spoke the words aloud, pressed the card close to her breast then, startled at her action, threw it from her into the fire where the flames caught it and shrivelled it up.

The sun was up early the next morning. Daisy opened the back door and looked across the rolling fields to where the hills rose majestically into a cloudless sky. Already the warmth of the sun had chased away the last lingering fingers of mist, promising an Indian summer's day.

A perfect day for giving the cottage a thoroughly good airing, for baking a batch of bread, Daisy thought, feeling as housewifely as Mrs Beeton, realizing suddenly that she felt *happy*. Guiltily she amended this: well, at least not *unhappy*.

At breakfast-time the children looked and behaved like little angels, spooning up their Force without squabbling as to who had Sunny Jim facing them from the cereal packet. Was she imagining it, or were they beginning to look like country children already, with their rosy shining cheeks and bright eyes?

'Miss Birtwistle's going to take us for a nature walk today.' Oliver smirked at his sister. 'Just the First class, not the babies.'

'Stop banging on the table with your spoon,' Daisy said.

'It's not my spoon. It's Sally's spoon.'

'Well, stop doing it with Sally's spoon.'

'*My* spoon is on the floor.'

'Well, pick it up then.'

'And eat with it?'

'Of course.'

'Even though it's filthy?'

On the way to school Sally asked her mother when they would be going back home.

'But *this* is your home now.' Daisy looked down at the bright little face framed by a knitted pixie cap. 'You like it here, don't you?'

'Sometimes,' Sally conceded, perking up at the sight of a hedgehog slowly crossing the grass verge.

'Winnie said we wouldn't be here very long.' Oliver was steadfastly refusing to hold Daisy's hand. 'She said we wouldn't like living here.'

'Why doesn't Winnie come and see us?' There was a tremulous quiver in Sally's voice.

'Because she's going to have a baby, dope.' Oliver's lip curled. 'It's inside her stomach.'

'I *know* that,' Sally said, as they turned in at the school gate. 'For goodness' sake, I *know* that!'

'Winnie used to give us a toffee apiece to eat on the way to school.' Oliver ran to join the line-up by the door waiting for Miss Birtwistle to come out with the bell. 'And she used to give us another one to keep for playtime.'

'I wish Winnie lived with us now,' Sally said, breaking away from Daisy to run across the yard to greet a group of small girls playing hopscotch . . .

Winnie was no good at letter writing. One day she sat down and poured out her heart to Daisy but when she read it through it sounded so false she tore it up and flushed the pieces of paper away down the lavatory.

She read the letters coming from Daisy over and over again, carrying them around in her apron pocket for days.

'You were quite right in what you said about the country. It is even worse than you described it to me.'

But Winnie could see Daisy smiling as she wrote that, because the real truth was that nothing at all was terrible with Daisy there to make the best of it. Daisy might even have ended up being best buddies with old Mrs Smalley.

Winnie looked down at the bruise marks on her left arm where Leonard had nipped her with one hand while holding the other over her mouth to stop her yelling out. In case his mother heard them rowing.

Winnie pushed back the sleeve on her other arm where the previous bruises had faded to a smudged and dirty yellow. She went over to the bedroom window and stared down into the street.

Dear Daisy (she imagined herself writing), Leonard has taken to *nipping* me. He has little hard busy fingers and when he nips his eyes go little and hard as well. It hurts so much I want to scream but he holds a hand across my mouth so his mother won't hear what's going on. He nips me if I complain about it being impossible to do all the work in this house *and* sit with his mother as well. He nips me in bed because he gets more of a

197

kick out of nipping than doing the other thing. I wish
he would hit me because it would be more manly, but
he can't do that for fear of being overheard. (Winnie
swallowed a lump in her throat and imagined Daisy
getting a letter like that. She would know it was true
because it was far too ridiculous and far too terrible to
be another of Winnie's exaggerations.)

And if Daisy believed it she would be on the very
next bus to see for herself what was going on. She would
want to know what had happened to change the Winnie
she knew so much that she *allowed* herself to be bullied
and abused like this. The Winnie who used to be would
have given back far more than she got. But that Winnie
was dead . . .

'Coming,' she shouted in answer to the demanding
voice spiralling upstairs. 'I'll not be a minute.'

The sad thing was that she had really and truly
wanted to like Leonard's mother. She had felt sorry for
her at first, watching her struggle to do up buttons and
raise her arms to comb her white hair.

'I've tried to *love* you!' she had shouted one day. 'But
you won't bleedin' well let me!'

'I have tried to understand her,' Mrs Smalley had
told her son that evening, 'but it's impossible. She's one
on her own and always will be.'

Winnie knew she looked awful with her stick-thin
arms and legs and her enormous swelling stomach.
Apart from that one place, the flesh had dropped from
her, making her face look more pointed than ever, her
sharp nose sharper, and her wrists no thicker than a
poss stick. She knew that she walked badly too, leaning
backward and shuffling her feet as if to balance the
weight and stop herself from falling over.

Leonard's mother was sitting crouched forward, holding out her hands to the fire, as if there were a freezing

wind outside and not hot sunshine spilling down from a cloudless sky.

'That stew you gave me's repeating on me,' she grumbled, giving a little belch to prove it. 'There's a packet of Rennies in the sideboard drawer.'

'I don't feel very well, Mrs Smalley.'

Suddenly the overheated dark room with its heavy furniture and long velvet curtains seemed to be closing in on Winnie. She looked down at the plum swirls on the worn Wilton carpet, and saw them come up to hit her, smack in the face . . .

'She fainted,' Mrs Smalley told her son when he came in late after working a double shift. 'She's gone out to get some fresh air.'

'Did she say exactly where she was going?' Leonard was down on his knees building up the fire and sweeping the hearth with the brush from the brass tidy. 'I've had a notion lately that she might be having twins.' He sat back on his heels. 'They're only hearing one heart beating at the clinic, but twins can sometimes lie in the womb one *behind* the other.' He demonstrated with his tiny hands. 'Like this.'

'You should have been a doctor.' Mrs Smalley leaned forward for her son to adjust the cushion at her back. 'If your father had lived things would have been very different.'

Leonard went to the door to see if Winnie was coming up the street. She had no right to disappear like this without saying where she was going. He rubbed his hands together. She would have to be punished. A small frisson of excitement tightened his loins as he went in and closed the door.

Percy Bulcock opened the door of Shangri-La to see Winnie standing there looking as if she had half a barrel clamped to her belly. He couldn't place her at first, then light dawned.

'I've come to see Miss Grimshaw.' Winnie tried to peer round him down the familiar hall, but he put out an arm to block her way.

'Miss Grimshaw doesn't live here now.' Percy thumbed a dangling brace and pulled it back over his shoulder. 'She needed special care.'

'What special care?' Winnie's white face turned brick red. 'The only extra care Miss Grimshaw needed was her food mashed for her on account of her bad digestion. And the crusts cut off her bread. She wasn't *ill* or anything.'

'For her own sake we had her admitted to a home.' Percy stepped back a pace. 'The stairs got too much for her and she got on the guests' nerves always hogging the fire.' He began to close the door. 'We weren't her *relatives*. We weren't obliged to take responsibility for her. She would have died anyway, considering her age.'

'*Died*?' Winnie was suddenly inside the house and beside him there in the hall, poking her finger at him and shouting at the top of her voice.

'*Died*? Miss Grimshaw died? She was as fit as a fiddle when me and Daisy left.' Emotion closed Winnie's throat. 'You wanted her room, didn't you? You promised Daisy you would keep her here paying the same board and lodging and then you turned her out. This was her *home*!'

Percy held the door wide open, jerking his thumb in the direction of the street. 'If I were you I would restrain yourself. Unless you want that baby to be born any minute.'

Winnie glared at him. She hated him so much at that minute she was sure her very blood was actually boiling. There was a pain low down in her back and she was scared she might be going to faint again. She could never have told little Miss Grimshaw what marriage to Leonard had turned out like. Not with her being a

200

spinster and refined as well. But Miss Grimshaw would have *talked* to her; they would have remembered how it used to be when Winnie and Daisy were a team and this house was filled with the smells of cooking and Daisy came out of her kitchen to greet her guests with her hair nicely done and a nice clean blouse on.

Now the only smell was of wet cabbage, and Percy Bulcock was wearing a shirt that should have been in yesterday's wash. The house was quiet because the sun was shining outside. The guests would all be down on the sands making the best of it. There was sand on the stairs and the coat-stand had broken one if its antlers.

With as much dignity as her ungainly shape would allow her, Winnie walked down the steps to the pavement, turning at the bottom.

'When you are old, Mr Bulcock,' she said in a clear ringing voice, 'remember that once you were young. And now you are young, remember that one day you will be old. Shakespeare! And by the way, your hair is on back to front. Goodbye.'

The Winnie who used to be could have done much better than that, but it kept her going until she reached the street where Leonard and his mother lived. Then her shoulders drooped and the sight of her husband coming to meet her filled her heart with dread.

Walking back to the cottage, Daisy had the feeling she had aged ten years since getting out of bed that morning. Even the bright promise of the day seemed to be drifting away, with high ragged clouds covering the sun. When she saw the postman turning in at her gate she was sure it would be another unexpected bill to add to the growing pile on the kitchen dresser. Probably from the Bulcocks claiming prompt payment for more repairs they were prepared to swear on their respective oaths were Daisy's responsibility. Or from Mrs Rothwell's son

Walter apologizing for not remembering to tell her that the cottage was on the condemned list.

But the envelope lying behind the door was addressed in David's spidery writing, postmarked Washington DC. Daisy opened it without waiting to take off her hat and coat.

> My dear Daisy,
> You will be surprised to hear from me again so quickly, but today I drove out into Virginia, and I wish I had a poetical turn of phrase so that I could describe to you the breathtaking glory of what I saw.
>
> Miles and miles of colour. Miles and miles of trees in russet-gold, bronze, yellow, mixed in with the fading green of summer. The Americans call this time of the year the 'fall', and they seem to take all this beauty so much for granted, believing as they do that because it is America then it must be well nigh perfect.
>
> Everything is *more* here. More colourful, alive and more vast. They work so hard and are so proud of this beautiful city with its white buildings etched against a sky of vivid blue. They tell me that the winters can be bitterly cold, but at the moment it is blissfully warm. They call me The Englishman at the hospital, because they say I look exactly like what they imagine an Englishman should look.
>
> I think of you alone with the children in that cottage in the shadow of those bleak hills, and I wish I could whisk you across the sea to share all this with me.
>
> Write to me often.
>
> > Yours,
> > David

Daisy pushed the letter deep inside the placket pocket of her skirt. She felt it crackle now and again as she scrubbed out the accumulated dirt òf what she was sure must be years from the floor of the little shop. It sounded as if David was happy out there. She could just see him, striding about the hospital in a white coat flying open like doctors' coats always did on the pictures, his stethoscope pushed nonchalantly into the pocket. *The Englishman* . . . well, that was true enough. She hoped he hadn't told them, as he had once told her, that his mother was a Kelly from Dublin and his father's mother a MacTavish from Inverness.

Joshua would have been fascinated hearing about America. He would have got books from the library and looked up Washington DC. He would have written long letters to David telling him to make sure to see this museum and that art gallery, and be sure to tell him all about it when next he wrote.

Daisy carried a pail of filthy water out of the open front door and emptied it down an outside drain, her mind three thousand miles away.

'Good morning, gorgeous!'

Bill Tattersall waved at her from across the road, his face alive with impudent laughter. 'How did the bun fight go yesterday?'

Daisy could hardly bear to smile at him. He would know full well how the meeting went yesterday, for the simple reason that Shirley would have told him about it when he took her out to tea and to the pictures. He might be a mystery man to Mrs Tomlinson and her friend Mrs Smith, but to Daisy he was as transparent as a sheet of tracing paper. And oh, flippin' 'eck, he was coming across the road to speak to her.

'How's it going, gorgeous?'

Daisy knew she was looking anything but that with her hair tied up in a scarf and her stockings damp and wrinkled over her knees. How could she put on airs and graces when she was looking such a tuttle? To be coolly dismissive you had to be wearing lipstick, have your hair nicely waved and be wearing your best frock.

'Give that to me, love.' He took the bucket from her and without a by-your-leave carried it into the cottage. 'You're making a good job of this place. You thinking of opening it up as a shop again?'

It was no good. You couldn't be on your high horse with this twinkly-eyed outspoken man for long. Shirley had said he was a good bloke, and Daisy was prepared to think she could be right. She was also prepared to try to stop seeing him as Shirley's lover. What he did in his spare time was his own business, no concern of hers. Oliver certainly thought he was the cat's whiskers because Bill allowed him to help with odd jobs around the garage.

'You've polished that counter up a treat,' he was saying now. 'Did you know those shelves are out of flunter? If you've got a hammer I'll fix it for you.'

'Are you the sort of person who can't live with himself if something is a bit skewwhiff?' Daisy could hear herself being unfairly nasty.

Bill considered this. 'You could be right at that. If I'm eating a bag of chips and they're not all of equal length, I must admit it causes me real pain.'

Daisy gave up. 'You're a crack-pot. Did you know that?'

'So they tell me,' Bill said.

'Mrs Tomlinson thinks you're a bit of a mystery.' The urge to say that was somehow irresistible.

'So I believe,' said Bill, accepting the hammer and climbing on to a kitchen chair to line up the shelves. 'You strike me as being a bit of a two-headed woman yourself.' He wielded the hammer with dexterity. When he turned round there was a smile on his face like the smile a child draws on a picture of Mr Moon – with a watermelon curl at its edges. 'One of these days I'm going to find out for myself what makes you tick.'

'*Indeed?*' Daisy stretched out a hand for the hammer, hoping she looked as exasperated as she felt. 'My friend *Shirley* is meeting me after school with the children and taking us to see the farm.'

She narrowed her eyes, scrutinizing his face for a sign of guilt.

'Is that so?' Bill's bland expression would have made a Chinese mandarin look animated. 'You want to watch our Shirl doesn't lead you into bad ways.'

Chapter Two

The farmhouse was at the top of a lane bordered by stone walls so high it was impossible to see what lay behind them. Daisy could hear a dog barking, but it was like walking through a maze, with noises coming at you from you knew not where. Shirley had said she would come down and meet them, but she still hadn't appeared when they rounded a sharp corner and saw a long white house so covered with ivy Daisy decided it wouldn't have mattered if the walls themselves had crumbled away.

It was so isolated up there at the top of its own lane, it was no wonder Shirley had said that during the Big Freeze they were cut off from civilization for three months. 'I went berserk at my first sighting of a handsome man when we finally thawed out,' she'd said.

There was a round pond over to the left complete with ducks swimming round and round, whilst in the wide porch a fat cat slept on a wide stone ledge. It was so beautiful Daisy felt the prick of sentimental tears behind her eyelids. Surely Virginia, USA, couldn't be any lovelier than this?

She wished Shirley would appear. All the windows and the door were wide open. She could see down a long flagged passage with doors leading from it. She could hear voices, but they sounded as if they were coming from round the back of the house.

Sally and Oliver were on their knees by the pond holding out clumps of grass to the ducks. Daisy wished she'd brought a bag of crusts.

She felt foolish standing there not knowing what to do, so she knocked on the open door.

She guessed that the man coming from the back of the house was Tom Hindle before he introduced himself.

Mrs Tomlinson had called in that morning and briefed Daisy well. Tom wore a beard to hide bad scars which were a legacy of the time he'd been shot down during the war and landed smack in the middle of a glass roof. He didn't mix well, though he was matey with Bill from the garage. He gave fruit and vegetables to the church for the Harvest Festival though he didn't go himself, being 'antagonistic'. He had been a regular in the Air Force, going straight in from university, and he'd met Shirley when she was in the WAAF.

'She wasn't out of the same drawer as nim,' Bertha had added.

Daisy took to the big man straight away. She thought that with dark hair instead of his own pale ginger, he would have a distinct look of Gary Cooper. There was the same gangling way he had of walking.

'Shirley asked me to tell you she could be delayed.'

Two of his front teeth were obviously false. Another result of the terrible fall through the glass roof, Daisy decided. She wished Mrs T hadn't been so detailed in her description. It was like talking to a character met in a magazine serial. You knew a lot about them while they knew nothing at all about you.

When she called the children over he crouched down to talk to them. It was obvious he loved children. Mrs T had said she was sure the glass roof had severed his chances of ever having any of his own. Daisy winced.

'Would you like a drink of milk straight from one of my cows?' He was standing up and holding out his hands.

The cows, he explained, as they went into the shippon, were models of self-sufficiency. Their milk fed the chickens, whose droppings fertilized the fruit trees, which in their turn fed the bees, who pollinated *them* in turn.

He took a stool down from a nail, and mingling his beard with a cow's rough flank, began to milk it into a spotlessly clean pail.

Daisy closed her eyes in horror. She knew quite definitely that if she was offered some she would have to forget good manners and refuse. The very thought was churning her insides already. And yet why? It was just the same milk she drank cold from a bottle. It was the *association*, she decided.

But in the farm kitchen, not wanting to hurt the feelings of this ginger-haired giant of a man, she held a mug of the pure sweet-smelling milk to her mouth, closed her eyes and drank deeply of the warm frothy liquid.

'Well?' His bright blue eyes were teasing her.

'Quite nice,' she said. 'As long as you don't dwell on where it's *been*.'

'Come with me.' Tom ushered them out of the kitchen, down a flagged passage, through a small penned-in yard and into an outhouse.

'There!' He pointed to a corner, where in a large basket a brown and white dog nuzzled four brown and white puppies. 'They're only three days old.'

The children fell on their knees in an act of pure worship.

Oliver's brown eyes rolled heavenwards. 'Our dad said we could have a dog when we lived in the country.'

'A lickle, wickle puppy.' Sally was stroking a wriggling tiny body. 'This one keeps slipping off the nobble.'

'Our dad has died,' Oliver told Tom, in the touting-for-sympathy voice Daisy recognized.

All at once she remembered that last evening when, rosy from their baths, they had sat on Joshua's knees in their pyjamas listening to him telling them how it was all going to be.

Tom spoke softly to Daisy in a kind of verbal short-hand. 'These are too young, but I have a similar almost house-trained mongrel from another litter. If you think you could be bothered with all it entails . . .'

'Can we take it now?' Oliver didn't miss a trick. 'It can sleep on my bed.'

'On *my* bed.'

To avoid what Daisy knew could have developed into mortal combat, she spoke quickly. 'If we accept Mr Hindle's kind offer, *if* we do, the puppy will sleep downstairs.'

'Did you see the way my son looked at me, as if me agreeing to have the dog was the first kind deed he'd known me do?' Later, Daisy stood with Tom at the window, watching the children playing with the tan and white puppy on the grass, rolling over and over with it, as abandoned as the puppy itself. 'Since Joshua – my husband – died, that's the way it's been.'

'He's punishing you,' Tom said at once. 'The only way the little lad can show his grief is in anger. He has to blame someone for the dreadful thing he can't understand, and who else is there but you?'

'They used to spend hours and hours with their father. I ran a busy boarding house at Blackpool, so the time I could spend with them was limited.' Daisy sighed. 'He used to read to them, and bath them, when I was busy with the evening meal.' Her voice broke. 'Now I have all the time in the world to be with them and talk to them they don't seem to need me.'

'It will all solve itself, given time.'

Daisy felt ashamed of her outburst. Her emotions were so near the surface, she would have told her entire life story to the first person who looked willing to listen.

She glanced up into Tom Hindle's kind hairy face. What a lovely lovely man he was, and yet his wife was out somewhere busily deceiving him. In a wild flight of imagination Daisy saw Shirley making passionate love with Bill Tattersall, lying on a carpet of dead bracken, shuddering with pleasure as they assuaged their fevered longing for each other.

When Shirley walked into the room, smiling broadly, Daisy could hardly bring herself to look at her.

'The flamin' car broke down,' Shirley whispered, 'but he got it going eventually, thank God.'

Shirley was talking out of the side of her mouth, like a gangster. Daisy could see Tom watching her.

'Yes, we have had quite a nice back end,' Daisy said in a silly false voice. 'Considering the terrible winter,' she added, willing Shirley to straighten her mouth and behave.

They met up with Bill Tattersall as they walked back down the narrow lane. For decency's sake Daisy thought he would have given the farmhouse a wide berth, but no. There he was large as life, trudging along carrying an empty jug.

'Run out of milk,' he told them cheerfully, then caught sight of the puppy cradled in Daisy's arms. 'Tom told me he was looking for a good home for this little chap.' He looked down at Oliver. 'What are you going to call him?'

'Jasper.' Oliver was beside himself. He ran on ahead, waving a makeshift lead round his head like a lasso, overcome with the joy of the moment.

Bill tickled the puppy behind the soft flop of an ear. And was rewarded by a melting look of devotion from chocolate-drop eyes. He stepped round Daisy. 'I'll call in and see you when I've got the milk, to check your fencing is secure. He'll be off like a shot if he gets the chance. He looks like a bit of a villain to me.'

'Takes one to know one,' Daisy said, walking off.

He arrived at the cottage later that evening, carrying four lengths of wood and a tin box filled with nails. The children were in bed, worn out by the excitement of the day, and the puppy was fast asleep in a cardboard carton by the fire, covered with the blankets and frilled eiderdown from Sally's doll's cot.

'I'd like to get this done before it goes dark,' he said, 'while it's light enough to see the gaps in the fence. That was a loaded remark you made when I met you coming down from the farm. It referred indirectly to our Shirl, didn't it?'

'If you mean Tom's wife, then yes, it did.'

Bill laughed out loud. 'You've no idea how righteous indignation suits you. You don't let fly very often, do you, love? You should do it more often. It makes you look very desirable.'

Daisy blinked. He was impossible – he had the cheek of the devil. But she followed him down the garden just the same, standing right behind him whilst he knocked in the extra stakes with a few deft strokes of the hammer. So that the least she could do was to offer him a cup of tea when he'd finished.

He turned round from washing his hands at the stone slopstone. 'I'm a cocoa man, really. That is, if you've got some.' He walked through into the living room and stared down at the puppy. 'That little fella looks like I feel today. Completely jiggered. I was out on the top road at three o'clock this morning rescuing a couple who'd been to a late dance in Whalley. The bloke had walked miles to a phone box, leaving his wife having the screaming ab-dabs in the car because a sheep had

211

stared at her through the car window. She thought it was the devil himself come to get her.'

He sat down on what had once been old Mrs Rothwell's chair, unrecognizable now since Daisy had washed the covers. 'Can a man ask more than a glowing fire, a sleeping puppy, and a fantastic looking woman bringing him a hot mug of cocoa with the steam coming through the froth? How about coming out with me one night, Mrs Penny? We could go to the pictures – that is if you could find someone to look after the children. I know where there's a Gary Cooper film on.'

Daisy stared at him in disbelief, overwhelmed by the sheer audacity of the man. 'Tom Hindle is the spitting image of Gary Cooper – that is he *would* be if he didn't have a ginger beard.' Daisy felt she couldn't have been more pointed than that. 'And no thank you. I won't go to the pictures with you, if you don't mind.'

'But I *do* mind!' Bill surprised her by laying his mug of cocoa carefully down in the hearth and coming to sit beside her on what had been the Rothwells' sofa. 'Here, hand that over and listen to me.' Just as carefully he settled Daisy's mug of cocoa next to his own. 'I think it's time you and me got a few things straight. Right?'

Looking into his set face, Daisy realized it was the first time she'd seen him looking even remotely serious, almost angry.

'Right,' she whispered.

'Tom Hindle is a man in a million. He was flying on operations for almost two years. He got shot down once and escaped back to England all in one piece, but the second time his parachute landed him straight through a glass roof, and by the time he was found he'd lost an amount of blood that would have finished a lesser man off.' Bill stared into the fire for a minute. 'But his injuries go far deeper than what could be seen or treated. His *mind* was cut to ribbons, and what's left is a sheer

212

will to work till he drops. Without stopping. Without relaxing, *ever*. Can you think what that means to a girl like our Shirl? A girl who has to be made a fuss of, flattered, and, okay, *made love to* before she can begin to function?'

'So you are really doing her a kindness?'

'Oh, my God!' Bill balled his hand into a fist and banged his forehead. 'Where have you come from, Daisygirl? From another world than this, that's for sure. Did your mother never teach you about a colour that's neither black nor white, but a compromising shade of grey?' He stood up. 'I'll be on my way.' He picked up the box of nails. 'Forget what I said about the pictures. Just keep on sitting there thinking your noble thoughts and closing your eyes to reality. Good luck to you, love.'

'You're misjudging me!'

Daisy could hardly believe what was happening. She, who hated rows, was having words with this man she hardly knew. For two pins she would snatch his flamin' box of nails from him and empty the lot over his head. 'I'm not lacking in compassion,' she told him coldly. 'Or understanding. It's good luck to Shirley if what she's doing makes her happy. If what she's doing makes *both* of you happy.'

'I'm not the man she's going out with, for God's sake!'

Daisy saw that the eyes staring straight into hers had completely lost their twinkly expression. Now they were hard, weighing her up – and obviously finding her wanting. He was so close to her she could see the sunburst wrinkles round his eyes, and the way his unbuttoned shirt showed a strong tanned neck.

He was shaking his head at her. 'Tom Hindle's a good friend of mine, and whilst his wife might be a real bobby-dazzler, she's not my type.' He turned on his heel. 'No, *you're* my type, Daisygirl.'

213

To compose herself Daisy went through into the shop. There was so much to do and so little time in which to do it. The stupid scene with Bill Tattersall had upset her a bit. She'd never met anyone quite like him before. He was a man totally free of inhibitions. She stared down at a disintegrating floorboard, tucking and retucking a strand of hair behind an ear. A sure sign that her normal serenity had been rattled.

All right then, she had misjudged him. But that was no excuse for him to misjudge her! She'd never closed her eyes to reality. Never! Watching Joshua slowly dying over the years had been real enough. Deciding to follow Joshua's dream and bring the children out here to give them a better life – had *that* been a selfish thing to do? She could have done what she knew David wanted her to do after Joshua died. She could have stayed on in Shangri-La, doing the job she was best at instead of hopelessly trying to start all over again.

She dragged a rickety three-legged stool over to a wall cupboard. The shelves she'd painted were dry now, and it wouldn't take long to arrange glass tumblers on them. It might be getting a bit late in the season for sarsaparilla and dandelion and burdock, but what about Bovril on a cold day? She took three tumblers from the carton on the counter and climbed on to the stool.

And whilst she was busy justifying herself, had advising Winnie not to tell Leonard that it was doubtful he was the father of her child been the act of a *prude* who saw everything as either black or white? The less she saw of Bill Tattersall the better. He'd *disturbed* her. Not offended her, for goodness' sake, just set her pattern of thinking out of flunter.

As she reached downwards and backwards for more tumblers, the stool collapsed beneath her. For the fraction of a terrifying second she flayed about her, trying desperately to keep her balance, clutching at air. Only to fall heavily on to the hard floor.

There was no pain at first. In fact Daisy pulled herself up by the edge of the counter almost straight away. She had always been a child who got up the minute she fell down, a grown woman who had given birth to both her children with the minimum of fuss, but there was a jagged tear in her left knee with a piece of broken glass sticking out of it; there was blood running down her leg; it was the last flamin' straw!

Suddenly Daisy let rip: 'Oh, flamin' hell!' she shouted to the curtainless windows. 'I'm not flamin' noble! I don't set meself up as judge and jury to nobody! An' while I'm at it, I'm no flamin' martyr either!' She began to hobble through to the scullery. 'I'm trying to get this place to rights all on me own while it's dropping to bits all round me.' She glared at the defenceless sleeping puppy. 'An' if you make more hard work for me I'll tie a brick round your neck and throw you in the river!'

The glass sliver came out easily, but the blood flowed even more freely. Daisy hopped about, dripping gore everywhere. By the time she had washed the wound clean, covered it with a piece of white lint layered with Germolene, and tied strips of an old pillowcase round her knee as tightly as she could bear them, she was feeling sick and exhausted.

The puppy slept on. He looked acutely uncomfortable with his head lolling over the hard edge of the box so, ignoring the heavy throbbing of her leg, Daisy took a small cushion from the sofa and settled him on to it.

'I didn't mean it about tying a brick round your neck and throwing you in the river,' she told him, touching the soft mound of his head. From his shallow fluttering sleep he summoned up the energy to open one eye at her before sinking into sleep again. Forgiving her, she felt.

There was nothing for it but to rest up for a while till the throbbing stopped. Even though sitting still doing nothing always made her twitch. She folded her arms and stared into the fire.

So Bill Tattersall wasn't Shirley's secret lover. It was a bit disconcerting when all the clues had pointed in that direction. Perhaps he was having her on? Daisy thought not. His temper had been real enough. For a moment she had thought he was going to hit her.

Daisy closed her eyes. Before she met Joshua she'd known a man stamped with a similar dye to the garage man. Sam Barnet, a chauffeur from London, who had walked into her mother's pie shop in Blackburn and stolen her heart. All cheek and dimpled impudence, reminding her of Clark Gable. Daisy opened her eyes and saw that the blood had seeped through the makeshift bandage. She decided to ignore it.

If she didn't watch herself she was going to fall asleep – with a million and one things to do before she went up to bed.

Bill Tattersall didn't have dimples, nor did he look in the least like Clark Gable. As a matter of fact, for once in her life she'd met a man who didn't remind her of anyone.

Daisy crossed her hands on her chest. There were curtains to hem, a tartan kilt of Sally's to let down, a hole in the elbow of Oliver's green jersey to darn, letters to write. And the stain on her bandage was spreading. She hoped there was plenty more blood where that came from, but she didn't know what she was going to do about it if there wasn't.

Perhaps if she wrote a letter to David it would take her mind off her leg. She would tell him about the farm and the puppy and the warm frothy milk drunk straight

216

from the cow. David said her letters made him laugh, that sometimes he read bits out to his friends Kitty and Ben Coogan. He asked her to tell him everything; wrote that receiving her letters wiped out the miles between them. She was lucky to have a loving friend like David. He took what he saw as his responsibilities as Joshua's friend very seriously. But then, David was a gentleman, just as Joshua had been a gentleman. And Tom Hindle was a gentleman. Daisy's eyelids drooped. Three perfect gentlemen.

Forcing herself to stop wasting valuable time, she hopped over to the sideboard and took a pad of writing paper from a drawer. She would write to David, making everything that had happened to her that day sound so funny it would have him and the Washington Coogans in stitches.

Dear David,
At last I'm getting the measure of old Mrs Rothwell's gas stove. I baked a cake yesterday and shoved it in without feeling I should have lined the tin with an obituary notice . . .

Daisy lowered a hand and touched the puppy's head, feeling it pulsating gently beneath her fingers.

So if Bill Tattersall wasn't Shirley's secret lover, then who was?

It was no use, she couldn't keep her eyes open a minute longer . . .

The pad of writing paper slid from her grasp, her fingers loosed their hold on her pen. She joined the puppy in a dreaming, twitching doze.

She spent a restless night and found it hard to leave the warm hollow in her bed the next morning. Jasper had made a slight mistake on the carpet, but Oliver had let him out into the garden as soon as he came down, just as Tom had explained he must do.

Sally, when her mother wasn't looking, lowered her cereal bowl to the floor and watched in rapture as Jasper's nose disappeared into the warm sugary milk, his rear end quivering in ecstasy.

'He eats from his *own* bowl. Never from yours.' Daisy retrieved Sally's shoe from underneath the dresser. She stood up feeling she could easily faint. There hadn't been time to change the dressing on her knee, so she had pulled her stocking on over it and hoped for the best. When she looked at herself in the mirror her face was green-tinged. When she tried to run upstairs to find Oliver's tie she felt the bleeding beginning again.

The morning outside was dismal and raw, more like November than late September, with leaves floating down from trees twisted into nebulous shapes. They hadn't got far down the road before their coats were beaded with drizzle. Overnight the Indian summer had vanished. The hills were shrouded in mist, and the fog rising from the river chilled Daisy to the bone.

In the middle of the road a hedgehog lay spreadeagled in a mess of bloody spines. Daisy hurried the children past the corpse before the questions could begin. Each time she put her foot down her knee shot daggers of pain right up to her thigh.

Outside the garage Bill was giving his good-looking apprentice his instructions for the day. Keith would have finished his apprenticeship before Christmas, when Bill knew he would be off, as far away as he could get from the village. Vague problems with his feet had kept him out of the army, but Bill could see no sign of them bothering him overmuch. He arrived, late more often than not, on his bicycle; rode a motorbike when he could scrounge the petrol, and took repaired cars for far longer test drives than Bill sometimes thought was necessary.

'I'd be a racing driver if I had the money,' he'd told Bill many times.

There were occasions, like this morning, when Bill wondered if Keith listened to a word he was saying. There was often a strangely distant look in the grey eyes fringed with long girlish eyelashes. Keith was a looker all right, with his even features and perfect white teeth. Bill would have suspected him of being a jessie if he hadn't known different.

He was finding keeping his own mind on the subject in hand a bit difficult at the moment. Daisy had just passed by on the other side of the road, walking with a decided limp. She was pretending she hadn't seen him, holding her head high and talking non-stop to the children. Bill forced himself to concentrate on the serious matter of a car brought in that week with transmission trouble.

Why was Daisy limping? She'd been all right when he'd left the cottage. What job had she tackled last night in that musty old place? Why hadn't she realized that the cottage was rotting away and needed good money spending on it?

'We'll have to get the car over the pit,' he told Keith. 'My guess is the trouble's due to it being garaged all through the war.'

Tom Hindle's battered old Ford van was outside the cottage when Daisy arrived home.

'I'm on my way to the market,' he explained, 'so I thought I would just call in and see how the puppy was faring. I hope he didn't keep you up last night. Some of them whimper for a few nights just at first.'

As they went up the path together Daisy saw Mrs Tomlinson's net curtain twitch. She subdued a mischievous inclination to wave. Mrs T had appeared in her own garden the evening before when Bill was repairing the fence, cracking on she was picking up the day's windfall apples.

'You couldn't bring yourself to give me just the slightest loving peck on the cheek, could you?' Bill had asked as they'd gone back into the cottage together. 'That would set her up for a fortnight.'

'She thinks you're a bit of a mystery,' Daisy had confided tactlessly, 'because you go into Blackburn most weekends without telling her why.'

Was that what had sparked off his belligerent mood later on? He had certainly set his mouth hard for a moment.

'Bill from the garage came and made the fence secure last night,' she told Tom now. 'So Jasper can't get out, thank goodness,' she said, remembering the dead hedgehog in the road.

'Jasper?' Tom smiled. 'A good name for a puppy. I like it.'

How shy and reserved he was. He sat down only when he was told to, looking big and bulky in his hairy jacket worn over a rollneck jersey. He accepted a mug of tea and asked Daisy how on earth she had produced it so quickly. 'One minute you were offering me one, the next you were coming through the door with it. You must have had the kettle on the boil.'

Daisy limped over to a chair. 'Back in the boarding house the whole day revolved round cups of tea.'

'You must find it pretty lonely out here after having a house full of guests.'

'I would if I'd nothing to do.'

'Oh, yes, the shop you're going to open. Shirley told me all about it.' Tom moved back from the fire. 'Giving you a hand with it will be a marvellous thing for her.

I'm glad you asked her. She'll enjoy the company. She's not really cut out to be a farmer's wife.'

To hide her embarrassment Daisy took Tom's mug through into the kitchen. For the life of her she couldn't remember asking Shirley to help her with the shop. In fact, as far as she *could* remember, she'd only mentioned it in passing.

'Poor Shirley,' Tom said, when she went back. 'She married me when I was a dashing pilot. Silver wings stitched on my tunic, DFC and Bar kind of thing. That didn't prepare her for life on an isolated farm with no neighbour within waving distance. Shirley likes people round her all the time, not animals.'

'But she must have known you were a farmer before the war, and that you'd go back to it in the future.'

'But there wasn't going to *be* a future, was there? Not in those days.' Tom smiled his twisted smile. 'I was one of the death or glory boyos. Shirley was in the WAAFs. She managed, even in those days, to get kitted out with a uniform skirt that was tight in all the right places.' He smiled at the memory. 'We had a forty-eight hour honeymoon in the December of forty-two in a blacked-out Southport, and went to the pictures to see Jeanette MacDonald and Nelson Eddie in *Bittersweet*. On the way back we got off the train at Preston and saw *Gone with the Wind*. I used to think that Shirley was a lot like Vivien Leigh in those days, before she went blonde.'

'She *does* look a lot like Vivien Leigh. Even now.' Daisy was on firm ground at last. 'It's the delicacy of her features, and the way she has of pouting.'

'When she doesn't get her own way,' Tom smiled.

'I wouldn't know about that.' Daisy stood up and groaned. 'It's all right. It only hurts when I laugh. I fell off a chair and cut my knee on the glass from a broken tumbler. I reckon I'll live.'

Tom stood up, towering over her. His reserve was

difficult to cope with, his meticulous politeness even more so. Daisy knew she was good at putting people at their ease, but Tom's diffidence was getting through to her.

'I'd take good care of that knee,' he mumbled into his beard before he left. 'Cuts can turn nasty if they're neglected.'

She was just about to close the door behind Tom when Bill Tattersall came up the path, dangling a red leather lead from his hand.

'I found this at the bottom of a bag of tools,' he told her. 'It's none of your utility stuff either. I reckon it's been there for years.'

Not a word of apology for the way he'd spoken to her the night before, not even a sign that he was sorry for having so badly misjudged her.

'Why are you limping?' he asked abruptly. 'What damn fool trick did you get up to when I'd gone last night?' Without as much as a by-your-leave again he stepped inside. 'What's up with that bloody stocking?'

He walked straight through into the scullery, then rounded on her. 'Off with that stocking, lass. And you can stop looking at me like that. I spent two years in the desert during the war, seeing more bare legs than you've had hot dinners. Sit down on that chair and don't look so worried. I'm not going to chase you round the furniture at the flash of a kneecap.'

He hadn't even the grace to turn away as she fiddled with a suspender. He just knelt there, waiting, making Daisy feel awkward and silly at being so embarrassed.

'*I'll* do it,' she said, beginning to unwind the strips of pillowcase, but when she got down to the lint it was stuck fast to her knee with congealed blood. '*I* can do it' she said again, but when she lifted a corner of the dressing the pain shot straight up to her head.

'I'll bathe it off, love.' Bill poured water from the

222

kettle into a saucer and dipped the corner of a clean towel into it.

He wasn't prepared for what he saw when he got the dressing off at last. The cut extended to below the knee, and was more of an open gash, so through to the bone that he could see the tiny beads of fat beneath the skin. Daisy was biting her lips, looking away from a fresh flow of blood. She was green to the gills. Not uttering a sound.

'There's no medals for not crying, lass.' Swiftly he replaced the dressing and bound the leg up tightly. 'How you've managed to walk on that beats me.' He touched a puffy ankle. 'You've twisted this as well. What did you fall off? The mantelpiece?'

'I have never fainted in my life,' said Daisy.

And did.

'You must have *somebody* you can call on,' Bill said as he drove Daisy back from the cottage hospital. 'You heard what the doctor told you. That leg has to be kept up as much as possible till the stitches come out.'

'I can manage perfectly well.' Daisy's chin was up, he noticed. 'I've come through a lot worse than this. Fusspots bore me.'

'You've been brought up in a hard school, haven't you, lass?' Bill waved to an old man wearing a sacking cape mending a dry-stone wall. 'Did your mother never allow you to be ill?'

Daisy couldn't answer for a minute. She was too busy resurrecting her mother. Seeing her bent double with chest pains over the back of a chair, then going into the shop blue-lipped to carry on serving cakes and bread. Seeing her treating the doctor's advice with contempt, and refusing to talk about her health.

'I'll go out till the day I die!' she had said. And had done just that, swanning off to Blackpool and dying in

223

a deckchair on the sands, with the sun shining down into her dead eyes.

'My mother was a weaver when she left school,' she said at last. 'She thought mardy women deserved to be shot at dawn. I was told she was kneading dough a few hours before having me, and she almost died of the Spanish flu through not having the doctor sent for till her cough was taken for the death rattle.'

'*My* mother was a weaver, too, *and* her mother before her.' Bill's eyes were steady on the winding road. 'They were both riddled with rheumatism, and no wonder. The winters were the worst, when they had to stand all day on stone flags with hardly any heating in the sheds. The looms were made of iron so everything they touched was cold. My grandma had a five-mile walk to work and if she got wet she stayed wet all day.'

'*My* father said the light from the gas lamps was so poor that some of the men took their bicycle lamps to work in case they were asked to work on a warp with black on it.'

'The workers won't stand for that now. Not after going through a war.'

'So you're one of those who believe that the peace we've won will herald a new dawn once the country's back on its feet?'

'I'm not an idealist, if that's what you mean.' Daisy had the feeling he was getting at her again. 'If you'd seen me in a mile, long queue at the Food Office yesterday, you'd have seen me wondering just who had won the war. I've never had anything I haven't worked flamin' hard for, and I can't see that things are going to be much different – well, not for the next few years at anyroad.'

As he negotiated a hairpin bend in the road, Bill had to swerve to avoid a car badly parked by the side of a sloping grass verge. The near collision was avoided in a matter of seconds, but Daisy had time to recognize the couple in the back of the car entwined in each other's arms.

'In broad daylight!' Bill stepped on the accelerator as if to put as much distance between him and the parked car as quickly as possible. 'Doesn't the stupid flibbertigibbet know that Tom often comes this way back from market? Couldn't they at least have backed into a field, or driven on down the path through the wood? Apart from the fact that I'd promised a bloke in Clitheroe he could have that car back, going like a bird and clean as a whistle, by this afternoon.'

Daisy said nothing. Shock was keeping her quiet for the time being. *Uncritical* shock, of course. She was far more worldly wise than the man at her side believed her to be. But the couple had been kissing so *hungrily*. Shirley had looked completely abandoned with her long fall of blonde hair hanging down and her eyes tightly closed. They had been oblivious to the world, and yet in that second she had seen them as clearly as if she'd spent half an hour posing them for a photograph.

'So now you know,' Bill said.

'Now I know,' Daisy said back, in a tone she hoped conveyed not black disapproval but a sophisticated grey acceptance. 'It goes on all the time.'

Outside the cottage Daisy got out of the car and winced as she put the whole of her weight on her leg. 'I'm so grateful for your help. It never occurred to me that my leg needed stitching.'

'Or that a tetanus injection was called for.' Bill stared at the big iron key in her hand with open surprise. 'That monstrosity looks as if it's been around since Adam was a lad.'

'The Rothwells never got round to Yale.' Daisy turned the rusty key in the large old-fashioned keyhole with difficulty. 'I'll give it a drop of oil from my sewing machine can. That'll do the trick.'

'You mean right now?'

'Why not?'

Bill took her by the arms and whirled her round to face him. 'Right now you go inside and sit with that leg up. Okay?'

'That rusty lock will bother me till I see to it.'

Bill gave her a little push. 'Inside! Right? Resting that leg. Okay?'

Daisy thanked him for his kindness, went in and closed the door. Glancing at the clock on the mantelpiece and hopping from one side of the kitchen to the other, she began to gather the ingredients together to make a corned beef hash for the children's dinner.

Outside in the road Bill started the engine of his car and executed a perfect U-turn in the middle of the road.

'If she bursts those ruddy stitches I'll swing for her,' he muttered, driving the car into the forecourt of the garage, and finding old Eli sitting on his backside in the office reading the *Daily Mirror*.

'I've been sent,' Shirley said, appearing half an hour later to find Daisy oiling the lock on the front door. 'Bill said you couldn't put a foot to the ground.' She stared down at Daisy's bandaged leg. 'Do you know your ankle's swollen up like a balloon?'

'They've bandaged it too tight, that's all.' Daisy led the way through into the kitchen. Shirley looked marvellous, as radiant as a bride. Her glittery hair was brushed over one side of her face, but the eye Daisy could see had a wary look about it.

'What's that you're making? It smells good.'

When she came close it was like falling head-first into a bed of April violets. When she shrugged off her white fluffy coat and leaned over the pan, Daisy could see right down the front of her low-cut crêpe-de-Chine blouse.

'It's corned beef hash, because it's quick and easy. You just shove the lot into a pan. I've skinned some soft tomatoes in that dish over there.'

'Want them now?'

'Not till the children come in. You add the tomatoes at the last minute.' Daisy couldn't get over the see-through blouse, though she did think it needed a bustier person to fill it out. 'Mrs Tomlinson is picking them up from school. She saw Bill dropping me off at the gate.'

'I hope you told her you'd hurt your leg making such passionate love with him that you fell out of bed.' Shirley stared round her at the newly washed walls and the hanging pans that were clean enough to show their bottoms. Fresh gingham curtains hung from the window, and a fresh sheet of newspaper protected the scrubbed linoleum from the puppy's dish.

'Talk about Mary and Martha. Did you learn about them at Sunday School?' Shirley preened herself in the round mirror fastened to the wall. 'Mary knelt at Jesus' feet while Martha got on with the washing-up. I'm the helpless Mary, aren't I, while you're the hard-working practical Martha.'

'Oh, I don't know,' Daisy said, feeling a bit miffed.

'You're a *proper* homemaker. And I'm a *proper* slummock. I'm neither use nor ornament at the moment. Oh, for God's sake, sit down, Daisy and let me do the stirring.'

'I'd rather be a bit helpless and look like you do in that blouse,' Daisy said, envying Shirley's glamour.

After a minute Shirley left the pan and began walking up and down wringing her hands. On the third turn past the table she burst into noisy sobs.

'Keith's going to go away soon. He says there's

nothing here for him in the village. He says they might as well dig him in and cover him with topsoil.' She groped in the placket pocket of her skirt for a handkerchief. 'I won't be able to go on living without him. He's the only thing that makes this horrible life worth living for me. I never thought I could love anyone as much as I love Keith. And you needn't laugh!' she told Daisy, who felt more like crying. 'I know you know who I'm talking about, because Bill told me you'd seen us together. He was livid about us taking the car, but what else could we do? Where was there to go? We had to talk, and that ancient monument who works for Bill was sitting in the office slurping tea through his walrus moustache. And you needn't say a word!' she flung at Daisy, who hadn't even opened her mouth. 'I know Keith's nine years younger than me. But what's nine years? It's how you feel in here.' She thumped her chest. 'When I'm with him I feel about sixteen. I *am* sixteen!'

Daisy was at a loss. She could hear a faint sizzling sound coming from the pan Shirley had forgotten about, and she knew that the thick potato hash was beginning to stick to the bottom. The sedative she'd been given at the hospital was starting to wear off, and the pain was beginning to come out of the top of her head again. Shirley was standing by the slopstone with her hair hanging down, her visible eye swollen with weeping.

'I know you're thinking I'm a silly woman,' she cried.

'I'm thinking that if I don't get up and turn that gas off, the children's dinner will be burnt to a cinder.' Daisy struggled to her feet.

'You see!' Shirley moaned, folding her arms and swaying backwards and forwards. 'I told you I was useless. Men only want me for one thing.'

'You're upset because Bill saw you.' Daisy turned off the gas. 'What you should be upset about is that *Tom* might have seen you. He could easily have passed along that road on his way back from the market.'

Shirley wasn't listening. 'If Keith goes away I'll die.' She lowered her voice to a whisper. 'Have you ever been kissed on every single part of you? Till you wanted to faint with the joy of it?' She sat down at the table and closed her eyes. 'Was Joshua a passionate man?'

Daisy's face was a study.

'You don't need to answer me.' Shirley opened her eyes. 'You have a lovely face, but it lacks the look of a satisfied woman. Joshua was older than you, and a sick man. In his own way Joshua was a Tom.'

'I loved him very much, Shirley.'

'And I love Tom. Don't you see? But I can't turn myself into a farmer's boy for him! I won't drag myself out of bed at half-past four, summer and winter, to milk the flamin' cows. I won't tie a piece of sacking round my waist to go hedging and ditching like a Russian peasant. Nor will I bend double in the mud lifting a flamin' ton of carrots.' Anguish stared from her uncovered eye. 'What I'm really cut out to be is a French whore, lying on a chaise longue on a balcony overlooking the Mediterranean, with regular clients queueing up for my favours.'

'I must admit there's no comparison,' Daisy admitted. She sat down opposite Shirley. 'Tom told me you were going to come and help me in the shop when it's open.'

'That was before I knew Keith was going away.' Shirley stared tragically into space. 'I was going to use you as an alibi.'

Daisy reached across the table and took Shirley's hand. 'We could have fun, you know. I'm going to put two or three tables in and serve hot home-made soup, or Bovril, and maybe toasted barmcakes. There's a lot of traffic uses this road, and a lot more to come when things get going again. Then there's the weekend ramblers – they always use this route on their way to the fell road. There's nowhere else they can get a drink when the pubs are closed. I know, because I've checked.' She jiggled Shirley's hand up and down. 'And Mr Waring at the grocer's says he'll be glad if I start selling bread. The stuff he gets from the wholesaler's takes a lot of his shelf room.'

'It's not as if Keith has any money.' Shirley sighed deeply.

'Maybe you could wear some kind of uniform?'

'Like a French maid?'

'Well, not *unlike*.'

'Sometimes I think he's going just to get away from me.'

They stared at each other for a long moment.

'You don't look a bit well,' Shirley said at last. 'I'm a selfish so-and-so going on about my troubles when you're in so much pain.'

Daisy pulled herself up by the edge of the table. 'That's Mrs Tomlinson at the door with the children.'

'And that's me doing a skedaddle.' Shirley grabbed her coat. 'She hasn't found out about me and Keith yet, but give her time!'

'That flibbertigibbet is lying up with that young jessie at the garage,' Bertha told Daisy when the children had eaten and been sent on their way back to school. 'They don't seem to mind where they perform. For want of a better word.' She turned round from washing up the dinner pots. 'Fields, backs of cars, on the back row at the pictures. Mrs Smith's husband says he's seen them at it by the war memorial. They're worse than animals. At least with animals you know it's natural.'

Chapter Three

Winnie decided not to bother writing to tell Daisy about little Miss Grimshaw dying. In her strangely apathetic mood she couldn't see that it would make an 'aporth of difference. Off with the old, on with the new, that was Daisy now.

Besides, she was too tired to write a letter. Too tired to argue with Leonard when they went to bed, which meant he didn't have the same excuse for 'punishing' her. Winnie couldn't make him out ... On the one hand he was kind and gentle in the way he made sure she was taking her daily vitamin tablet and her bottled orange juice, and on the other he was sadistic and cruel, turning into a fiend when he tried to force her to respond to his lovemaking.

There was a hope inside Winnie's head which told her that after the baby was born everything would be different. Not between her and Leonard. There was no hope there, but in a way as yet unknown.

Maybe she would die giving birth. They would put the dead baby in the coffin with her, and Leonard and his mother would spend the rest of their lives in overwhelming remorse, remembering how they'd treated her.

Daisy would come to the funeral in her red hat, just to be awkward; Sally would wear a black bow in her hair, and Oliver a black arm band. They would have to be led weeping from the graveside, and Daisy would have to be restrained from hurling herself on to the coffin, a white rose clutched in her hand.

As time went on Winnie added other people to her fantasy. Her mother turned up at the funeral prostrate with grief. Doctor David sent a wreath from America twice as big as anyone else's, and the neighbours, heads bowed, lined the street.

'What if I die?' she asked Leonard, and he got out his Red Cross Manual and explained to her that having a baby was as easy as shelling a pea from a pod.

When Daisy's leg was almost healed Bill offered to drive her into Blackburn to visit the auntie and uncle she was always talking about.

'I've got to go anyway,' he told her, in what she thought was an over-nonchalant manner. 'On business.'

Daisy knew better than to ask him any questions. She was certain of one thing, though. If he *was* having a torrid affair it wasn't doing him much good. He wasn't bubbling over with excitement, whistling as he drove along; there was no gleam of anticipation in his eyes, as far as she could see. In fact, he was so quiet, so obviously downcast, she thought his face looked like he'd been mopping the floor with it.

It was a morning of grey skies with sudden bursts of slanting sunshine through breaks in the low clouds. On the outskirts of the town they drove past solidly built semi-detached houses, their grey pebbledash flanked by leaded-light windows. Every so often tributary avenues, crescents and closes meandered away into rolling fields, segmented by green hedges.

As they drove through the town's centre the sky seemed to close in on them, and now the houses, soot-blackened and identical, huddled together in rows, front doors opening directly on to the pavement.

'Nearly there,' Daisy said.

'Who's yon chap?'

Edna was doing her level best not to look chuffed to little mint balls at seeing her niece standing there when she opened her vestibule door. 'Are you fetching him in for me to have a proper look at?'

'He's coming back for me in about an hour.' Daisy followed Edna's straight back down the familiar lobby. 'He's the man who runs the garage not far from the cottage. He had to come to Blackburn today. On business.'

'What's he called?' Edna led the way into the back living room with the inevitable fire leaping in the grate. 'Take your coat off, love, or you won't feel the benefit when you go out. It can get parky at this time of the year.' She poked her head forward. 'Nay! What on earth have you done to your leg? Tripped over your shoelaces?' She bustled through into the kitchen without waiting for an answer. 'The kettle's on the boil and there's a nice piece of slab cake in the tin. I made it with proper eggs, none of your dried muck. I'll not be a minute.'

Daisy sat back in the rocking chair, setting it going with her foot. It was like coming home. It was the next best to coming home. Edna reminded her so much of her mother, especially now she was more or less the same age Martha had been when she died.

'Never a day passes but what I think about your mother,' Edna shouted from the back. 'Not many sisters can say they never had a cross word.'

'Except for the months and months you and she never spoke to each other,' Daisy muttered underneath her breath. 'Where's Uncle Arnold?'

'Where he always is. Up his flamin' allotment. I don't know why he doesn't take his bed up there. I won't see hide nor hair of him till his dinner's ready to go on the table.' Edna reappeared, carrying a tray. 'Then if it keeps fine he'll be back up there all afternoon. I don't think him and his cronies know the war's over. They're still digging away for flamin' victory, the silly beggars. She passed Daisy a cup of steaming tea. 'Still, it gets him from under my feet. Goodness knows he's been under them in a manner of speaking since he first trod on them at a Band of Hope dance.'

'How is he?'

'Fair to middlin'. He doesn't improve with keeping, but then who does? He misses our Betty, bless her, and our Edwin. It's not the same without yon little lad running in and out.'

'Does Betty like living down in London?'

'Well, *Cyril* does, so it's blow what our Betty thinks, isn't it? Cyril's dad's down there now, stopping with them. What did you say that chap who brought you was called?'

'Bill Tattersall.'

'Was his mother a Worswick? And did his grandfather have a second-hand clothes stall on the market?'

'I shouldn't think so. He comes from Liverpool. His parents were killed when their house was bombed.' Daisy sipped her tea, made the way her mother used to make it – so strong a fly could walk across it without sinking.

'Cyril's mother used to make tea like gnat's pee,' said Edna, reading her thoughts again. She chewed on nothing for a moment. There had been something familiar about the man at the wheel of the car drawn up outside the house. She'd seen him before – more than once. She narrowed her eyes in frenzied concentration. 'Has he got a little lad?'

'Not that I know of.'

'Is he married?'

'I don't think so.' Daisy shook her head. 'If he is he doesn't live with his wife. He doesn't talk about himself much.'

'Well, he's got a little lad.' Edna's button eyes glistened with triumph. 'He walks down the street with him. Mostly of a Sunday. I *know* because I sit by the window in the front parlour reading the paper. He goes by on the other side, and I've often wondered who he is. I've never seen a woman with them.'

'How do you *know* they're father and son?'

'How do I know they're father and son?' Edna snatched the knitted cosy off the teapot. 'Because they're the dead spitting image of each other, that's why. Same walk, same black heads, same way of sticking their hands in their pockets. They're father and son all right.'

'Ask him about it,' Edna said, when Bill sounded the car's horn outside. With a swift movement she whipped off her pinny. 'I'll come out and ask him myself. I'll just mention it casual like.'

'No!' Daisy was horrified. 'He doesn't want it known about the boy or he'd have talked about it.' She gave her aunt a swift peck on the cheek. 'Give my love to Uncle Arnold.'

A thin cat appeared from nowhere and streaked past their legs into the house. Edna spun round like a whirling dervish. 'That old moggy's jumping with fleas! I only need to open the door a crack for it to be in. It's your Uncle Arnold's fault for feeding it, soft 'aporth that he is.'

She was off down the lobby, heels plopping from her shabby slippers, screeching at the cat in her tinny voice.

Leaving Daisy to make a quick and thankful dash across the pavement. To dive into Bill's car before anything untoward could be said.

There was an agitation about him on the way back. He'd been quiet enough on the way there, but now he seemed to have forgotten Daisy was sitting beside him.

235

She could see a nerve twitching in his jawline, and although as usual he drove as smoothly as if the car were an extension of himself, he drove aggressively. Once, he set his face hard and tooted the horn at a young girl who dawdled across the road pushing a baby strapped in a go-chair.

'Silly young beggar,' he muttered, overtaking a bus at such speed the driver leaned out of his cab to shake a fist at him.

Daisy asked him in when he pulled up with a squeal of brakes outside the cottage. She had a shepherd's pie just ready to warm up in the oven, she told him, and one more wouldn't make any difference as she still hadn't got used to catering for only three. She wasn't surprised when he refused.

'I'm in no mood for company,' he told her.

'I gathered that,' she said wryly, and thanked him again for giving her the chance to visit her auntie.

'Any time,' he said, driving away the second the car door slammed.

There was a letter from David behind the door. Daisy picked it up and sat at the living-room table with it without waiting to take her coat off. She wanted to have a bit of a think about Bill Tattersall's strange behaviour. Obviously the young boy Edna had talked about was his son. It *had* to be his son. But why the mystery? Almost without volition Daisy slit open the envelope. Bill was marvellous with children, especially little boys. Oliver thought he was wonderful, and Daisy suspected the admiration was mutual: Bill allowed Oliver to 'help' him at the garage. He was very much like Joshua in knowing how to talk to children.

'Joshua,' Daisy whispered, blinking her eyes to hold back the tears. 'Oh, Joshua, why did you have to die?'

'Dear Daisy. Very dear Daisy.'

She got up and took her glasses case down from the mantelpiece. David's writing was shocking, more like a child's scribble. She put the horn-rimmed glasses on and began again:

'Dear Daisy. Very dear Daisy.'

She read on, dwelling on the last page, in total disbelief. Then she pushed the letter back in the envelope and went through into the kitchen to light the gas oven.

All that talk of David's about missing her, wishing she was there with him in America – she had dismissed it as the heartache of a lonely man who had suffered too much loneliness already. He had come and gone so quietly from the tall house in Blackpool when Joshua was alive. Always polite, often apologetic when there was nothing to apologize for. Joshua had said David was a lost soul; that it was more than likely that because of what had happened to him in the war he would *always* be a lost soul.

'He needs a woman,' Joshua had said once. 'If ever a man needed warmth and light and the feel of a woman's skin against his own, then that man is our Doctor David. A pity his wife wasn't waiting for him when he came back. It must have been a desolate homecoming.'

Daisy trembled. It was too soon. *Far* too soon for any man to say the things to her David had said in his letter. With shaking fingers she forked up the mashed potato on the top of the shepherd's pie and opened the oven door.

'Flippin' eck, you look hot,' Shirley said, coming in by the back door without knocking. 'I've just seen Oliver and Sally coming down the road with a bunch of kids from school. They're taking their time, but you were quite right to stop taking and fetching them. I went to school on my own when I was four.'

'So did I,' said Daisy, in a far-away voice.

Shirley saw the letter on the table and nodded knowingly. 'From the secret lover? That's why you look like you're running a fever.' She put a hand on her own heart. 'Can you feel desire throbbing in your veins? Are you just living for the moment he comes home and smothers you with burning kisses, not missing a single inch of your soft white body?'

'He wants to marry me,' Daisy said, then put a finger to her lips as the children came in, buttoned untidily into their coats, shoelaces trailing, cheeks glowing with health.

'Little pigs . . .' Shirley said at once, giving Sally's ponytail a gentle tweak.

'Is there any of that going spare?' she said when the pie came from the oven with dark brown gravy bubbling through the golden peaks of mashed potato. 'Tom's taken a boiled-ham butty down to the bottom field to have for *his* dinner. He's upset because he's had to call the knacker in to a cow with a terminal illness. He's been massaging its legs for over a week now.'

'And speaking of massaging legs,' she whispered, pulling a chair up to the table, winking at Daisy, 'when is the one in question coming home to have his evil way with someone not a million miles from here?'

'*Why* can't you marry him?'

Shirley was helping Daisy to tack frills of coloured paper along the edges of the shelves in the shop.

'Nobody bothers about waiting a year after a funeral these days. The war put a stop to all that. I had a friend in the WAAFs who bitterly regretted having a pink coat dyed black for her husband's funeral. It would have come in nicely when she married again six months later.' Shirley hammered a drawing pin in with the heel of her shoe. 'Did David desire you when you were Joshua's wife?'

'Stop talking about desire!' Daisy jumped down from

a box, forgetting her leg. She winced and looked down at it, thankful that she hadn't started it off bleeding again.

She began to scallop another length of the green crêpe paper, in her mind a clear picture of David the day he came to say goodbye before he left for America. Standing thin and tall in the hall of Shangri-La by the antler coat-rack, the limpid blue of his eyes dimmed with unshed tears.

'You don't know how fond of you I am,' he'd said. She had felt him trembling as he pulled her into his arms. And, God forgive her, she had thought it was his malaria coming on again.

'Why can't you marry him?' Shirley was looking at her strangely. 'What's he like to look at?'

'Leslie Howard,' Daisy said at once. 'But taller. A bit stoop-shouldered because his back was damaged while he was a prisoner of war in the Far East. A posh sort of accent because he was sent away to a boarding school when he was eight years old.'

'Plenty of brass?'

'Not short of a bob or two.'

'Well, then!'

Daisy accidentally stuck a drawing pin through the cushion of her right thumb. She watched a bead of blood appear. 'I like him a lot. As a *friend*. As Joshua's friend.' She sucked the blood away. 'He's a *doctor*, for heaven's sake! Like a priest. I can't see him as just a man.'

'He's a man longing to make wild passionate love to you. Aching with frustration because of the miles dividing you.'

'Is that *all* you think about?' Daisy cried, sucking away at her injured thumb.

'Of course,' said Shirley, unabashed. 'Show me the letter, Daisy. Go on!'

'I can't do that!'

'Why? Has it got rude words in it?'

Daisy threw down a green frill with an air of resignation. 'I'll never be ready to open on Monday at this rate. Well, all right then. I *will* show you the letter. It's not as if you know David. I've got to talk it over with *someone* or bust. I've got to *reply* to it for heaven's sake.' She put a hand over her mouth. 'Oh, I *wish* he hadn't brought his feelings out into the open just yet. I'm not *ready* to make decisions. I keep on thinking I made the wrong one when we came out here. I've hardly touched the garden yet and the plants I've pulled up are probably the ones I should have left in, anyway. The bloomin' fuchsias are standing there leafless, and the petunias are crouching in their little pots like fossilized ferrets. I still can't get the smell of mould out of the bedrooms, though I've done so much scrubbing with hot water and Lysol I'll soon be able to peel the skin off my hands like a pair of gloves. And I'm not even sure whether opening this shop is a good idea. I seem to be doing all the wrong things for the *right* reasons.'

'The letter?' Shirley held out a hand.

'It's just between you and me, then. Promise?'

'May I spit on my mother's grave,' said Shirley, wetting a finger and drawing it across her throat. 'Pass it over.'

They read the letter together, leaning over the newly polished counter with its weigh scales at one end and its old-fashioned till at the other. Daisy didn't need to wear her glasses this time, because the first reading had imprinted almost every single word on her mind.

'Even his writing looks frustrated,' Shirley said, gloating.

Dear Daisy, Very dear Daisy,

I've just come back from a trip to New Orleans

where I lectured on nutrition at two of the colleges. How I wish you'd been with me. The city has a real French feeling, which isn't surprising as it belonged to the French not all that long ago. The architecture, the food and the people - all predominantly French, or French Canadian. It's right at the heart of the jazz world, and a couple of students took me to a room where they say it all began. It was a dirty old place with broken benches and chairs, a rusty iron piano, and windows yellow with dirt and cigarette smoke. The wooden floors were uneven, the walls covered with faded jazz posters, and yet there, in that incredible setting, six old negros with grizzled faces and white fuzzy hair were playing music that made your toes tingle . . .

'When do we come to the bit that matters?' Shirley wanted to know.

'The last page.' Daisy pushed it forward. 'Starting there . . .'

I promised myself that I would stay over here for at least a year, and my work schedule commits me to this. But a year is a long way ahead. First there is the winter here, which I've been told can be even colder than our last winter was, then there's the spring and most of the summer.

What I am trying to say is that I can't face all those months without first telling you how much I love you.

I am in a suspended existence over here. I work, I eat, I sleep, I am not unhappy. I only have to think of you to be happy. Do you know that you are a very special person, Daisy? All the more unique because you haven't the faintest idea.

Joshua knew the warmth of you, the kindness of you, the way you have of holding out your arms as if you would embrace the world. I believe he taught me how to love you.

And because I loved him, it is right and good and proper that I should love you, too.

Will you marry me when I come home?

David

'It's like poetry,' Shirley said in a hushed voice. Her small face, smothered in the white-blonde hair, was wistful. 'I've known a lot of fellas, but not one of them has ever written me a letter like that. You must have egged him on a bit for him to write to *you* like that. Given him some kind of hope.'

'He was *Joshua's* friend.' Daisy tried to make Shirley understand. 'David lost most of his men during the war. He told me that those who were left became like brothers. Then they all died, or were killed, one after the other. He was in a terrible state when he came home. Like a walking skeleton. His wife had left him; he was a lost soul, so it seemed natural that Joshua would become his close companion. Joshua made no demands on him. They sat together listening to music, playing chess, talking. I've only realized recently how two of a kind they were. And I was there, always busy, too busy to sit with them, but David would come into the kitchen on his way in or out, and gradually we became friends, too.'

'So now you think that he is *imagining* his love for you because he hasn't yet come to terms with his friend Joshua dying?'

Daisy nodded, surprised at Shirley's unexpected perceptiveness.

'Oh, I'm not just a pretty face, you know. I can do joined up writing, too.' Shirley reached for her handbag.

'I have to go, love. Tom will make do with a butty for his dinner any day as long as he gets a proper meal at five o'clock.' She outlined her lips in a stinging scarlet. 'You'd think with a herd of flamin' cows and a hillside teeming with flamin' sheep there'd be more for me to cook than four sausages.' She stared pointedly at the top shelf laden with rows of Daisy's home-made chutney. 'Where did you get the sugar from to make that lot?'

'I brought a lot of it with me. When you've twenty to thirty ration books to juggle with you can always put a bit away here and there.' Risking life and limb again, Daisy climbed up and passed a jar over to Shirley. 'Here, put a good dollop of this on Tom's plate and he won't notice it's just sausages. Better still, if you core two large potatoes and fill the cavity with the skinned sausages, then bake them in the usual way, he'll think it's his birthday.'

Shirley burst out laughing. 'Lover boy is right. You *are* unique! Bloody unique! Giving me a recipe for stuffing potatoes with sausage meat when you've just received a proposal of marriage from a man with pots of money who looks like Leslie Howard! I'd be jumping up on that counter and running up and down on it and throwing all those jars of home-made chutney straight through the window.'

With a swirl of her full skirt and a toss of long blonde hair, she was gone, leaving the new shop bell tinkling.

Immediately Daisy picked up the letter and began to read it again. She didn't feel like jumping on the counter and throwing things through the window. The truth was that since the letter arrived she hadn't had time to think straight. Yet, all the time, somewhere deep inside her subconscious there was a small frisson of excitement, and overriding it all the knowledge that her mother would have been beyond herself with pride at the very idea of her daughter getting a proposal of marriage from a doctor. A man with letters behind his name, as she would have said. Nobody in her mother's circle had ever been on first-name terms with a doctor, let alone have one in the family.

Daisy started guiltily as the shop bell pinged. She pushed the letter deep into her apron pocket.

Bertha Tomlinson had come in round the front way, because it was going to be a shop soon anyway. About her brow was a deeply ingrained red line where the net she wore in bed had bitten into the flesh.

'I've just seen that giddy young kipper from the top farm tripping off down the road laughing at nowt. She'll be laughing the other side of her face when her husband finds out she's deceiving him behind his back. Tom Hindle's not been the same since he fell through that glass roof during the war. They say he's a dangerous man when he gets in a paddy. That young jessie at the garage will wonder what's hit him when Tom Hindle takes his shotgun to him. Is it right you're going to have that young Jezebel helping you out when you open the shop?'

Daisy nodded. All at once she felt drained and numb, bewildered by her feelings, wanting time alone to sort them out. She wished she'd remembered to lock the door behind Shirley, even as she accepted that Mrs Tomlinson would merely have walked down the ginnel and in at the back door. A locked and bolted back door in the village, Shirley had told her, meant that the woman inside was either lying dead on the floor, or upstairs enjoying a bit of 'anky-panky.

Bertha's head went to one side, the hairless lids blinking rapidly. 'There's a letter sticking out of your pocket. I saw the postman fetch it. You've been out with Bill Tattersall, haven't you?'

Daisy could hardly bear to look at her. Since reading David's letter she hadn't had a minute to herself; had been all at sixes and sevens. One moment elated, the next despairing.

'A nice letter, is it?' Bertha wanted to know.

'Look at it this way,' Bill said. 'I don't mind Mrs Hindle calling in to see you, Keith. What you choose to do with your private life has nothing to do with me. But when I come into my own office in the middle of the afternoon and find you necking then it has a *lot* to do with me.'

'One kiss,' Keith said, lounging against the wall. 'She wasn't here for more than five minutes.' He took a brown comb from his top pocket and ran it through his hair. 'I can't help it if I'm God's gift to women, can I?'

'You're a cheeky young blighter.' Bill pushed a work-shop manual off a chair and sat up to his desk. He drew a sheaf of invoices towards him and rifled through them. He was in no mood for any kind of confrontation. He reminded himself that Keith would be leaving soon, shaking the dust of the village off his smart two-tone shoes and heading for London.

But the hard truth had to be said. 'You'll be for the high jump if Tom Hindle finds out. I've seen him raise a whip to one of his farm hands before now. God knows what might have happened if I hadn't intervened. His temper's on a short rein. You must know that.'

Keith's girlish mouth curved into a sneer. 'He won't find out. He's out in the fields communing with Mother bleedin' Nature all day. Shirley might just as well be one of his cows. She'd be better off if she *was* for all the notice he takes of her. He's not the man she married, that's for sure.'

'And do you know why?' Bill's voice was steel.

'I should do. I've heard it often enough. Bleedin' heroes are two a penny these days.'

Bill stared at Keith with distaste. More than anything

245

he wanted to sack his apprentice on the spot. Chuck his cards at him and tell him to get the hell out of there. But Keith was within a few weeks of finishing his apprenticeship. He had served his time first with the previous owner of the garage, and for the last two years with Bill, and Bill knew how important it was to leave with a clean slate. There was a studied insolence about the handsome bony face that made Bill want to grip him by the seat of his overalls and throw him out of the office. Keith was a bad lot. Suddenly Bill knew that for sure. Keith didn't care a toss whether Tom Hindle found out or not. He would probably find a perverted satisfaction in the situation if he did.

Bill flicked a cigarette out of the packet on the desk and lit it. Shirley Hindle was merely a silly young woman who would go with any personable man who flattered her. But Keith was bad. Through and through.

'Oh, by the way,' Keith was saying now, 'Shirley just told me that the little widow woman in the Rothwells' cottage is getting married. To her husband's best friend when he comes back from America.' He turned on his heel. 'They've not let the grass grow underneath their feet, have they?'

The door swung to behind him. Bill heard him whistling out there on the forecourt: 'We'll meet again. Don't know where, don't know when . . .'

The sound went through Bill, setting his teeth on edge, as if a nailfile had been screeched across a pane of glass.

Daisy thought that Bill might have dropped in over the weekend, knowing full well she was opening the shop on Monday. She would have welcomed his cheery face, and a bit of help too in dragging the heavy stuff through into the room at the back she had earmarked as a storeroom.

She wouldn't have believed the rigmarole to be gone through before she could say she was in business. If old Mrs Rothwell hadn't retained the licence, Daisy would have given up before now. Meals in restaurants were still restricted to three courses at a ceiling cost of five shillings, and although Daisy had informed the Ministry that the permit she was applying for was for drinks and basic snacks only, she felt she could have papered a wall with the number of forms she'd filled in.

'Why do you bother?' Shirley had wanted to know, when she'd turned up on the Sunday evening to find Daisy elbow deep in flour. 'It's not the money, surely, because what you're going to make on this little venture won't exactly keep you in clover.'

Daisy just smiled. She thought about the dwindling capital in the bank, a capital that Joshua had worked out on the night he died, never knowing about the enormous bills that would have to be paid for the dry rot crumbling the guest house away. A more practical man would have noticed the signs of decay, and recognized them for what they were, but not even Joshua's own mother could have described her only son as a man born with a slide rule in one hand and a spirit level in the other. Then on his one brief visit to the cottage – blinded by the glory of the garden on that sunny day – he had seen, Daisy guessed, only what he wanted to see.

'On paper,' she told Shirley, 'I can just about manage, but nothing's finally settled up yet. I know I'm going to have to watch pennies, even though it won't be as bad, I hope, as wondering where the next butty's coming from.'

She turned the gritty oatmeal dough out on to the floured table and began to roll it with deft strokes of a well-used rolling pin.

Shirley watched mesmerized as Daisy cut out even

squares, laid them in rows on a greased baking tin and slid it into the oven, turning round to roll out a second batch quick as a lick.

'If you were wearing a striped blouse I'd be dizzy before this. You're like greased lightning. Did you ever stand still long enough for lover-boy to have his wicked way with you?' Shirley watched Daisy gather together the last of the dough to form it into a decent shape for the last biscuit. 'You won't need to make oatmeal biscuits to stay alive when you're married. If you must work you can always be his receptionist in a white coat, nipped in at the waist. Or answer the telephone for him in a deeply sympathetic voice. You *are* going to marry him, aren't you? You wouldn't pass up a chance like that to be made love to every single night by a man who looks like Leslie Howard. Didn't you just love the way he used to drive his women wild by ignoring them in his films? How could Vivien Leigh have preferred beefy old Clark Gable to him in *Gone with the Wind*? Fair hair and blue eyes have always been my downfall. Was Joshua fair?'

Brown. Brown of hair, eyes and clothes. If he bought a new jacket it was always brown.'

'Keith suits grey.' Shirley's voice was dreamy. 'Tom never even looks at his clothing coupons, so I pinched some and bought Keith a shirt. Grey. The exact shade of his eyes.' She rubbed her arms up and down and closed her eyes. 'Do you know, Daisy, I only have to say his name to go all of a doo-dah.' She opened her eyes. 'What are you doing now?'

Daisy drew a large earthenware bowl towards her and emptied a bag of flour into it. 'I'm making an extra ginger parkin. Cut into squares this was always a sure-fire seller in my mother's shop, though we could use proper ingredients then.' She chopped cooking fat and margarine together in thumb-end sized lumps, then

248

dropped them into the flour. 'Of course, in the bakehouse we had machinery for mixing. But then we made larger quantities. Naturally.'

Shirley went to get herself a drink of water, swaying from the hips, managing somehow to look as if she weren't wearing any knickers. She turned round from the sink, sipping the water as if it were sherry, staring at Daisy with her showing eye narrowed.

'You're enjoying yourself, aren't you? You've been on your feet all day, and yet you're in your element making ginger parkin and flamin' oatmeal squares. You know it's all a substitute for a normal sex life, don't you?'

'I beg your pardon?' Daisy had to laugh. 'There are other things in life, you know.'

'Such as?'

'Friendship. Children. A job you enjoy.'

'Joshua wasn't very good at it, was he?'

'Shirley!' Daisy's face went brick red. 'You don't *say* things like that!'

'Why not?'

'Because you just don't, that's why.'

'Because it's a rude subject?'

'Because it's *personal*. Private. It's sacrilege to talk about what goes on between a husband and wife.'

'Or what doesn't.'

'Stop it, Shirley! If my mother had heard the way you talk she'd have shown you the door.'

'She sounds like old Bertha next door. I bet *she'd* do a faint if you said "lavatory paper".'

'She knows about you and Keith.' Daisy resumed rubbing the lumps of fat into the bowl of flour. 'And what she knows today the world knows tomorrow.'

'I'll probably tell Tom, anyway.' Shirley picked up her coat from the back of a chair. 'I can't keep going home with grass stains on my skirts, and I can't keep telling him that the love bites on my neck are heat spots.' She lingered at the door. 'I'd best go. They'll be coming out of church and that's where Tom thinks I am.'

'You don't need to lie when you come down here, surely?'

'I was meeting Keith.' Shirley sighed. 'But he didn't turn up.' She came back into the room. 'Daisy? Did you go all weak at the knees when you saw David's letter lying on the mat when you came in?'

'I was pleased to see it.' Daisy dribbled a steady stream of golden syrup into the bowl. 'He writes every other day, and yes, okay, I miss him a lot.'

'Miss his touch, and his skin, and his smell? And ache down in your guts for the feel of his mouth on yours?'

'For heaven's sake!'

'Then you don't love him,' Shirley said, disappearing into the gloom of an evening as dank and soggy as a dripping face flannel.

It was long after midnight when Daisy got to bed, but she was used to that. Conditioned over the years to making do with the minimum of sleep, she was planning to be up before six to put the finishing touches to the little front room that was now the shop.

She felt happier and more alive than she'd felt for months. Everything had turned out right: the little moist and golden ginger parkin squares, the trays of nutty oatmeal biscuits, the chocolate cakes made with Bournville cocoa, dried eggs and saccharin tablets. Before the children got up that morning she would make a basin of mock cream with cornflour, milk and a few drops of vanilla essence, and fill the cakes to give them that before-the-war look.

She crossed her hands over the front of her winceyette nightie. She would make time to bake a special tray of gingerbread men for any children coming into the shop on their way home from school. She would put up a notice saying she was taking orders for Christmas cakes. She would pile a basket with apples from the trees at the bottom of the garden and offer them free. She might even put the basket outside for passing motorists to see.

She was far too tired and wound up to sleep. Her thoughts were jumping from one subject to another, whizzing round and round in her head like moths trapped in a light-fitting.

She would wait a few days before answering David's letter, so that she could tell him about the first few days in the shop. She would explain that she wasn't ready to think about marrying again, that she thought of him as a loving *friend* and missed him a lot.

Oliver cried out in his sleep and she sat up, listening with her head on one side, wide awake again.

Oliver had always been just a little in awe of David. Daisy lay down again. That could have been because David was a doctor, and not as ordinary men.

All at once Daisy heard her mother's voice as clear as if she'd appeared at the foot of the bed: 'Oh, yes, me daughter's married to a doctor, you know.' A little tin god who caused consternation and chaos before he'd even set foot in the house, which had to be cleaned from top to bottom, the sheets changed and apologies tendered for troubling him. Doctors were a breed apart. To be friendly with one out of surgery hours meant you had arrived. To *marry* one set you above and beyond the pale for ever. Daisy sighed, got out of bed and switched on the light. Maybe if she read for a while her brain would calm down. Maybe she'd find time one of these days to have a go at putting up shelves for the books still piled in rows along the skirting board. She opened her book.

'She took him into her arms, and he lay with his face on her bosom, weeping.'

She quite liked the thought of that. Warwick Deeping had such a gentle way with words. Even the faces he described were calm, grave, even luminous. His characters could sit for long periods just watching the smoke from their pipes.

Daisy closed her eyes and imagined herself lying in bed with David's face on her bosom. She imagined it would be quite difficult for a doctor to do that without automatically counting the rate of his loved one's heart-beats. And where would be the mystery of his loved one's first disrobing before him when every single inch of a woman's anatomy was known to him, and had probably been drawn in detail with suitable headings?

'Dear David (she wrote in her mind), I wish you were here so that I could remember the way you look and the way you talk, and the way you smile at me. Your tender friendship drew me out of the shadows after Joshua died, so that now I can go on, filling my days with work so there is no time for too much thought.

But I cannot write that I will marry you, because it's too soon . . .'

Her breathing slowed, the hand holding the book fell slowly to the turned-down sheet.

Too soon . . . too soon . . .

Suddenly, with the stark white light from the naked bulb hanging from the newly whitewashed ceiling falling full on her face, she was asleep.

Chapter Four

Daisy received one of Winnie's postcards just as she was opening up the shop.

It showed a big fat lady with her dress tucked up into her knickers paddling in the sea. By her side a tiny man with a flat cap on his head was bemoaning the fact that he'd lost his little Willie.

'Dear Daisy,' Winnie had written on the reverse side, 'Thank you for your nice letter. I am as well as can be expected. Give my love to the children. Leonard sends all the best. Love, Winnie.'

Daisy put it on the mantelpiece next to David's last letter, worried a little about the cold impersonal words then got on with the million and one things she had to do, hoping the driving rain slanting down from a dull grey sky wouldn't keep too many customers away.

At half past three in the afternoon Bill came into the shop. Daisy flashed him a dazzling smile.

He stood there wishing she wouldn't try so hard to be cheerful. He would have known what to say, and even better, what to *do* if Daisy had wept on his shoulder. It was obvious she'd sold practically nothing all day.

'I'll take a dozen of those,' he said at random, and pointed to a tray of macaroons. 'And four of those.'

'*Gingerbread men?*'

'Gingerbread men. And include the little chap with only one eye – you could find him left on your hands.'

She was wearing a dazzling white overall, to match the smile. The disappointment of the long, wet, dreary

Monday must have depressed her, but no, there she was, sliding the biscuits he'd bought into bags and handing them across the counter to him as if she'd been doing it all day. Run off her feet in fact.

Bill was very wet. He'd been forced to change a wheel on a car high up on the fell road, and the khaki battledress top he was wearing looked as sodden as a piece of wet blotting paper.

When he turned to go Daisy called after him. 'The kettle's on if you fancy a hot drink and a warm by the fire.'

He followed her through into the living room, watched her disappear then reappear with a mug of cocoa faster than if Aladdin had rubbed his lamp.

'You didn't have to buy all that stuff just because you were sorry for me,' she told him. 'You're not my only customer, oh dear me, no. Mrs Smith from the post office bought one of my sponge cakes made without fat. She was going to give it a quick warm-up in the oven, pour custard over it and present it to Mr Smith as a pudding she'd made herself.'

'The women round here don't go much on shop cakes.' Bill took a sip of the frothy cocoa. 'They reckon only women with more money than sense and with nothing better to do buy cakes from a shop.'

'I don't remember you ever telling me that!'

'Would you have listened?'

'No.' Daisy sat down opposite to him. 'But I did my homework properly. I made sure there wasn't another shop for miles selling cakes. I *walked* flamin' miles finding out.' She waved an arm in the direction of the door leading through to the shop. 'That lot would have sold in less than an hour in my mother's shop in Blackburn. We couldn't serve the women fast enough when they came out of the mill.'

'There you have it, Daisygirl. A lot of the women in

254

the village did go out to work during the war, doing men's jobs mainly. The vicar's wife did a postal round and Mrs Smith ran the post office on her own so her husband could catch the bus to the ordnance factory every day.'

'Now they stay at home cleaning their husbands' shoes. And baking cakes.' Daisy followed Bill back into the shop and stood with him at the door.

'It'll turn out right,' he said. 'Things usually do.' He stepped out into the rain. 'Anyway, once you're married you'll be leaving the village, so why worry?'

As she stared after him, she could see the children coming out of school, straggling along the road in ones and twos, heads bowed against the driving rain. Stopping now and again to jump in a puddle to try it out for splashing potential.

Shirley followed Oliver and Sally into the cottage, looking like a film star in a blue gaberdine raincoat with a hood framing her face.

'I'll take over in the shop while you give the kids their tea.' She unbuttoned the long coat. 'Have you got much stuff left?'

'Go through and see for yourself.'

Daisy was down on her knees peeling Sally out of her wet things, ignoring her protests.

'I've always did it myself,' Sally wailed.

'There are three different kinds of cake for tea.' Daisy took their wellingtons through to the back-door porch and set them to dry. 'Then when you've finished we'll have a game of tiddlywinks.'

The children exchanged glances.

'We don't like tiddlywinks,' they said together.

'Well, snakes and ladders, then.'

'Sally's frightened of the snakes,' Oliver informed her through a cream moustache.

'She's cross,' Sally said when Daisy walked off into the shop.

'We'll play just one game with her,' Oliver said kindly, reaching for a coconut macaroon which he managed to cram in his mouth whole.

'You mean you've only had two customers?'

Shirley stood in the middle of the shop. She looked genuinely upset. 'I can only stop for an hour because I'm meeting Keith, but I'll buy one of those chocolate cakes, and most of the biscuits. Oh God, what a shame! What an absolute flamin' shame.'

'You told Keith I was getting married, after swearing on your mother's grave you wouldn't say a word.'

'Well, I was *thrilled* for you.' Shirley sat down at one of the little tables. 'You don't know how lucky you are having the chance to go off and live with a man who worships you.'

'I haven't even answered the letter, yet!' Daisy began to put the smaller cakes away in tins. 'And I'm certainly not going off to live with anyone. Anywhere!'

'You'd have a swimming pool in America. Everybody has. And at midnight you could run naked across the lawn together and swim.' Shirley lowered her voice to a whisper. 'And make love under water. Keith says he read a book describing the sensation.' She started to pull the blue coat back on again. 'If you're going to shut up shop I might as well go. Keith said he can get away without Bill knowing.'

Daisy didn't need telling that Shirley was in a restless, hang the consequences kind of mood. Her face, framed once again in the flattering blue hood, was flushed, her blue eyes looked dazed. She exuded sex appeal – there was no getting away from it. She reminded Daisy of Rita Hayworth in *Gilda*, parting shiny pouting lips, peeling off long silky gloves, letting her glorious hair

256

fall down over her face, then lifting her head and tossing it back to reveal come-to-bed eyes. Rita Hayworth had glamour, so did Shirley. Daisy had always set great store on glamour.

She opened the door for Shirley, letting in the wind and the rain, then she closed it behind her and reached up to shoot the bolt into place.

No one would come into the shop now. She might as well admit it. She was a failure. A failure without sex appeal, and minus even a suspicion of glamour.

She sat down at one of the little tables and stared at the wall. Even her own children rejected her. They were paying her back for neglecting them when they were no more than babies. She'd forced them to be so independent that now they didn't need her. As tiny babies in their cots they had seemed to know instinctively that there were certain times in the busy boarding house when their mother was too frantically busy even to pick them up for a cuddle.

Daisy raised anguished eyes to the ceiling. Those two poor little creatures had been forced to play alone, making up their own games. Was it any wonder they were bewildered now?

She gloomed at the unsold cakes and biscuits. Everything was turning out wrong. Why not admit it? What good were positive thoughts at a time like this? Daisy dismissed positive thinking and lowered her head for another good wallow in misery.

She should never have bought the cottage. She had made the important decision in a state of shock. In her fevered imagination she had seen russet leaves against a pastel-blue sky, bees buzzing in and out of a hedge of honeysuckle and fox cubs playing like puppies on the lawn.

Jasper had followed her. As he sniffed his way round the walls his fat rear end quivered in expectation that the sweet sugary smells meant an extra feed. Already he was Daisy's dog, looking up at her with blind devotion. Because she was the one feeding him, Daisy reasoned. That was all. Cupboard love, nothing more.

She would answer David's letter when the children were in bed. She would be absolutely honest with him. It was too soon to think of marrying again, she would say, but she would tell him truthfully that he was never far from her thoughts. She closed her eyes for a moment, trying to picture the way he looked and walked and talked. And knew that if he had walked into the cottage right that moment she would have gone straight into his arms.

She remembered how, after he had kissed her on that last day before he went away, he had lowered his head and buried it against her neck. So that for a moment his pain was hers. It would be so easy to love a man like David. He was in such *need* of loving, after all that had happened to him on the far side of the world during the war. He had suffered so much . . . Daisy bent down and picked up the puppy, nuzzling the soft dome of his head beneath her chin.

'Daisy! Oh, Daisy!'

When the loud knocking came at the door, she nearly jumped out of her skin.

Shirley's voice was not her own; she sounded half demented, banging at the door and shouting. 'Daisy! For God's sake, let me in!'

When Daisy fumbled with the high bolt on the door, drew it back and opened the heavy door, Shirley almost fell over the step.

The long blue gaberdine coat was open, the hood laid back, the long bleached hair dark-wet with rain. Quickly Daisy drew her inside and closed the door.

'It's Tom!' The fresh colour in Shirley's face was fading already, leaving it grey-white, like putty. She was gasping for breath, clutching her side where the stabbing pain raged.

Daisy helped her into a chair, knelt down beside her and tried to push the curtain of hair away from Shirley's face.

'Try to tell me, love. What has happened to Tom?'

The chair was flung on its side as Shirley got to her feet. Her china-blue eyes started from her head with fear.

Daisy gripped her arms, forcing her to speak. 'Tom? What has happened to Tom?'

'Nothing has happened to *Tom*!' The words came from Shirley in a great drawn-out wail. 'It's Keith! Tom found us together in the low barn.'

'And . . . ?' Daisy shook Shirley hard. 'He hit him?'

'I think he's killed him! Oh Daisy – oh, dear God in heaven! I don't know what to do! There's blood everywhere!'

'Mummy has to go out.' Daisy spoke with a quiet firmness. 'Auntie Shirley isn't well and I'm just taking her home.' She pointed to the fireguard. 'You don't *touch* that. Promise?'

'Can I have another cake?' Oliver looked up from the Plasticine he was modelling into a recognizable racing car.

Daisy pulled on a coat and went back into the shop, relieved to find that Shirley had pulled herself together enough to stand up holding on to the table, swaying from side to side like a metronome.

Daisy again spoke in the deceptively calm voice. 'We'll go up to the barn *together*. *Now*.' She held out a hand. 'It might not be as bad as you think. We can't leave Keith there if he's badly hurt. A bit of blood goes a long way,' she added in a soothing voice.

It was as if she had never spoken.

'I can't go back.' Shirley swiped Daisy's hand away. 'Tom will kill *me*!' She backed away suddenly, her eyes wide, so that Daisy turned round quickly, expecting to see the ginger-bearded farmer's huge frame blocking the doorway. 'Tom was carrying a storm lamp, Daisy. It swayed to and fro. We scrambled away trying to avoid its light, but it was no good. He'd been prowling about outside the barn. *Listening!* He burst in and held the lamp up high and saw us in the hay, and I swear to God there was murder in his eyes.' She began to sob. 'I *daren't* go back, Daisy. He'll be sitting there waiting for me, brooding. With his gun across his knees.'

'His *gun*?'

'He always walks his last round of the day carrying a gun. Foxes. One got the hens last week.' Shirley raised an agonized face. 'He's unhinged, Daisy! He'll be hiding in the lane somewhere. He can move like a cat in the dark. He can *see* like a cat.' She covered her face with her hands, the scarlet fingernails vivid against the pallor of her skin.

'But what about Keith? Someone will have to go to see to Keith.'

'Keith is dead,' Shirley said. 'Tom smashed his face to a pulp.'

It was a night without moon or stars to light the way as Daisy stumbled along the road. It was a darkness worse than any she remembered during the black-out in the war. Only the week before it had been decided to switch off the few street lamps as an economy measure, and in her upset state Daisy hadn't even thought about taking a torch. The cottages loomed up on either side of the road, their windows merging with the night-black walls, their occupants snug round the fires of their back living rooms.

Without seeing as much as the bare outline of it, she

260

could sense the brooding hump of Pendle Hill; she could hear, she swore, the ghostly bleating of grey hill sheep wandering over the wiry grass. She cursed her short-sightedness which turned the familiar horse-trough into a crouching bear, the outline of Bill Tattersall's little office into a misty mirage which would vanish even as she approached it.

Halfway up the steep farm track a twig broke with a noisy snap behind her; to her left a bird rose from a hedge with a sudden frenzied flutter of wings. Something or someone was stalking her.

Daisy felt a trickle of terror meander its way down the full length of her spine. It was either some wild beast come down from the hills, or the long-lost ghost of a Pendle witch stretching out fingers like talons towards her. Daisy stopped, holding a hand over her wildly beating heart. A dog barked, freezing her blood.

The rustling sounds were in front of her now, a soft rhythmic swish as if a path were being scythed through the long grass. She imagined Tom creeping along behind the hedge, peering through the darkness with his crazed blue eyes. Trying to get her in the wavering sights of his gun, because he was sure she was Shirley come back to find her dead lover.

Daisy whimpered aloud, the sound shocking her. She had thought she was brave, but she was not. She was so scared she could actually feel the hairs rise on the back of her neck. She tried to turn and run but her thin house shoes slithered over the sharp stones of the deeply rutted lane.

The wind tore at her hair, watered her eyes, rasped her breath in her throat. Her heart was racing as if it would burst.

Who would bring up her fatherless children if she ended up sprawled face down in a muddy lane with a bullet hole in her forehead? She ran with arms

261

outstretched, half-demented in her terror. Keith was dead. Shirley had said so. There was nothing she could do for him. Her duty lay with Oliver and Sally, playing like little angels on the rug with their modelling clay. Safe in the cottage ...

Safe? Oh, dear God! *Safe?*

Daisy felt her ankle turn with a painful wrench, but she ran on. *Shirley* was with the children, and it would be Shirley Tom was looking for. Even as she had toiled her way up the hill he could have burst into the cottage, kicking the door to behind him, huge and hairy, gun blazing, frightening the children out of their little lives. Killing them as well because the smell of death was in his nostrils.

She had turned out of the lane on to the main road now. All at once she could see. Her eyes, grown used to the dark, showed her a square of light coming from Bill's little office across the road. Daisy stopped to try and catch her breath, holding a hand to the fiery stitch raging in her side.

That was what she should have done in the first place. She should have gone for Bill, not chased up the lane on her own. Trying to be all things to all men as usual, thinking she could put things right for everybody when the truth was she couldn't even put things right for herself.

When the man loomed up in front of her she screamed so loudly he was forced to clamp a work-roughened hand across her mouth.

In her headlong dash out into the night, Daisy had forgotten that the door to the cottage was still on the latch.

So that Bill walked straight in without knocking.

The children looked up from the rug where they

262

were squabbling half-heartedly over the last stick of yellow Plasticine which Sally wanted for a sun.

'Shirley's gone,' Oliver told Bill. 'She was crying.'

'But Mummy's coming back soon,' Sally told him pleasantly. 'She'll be back in a minute.'

Bill knelt down beside them and forced himself to speak in a casual voice. 'I'm going out again now, but not for long.' He cuffed Oliver on the shoulder. 'I'm going to bring your mum back. Okay?'

'Okay.' Oliver had taken advantage of the unexpected interruption to palm the stick of yellow clay and stick it underneath the rim of the fender. As the cottage door slammed to yet again after another flying figure, he offered to help Sally search for it.

'I should think Jasper ate it,' he suggested.

'He eats *everything*,' Sally agreed placidly, making do with a bright green sun.

Daisy beat at the man's rock-hard chest with clenched fists.

'Steady on!' Bill held her away from him. 'It's only me, Daisygirl! Not Jack the Ripper!'

There was just enough breath left in her body to say his name before she collapsed against him.

'I thought you were Tom,' she said, when she could speak. 'I've got to get home; there's no time . . .'

Bill caught her easily and whirled her round to face him.

'Tom's given Keith the hiding of his life. The lad's got a busted nose, a few loose teeth and a couple of slits for his eyes, but he'll survive.' He held Daisy by the arms, forcing her to listen. 'Tom Hindle, being the kind of man he is, half carried Keith down the lane to the garage, dumped him in the doorway like a sack of potatoes and asked me to see to him.' His grip tightened. '*Listen*, Daisygirl! It's all over bar the shouting. Shirley's over there in the office bathing what's left of Keith's face, and Tom's back at the farm waiting for her.'

'To kill her!'

'To *forgive* her, the blessed saint that he is. And not for the first time, not by a long chalk. He's one in a million is old Tom. He deserves a *wife* in a million instead of that daft woman chasing after any man who looks at her twice.'

'She loves Keith,' Daisy said. 'She's carried away by the force of her emotions.'

'Stop talking like an 'apenny book,' Bill said, giving her a none too gentle push along the road towards the cottage.

Bill seemed in no hurry to go after he'd helped Daisy see the children to bed, with Oliver fighting a rearguard action on every step.

'Sit down,' he ordered. 'Take the weight off your feet. You look done in.' He almost forced her down into a chair. 'That was a brave thing you did tonight, going out all alone to face a man crazed with jealousy.'

Daisy agreed at once. 'A man with a gun, don't forget.'

'Filled with a lust to kill.'

'Sure I was Shirley coming up the lane. Ready to take a pot shot.'

'You deserve a medal.'

Daisy nodded. 'Except that I changed my mind about being brave halfway up to the barn.' She rolled her eyes ceilingwards. 'I came back down that lane faster than a streak of greased lightning.'

Bill smiled at her. 'When did you eat last, lass?' He put up a hand. 'Okay, okay, I know. That's changing the subject, but you look in dire need of sustenance. Stop where you are and I'll go through and make your tea.'

'I can't let you do that!' Daisy got to her feet.

'Why not?'

'Because . . .' she floundered. 'Because, well . . .'

'Has nobody made you your tea before, Daisygirl?' He shook his head at her. 'For God's sake, lass, let somebody do something for *you* for a change! God love us, the world won't stop turning because Daisy Penny puts her feet up and lets somebody else do the waiting for once. Tell me what you fancy and I'll make it. I'm a good cook, believe it or not!'

The events of the long day had taken their toll. Daisy sank back into her chair. 'A cup of tea will do me.' Her face was so tired she found she was having difficulty stretching her mouth round the words. 'And perhaps a piece of cake. You'll find you're spoilt for choice.'

She was asleep when he came back with the tray, but even the slight sound of him putting it down on the table beside her woke her. He thought she looked far younger than her years, wind-tossed and achingly vulnerable. So tired he felt he could weep for her. Instead his emotion came out as a kind of anger.

'When's that bloke of yours coming back from America?' He jerked his chin towards the mantelpiece where David's last letter lurked in its usual place behind the clock. 'It strikes me it's time someone watched over you instead of what I think has always been the other way round.' He passed her a cup of tea. 'My guess is you were playing nursemaid to your husband for a long time before he died.'

'You don't exactly mince your words, do you?' Daisy took a sip of the tea, savouring its comforting smell. It was made just how she liked it, with exactly the right amount of milk, and no tea leaves floating on the top.

'The very first time I met and talked to Joshua he made me a cup of tea that tasted of nothing else but warm steam. It was horrible.'

'And the one you're drinking now?'

'Perfect. Just what the doctor ordered.'

Bill folded his arms. 'Tell me about him. The doctor I mean.'

The urge to talk about David was suddenly overwhelming. Daisy leaned back and closed her eyes.

'Well, he's like Leslie Howard to look at. You remember Leslie Howard?'

'The Scarlet Pimpernel?'

'Yes. Most people I meet remind me of some film star or other. Joshua was Herbert Marshall; Shirley, Veronica Lake of course, and if you forget the beard, Tom could be the image of Gary Cooper.'

'And I remind you of Boris Karloff, but you don't like saying.'

Daisy opened her eyes and stared gravely at Bill's face.

'That's a funny thing. You don't remind me of anyone.' She began to laugh. 'I've just thought how furious Mrs T will be when she comes back from her sister's tomorrow and finds she's missed all the goings-on.'

Bill startled her by standing up abruptly. 'If you laugh like that again I'll have to kiss you.'

'Oh, I wish you would,' Daisy said at once. 'It's been such a terrible day, a nice friendly little kiss would be quite welcome.' She held up her face and pursed her lips.

When the door slammed behind him she wondered what could have flared his anger to the point when she thought he was going to hit her. She touched her mouth gently, the way he had done before storming out like that – running his finger round the outline of her lips, lingering and gentle. She shuddered as a creeping sensation of pleasure shivered through her.

She got up, carried the tray back into the kitchen

and ran the tap on to the cups and plates. There had been an expression in his eyes that had brought Charles Boyer to mind. For a moment her hands were still. Now *there* was a man for you. Good old Charles Boyer, smouldering away even when he was laughing his socks off.

Daisy upended the cups and saucers on the wooden draining board. She hoped Bill wasn't going to spoil a nice friendship. Reverting to type, she supposed. Doing what came naturally. To a *man*. She stared at the clock ticking away on the wall till her eyes went out of focus. She wasn't turning into a replica of her mother, *nor* her Auntie Edna. Not for a minute she wasn't. They weren't happy unless they were slapping men down a peg, emasculating them, making out that men's brains were in their trousers and that they rampaged through life lusting after women. Oh, no, *she* was quite open-minded about men.

Daisy put a hand to her mouth to cover a huge yawn. The answer to David's letter would have to wait. If she tried to write it now, the way she was feeling, she might say things she'd regret. Her pen might carry her away as she tried to express the sudden inexplicable longing she was feeling, making her want to do crazy things. Like taking off all her clothes and running out into the wet and tangled back garden. Holding up her arms to the sky and feeling the rain on her skin.

'Signs of an early change,' her mother would undoubtedly have said, had she been alive.

The memory of the acid-tongued little woman steadied Daisy as nothing else could. She'd let Jasper out then she'd fill her hot water bottle, climb up the narrow squeaking stairs, say her prayers in bed because the room was a freezing ice-box. Rome wasn't built in a day, and she might open up the shop in the morning to find a mile-long queue going crazy to snap up her coconut macaroons.

Jasper had to be called twice before he would leave the warmth of his box by the fire to slink past her, ears flattened against his head, tail drooping, obedient but far from willing.

As she waited for him, Daisy stood at the back door staring out into the darkness, listening to the sounds of the night.

The rain had almost stopped and the wind was no more than a sighing in the trees. She could hear the far barking of a dog and thought she heard a curlew's repetitive cry. Pendle Hill would be shrouded in dank dark fog. Tom Hindle's grey-stoned farm would be wreathed in mist and inside, by a blazing log fire, Tom would be forgiving Shirley, and she would be promising him that she would never be unfaithful to him again.

Or would she? Was Keith really the one true love of Shirley's life? Daisy sighed deeply. Jasper padded back on muddy paws. She closed the door and stood on tiptoe to shoot the bolt into place.

In the living room she banked up the fire with slack, put the fireguard round, half reached up to take David's letter down from the mantelpiece, then left it where it was. To answer when she was in a more normal frame of mind. Less *unsettled*, she told herself wisely.

Bill Tattersall was in a strange restless mood. He could smell the sweet clean scent of cold rain in the air. He didn't want to go home – if you could call the corrugated hut he lived in a home.

There was a clear picture in the forefront of his mind of Daisy Penny holding up her laughing face for a 'friendly' kiss. What was she, for God's sake? A naive innocent, or a practised tease? She was no Shirley Hindle, he was sure of that. There wasn't enough room for two Shirleys in one village. He stopped and leaned against a low stone wall, staring up into the dark sky for all the world as if he were feeling the warmth of the sun on his face.

Clenching his fists deep in his pockets he crossed the road to the garage, opened the door of his little office, clicked on the light and saw the sheet of blue notepaper propped conspicuously against the telephone.

Shirley's handwriting was as flighty as her disposition, he thought, as he read the note, all swirls and sudden changes in style.

> Dear Bill,
> Keith is taking me to his mam's house. I am never going back to the farm. I would like you to tell Tom for me and say how sorry I am that it has to be like this. I will collect my things, tell Tom, when he's calmed down a bit.
>
> > Shirley

Bill shook a cigarette from a crumpled packet and sat down at his desk. Of all the stupid, silly, misguided little twerps . . .

Screwing up the note he hurled it from him, in his mind a clear picture of Keith with his head choirboy's face, the fair stubble on his chin no thicker than the down on a chicken's breast. Living with his widowed mother who had breast-fed him, it was rumoured in the village, till he was two years old.

Bill stubbed out the unwanted cigarette in a tin lid overflowing with old Eli's squashed dog-ends. Did Shirley, with her bottle-blonde hair and her undulating backside, think she could take the place of Keith's mother, waiting on him hand and foot, accepting uncomplainingly that never once would he give a passing thought as to how the food reached his plate?

269

Bill stood up, and on his way to the door kicked the ball of blue paper into a dusty corner. God only knew how he was going to tell Tom that his wife was never coming back. The last time Bill had seen him, he had looked like a man at the far end of his tether.

'See to him, Bill,' he'd growled, pushing the battered Keith through the door. Then he'd turned on his heel and disappeared, his bomber-jacket black-wet with rain, his hair clinging to his scalp as if every strand had been separately oiled.

The rain had started again, but Bill chose to take the short cut up to the farm, following a thread of a stream which sounded now like a raging torrent. If his army manoeuvres had taught him one thing, it was the ability to see in the dark. Like a ruddy cat, he told himself, slithering and slipping in muddied boots over tree roots and jagged stones.

As he approached the farm he saw lights blazing from the hall and lounge windows, knew that Tom had left them on for Shirley, imagined him waiting there by the massive fireplace, staring into the embers, waiting for her to come home.

By the noise the dogs were making it was obvious they were not in the house. The sound of Bill's footsteps as he skirted the long barn sent them mad. Hurling their bodies against the massive door, bulging it outwards as it strained at the padlock.

Something was very wrong. Bill ran up the slope of lawn, his feet sinking into ground as soggy as a wet sponge. Tom Hindle never shut his dogs away. His so-called barmy way with his animals was a joke down at the pub. As far as Bill had been able to judge, the dogs had the run of the house, lolloping on muddy paws down the long stone corridors, settling to sleep on chairs as if by divine right.

The impact of the ferocious barking was a devastating

pulse-beat in his head – continuous, frenzied, rhythmic, never letting up for a second, alerting him to God knew what. Bill tried the front door, found it locked, stepped out of the porch back on to the gravel path. The lights were on all right, but the downstairs curtains were drawn tight, the pink curtains that Shirley had chosen because pink was her favourite colour.

'Pink to make the boys wink,' she'd giggled on the day Bill had called in at the farm and found her halfway up a ladder hanging them, showing everything she'd got. On purpose.

Bill's mouth set in a grim line. His boots crunched on the wet shale as he ran round to the back of the house. Why was he running? He was damned if he knew. It was the mind-blowing noise of the loud barking; it was the numb feeling there in his chest. It was the memory of Tom Hindle's face as he'd turned and walked away from the garage earlier on. But most of all it was the knowing that Tom had always said that his door would never be locked against his wife.

'Tom?' Bill found the door leading straight into the kitchen only needed a push to open it. He moved swiftly, blundering into the big scrubbed table, clattering a plate to the floor.

'Tom?' He crossed the lighted hall and went into the lounge where, just as he had imagined, a huge log fire crackled in the grate.

What he saw had him down on his knees, turning his friend's body over, wincing away from the sightless eyes staring up with a blue and chilling intensity.

At nothing.

There was no other way to tell Daisy but to come straight out with it. Not at five o'clock in the morning when Bill had finally come down from the farm and seen by the light shining through from Daisy's kitchen that she was already up and doing.

'You look terrible,' she told him, drawing him inside, reaching with an almost reflex action for the kettle. 'Where did you sleep last night? Under a hedge?' She struck a match and bent down to light the gas. 'I didn't sleep much, either. I kept waking and fancying I could hear dogs barking.' She busied herself putting cups on saucers, spooning tea into the brown pot, taking the beaded net cover off the sugar basin.

'Leave that!'

She blinked at the tone of his voice, then when he told her about Tom she sat down abruptly on a kitchen chair, the fresh colour fading from her cheeks.

'Shirley will have to try and live with that for the rest of her life,' she said slowly. 'She'll think she killed him as surely as if she'd pulled the trigger of his gun herself. Daisy groped in her dressing-gown pocket for a handkerchief, held it to her eyes. 'She's not half as bad as you think she is. Just unthinking and unhappy. Desperately unhappy. Always searching for admiration, believing she knew the only way to get it.'

The sound Bill made brought her head up with a jerk.

'You expect me to feel sorry for *Shirley*?' He turned his head away as if he couldn't bear to look at her. 'Oh, she came up to the farm when she was sent for. A police car brought her from Keith's mam's house. At least she had the sense not to bring him with her, though I wouldn't have put that past her. No, by God, I wouldn't.' He began to pace backwards and forwards. 'The performance she put on would have shamed Greta Garbo. She was wailing and weeping over Tom's body with that great daft sergeant looking on, I swear, with tears in his eyes.' He whirled round. 'She was leaving Tom this time. For good. Going away with Keith, though

God knows where to, or what they thought they'd live on.'

'Tom knew that?'

'Oh, aye, he knew that without her ever getting the chance to tell him. He knew it was all over when he stepped out of character and lashed out at Keith. Tom knew he'd had his chips as far as Shirley was concerned from the minute he landed the first blow.'

'She'll never get over it,' Daisy persisted, getting up to brew the tea. 'Her marriage to Tom didn't stand a chance from the day his plane was shot down during the war. Shirley told me he was a changed man.' She brought the teapot to the table. 'A man like that needs special care.'

'And *you* should know?'

'I should know.' Daisy poured milk into the two cups. 'Tom Hindle came home but he was still a casualty of war.'

'Just as Joshua was?'

'In just the same way.'

'An' you're going to marry yet another of them! Your doctor friend was a prisoner of the Japs, so *he'll* need plenty of mothering too, won't he?'

Bill spoke through his shock and grief, hardly knowing what he was saying. 'What are you, Daisygirl? A martyr? A masochist? Is there something in you that can only respond to a half-wick man?'

His mouth on hers was hard and demanding, his arms round her bands of steel. When he let her go she almost fell.

'And now what, Daisygirl?' he whispered. '*Now* what?'

For the third time in the past twenty-four hours he closed the front door of the cottage none too gently behind him.

Leaving Daisy standing there in her kitchen, holding

a hand to her mouth, weeping silently. For who or what, she was no longer sure.

Chapter Five

Bertha Tomlinson would never forgive herself for being over at her sister's on the night Tom Hindle did away with himself.

'It goes without saying he found out his wife had been laying up with that jessie from the garage,' she told her friend Mrs Smith. 'There's something fishy about the way young Keith did a skedaddle the day before the funeral.'

'His mother says he's got a job with a big firm down south. He'd served an apprenticeship, you know. She says the money's better the further south you go. That's why he went.'

'Well, she'd say owt, wouldn't she?' Bertha's eyes did a full circuit. 'She thinks that son of hers is the best thing to happen round here since piped water came up to the village. She breast-fed him for that long he used to stand by her knee and unbutton her blouse.'

Bertha was furious because she hadn't managed to get as much as a dicky-bird out of Daisy about Shirley Hindle and what was going on, not even by asking her straight out. All she knew was that Shirley had gone to live with a brother nobody knew she had over Oswaldtwistle way, leaving the farm to be run in a slipshod way by Tom Hindle's assistant, till somebody could be found to buy it.

She *hated* not knowing the full details, but it had all happened so quickly behind her back, and everyone in the know seemed to have entered into a vow of silence. Little Mrs Penny was in on it – Bertha was sure of that.

'Bill Tattersall isn't always in and out of next door the way he used to be.' Bertha passed her cup over for a warm-up. 'I had the feeling once that he fancied his chances there.'

'That lad he's taken on at the garage in Keith's place looks a penny short to me,' Mrs Smith said pleasantly. 'Sorry I've only got Marie biscuits.'

'Mrs Penny's started taking orders to the big houses. She delivers them herself. I've seen her pass my house looking like a pack-horse. She'll kill herself one of these days,' Bertha said cheerfully, refusing a pallid biscuit. 'Did you see the vicar's wife at the funeral?'

'Yes. Why?'

'Didn't you think she'd aged?'

'We all have, Bertha.'

'Aye, but not like *her*. She's put ten years on since last Christmas.'

Bertha shook her head, making a mental note of the layer of dust on the gate-leg of the table, and the way her friend hadn't bothered to put a doyley on the plate.

From where he was lying underneath a car on the forecourt of the garage Bill saw Daisy walking by on the other side of the road carrying two baskets. He knew where she was going because Mrs Birtwistle of Willow House had called in for two gallons of petrol the other day and told him that she had asked Mrs Penny to cater for the afternoon tea party she was giving in aid of the Red Cross.

'She's marvellous,' she'd enthused. 'She made an iced walnut sponge for Mrs Appleby at Westwinds that defied description. I can't thank you enough for telling me about her.'

Bill slid from beneath the car to watch Daisy walk on down the road. Mrs Birtwistle's house was a good mile and a half away. There was rain in the wind and he was tempted to jump in the van and drive after her to offer her a lift. He wiped his hands on an oily rag and pushed his beret to the back of his head.

Things had been more than a little bit strained since he'd blotted his copybook on the night Tom Hindle died. Daisy was her cheerful self when they met, but she kept her distance, a wary look in her eyes. As if she was afraid he was going to pounce again, he thought angrily. She'd made a point too of mentioning her pen-friend, the good doctor, as if reminding Bill that she was spoken for.

He turned his back on the sight of the little widow woman – as Keith used to call her – and went back into his office. He wondered what Daisy would say if she ever found out that he'd told some of his wealthier customers that he knew where they could buy the best home-made cakes this side of Manchester? That her new-found success was directly due to his initial inter-vention?

He kicked at a heap of tyres. Trust Daisy to offer to do the deliveries as well. If ever there was a woman who was a glutton for punishment it was Daisy Penny. If she'd been a suffragette before the First War she'd have been in a queue to chain herself to flamin' railings. He moved an old chest of drawers out of its corner, deciding to have a bit of a tidy-up while things were slack.

And saw the bicycle propped against the wall.

There were some days, and this was one of them, when Daisy went to bed realizing that she had gone all day without once thinking about Joshua. Or about David, either, if she wanted to be honest with herself.

It struck her sometimes on one of her more fanciful days – and this too was one of them – that the brooding shape of Pendle Hill put problems into a kind of perspective. The whale-shaped hill had been there for ever. It was there when Roman soldiers marched in its shadow from Ribchester; it had brooded over the monks as they built Whalley Abbey, and it alone knew the truth about the Lancashire witches more than three hundred years ago when they terrified the good people of the surrounding villages, whipping them into a frenzy of superstitious terror. Today Pendle hid in a cloud of purple mist.

Daisy was in one of her reckless moods. If she hadn't had to get back in time for the children coming home from school she would have handed over her order to Mrs Birtwistle at the grey-stone house with its beautiful mullioned windows, and walked on into the ever-changing light, through the grey-yellow grass, past the remains of farmhouses, deserted long ago. Emily Brontë wandering her beloved moors, stretching out her arms to the sky, the wind blowing her long dark hair in sweet disorder round her pale sad face.

What did it matter that the Brontë moors were the other side of the Pennines, or that Daisy's own dark hair was far too short to be tossed by the wind? All she knew was that she was enjoying this strange mood of exhilaration. She pretended that from somewhere in the far distance a handsome man on a black horse was riding towards her, his aquiline features etched against the grey sky, his thin lips curving up into a sardonic smile as his hawk-like eyes spotted her.

On the way back, swinging her empty baskets, she glanced across the road and saw Bill Tattersall down on his knees pumping up the tyres of a bicycle that looked as if Adam might have ridden it when he was a lad. If he saw her he gave no sign, and when she let herself into the cottage there was Edmundo Ross doing his nut in tango rhythm from the wireless she'd forgotten to switch off.

At once Daisy picked up the long yard-brush and led it out on to the kitchen floor, swaying her hips and twinkling her feet in rhythm to the music.

It was a long long time since Winnie had danced with anyone, let alone a long brush.

The baby was due in three weeks' time and was kicking so heftily inside her she felt absolutely certain that Leonard could not possibly be the father. She had started sleeping in the spare room, locking the door against him, going to bed before he helped his mother upstairs. When he rattled the door handle she stuffed the sheet in her mouth to stop herself from crying out, knowing that he would give up and go away in case his mother heard.

She felt so ill, so *heavy*, there were days when she thought she might die. There was a continual pain in her side and the agony of bleeding piles made sitting down a torture. Her ankles swelled so much that at the end of a long day her feet turned almost black. She cut the straps of her sandals, not caring what they looked like – she couldn't see them anyway.

She accepted that marrying Leonard had been the worst mistake of her life. His mother was determined to be nasty to her, and Winnie didn't give a monkeys. All that was left of her energy went into getting through each day. Daisy's letters kept her going; they were so full of what she was doing, and what the children were doing ... the country wasn't turning out to be such a bad place after all.

Winnie pulled a face as the kipper she had eaten for breakfast repeated on her. Levering herself out of the low kitchen chair she waddled over to the cupboard and took down a bottle of Tizer. The fizzy yellow drink wouldn't mix well with the kipper, but she didn't give a monkeys about that either. She poured herself a cupful

and drank it down so fast the bubbles pinged in her
nose. She heard Leonard's mother banging with her
stick, and with an upsurge of her old spirit gave a rude
sign at the ceiling. The old woman called out and
Winnie said a word so filthy Leonard would have killed
her if he'd heard it.

'Winnie!'

The voice from upstairs was a clarion call. 'What do
you think you're doing down there? Have you gone
deaf?'

Winnie took no notice.

She drained the cup and slammed it down on the
draining board. Some day she'd walk out of this house
and never come back. Not even if Leonard sent a team
of wild horses to drag her back by the roots of her hair.

The kipper and the Tizer gave up the struggle to
settle down with each other. Winnie lumbered as fast
as she could up the stairs to the toilet, holding her hand
over her mouth, trusting she would get there in time.

Nora Jolly felt sick. She had read the letter at least
six times. David's replies to her long screeds were so
unsatisfactory, so obviously polite acknowledgements,
they were hardly worth reading twice.

This one was different:

Dear Nora,

Your long newsy letters fill me with shame when
I think of my own brief replies. Yes, I can tell you
quite truthfully, the Royal Wedding is creating a
lot of excitement over here. The Americans love
our Royal Family, and when I told the dietician
here that people were preparing to sleep all night
on the pavements, she was fascinated. (I must tell
you about her some day; she has a most unusual
background.)

'*Must* you?' Nora muttered, turning over a page.

> In her last letter Daisy told me that The Mall is
> considered to be the best place to be sure of a good
> view. She also tells me the little shop she's opened
> isn't doing too well yet – the wrong time of the
> year probably – but she seems to think there could
> be a growing market for her in deliveries to the
> big houses on the outskirts of the village. She says
> if only she could find someone willing to look after
> the children she would be prepared to go out and
> cook whole meals for the dinner parties starting to
> be given again now that the war is over. You know
> the kind of thing. The hostess sits down at the table
> cool and unruffled whilst someone else slaves away
> in the kitchen. Trust Daisy to think of a scheme
> like that! You have to admit she's a trier.

Nora didn't bother to read down to the end of that
page. Daisy! Daisy! Daisy! – with her big brown eyes,
her childish laugh and the irritating way she had of
making the best of everything.

Nora forced herself to read the last page:

> I hope you won't be too surprised when I tell you
> that I've asked Daisy to marry me when I come
> home in the summer. I wanted you to be the first
> of my friends to know.

Oh, my love, Nora thought. He was trying to let her
down gently, anxious that she understood. He still *felt*
for her. It could only mean that.

She read on:

> Daisy hasn't said a definite yes as yet, and knowing
> her as well as I do I suspect she feels it's all too

soon after Joshua's death. He once told me she was a great stickler for the formalities.

'True to her superstitious working-class mentality,' Nora muttered. Her eyes filled with tears. Daisy . . . Daisy . . . Daisy . . . devoid of even a semblance of culture. The hatred Nora felt for her sparked the air around her. What did Daisy Penny have that she, Nora Jolly, didn't have in abundance?

The cry coming unbidden from her throat was a great wail of despair. She couldn't believe that David could be such a fool, such a poor misguided fool. She picked up a sofa cushion and beat it so hard on the wooden arm-rest of her chair that feathers flew from it and danced around the room like snowflakes.

Her lovely gentlemanly David, married to that . . . that little pastrycook? Dear God, if someone pinched Daisy Penny's egg whisk or her wooden spoon, she'd be as nothing. Sunk, lost, bereft, like a medical student without his stethoscope.

David was on the up and up. Once he'd recovered from his wartime experiences as a prisoner of war – and time was the greatest of healers – there'd be no stopping him. Nora lit a cigarette with shaking fingers. Nutrition was the coming field in which to practise. Making the rations go round had made women food conscious. The orange juice and cod-liver oil handed out to pregnant women had taught them the value of correct vitamins and minerals. *She* understood all that.

Nora was almost beside herself. Her mind raced ahead.

The research potentiality was enormous. Doctors had come a long way since recognizing that lack of vitamin C caused scurvy, and that rickets were symptomatic of malnutrition. A swollen belly and hollow eyes weren't the only evidence of starvation.

David had talked to *her* about all this. And *she* had been able to talk back. With intelligent comprehension.

Nora was drawing so deeply on the cigarette it was making her cough. The hurt inside her was a physical pain she didn't know how to bear.

Why had she never suspected that David's feelings for his friend's widow ran so deep? Why had she lived on hope ever since he went away, rehearsed how she would greet him when he came back, cured of his memories of what had happened to him during the war?

It was ludicrous to imagine a man like David married to a woman like Daisy Penny. She would ruin him. She would grind him down to her own level. She would answer his telephone in that Lancashire accent of hers; she would answer his door with flour on her nose, wearing a crossover pinny. She would probably sit down at David's table still *wearing* the pinny.

Nora ground out the cigarette with such fury that she scorched her fingertips. The pain was the last straw.

Shaking with anger she ran through into her bedroom and positioned herself tragically in front of a long white swing mirror. Even today when she had taken a day's sick leave from the office because David's letter had made her feel ill, even though she wasn't planning on leaving the flat, she was wearing a neatly pressed navy gaberdine skirt with a pale-blue Viyella blouse with tiny box pleats down the front. For all her anguish she just wasn't the type to slop about after nine o'clock in a dressing gown, with her hair any old how and a nose shining like a beacon.

'I could have made him love me,' she cried out loud to her reflection. 'I am *right* for him. And *she* is wrong.'

The sound of her voice startled her, but she made no attempt to latch on to her fast ebbing control. Through the mirror she could see her bed, boxed in its pleated spread, the day pillow in its pale green linen cover propped against the headboard.

A nun's bed. A virginal spinster's lonely loveless bed.

Nora held her hand to her heart, spun round and threw herself face downwards on to the bed, kicking her heels and drumming with her fists in a frenzy of unladylike passion.

When it was over she turned on her back, sat up and smoothed down her skirt. She was calm now, filled with an icy resolution. Summer was a long way off. A lot could happen before next summer, and David wasn't lost to her yet. Some time before now and then she was determined to make him come to his senses.

All that emotion rampaging through her blood stream had made her feel hungry. Swaying from the hips like a mannequin on a catwalk, her dark eyes huge orbs of despair, she made for her tiny kitchen. For the solace of a cup of coffee and another Russian cigarette.

Bill Tattersall dropped his cigarette end and ground it out with his foot. That night the wind was boisterous. He had tried out the bicycle without wearing gloves and his fingers were numbed and stiff. It was late, almost eleven o'clock, but he had seen by the light streaming through from the back of the cottage that Daisy was still up. So, acting on impulse, he had clicked open the gate and wheeled the newly furbished bicycle up to her front door.

'Would this be any good to you?' He spoke without preamble, pushing the machine forward. 'I've checked the brakes and tyres and fitted a basket on the front handlebars. All that's missing is a bell.' He pointed to the carrier at the back. 'You could strap another basket on here if you wanted to.'

'How much do you want for it?'

Daisy hadn't meant to say that, but the knock at the door late at night had startled her. Her mood of exhilaration had drifted away late that afternoon along with the dark clouds scudding across a leaden sky.

Bill looked as hurt and angry as she immediately felt he had every right to be. 'I'm not selling it. I'm offering it to you. I *found* it, for Pete's sake. It would have gone on the scrap heap.' He turned to walk away. 'Do what you like with it. It was only a thought.'

'I wouldn't have been so stroppy with you if I hadn't had me curlers in,' Daisy told him over cups of steaming cocoa. She had poked the fire back into life and snatched the few steel curlers from the front of her hair. 'I have a thing about being seen in them. It really embarrasses me.' She smiled at him. 'The bicycle will be just the job. Thank you very much. There is just one snag, though.'

'Which is?'

'I've never ridden a bicycle in me life!'

'Everybody can ride a bike, lass.'

'Well, *I* can't. I've never had no need for one. I've always lived in a town, remember, with shops round the corner and a bus stop at the end of the street.'

Bill thought she'd be even more embarrassed if she realized that her dressing gown, open at the neck, showed the hollow between her full breasts when she leaned forward.

'I see you were writing a letter,' he said abruptly, nodding towards the table and the open writing pad. 'I wonder what the good doctor would say if he knew you were sitting round the fire late at night wearing your nightie and drinking steamy cocoa with a man just aching to have his wicked way with you?'

For a moment Daisy's quick wit deserted her.

'David trusts me,' she said, feeling as priggish as she sounded.

'Then he's a fool.' Bill held out his numbed hands to the fire. 'Do you honestly love him?'

Daisy didn't give herself time to think. 'I don't know. All I know is that he needs me.' She flinched at the expression on Bill's face. 'I know what you're thinking, but you're wrong.' She leaned forward, giving Bill a ringside view of a deep cleavage. 'Maybe there *is* a motherly streak in me. But I enjoy looking after people. I like *giving*. I don't mind hard work. If someone needs me I have to respond. It's just the way I am. Does that turn me into some kind of a freak?'

'You're showing the tops of your bosoms,' Bill said.

What could she do but laugh? He was so cheeky and impertinent, sitting there on the sofa grinning, his eyes dancing with triumph at having shocked her once again. His hands were almost purple now that the feeling was coming back into them. She remembered seeing him kneeling down outside the garage that morning, pumping up the bicycle tyres. Working on it. In the cold. For *her*.

'Are you ever serious?' she asked him. 'Does anything really bother you?'

A small nugget of coal fell from the fire into the hearth. Daisy leaned forward to pick it up with the brass tongs, remembering to clutch her dressing gown tightly round her throat. 'Life's one big laugh to *you*, isn't it?'

'Not at the moment it isn't.'

Daisy looked away, wary of the seriousness lying like a shadow across his face. This man she could cope with as long as he kept the jokes coming, but he was staring straight at her with an expression of great sadness.

'You can't get warm, can you?' She threw a log on to the fire, saying the first thing that came into her mind. 'You must have been mad trying that bike out on a night like this.'

'On and on for miles,' he agreed. 'To make sure it was roadworthy.' He got up to go. 'But that's the way I am. Still a Boy Scout at heart. They don't grow men like me these days.'

She went with him to the door, standing there in the square of light. 'I'm going into Blackburn next Tuesday,' he told her. 'If you feel like seeing your auntie again you're welcome to a lift.' He walked backwards down the short path, hands thrust deep in his trouser pockets. 'It will most likely be the last time I go, so you'd best take advantage of me.' He grinned. 'I wish you would.'

'I'd like to go,' Daisy said.

He came back to her. 'I'm glad you said that. I'd like very much to have you with me,' he said.

Then he was off, away down the road with his jaunty springing walk. Leaving Daisy to go back to the fire which looked set to blaze for a long time yet.

Daisy reckoned that the only way to learn how to ride the bicycle was to climb on the wretched thing and start pedalling. And the only way to do this in private was to wheel the bicycle along the main road well away from the garage, making for the first secluded lane. If anyone stared at her wondering why she was wheeling instead of riding she would pretend she had a flat tyre, and if they offered to blow it up for her she would say she'd left her pump at home and what a shame, wasn't it?

The lane she chose was bordered with beech trees, giving way further down to holly and hawthorn. From across a field she saw lapwings flying gracefully in slow motion. Daisy wished with all her heart and soul she was going for a nice long walk.

She wheeled the bicycle to a good stretch of flat road bordering a grassy verge. At least if she fell off she'd land on something soft, she muttered, hoisting herself

on to the saddle. Bill had told her the saddle was exactly
the correct height for her, but he hadn't explained how
to get on to it. Within two seconds flat Daisy's foot had
slipped from the pedal, the machine had keeled over,
taking her with it so that she found herself flat on her
back staring through a tracery of beech trees at a
lowering sky.

'Need any help, love?'

The man coming round the bend of the lane wore a
large sack round his shoulders and two smaller versions
tied with string round his knees. Daisy knew she had
seen him before, but couldn't quite place him. She
smiled, sending up a small prayer of thanks that at least
she was back on her feet.

'Bit parky this morning?'

Daisy said indeed it was.

'Dratted mice are on the move. They've got at the
apples but I'll settle the little buggers. One of the cheeky
young blighters made a home for itself behind the
kitchen dresser, coming out at night to nibble ears of
barley from the corn dolly the missus got from the
autumn bazaar.' He lifted his cap to scratch his head.
'I don't suppose tha'd say no to a dozen pullet eggs?
They're noan much bigger than a rabbit's droppings,
but childer'll like 'em.'

'That's very kind of you.' Daisy wished she could
bring to mind where she'd seen him before. She remembered the sacks, but not the man wearing them.

'Reet then.' He backed away from her. 'I'll fetch 'em
round to thi place, Mrs Penny, and if I were thee, I'd
fettle that chain back on that contraption. You might
find it'll go better.'

Halfway through struggling to get the greasy chain
back into what she hoped was the right position, Daisy
remembered that the old man used to work for Tom
Hindle. She had seen him mending a dry-stone wall,

and she had heard him calling the cows in for milking, shouting their names at the top of his voice. One day, as she walked up the hill to the farm with Shirley, he had yelled at them, asking where they were going all dolled up.

Shirley ... For a moment the job on hand was forgotten as Daisy clearly recalled how Shirley had looked that day. She'd been wearing a tight green skirt with a fluffy teddy-bear swagger coat, her hair arranged up on top for a change, each coiled curl secured with a kirby grip. Her lips couldn't have looked redder and fuller if a bee had stung them. Daisy had thought she looked glorious and didn't wonder that men did a double-take when they first saw her. Shirley ... who would have Tom's death on her conscience for as long as she lived. And Keith? Would what had happened destroy the love they felt for each other? In spite of her genuine sadness Daisy was fascinated by the drama of it all. It was a film happening in real life. It was terrible, wicked, beautiful, tragic, all mixed up together. Daisy looked down at the chain and wondered for a split second what it was.

By the state of it she calculated that Bill had used enough oil to lubricate the looms in a dozen weaving sheds. Not the man to do anything by halves, she told herself grimly, mounting the saddle again and groping desperately for the pedals which she wished would stop whizzing round. If only the handlebars would keep still. No matter how firmly she held on to them they juddered and jerked as if they had a mind and a will of their own. But she hadn't fallen off for at least a hundred yards, though she had already decided that if a car should suddenly appear she would get off and pretend she was adjusting the straps holding the front basket in place. Alternatively, she would just steer for the ditch and fling herself and the bike into it.

But after four more false stops and starts she felt she was getting the hang of it. The sit-up-and-beg handlebars were steadier now and she could squeeze the brakes on gently without risking catapulting herself over them. She could free-wheel down the more gentle slopes, though going up hills meant she had to get off and push.

For the next quarter of an hour she practised getting on and off with grace. She was sure that jamming on the brakes and straddling the road with her legs apart wasn't the right way. No, the correct way was to brake slowly, then as she came to a stop allow her right leg to cross over so that she pulled up in one flowing motion. In her films Judy Garland could even *sing* as she dismounted without missing a flippin' note. Daisy decided a bit of a sing-song might help.

'There'll be blue birds over . . .'

She was pedalling so fast and furiously she felt the bike could lift into the air at any minute. This was really marvellous . . . As the wheels spun round they gave off an attractive ticking sound. The pumped-up tyres skimmed the surface of the road with their own swishing noise. Judy Garland? Daisy felt sorry for her.

When the dog suddenly appeared as if from nowhere to saunter across the road ahead of her, Daisy jammed the brakes on hard.

It took a lot of nerve to force herself to get back on to the bicycle. First she had to re-align the handlebars, then for a while she wobbled dangerously from one side of the road to the other. She could feel a lump coming up on her forehead, and pain from a grazed ankle sent shock waves up her leg.

A farm tractor rumbled slowly towards her, and by a miracle she kept on pedalling . . .

'Nothing to it,' she told Bill when he picked her up in

his car the following Tuesday morning. 'You were quite right. Riding a bike is an instinctive skill. Anybody can do it. It's as easy as falling off a log.'

He was in the same twitchy mood he'd been in the first time he'd taken her into Blackburn, but this time it was worse. Now he looked ill, with dark shadows beneath his eyes. A tiny pulse jumped and throbbed by his jawline. Daisy couldn't take her eyes off it, having only read about such a phenomenon in romantic novels.

'Matthew Bolton, Tom Hindle's old cowman, told me he'd seen you lying as if for dead by the side of the road the other morning, pondering why the wheels wouldn't turn without the chain in place. When I dropped my washing in at Mrs T's just now she told me Mrs Greenhalgh from the almshouses saw you flying over the handlebars right outside her front gate.'

Daisy fingered the strip of sticking plaster on her forehead. So much for the time she'd spent trying to conceal it with a fringe of loose curls.

'I bet you can tell me exactly what I had for breakfast this morning?'

'You didn't have any,' Bill answered promptly. 'You were too busy getting the shop ready to open at one o'clock. Oliver didn't eat his, either, because he looked as if he was coming down with a cold.'

Daisy gritted her teeth. 'Mrs T. She came in to borrow a cup of plain flour to make some paste to stick the wallpaper back behind her bed. She's okay really. As long as you tell her everything, she's your friend for life.'

Bill had lost interest in the conversation. He was driving with his usual casual skill, but when he turned his head to the left to check that a woman with a child in a pushchair wasn't going to step off the kerb, there was a bleakness about his eyes that startled Daisy.

'What's the matter, Bill?'

291

His mouth set tight at the question, but Daisy persisted.

'Look. I know it's none of my business, and I respect your wish for privacy, but these trips to Blackburn? They *upset* you.' She swallowed hard. 'You're going to see your little boy, aren't you?'

For a moment she thought he was going to slam the brakes on, lean across her, open the door and order her out of the car. She saw his face darken, and his eyebrows draw together in an angry frown. He drove on for a while without speaking, then at the next lay-by pulled in to the kerb.

'Need I ask who's been gabbing? Mrs T?'

Daisy shook her head, miserable now that she'd forced the issue. 'Not this time. I'm sorry, Bill. I ought not to have said anything, but . . .' She turned towards him, her eyes pleading. 'It *does* help sometimes to talk to someone, and since Tom . . .' she hesitated, 'did what he did, I've sensed that you miss walking up to the farm and talking things over with him.'

'So you know about *that*, do you?' His voice had a rough edge to it. 'Is nothing sacred?'

'What is sacred is your own secret life, if you *wish* it to be secret,' Daisy said softly. 'But my guess is you need to confide in someone so badly that the need is eating away at you.' She risked touching his arm. '*I'm* here, Bill.'

He didn't say anything for at least five minutes, just sat there drumming with his fingers on the wheel. Trying to make up his mind, Daisy guessed. But at least his anger seemed to have evaporated. Now he looked like a man almost weak with relief, a man who had decided to unburden himself. She waited, scarcely daring to breathe.

'I was away for five years during the war,' he began. 'Many of us were. France, Tobruk, El Alamein, Tripoli.

292

But before I went . . .' He turned his face from her. 'I made love to a girl instead of just kissing her goodbye.'

He glanced quickly at Daisy, but she forced herself to show no reaction at all.

'We hardly knew each other. We weren't engaged or anything. In fact, I'd never been to her house, never met her parents.' He ran a finger round his collar. 'What I didn't know, and what she didn't tell me was that she was barely seventeen, not the nineteen she'd claimed to be.' He gave a short laugh. 'She wrote to me telling me she never wanted to see me again, but that she wished me luck and would remember me in her prayers. What she left out was that she was pregnant.'

He sat up straight and squared his shoulders, avoiding looking at Daisy. 'I accepted what she said. I wasn't remotely in love with her. She'd been a pretty girl, out for fun, and she made the last week of my leave one of the happiest times I'll ever remember. I didn't force her,' he said, raising his voice and banging with his hand on the wheel. 'Thank God I don't have rape on my conscience.'

A busload of people passed the car. Daisy saw some of the passengers glance idly at the two of them sitting there, cocooned in their own little private world halfway down a busy street. Bill had paused for a moment, but from her own stillness she willed him to go on.

'So that was that. Unbelievably, that was that. I wondered about her from time to time, even started a letter to her once or twice, but I've never been one to force my attentions where they weren't wanted, so in a very short time I had forgotten her. I couldn't remember her face. I can't even now. But she had an unusual and pretty name – Denise.'

'And when you came back?' Daisy prompted him gently.

'It was like coming back to a strange country. Everything drab, and the skies so grey after all that sunshine. Shortages of everything. I wandered round Liverpool staring at the gaps where buildings used to be. My parents were dead and all my old pals were married. Every man Jack of them! I couldn't get a job even though I was assured the unemployment situation was only temporary, so I decided to sink my savings and my gratuity in a little business of my own. When I came out to the village and saw the garage I knew that was where I wanted to be, where I wanted to live for the rest of my life. I knew, you see, that petrol wouldn't be rationed for much longer, and I reckoned on many more cars coming back on the road. I didn't aspire to be a millionaire, but if I'd dreamed at all of the future during the long years I was abroad, it must have been of the place where I live.'

'I know what you mean.' Daisy's voice was soft. 'Go on, Bill. Try and go on.'

It was some seconds before he could continue. 'I went over to Blackburn one evening. After weeks of working non-stop at the garage I felt ready for a bit of a night out. So I went dancing. To the same place where I'd met Denise.' He began to talk rapidly. 'Like a fool I looked around for her. Being away in the war for a long time did that to you. Other blokes told me the same. You come back surprised because everything isn't just the same. Denise wasn't there, but I thought I recognized a friend of hers. It wasn't all that much of a coincidence really. It was a Saturday night and there's not much else to do but go pubbing or dancing. I asked this girl for a dance and asked her did she ever see Denise . . .' His voice dropped to a whisper. 'What she told me nearly sent me wild. I left her standing there in the middle of the floor with the band playing and couples waltzing, and I went straight round to Denise's house.'

He was looking straight into Daisy's eyes as he said: 'Denise had *died*, giving birth to a baby, and the date fitted. It could have been my baby, and by God I had to find out! So I ran up the street, I banged on the door, and they let me in.'

He lowered his head. 'Denise had told them my name and that I was stationed abroad, but she had made them promise not to contact me. She never wanted to see me again, definitely not marry me. Not even after the war ended. It was a reaction a lot of girls have, I believe, when they are having a baby by someone they hardly know. They want to cross him from their mind completely.'

He shook his head from side to side. 'Her parents were much younger than I'd expected them to be. Middle forties, no more. The grandma looked about twenty-nine, with her daughter's round blue eyes and brown curly hair. It was seeing her that brought the face I'd forgotten back to me.

'She was staring at me with an expression on her face I'll never forget. "He's your son," she said quietly. "There's no mistaking the likeness. It's uncanny. And besides, Denise wouldn't lie to us about a thing like that. Not when she knew she was dying."

'She had a heart complaint, her father told me. He hadn't said a word up till then. The operation would have been too tricky to put it right.'

Bill put his hand over his eyes. 'I wanted to make amends. I wanted to offer to support him. I was shouting at two people I'd never seen before, so shocked I didn't know what I was saying. I wanted to see him, so the mother took me upstairs and even lying asleep sucking his thumb he was so much like me it was laughable. I wanted to wrap him in a blanket there and then, tell him I was his dad come back from the war, and take him with me. In my unthinking blindness I wanted to do that.'

A lorry delivering utility furniture into a shop across the wide pavement tooted its horn, requesting parking space. Bill switched on the ignition, raised a hand, and drove off.

'We went back downstairs. Halfway down Denise's mother stopped, so I had to stop too. She said that Denise had told her I was the first man she had made love with, and was it true?'

Bill signalled left, driving automatically. 'It was one of the worst moments of my life, I can tell you. But I told her that until I had come along her daughter had been a virgin, and that I accepted full responsibility. Oh, dear God, how they must have hated my guts.

'They told me that the boy was *their* child. They had lost their only one, they reminded me, but no one was going to take away their grandson. "He calls us Mum and Dad," they said. "He's happy. He's just started school. He's *ours*," they kept on saying.'

'But you would never have taken him away?'

'Never! I'm not that cruel. I offered to make regular payments towards his keep and they said they'd chuck the money on the fire if I did. I could understand it, Daisy. They obviously worshipped the little nipper. There was a three-wheeled bike in the lobby, and a posed studio photograph on the sideboard. There were toys in a box and a red jersey airing by the fire. They were nice people. Lovely people, Daisy, and when I said I'd like to see the boy and take him out occasionally, as a kind of uncle, they agreed.'

'And you're going to see him this morning?'

'No. He's at school. I'm going to see *them*. To give them the news they've been praying for.'

Bill pressed his foot down hard on the accelerator. 'The last time I went the kid must have got it into his head that I was trying to take him away from his mum and dad. You know how kids pick up atmosphere?' His voice had heartbreak in it. 'I lifted him up and he kicked out at me – almost kicked my shins raw. And that was the moment I realized I was an intruder in his life. A strange man who called and took him for walks when he would rather have been stopping in with his mum and dad. A man who ruffled his hair and sometimes terrified him by hugging and kissing him.'

He gave a short laugh. 'I'm going to give them my word that this is the last time they'll see me. I'm going to promise never to contact them again. I'm going to do what's right.'

Edna was at the door waiting for Arnold when he came down the street. To tell him she'd had a visitor.

'Our Daisy was really sharp with me once or twice,' she said. 'There's a lot of her mother in her. She didn't look so well to me. Last time she came she was bandaged up like an Egyptian mummy, and this morning she looked as if she'd been in the wars. She said nowt, though. She always kept things close to her chest, did Daisy.'

Arnold wished his wife would hurry up and get his dinner on the table. It had been bitter cold up the allotment, even though he'd huddled with his pals round a coke stove in Bert Wainwright's greenhouse. He was sorry he'd missed Daisy again, but he never worried overmuch about her. In his opinion his favourite niece had been born with two feet not only on the ground but a yard or two underneath.

'I asked her was she having money troubles.' Edna went into the back kitchen and returned with a bottle of HP Sauce and nothing else. 'She flashed out at me quick as a lick saying she wasn't quite reduced to searching down t'backs of chairs and robbing t'gas meter.'

Arnold laughed. 'She's a proper caution.'

'She asked us for Christmas.'

Arnold bided his time before he spoke. Christmas had been a touchy subject for a long while, ever since their Betty had written to say that Cyril's father was going down to stop with them in London, but adding that Edna and Arnold were welcome too as they'd bought one of the new bed-settees and could fit them all in nicely.

'Aye.' Arnold spoke over the rumbling of his stomach. 'Why don't we do that, lass? Daisy'll be out there in the back of beyond all on her own if we don't go. I can't rightly see how we can refuse.'

'And it'll show that son-in-law of mine that we're not beholden to them. That even if he moves his father in next door we've still got a life of us own to live.'

'So you told Daisy we'd go?'

'Well, of course I did.' Edna bustled into the kitchen, coming back with a nicely browned corned beef and potato pie. 'You being so slow on the uptake aggravates me that much I think I'll run away and take the veil.'

'It's me age, love,' Arnold said, happily drawing up his chair. Getting his feet underneath the table.

'That chap fetched her again.'

'Oh aye?'

'Daisy snapped me head off when I tried to ask her about him.'

'Well, it's none of our business, lass.'

'If he's there at Christmas I'll know there's something going on.'

Arnold forked up a mouthful of pie, savouring the smell.

'By the left, lass. But this is better than a slap round the earhole with a wet flannel any old day.'

Bill followed Daisy into the cottage, going straight through and sitting himself down on the chintz-covered sofa. He had been silent, preoccupied all the way back, so Daisy had left him alone, sure that was the kindest way.

He didn't lean back against the cushions but sat on the very edge, clenching his hands together between his knees.

'I've done the right thing,' he said suddenly, raising his head and looking at her with pain-filled eyes. 'Haven't I? The best for *him*.'

'Oh, love . . .' Daisy sat down beside him. 'You've done the *only* thing.' She stretched out a hand and touched his hair. 'You wouldn't have done it if you hadn't known he was happy. Known that he had a loving, secure home.'

'But will he ever *blame* me?' The words came out thick. 'He'll find out. Kids always do. And when he does will he hate me as much as *they* hate me?' He shook his head. 'No, the hating me doesn't matter. What I am asking myself is will he think I *rejected* him? That I caused his mother's death then turned my back on him?'

His whole expression was tense. He looked angry, sad and bewildered at the same time. Instinctively Daisy reached for him.

'Come here, love. Don't be so unhappy. It'll work out right, you'll see.'

She held him in her arms, rocking him, soothing, comforting, a friend and a mother, holding him close.

Then all at once he was holding *her*, and they were kissing, tenderly at first, then with longing. His hands were moving over her, feeling her soft and yielding. He could feel her heart thudding as he touched the rounded swell of her breast. He was so charged with emotion he hardly knew what he was doing.

299

'Don't be so sad,' he heard her whisper against his cheek.

But in that moment all sadness was gone. He wanted her so badly, needed her so badly there was nothing left in the world but his need of her.

He would take her upstairs. He would *carry* her upstairs if needs be. This woman was special. There would be no embarrassed fumblings with buttons and zips there in the living room with the chance of a neighbour walking in on them. He would draw the bedroom curtains against the raw November light. He would slowly undress her and she would lie on the bed waiting for him.

He lifted his head. And looked straight at the familiar envelope on the mantelpiece, halfway tucked behind the clock.

'I've made you feel sorry for me, haven't I?' The words burst from him uncontrolled. 'I'm one of your lame dogs now, aren't I? To be petted and loved to make me feel better.'

He looked down on her astonished face. 'I'm not going to ask you to forgive me, because I know you will.'

'Bill? What is it?' She lay back on the cushions, flushed and unhappy. 'Have I done something wrong?'

He stood up, his dark eyes bleak. 'Did *he* enjoy you comforting him, the good doctor? Did you kiss him better, too?'

She reminded herself when he'd gone that he had been overwrought, ravaged by guilt, and immeasurably unhappy. She tidied her hair and straightened the rumpled cushions.

She imagined what might have happened, what so nearly happened. And found herself thinking, for a

300

fleeting moment, how wonderful she just knew it would have been.

Chapter Six

Daisy was feeling so worried about Oliver she barely glanced at the card from Winnie.

This one showed a busty landlady holding out a hot water bottle and asking her young maid why she hadn't put it in Mr Smith's bed as she'd been told to.

The maid, scarlet of face was saying:

'I tried me best to, mum, but 'e wouldn't let me; 'e kept fast hold of the bedclothes!'

As usual Winnie had sent her love to the children, said she was in the pink as she hoped Daisy was too, and added an all-the-best from Leonard.

Daisy had felt for weeks now that it was time she paid a surprise visit to Blackpool, and the more it became obvious that Winnie was trying to put her off the more she became determined to go. Perhaps at the weekend when Oliver was better, but in the meantime he was producing so many vague and unconnected symptoms he was losing all credibility.

'My hand hurts,' he whined. 'My head aches. My legs are wibbly-wobberly.'

'A touch of flu,' Mrs T said. 'There's a lot of it about.'

'His head *is* a bit hot.' Daisy wished Mrs T would go away. Her feelings towards her next-door neighbour wavered as usual between gratitude and irritation. 'I'll keep him off school if he's no better tomorrow.'

'I lost three cousins with the flu. The Spanish flu after the first war. They were burying them by torchlight up the cemetery. Bad epidemics always seem to come after wars. People just don't have the stamina.'

'My mother nearly died of it,' Daisy said, panic settling on her and beating at her common sense with pulsating wings. 'Do you think I ought to send for the doctor?' Her eyes were wide and anxious. 'I've never thought about finding a local doctor since we came here. David – Doctor Armitage would have come round at once if we rang to say one of the children was ill. Or his father. But then, they were family friends.'

Mrs T's eyes went into orbit. 'Bit far for him to come from America.'

'He was so good with the children. Though he never had any of his own.'

Daisy was feeding Mrs T information that would be all round the village the next day and she knew it. But the mere thought of David walking in through the door, taking Oliver's temperature, making soothing reassurances that it was just a temporary fever, was an ache inside her. She glanced up at his latest letter behind the clock.

'A terrible thing his wife deserting him when he was in the hands of the Japanese. It was enough to finish him off,' Mrs T prompted her.

'It nearly did,' Daisy said softly.

It was nine o'clock before Oliver settled down into a feverish twitching sleep. Customers had been so thin on the ground for the past few days that Daisy had almost decided to close the little shop for the rest of the winter to concentrate on the swiftly expanding business of deliveries to the big houses around and on the perimeter of the village.

Word had got round that there was a little woman who would turn up with simply *everything* freshly prepared if one was having a tea or a coffee morning. There was a way this Mrs Penny had of cutting the crusts off slices of bread, layering them with delicious home-made fillings and fashioning them up like tiny Swiss rolls. So attractive set out on sandwich plates. And the scones! Feather-light without the teeniest hint of bicarbonate of soda in the flavour, and God alone knew how she produced sponge cakes as moist as if she'd used best butter in them. If only one could book her for dinner parties. It was said that at one time she'd run the best boarding house in Blackpool, with folks going back year after year just for the food.

Mrs Walker at Millstone Lodge would have willingly taken her on full time if Daisy hadn't had children to bring up alone. Though the days of live-in servants had gone since the very beginning of the war, when Mrs Walker's cook-cum-housekeeper had gone to be an oxyacetylene welder, and never bothered to come back.

Daisy left the door at the bottom of the stairs open in case Oliver called out, sacrificed a play she was going to listen to on the wireless, and decided to write to David.

Bill Tattersall saw her light was on as he walked past on his way back from the pub after chucking-out time had been called. He was slightly drunk, but nowhere near being sozzled. Sober enough anyroad to realize that knocking on Daisy's door would be a grave mistake.

He hadn't eaten since a slice of toast at breakfast-time, and the beer he'd got down him on an empty stomach had gone straight to his head. If his eyes hadn't searched out the safest places to put his feet as he stumbled along he would have fallen full length.

And if he'd found himself lying there, face down in the mud, then that would just about sum up the whole sorry day. He stopped suddenly, presenting his flushed face to the sky. A car sped past him in a cloud of spray.

304

There was more than a touch of sleet in the rain – the everlasting never-ending rain. God, how he missed the sun! He lurched across the road. What was it his old mate Tom used to say?

> If ice in November bear a duck,
> The rest of the winter'll be slush and muck.

Last winter had turned the fields bone white for weeks on end. The lower reaches of the river had iced over, and the ice had borne the weight of more than a duck. He had a sudden picture in his mind of Shirley skating with crossed hands between the two of them, Tom and Bill, not long back from the war. Casualties of war, both of them.

Ripe objects for Daisy Penny's pity and solicitude . . . The word had him beat. Too many sus's. Without being able to see more than the hand in front of his face, he sensed the upward flow of fields and hedges towards the sombre curve of Pendle Hill. As if the darkness enriched his memory, he went over every detail of the day. His cold renunciation of his son, given standing up in that toy-strewn room, as solemnly as if he stood with one hand on the pages of an open Bible. His drive back to the village with Daisy sitting quietly by his side.

Again and again, once he was inside his own place, he recalled how she took him in her arms and comforted him. Took *him* in *her* arms. Remember that, Tattersall. *Mothered* him. Was closer to him in that moment than she had ever been. But *only* because he had stirred up her sympathy.

Bill snatched the beret from his head and flung it to the far corner of the room. The beer he had drunk lay sourly in his stomach. He lay down fully dressed on top of his bed, closing his eyes when the ceiling seemed to dip and sway towards him.

Why, oh why, had he made such a fool of himself? Was his self-control so tenuous that the touch of a woman's hand on his cheek and the feel of her in his arms sent him wild? He would have married the girl whose face he couldn't remember. He would have done right by her.

He hadn't seduced her. She'd been more than willing, so come on, Tattersall, give yourself a break. Stop crucifying yourself for being no more wicked or irresponsible than the next man.

And as for the boy. He was never yours, Tattersall, so why not face it? You're his biological father, and what does that signify? Bloody nowt.

And as for that two-headed woman – that Daisygirl.

Come on, Tattersall. Face the truth again. Her body had curved into yours as if it belonged there. She had responded to your kisses like a woman in love. The *truth* now. She had responded like a woman who *ached*, yes *ached* for the physical expression of mutual desire.

She had clung to him moaning as his hands moved over her.

And he had pushed her away from him.

Why? Spit out the truth, Tattersall. The truth as you see it.

First, she'd been married to an invalid husband, years older than herself, coughing his life away. Then she'd taken a lover too weak from the notorious Jap camps to want to do more than cry on her shoulder and worship her from three thousand miles away.

Elliptical black shapes floated behind his closed eyelids.

He'd be *damned* before he'd let Daisy add *his* name to her collection of lame dogs. Life hadn't exactly been a bed of roses, but he was certainly no object of pity. She could save that ever-ready compassion of hers for someone who deserved it.

306

He tried to sit up but fell back on the bed, shaking his fist at the undulating ceiling.

This lame dog would look fate straight in the eye.

'I spit at fate,' he mumbled, as sleep at last penetrated the curtains of his pain.

'Mummy?'

Just when Daisy had thought Oliver was asleep his hoarse voice spiralled down the stairs.

'I want a drink of water. My head hurts.'

He was sweating now. That must mean the fever was breaking. Daisy lifted the hot little head and held the glass to the parched lips. Surely his eyes were not glittering quite so much?

At that moment she would have sold her soul for a thermometer, but Joshua had refused to have one in the house, telling Daisy that it was a known fact that children were constantly either up or down, feverish one minute and back to normal the next. He had said that the constant checking of a child's temperature was the sign of an over-anxious mother, and that a thermometer would mean a doctor would never be off the doorstep.

Daisy looked across at Sally fast asleep in her own bed, the corners of her mouth turned up as if she knew that tomorrow would be another day when teachers smiled on her, and the bigger girls at school squabbled for the privilege of walking round the playground holding her hand. Treating her like a doll. Daisy had long ago accepted the fact that her daughter would never be really naughty because she couldn't be bothered to step out of line; that her feelings ran no deeper than a dried-up stream.

She turned back to Oliver, felt his forehead again and decided his temperature had shot up in the last minute.

'Mummy? Can I go in your bed?'

That had always been the ritual when either of the children was off colour. Sally, prone to mysterious short-lived fevers, had spent many, many nights curled up on Daisy's knees in bed, facing the window, like spoons in a box. Only to wake up the next morning well enough to eat her breakfast.

Oliver was far too big to be carried, but Daisy managed it somehow rather than risk him catching further cold by walking bare-footed on the oilcloth covering all the upstairs rooms.

He asked for another drink of water, but when Daisy supported his head and held the cup to his lips, his teeth jittered against the rim.

Terrified, she laid him back against the pillows, tucked the blankets up close round his neck, thought of double pneumonia, yellow fever and illnesses so mind-shattering she dare not put a name to them. She took her nightdress through into the freezing bathroom, so that when she came up to bed she could wash and undress in there without disturbing him. She thought she heard him moan, but when she went back to him he was blessedly asleep, curled up in the middle of the bed.

As snug as a bug in a rug, Daisy told herself firmly, putting a match to a night-light standing in a saucer and placing it on the bedside table. Downstairs she banked up the living-room fire with slack. Tomorrow, if Oliver was still poorly, she would light a fire in the bedroom fireplace with its iron canopy. The grate was very tiny but she would carry a shovel of burning coals up from the living-room fire, remembering to walk backwards so that the flames and smoke trailed away from her.

She remembered lying in bed as a child, seeing her father come backwards into the room to tip his fiery burden into the grate, before kneeling down and putting the blower up to give it a chance to draw before he piled fresh coal on top. She remembered watching little flecks of smuts dancing round the room.

Having a fire in her bedroom was like living in Buckingham Palace. Lying in bed like a princess with the flames dancing on the walls and washing them to a warm apricot shade. Oliver could sit up and have his precious cars on a tray. She would make him egg custards to slip down his sore throat and nourishing beef tea to build him up.

David's father, old Doctor Armitage, had a reputation for prescribing a marvellous tonic bottle, made up by his own dispenser. It was a clear ruby-red and tasted of raspberries.

'Shake it up first,' he used to say to Oliver, 'but if you forget, just stand on your head for a few minutes. That should do the trick.'

David hadn't believed in tonics. 'Old-fashioned clap-trap,' he'd told Joshua once when Daisy was in the room. 'Good food gives all the body needs, and if the appetite needs stimulating then go without food for a while. You won't starve.'

But he nearly had starved out there in the heat swamps. Daisy drew his last letter towards her and read it through again.

Daisy, Very dear Daisy,
Yesterday a few of us from the hospital drove out to George Washington's house at Mount Vernon. I saw the outbuildings where the slaves used to sleep in wooden bunks. It was said that George Washington was embarrassed when he first saw their condition.

I think I've mentioned Donna Silver to you before. She's a dietician at the hospital. She's Jewish. Escaped with her brother from Berlin in the late thirties, leaving her parents to follow on by the same route. She smuggled jewellery to give them a start over here. They had converted all they possessed into diamonds. Well, the sad thing is that her parents never got here – they were both sent to Belsen and to make the tragedy even worse, Donna's brother died six months after he got here, from a bone marrow disease. Yet she's an amazing girl, completely without bitterness. To look at her you'd think her life had been totally uneventful.

I am working very hard. Staying most nights at the hospital. The Coogans say there's no point in me finding a place of my own as I'd never be in it. I think they quite like having me around. Kitty mothers me, and Ben is teaching me to play golf at the weekends. The weather is still like a coolish English summer's day, with blue skies and sunshine that fills every corner of the house.

I miss you and look forward to receiving your letters. I am beginning to know all the people you describe. Who is this chappie who lets Oliver help him round his garage? Ought I to be jealous of him?

All my love as ever,
David

P.S. Hope the shop is going well.

Dear David,

I'm beginning to think the shop was a mistake. I didn't spend enough time *thinking* about the possibilities. I took too much on myself, as Joshua was always telling me I was too fond of doing. I am still filling in forms, still waiting for my first delivery of chocolates and sweets. Maybe they think I am not capable of taking a pair of scissors and cutting tiny coupons from a ration book. Most of the time I bake for orders and this is the exciting part. I am getting a reputation as a freelance *travelling* cook, catering for coffee mornings and afternoon teas, birthday celebrations, anniversaries – you know the sort of thing. I arrive with the food plus my pinny and take over completely. Talk about how the other half lives –

Daisy paused, put down her pen to go to the foot of the stairs and listen intently. Satisfied that Oliver was obviously fast asleep, she went back to her letter.

That last sentence was a bit stupid. David would *know* how the other half lived. Mrs T had told her that his mother had been a wealthy woman in her own right. 'Came from a long line of mill owners,' she'd said. 'It stands to reason when you see Orchard House and remember it was only their holiday home.'

Daisy picked up her pen again, frowned into the fire, tried to think of something sparkling to say, and gave up. It was impossible to concentrate when she was so worried about Oliver; impossible to unburden herself to David when he was so far away. For a moment she tortured herself by imagining him coming into the cottage, running upstairs, taking Oliver's temperature, sounding his chest, examining him for spots and pronouncing him a bit of a fraud.

It was no use. She would finish the letter tomorrow when Oliver was sitting up and taking notice. She would get some goose grease from the farm and rub his chest with it. Old Doctor Marsden in Blackburn had sworn by it for most complaints.

As she put her writing things away in the sideboard drawer the last sentence in David's letter caught her eye.

'Ought I to be jealous of him?'

311

Even with no one there to see, Daisy felt a blush as hot as a scald creep up from her neck. She slammed the drawer on the half-written letter, and went to put the fireguard round the fire. If Oliver was no better she'd have the doctor to him first thing in the morning.

Oliver slept through the night, with Daisy lying rigid and wakeful beside him, but when he got out of bed the next morning to go to the bathroom across the landing, he fell flat on his face.

'My legs are tired,' he whimpered, and when he wept because he'd wet his pyjama trousers it was as much as Daisy could do to keep her voice calm and a reassuring smile on her face.

She stood at the cottage door waiting for the children to come past on their way to school. She handed Sally over to a big girl and asked her to give a note to Oliver's teacher. Right on cue Mrs T appeared from her front door.

'That little lad's not looked so well for a day or two,' she told Daisy, and yes, she would come and take a look at him, though it was a well-known fact children could be down one minute and tucking into their dinner the next.

'I'll tell you what,' she said. 'Old Mary Awkwright visits that potty old man who lives at the end cottage. She comes once a month to cut his toenails, and I know it's today because his daughter-in-law told me she personally wouldn't touch his feet with a brush handle! She says his feet are black as coal and his toenails as hard and yellow as their piano keys. She says he's taken to wearing his flat cap in bed. Old age is very sad, isn't it, even if it comes to us all in the end.'

'Who is Mary Awkwright?' Daisy interrupted.

Oliver had opened his eyes and stared at Mrs T as if he didn't know who she was. As if he had never seen her in his life before. His temperature was up again – she would swear to it.

'*Nurse* Awkwright,' Mrs T said, swivelling her eyes up to the ceiling and down again. 'She should be retired, but what with the war and everything she carried on. She's about seventy and skens like a basket of whelks, but she's as good as any doctor. Hang about a bit and I'll see if her bike's outside the end house. She comes about this time, regular as clockwork.'

Daisy watched her run with a waddling motion down the long length of the cottages, pom-pommed bedroom slippers on her feet, heedless of the drifting mist of rain. She felt drained by the much older woman's vitality, even as she accepted that most of it was derived from an obsessive interest in other people's affairs.

As she stood there, Mrs T turned into the end cottage and Bill went past in his van. If he had seen her he gave no sign, just drove on as if he was in a hurry to get somewhere fast.

'She's coming!' Mrs T shouted, waddling back along the narrow footpath. 'I'd heard the old fella wasn't able to hold his water and it must be true. You can smell ammonia before you've set a foot over the doorstep. No wonder she's forever washing. And that reminds me, I haven't had Bill Tattersall's washing yet this week. I've just seen him drive past looking scruffy. Men living on their own often let themselves go.'

Nurse Awkwright was the ugliest woman Daisy had ever seen. She had a profile like that of an emaciated Roman emperor, with a hawk-like nose hooked over a flourishing moustache. But she stood by Oliver's bed and looked down on him with a tender compassion that brought a lump to Daisy's throat.

'You're not feeling so gradely this morning, are you, pet?' She slipped an arm behind Oliver's back and raised him gently. She folded the bedclothes back and tested his reflexes with gentle hands, then she bent his fingers one by one.

'Has he been to the swimming baths?' She stood by the fire in the living room, beady eyes darting round the room. Missing nothing. 'Have you taken him to the pictures? Round crowded shops? Has he complained of aching limbs?'

Fear took hold of Daisy. She felt it trickle the full length of her spine. She refused to allow her thoughts to take her down a road so terrible her whole being screamed away from it. She had seen the hoardings and the warnings in the newspapers, telling people to stay away from swimming baths and public places. But that was in September. The danger was past. The epidemic was over. She wasn't the only mother who had said thankful prayers that her own children had been spared.

'I'm going to cycle straight down to the doctor's surgery.' Nurse Awkwright was buttoning up her coat. 'Mind if I go through into the kitchen and wash my hands?'

'Will the doctor come this morning?' Daisy followed her to the door, the fear a lead weight in her chest. She couldn't put her terror into words.

She just stared at the nurse, her face tense. 'You think he's got something bad, don't you?'

'Good gracious me, pet. I'm taking the right precautions, that's all. They call me Wary Mary round these parts. I'd rather make a fool of myself than be sorry afterwards.' She mounted her bike with a flourish. 'Don't worry, now. Children are . . .'

'Up one minute and down the next,' Daisy finished for her, going inside, closing the door and leaning against it.

And now the word she couldn't bring herself to say burst from her like a volcano erupting:

314

'Infantile paralysis!' Poliomyelitis, as it was called now. She remembered with a vivid clarity the outbreak in 1943. A little girl whose mother ran a boarding house across the street had caught it, but they didn't know how infectious it was then because the child had been put in the children's ward. The terrible creeping illness had taken its toll of the whole of her body, even her lungs, so that at the end of a week she had stopped struggling for breath and died.

Mrs MacDougal next door had said what a blessing that was, as she knew a boy who would have to be wheeled out in a reclining bathchair for the rest of his life after contracting the disease. 'It's as if he'd a boil on his spine,' she'd explained. 'An *inflammation*. If it festers and doesn't burst the poison spreads all through the body, but if it discharges there's a chance.'

Daisy ran upstairs and stood by the bed, forcing herself to smile down at Oliver.

The smile was wasted as his eyes were closed. Daisy leaned closer to him. His breathing was very shallow. She pulled down the bedclothes. His chest was hardly moving at all. She could hear someone letting themself in at the back door and knew it was Mrs T come to hear what the nurse had had to say. She ran downstairs.

'She's gone to fetch the doctor.' Panic shrilled Daisy's usually quiet voice. 'She thinks he's got something serious.'

Bertha thought that little Mrs Penny looked dreadful, but she wasn't going to say so. It was sad that she had no one of her own to turn to at a time like this. She was nobbut a lass herself when all was said and done.

'Now don't go jumping the gun.' She almost pressed Daisy down into a chair. 'I'll go through and put the kettle on. There's never a time when a nice cup of tea doesn't fit the bill. You wait till you see the doctor. He's a right bobby-dazzler, though what he ever saw in his

wife I've never been able to fathom. She's got a face on
her like the back of a fishcart.'

The minute the doctor finished his examination of
Oliver he went straight through into the bathroom.
Daisy followed him holding out a clean towel. She
wished with all her heart he was David who would
have broken the news to her gently. Old Doctor
Marsden from Blackburn would have talked round
things before frightening her to death by coming too
quickly to the point.

'He must go straight to the fever hospital,' this strangely impersonal man said, dropping the towel into the
bath, running downstairs in front of Daisy. 'I'll go back
to the surgery and telephone. I don't suppose . . .' He
looked round vaguely.

'No. I'm not on the telephone.' Daisy was so agitated
she didn't know what she was saying. 'It's infantile
paralysis, isn't it?'

'Poliomyelitis.' The doctor's voice was brisk. 'A classic
example, I'm afraid.' At the door he became suddenly
human. 'I've seen worse cases, Mrs Penny. Your little
boy's a fighter. He'll pull through.' He glanced at his
watch. 'Sorry to seem to be rushing away, but I've left
a full surgery.' Halfway down the short path he turned
round. 'Any other children in the house?'

'My small daughter.'

He nodded. 'I'll keep an eye on her. Try not to worry.
But keep her home from school.'

'Is there an even chance she'll get it?' Daisy thought
she was going to be sick. She was sure she would be sick
right then and there, standing by the doctor like his
shadow, only just controlling the urge she had to catch
hold of his coat sleeve. Beg him to promise her that all
would be well.

'Going by statistics I'd say she won't get it.' He opened

the car door. 'We don't know enough about it yet, but your little boy will have every attention.' He touched Daisy's shoulder, and she saw all at once that he wasn't an unfeeling man, just overworked and tired. Doing the best he could.

She went with Oliver in the ambulance, sitting opposite to him next to a nurse wearing her cloak and trying not to yawn.

'Night duty,' she explained. 'I should have gone off duty hours ago. God alone knows what time I'll get to bed.' She shivered and pulled the cloak closer round her throat. 'But I don't mind. Especially when it's children'.

Nurses had to be like that, Daisy reminded herself. Cool and detached, seemingly uncaring at times. Or how could they bear it? The nurse was taking Oliver's pulse now, holding her hand against his face, smoothing his hair back.

If he dies then I will die, Daisy thought, all control swept away. If anybody tells me he's gone up to heaven to join his father, I'll be sick. She stared blindly through the window, knowing that no one could see in, and it looked as if the ambulance was standing still while hedges rushed past them in a blur of green.

'Nearly there.' The nurse smiled. 'Try not to worry, dear. He'll be in the best place. The doctor will have a word with you before you go back home. Just to settle your mind.'

They allowed her to look in at Oliver through a tall outside window. She stood on a gravel path, alone, hardly feeling the cold which numbed her face and brought tears to her eyes. He was in a two-bedded room, small and defenceless in a high white bed. They had told her she could come back later in the day. They had asked her for the number of her nearest telephone and without pausing to think she gave them Bill's.

The doctor she had seen for a brief moment had said that while it was too early to be sure, the signs were good. Oliver was breathing of his own volition, and there was movement in both his arms. But the doctor hadn't mentioned his legs, and Daisy was too scared to want to know the truth.

There were two nurses and a doctor round his bed. Everything that could be done was being done. She was superfluous standing there on the windy hill outside the great gaunt hospital that had once been the dreaded workhouse. There was nothing she could do.

Daisy turned to walk away. Looking down at her feet she saw she was still wearing her slippers, realized that underneath her coat she was still wearing her apron. And knew that none of it mattered. Nothing in the whole wide world mattered but that small face on the white hospital pillow, that young body fighting to go on living.

She stood at the stop down the hill from the hospital, waiting for the bus that would take her to catch her connection direct to the village. Every moment that passed seemed like an hour. At this rate she would no sooner get back than she would have to start off again. She asked a woman in a shaggy sheepskin coat when the next bus was due. She was told she'd just missed one and that the next wasn't due for at least twenty-five minutes.

'The bus drivers form card-schools back at the garage,' the woman said. 'Sometimes there's two buses come together. You'd never guess we'd won the war, would you? I'm not sticking up for the Germans, God forbid, but at least they ran on time. I once went by train to the Black Forest with my hubby, and the trains were that punctual they'd have made Big Ben look like a rotten timekeeper.' She smiled. 'I'm looking forward to listening to the wedding on the wireless next week, aren't you?'

'Wedding?' The face Daisy turned to her was as blank as an unused piece of blotting paper. '*Wedding?*'

The woman moved on, sure she was talking to a barmpot.

With every part of her Daisy willed the bus to come, concentrating so hard she could almost see its red bulk lumbering towards her, hear the conductor ring his bell as she swung herself on to the boarding platform. Imagined herself explaining to a bewildered Sally that she had to go out again.

When the car drew up at the kerb she thought at first that it too was a figment of her imagination.

'Get in!' Bill leaned across the passenger seat and opened the door. He could hardly bear to look at her anxious face with all the normal vivacity wiped from it. When Mrs T had told him about Oliver he had felt an upsurge of unreasonable exasperation.

'Of all the obstinate, stupid women! She really takes the biscuit.' He had handed over his bundle of washing and made for the door. 'All she needed to do was to *ask*. I'd have followed the ambulance and brought her back. She knew I was about. She saw me drive by on my way back to the garage. But no! She'd lay her guts on the line for anybody needing help, but can she stretch out a hand herself?' He looked through the window to where Sally, in wellingtons and red pixie-hood, solemnly scattered corn for Bertha's scrawny hens. 'At least she's got you, Mrs T.'

Bertha followed him out to the front. There was some kind of situation going on she couldn't quite tune in to. She knew that Bill had taken Daisy out with him in his car yesterday, and gone into the cottage with her when they came back. But he hadn't stopped long because she'd heard the door slam not long after.

She flickered her puffy eyelids up and down. Today he was as mad as blazes with Daisy about something. Bertha began to put two and two together, coming up with an intriguing five. If she had sprouted antennae from the top of her head they would be quivering like reeds in a high wind.

She studied Bill's face carefully. 'It's a crying shame her doctor friend is so far away. He'd have been over like a flash. There's another letter waiting for her when she gets back from the hospital. He must write at least three or four times a week.'

Not a flicker of any kind of emotion passed across Bill's face. He hadn't shaved that morning though he was, in Bertha's opinion, one of those men who should shave twice a day to look decent. 'It upset me seeing her going off on her own in the ambulance with that little lad looking so poorly. I would have gone with her willingly if I hadn't been lumbered with t'other one.'

'How is the little lass taking it all?'

'Well, if she's bothered she's saying nowt.' Bertha jerked her head back towards the house. 'She's got an old head on her shoulders. I wouldn't have the responsibility of that one when she grows up, not for a gold clock.'

Bill got into his car, nodded briefly and roared off down the road, turning the bend before Bertha had time to ask him where he was going in such a hurry. She waddled back into the house. As if she didn't know! It was as plain as the nose on your face that he was off to the fever hospital to fetch Daisy home. Whipping off her apron she went to the back door and called Sally inside. She'd take her for a walk as far as the post office and back. Her friend Mrs Smith usually had a bit of a break about this time.

Bill was calming down a bit now he had found Daisy. She sat beside him in the passenger seat clutching a worn leather purse. The two front side pieces of her hair were anchored to her cheeks with kirby grips, and he wanted to stretch out a hand and remove them for her to save her even the slightest embarrassment when she realized she'd left them in. It was surprising how well he knew her. She was endearingly vain, for instance. He knew she wore glasses, but he'd never seen her in them. As if it would have mattered. Proud, too. She was fighting back the tears now; he could tell by the way she had her chin lifted away from the fur-trimmed collar of her speckled tweed coat.

'How is Oliver?'

She told him, averting her face as she did so. 'You found out about it from Mrs T?'

She tried to laugh but it turned into a little sob. 'She's really very kind. She has a good heart. But you soon learn not to tell her anything you wouldn't mind the whole world knowing.'

'Oliver will be all right, lass,' Bill told her. 'He's a tough little chap. He'll be all right. You'll see.'

Held up at the traffic lights, squeezed into the kerb by a double decker Ribble bus, he glanced sideways and saw that she was crying softly, making no sound at all.

Chapter Seven

The first thing Daisy did when they got back to the cottage was to pick up the letter from the mat.

'It's from David,' she said unnecessarily.

Bill saw the tapestry-worked spectacle case on the mantelpiece, and handed it over.

'Put these on. You'll see it better,' he said. 'I'll go through and put the kettle on.'

'He's coming over for Christmas!' She sat down at the square table and spread out the one-page letter in front of her, smoothing the folds in the blue notepaper. 'Flying this time,' she said, 'because he can't spare too much time from his work at the hospital.'

Bill noticed that her face had lost its frozen look. There was colour in her cheeks again and her voice held a tinge of hope.

'When the children were young David's *father* was their doctor, but they'd just got used to David before he went away again.' Her lips trembled. 'He had a way of coming into the house and running upstairs, and somehow you knew that everything was going to be okay.'

'Are you going to tell him about Oliver?'

'Not till . . . not till I know he's going to be all right. It would be cruel when there's nothing David can do. He's three thousand miles away, you know.'

When he saw the way her lips trembled again, Bill had to turn away. 'Don't cry,' he mumbled, fiddling with the box of matches at the stove, opening and shutting it and spilling a few of them on the floor. 'By the time David comes over at Christmas, Oliver will be home as lively as a cricket. You can have this thing bad or you can have it mild. You said yourself the doctor told you he was breathing all right. That means his lungs aren't affected.'

'But his legs are!' Daisy pushed the letter away from her and buried her face in her hands. 'He couldn't walk a step this morning. He told me last night his legs were wobbly and I thought he was putting it on. Since his father died he's changed a lot. He never used to be mean to Sally, but there are some days I think he hates her.'

'Normal.' Bill threw the box of matches down on the small table by the side of the gas cooker. 'It's just his way of showing her who's boss.'

'He's such a funny little boy, really. Shy, and yet determined to make himself join in with things. I was once outside the railings of the school playground without him knowing I was there. He was walking about with his hands in his pockets, whistling. All on his own. It almost broke my heart. I know that little girls are supposed to be softer and sweeter, but there's nothing quite as vulnerable as a small boy desperately trying to be tough.'

'I know . . .' Bill nodded. 'I know . . .'

At once her head came up, and she stared at him in silence for a full minute. 'Oh, Bill. Forgive me. I've been so full of myself and my own trouble, I'd forgotten about yesterday. How awful of me not to realize . . .'

'I'll pick you up early on, after tea.' As he walked past the table Bill pressed his hand into her shoulder. 'An' don't go saying you'll go on the bus because they're all full up at that time with factory workers.' He flicked the letter with his finger. 'I know *he'd* take you, but he's not here, is he?'

'I've come to say I'll see to Sally while you're at the hospital tonight.' Minnie Rostron had bumped into Bill as he was on his way out. 'Mrs Tomlinson tells me she's going to the pictures with her friend, Mrs Smith.' She placed a round familiar-looking tin on the table. 'I know that baking will be the last thing on your mind, so I've made you a batch of scones.' She prised off the lid and looked at them doubtfully. 'They're nicer toasted, I often find.'

She was wearing a hat like a chamber-pot with a cerise ribbon round it in moiré silk. Goodness shone from every contour of her angular face. She didn't give much for Oliver's chances of ever being the same, even if he lived. Her husband had buried three local children at the height of the forty-three epidemic, and the one who had lived dragged a useless leg behind him, supported by an ugly calliper.

Daisy Penny seemed so *alone* somehow. Mrs Tomlinson had said that the only relatives she talked about were an elderly aunt and uncle from Blackburn, and that her fiancé was across the sea. *Fiancé*? When Minnie had looked surprised, Mrs Tomlinson had confided that Mr Penny had been on his last for years and that the doctor was the one who tended him in his death throes. She said surely Minnie remembered the Armitages who used Orchard House for holidays and weekends? The boy had been a real turk, into everything, scrumping apples then swearing they were windfalls. But it turned out he'd been a prisoner of the Japs in the war, so thin he looked as if he'd been spoke-shaved. In her opinion Daisy Penny was jumping from the frying pan into the fire taking another half-wick fella on. But it wasn't for her to say, of course.

Minnie wished there was something she could do for Daisy. Some comfort she could give. Some way she could *promise* her that everything would be all right and that the little boy would be one of the lucky ones and get away unscathed, his limbs untouched by the dreaded paralysis. She would tell Daisy she was praying for Oliver, saying he was in God's good hands.

But she had thought her own boy was in God's good hands till the telegram came after Dunkirk, hadn't she? She wished with all her heart she had the uncomplicated simplistic faith of her husband.

'No fear. No doubts. Trust in Jesus,' he was always saying. As though it was as easy as that. He often used that phrase as the theme for his sermons. She would sit there in the high-backed pew, staring at him as though she were drinking in every word. All the time wondering if the dinner would turn out all right, or whether she'd dash into the rectory after the service was over and find it shrivelled to a frazzle.

'Don't be too independent,' she said before she left, giving a last anxious glance at the round tin on the table. The scone she'd tried had definitely tasted of bicarbonate of soda, though a pinch was all she'd given them. Still there were pinches and *pinches*, she supposed, hurrying down the road, wishing she didn't always feel so inadequate.

'Well, of course folks rally round. They always do in this part of the country. It comes natural.'

Bill had picked her up exactly as planned, settling her into the passenger seat, tucking a small tartan rug round her knees. At the hospital he stood gravely beside her as a doctor explained that Oliver was holding his own, that he was breathing normally and that while they were concerned about his lower limbs, the rest of him gave no cause for alarm.

'Do you think he knows we're here?'

They stood outside the tall window looking in on the small room where Oliver lay almost concealed by a large cradle which had lifted the sheets and blankets well away from his legs. A grey-haired nurse sat by his bed, so still that it looked as if she were asleep with her eyes fully open.

'She looks too old to be working.' Daisy stood on tiptoe to see better. 'She must be seventy if she's a day.' Daisy worried in case the still figure by the bed was really asleep. 'She hasn't moved a muscle.'

For twenty minutes they stood there with the wind freezing their ankles and turning their faces blue with cold. There was no point in it really, Bill knew that, but he could understand Daisy's reluctance to tear herself away. There were couples standing together outside every single window along the length of the north side of the big stone building. Bill saw a man in a flat cap gently lead his sobbing wife away, while further down two middle-aged women, thrown into soft focus by the light from the window, bowed their heads over their joined hands in prayer. It was terrible. It was *unreal*, like a scene from a film. Up there on the exposed hillside they stood enclosed in a cold clammy mist. He could see nothing else but the vast outline of the old workhouse with its illuminated windows. All that mattered was the frieze of silent couples standing motionless.

Often when he had walked the fells in an all-enfolding mist, Bill had felt as if the earthly cloud sharpened his senses, making him as alert as a sprinter waiting for the sound of the starting gun. Now, at that moment, he could see his *own* young son, not Daisy's, lying in the high white bed.

The lines on his forehead deepened. But it wouldn't be *him* standing there sending out waves of hope and prayer. He wouldn't even be told that his son was ill. Because he, Bill Tattersall, was the kind of man who could give his son away.

He had no choice! The words almost burst from him

as the bleakness of the surroundings pressed down on him. Only his concern for Daisy stopped him from walking away into the darkness, down the long hospital drive and into what he saw in his misery as the real world where healthy people laughed and talked, and where children knew their own fathers from the day they were born.

'Your mummy and daddy came to see you, dear.'

The grey-haired nurse laid her finger on Oliver's wrist and peered down at the fob-watch pinned to her starched apron. 'When they come tomorrow we must turn our heads and give them a smile and a wave.'

'My daddy is dead.'

Oliver closed his eyes again, missing seeing the look of consternation on the kindly red face. A look that he would have taken full advantage of if his head hadn't been hurting so much, and if he hadn't felt so tired and sleepy.

Bill saw Daisy into the cottage then drove away, refusing her invitation to go inside for a bowl of the warming soup she said wouldn't take a second to heat up. He left the car at the garage and walked away, turning up the fell road, hands thrust deep in the pockets of his jacket, his beret pulled low over his forehead.

If ever he needed to think clearly the time was now, so deliberately he walked up and up the steep hill until the mist no longer lay like a blanket, but trailed long scarves across his path.

Two miles further on he heard a stream rushing in furious torrent. Trees, battered by the recent gales, scattered their branches so that he tripped, cursed, and fought his way on, all the time gradually ascending. Feeling the springy turf respond like a sponge to his feet.

He had climbed this way many times in daylight. He had stopped and looked down, past the stone-built farmhouses to his village, huddled in its hollow, the church spire no bigger than a bodkin. Down there in the crumbling cottage with its overgrown garden Daisy would be sitting alone. No, not *sitting*. 'Getting on with things,' as she always said. Working at speed, moving from one room to another; going to bed at last to lie awake and worry about Oliver and how it was going to be for him.

Or writing a letter, making light of everything because the good doctor had suffered enough and must not be worried. Protecting him, shielding him, when all the time it was *she* who should be cherished, *she* who needed a man's arms round her, holding her safe.

He walked on, feeling the mist now like a cold creeping shroud wrapping him around. The vague outline of a hill-farm came through it, and as he came closer he saw that it was deserted, that whoever had lived there had gone away leaving a bedraggled shirt hanging on the clothesline in the yard. In the gloom and mist the shirt looked for all the world like a body drooping limply, headless in the gloom.

He was so wet that the state of being wet no longer registered with him. He had long passed the limit of feeling hungry or even cold, but he knocked loudly on the rickety farmhouse door, standing with head lowered as if he expected to hear the shuffle of feet coming towards him.

'You mean you slept all night long up yon? Nay, gaffir, it's a wonder tha's not cotched treble pneumonia.'

Old Eli had good reason for thinking the world of Bill Tattersall. He knew that at his age he should have retired years ago, that the time for putting his feet up had long since come and gone. He also knew that a week at home all day with his missus was more than flesh and blood could stand. Eli's wife kept to a routine so rigid that Eli had once had a duster shaken over him when he happened to find himself in the line of duty for the day. There was no room for him in that inflexible timetable, and he knew it.

Anyroad, what would the gaffir do without *him* there to answer the telephone and take messages? He could still get down on his knees and change a wheel, even if getting up again was a bit of a job.

Eli didn't like the look of the gaffir that morning. What the 'eck had he been thinking of, playing Boy Scouts up yon on a night cold enough to freeze the . . . He hesitated, remembering he'd been to church last Sunday . . . the *ears* off a man? Lighting a fire with the sticks left by the last tramp to take shelter there, and lying on the stone floor till it came light enough to find his way down to the bottom of the hill again.

There was something up. Eli chewed on the damp butt of a cigarette, rolling it from one side of his mouth to the other. Women's tittle-tattle wasn't for him, but he was in half a mind to ask his missus if she'd heard anything. The missus was a crony of Herbert Smith's wife at the post office. She in turn was a crony of that old bat Bertha Tomlinson.

Turning his head swiftly to the right, Eli spat out a shred or two of soggy tobacco. He reckoned *that* woman knew more about folks round here than what God did.

The Hon Mrs Singleton from Fold House sat in Daisy's cottage by the fire, toasting her knees.

'Just like an ordinary person,' Daisy could almost hear her mother saying. 'But then that's proper gentry for you. It's the jumped-up ones who put on all the airs and graces.'

'I came,' the Hon Mrs Singleton was saying, 'because

329

I heard about your little boy being taken to the fever hospital, and I wanted to tell you that under no consideration must you worry about the little finger-buffet I was giving for a few friends when we listen to the wireless on The Wedding Day.'

'Oh, yes. The Royal Wedding . . .'

Poor little Mrs Penny looked so apathetic, so numbed, most unlike her normal cheery self, Jane Singleton hardly recognized her. Surely she understood that to provide food from her kitchen at such a time was out of the question? Two of her friends had children of their own and though one knew very little about the dreadful disease – and thank God for that – it must be highly infectious, otherwise why the fever hospital? The medical profession had obviously discovered something fresh since the forty-three epidemic. She clearly remembered two of the village children being put in the children's ward in the cottage hospital.

'I was going to let you know I wouldn't be doing the buffet.' Daisy looked as if she were forcing herself to sit still. 'I've closed my little shop too.'

The Hon Mrs Singleton gathered her handbag and gloves together. Daisy studied her quite dispassionately. She had always believed, in her avid reading of the fashion pages in magazines, that a woman couldn't go wrong with good leather bag, shoes and gloves. But there was the Honourable Lady in her mustard tweeds and Robin Hood hat. Going wrong with a vengeance.

'You are in your element,' Bill said peevishly, 'coming through that door with a bowl of broth in a covered basket. Like Lady Bountiful dispensing succour to the old and needy.'

'You're not needy,' Daisy said, prising the lid off a round dish and revealing chicken soup with fresh vegetables, its surface glistening with golden globules of goodness. 'Anyway, you caught this chesty cold standing with me outside the hospital. So what else could I do?'

Before he could even begin to say he didn't want the soup thank you very much, she was tucking a linen napkin underneath his chin, sitting beside him on his bed, ordering him to open his mouth.

'I don't want . . .' he began, only to find his mouth full of the delicious-tasting broth.

He wasn't going to enlighten her as to where he had really picked up what he was sure was a bad dose of flu bordering on pneumonia. Only old Eli knew, and Bill could trust the man to keep his mouth shut. But Bill alone knew what had happened during the long night when he had lain there, listening to the wind howling round the deserted farmhouse and the rain pelting down outside. Out of the darkness had come his troubled thoughts, like ghosts, uncertain at first . . . The firelight had cast dancing shadows on the low ceiling and towards dawn he had said a last painful goodbye to his little boy. Some day maybe, when the boy was older and could think for himself, he would want to seek out his father, to discover exactly who he was. His youthful grandfather had told Bill to think of himself as no more than the *biological* father. And this he had to accept for the undoubted truth it happened to be.

'You're ill,' Daisy had told him when he turned up as usual to run her to the hospital. 'You're running a temperature.'

'I'm not,' he'd replied, furious with her for noticing.

That was the night the Sister had told her Oliver was improving steadily. 'You'll have him home for Christmas,' she'd said proudly, as if she'd arranged it herself.

'You're going to have yourself a very merry Christmas,' Bill said gloomily, standing outside the hospital in the cold, shivering, coughing, but swearing he felt in the pink.

'You're *ill*,' Daisy had told him again. 'Why don't you admit it?'

'I am *not*,' he'd said, buckling at the knees.

Now, after three days of being ministered to, he looked dreadful, Daisy thought. But not as dreadful as he had that night when she'd helped him to bed and poured whisky and hot milk down his throat, piled all the blankets she could find on his bed, and left him to sweat it out.

'Men,' she told him, wiping the soup from his chin with the clean white napkin she'd brought with her, 'are downright infantile when they're ill. No wonder your throat's sore, old Eli told me it should be red raw from shouting orders out to him. Bossing him about.'

'I've a bidness to run,' Bill said down his nose. 'I'm detting up tomorrow.'

On the wireless the commentator's voice was suitably hushed, his tones dulcet. He whispered that the trumpeters in their scarlet and gold were like a medieval painting. 'And now the glorious fanfare heralds the Bridal March,' he breathed.

'Through here,' Daisy told the ambulance man, who was carrying Oliver into the cottage in his arms. 'On the sofa.'

'A fairy-tale princess,' the wireless breathed. 'Wearing a fairy-tale gown spun from silver moonbeams.'

Daisy switched off the wireless. To be polite.

'He's not English,' the ambulance man said, depositing Oliver carefully on the settee drawn up at right angles to the blazing fire. 'Greek origin,' his mate said, following in with a small walking frame. 'Mountbatten's not his proper name.'

332

'Mountbatten's his uncle's name.'

'Oh, aye?'

They touched the neb of their navy-blue caps, thanked Daisy for her offer of a warming drink but explained that they'd best be on their way.

'There's a physiotherapist coming this afternoon,' Daisy told them. 'Thank you,' she said. 'Thank you very much.'

'Looks like Big Flossie's not waited till this afternoon.' The driver jerked his chin at a small car drawing up behind the ambulance. 'She's not wasted much time, has she?'

'Aren't you listening to the wedding?' Big Flossie Bates had prune-coloured badly dyed hair, hands like ham shanks and a habit of adding a slosh of brandy to every cup of tea she drank. 'Want some?' She proffered the small bottle to Daisy over the first cup of tea. 'Gives it a bit of a bite. You can forget it's tea you're drinking.' She stored the flask away in her bag, and winked. 'It works just the same with coffee or cocoa.'

As she massaged Oliver's legs with olive oil, he began to utter piteous little cries, so she told him how brave he was. She swore that her last patient had shinned up the bookcase and sat there hollering his head off. And that was before she'd removed her coat! She showed Daisy how to massage from the ankles upwards, with smooth firm strokes, three times a day without fail. And she said she would pop in every day till he was able to run up Pendle Hill without stopping to catch breath.

She gave the walking frame a lip-curling glance and said the best place for it was the muck-heap down the bottom of the garden. When Daisy remarked on the thinness of Oliver's legs she said another of her patients had legs so thin when he came out of hospital that his mother mistook them for her knitting needles and used them to cast on a jumper.

The little dog jumped on to the settee with Oliver, burrowing its way down underneath the blanket.

'Best thing out for him,' she said. 'He'll be chasing – what's his name? – Jasper, round the garden before long. One of my patients only started to get better when he began sleeping with his Alsatian again.' She followed Daisy through into the kitchen, making sure she had the portmanteau-like bag with her.

Daisy lowered her voice to a whisper. 'You really think he will walk normally again? They seemed evasive at the hospital. I'd like the truth. *Please*, Miss Bates.'

The wide nostrils flared. 'Oh, well, if we're going to take any notice of that lot up the fever hospital we might as well have him measured for a couple of callipers straight away. Faith and massage, that's the answer, Mrs Penny. I'll come and do the early one and you can carry on.' She accepted a second cup of tea, opened her bag and took out the flask. 'And a little drop of this now and again.'

When they went back into the living room Oliver was fast asleep with Jasper's head on his chest. Daisy's heart contracted as she looked down at the thin little face and the blue-veined hands. 'I wouldn't have believed how ill he could look in so short a time. Yet the doctor said he'd only had a mild attack.'

Flossie Bates buttoned her navy-blue single-breasted coat up over a massive bolster-shaped bosom. 'You mustn't even think about it. I had one patient so weak he couldn't have brushed a fleck of dandruff off his collar, but by the time I'd finished with him he could have won a medal as the next to the best weight-lifter in the world.' She plodded on plate-sized shoes to the door. '*I'm* the best.'

She drove away leaving Daisy smiling. Before Miss

Bates had arrived the cottage had seemed dark and depressing, the uneven plaster showing on the walls, the low ceilings making her feel claustrophobic and vaguely uneasy. A dank November drizzle had beaded the windows earlier on, but now there was a lightness in the air, a new confidence in her heart. Oliver *would* walk. Miss F. Bates had said so.

Chapter Eight

Oliver was definitely on the mend, but he still walked with a decided and worrying limp, in spite of all the olive oil massaged into his legs by Miss Bates's horny hands. He was a very bad patient, demanding and whining, watching Daisy from half-closed eyes. Making sure she had time for little else than running around after him.

Bill accused her of spoiling Oliver rotten. Twice he had buttoned the pathetic-looking little boy into layers of woollens and taken him out in the van for the day. Bringing him back rosy-cheeked and less clingy for a while.

'Are you my good friend?' he asked Oliver one day. 'I mean my real true buddy?'

'Sure,' Oliver told him, entering into the spirit of it.

'Well, why do you treat your ma like she was your slave? Why don't you go the whole hog and have her tied to a long rope so you can pull on it when you want something? She looks mighty tired to me.'

'She's okay,' Oliver mumbled, looking down at his gloved hands. 'She's okay. Honest Injun.'

'What did you say to him?' Daisy wanted to know. 'He was as good as gold for at least an hour. He actually offered to set the table.' She sighed. 'But the sight of him dragging himself about by clinging to the furniture upset me so much I told him to go and play with his cars again. Have you noticed the way he turns his right ankle inwards?'

'I've noticed his limp improves dramatically at certain times.'

'What certain times?' Daisy's eyes opened wide.

'Well, the other day . . .' Bill was watching her carefully. 'Oliver was at a bench in the workshop "helping" old Eli to clean up engine parts with oily rags. I had to check the wheel alignment on a car, which meant I had to lie underneath while someone else sat in the driving seat and moved the steering wheel to my shouted instructions.' He paused, his eyes holding hers. 'So I yelled out to Oliver to help me. He's done it before, and it gives him the feeling he's driving. Now I'm not going to say he *sprinted* across the forecourt, but he was over and into that car as quick as a lick. No sign of a limp.'

For a moment Daisy felt as if she'd been winded. 'Are you trying to tell me that a child that age is devious enough to *pretend* to limp?' Words almost failed her. 'To limp when he feels like it and walk normally when he wants to?' Her voice rose. 'He might just fool me, but have you seen the woman who comes to give him the morning massage? Nobody could get one over on her. She'd *kill* him if she suspected he was playing silly beggars with her. She knows her job, Bill! So flamin' enthusiastic she'd get limb movements from a man with no arms and legs. You expect me to believe Oliver could put one over on her? Not a chance!'

'Now listen . . .' He put out a hand. 'Don't you *want* to believe me?'

'Of *course* I want to believe you.' As tears choked her throat she put her apron to her face.

'Daisygirl . . .' He took a step towards her, but she sensed his intention and moved a step backwards.

'Do you think I enjoy seeing him struggle? It hurts like hell when Sally runs off to school with the other children.' To her everlasting shame she gave a great

337

sob. 'I have to carry him on my back upstairs to bed because I can't bear to see him struggle. I have to watch him sitting on that damned sofa all day long, and I'm scared that when his next appointment at the hospital comes round they're going to fit him with a calliper.' She was sobbing in earnest now. 'And that's the way he's going to be for the rest of his life. Always on the outside, watching other people run and dance and laugh. An' I'll tell you something else. I'm *glad* his father isn't alive to see it, because it would have broken his heart.'

She was tired. She was fighting depression. Last night, as she carried the shovel of burning coals from the downstairs fire up to the bedroom, she had dropped a red-hot cinder on to the stair carpet. By the time she could get to it with the tongs it had burnt a hole as big as a man's fist. Somehow it had seemed like the last straw.

She'd received a statement from her bank manager which showed her that for the first time in her life she was overdrawn. There were a couple of insurance payments to come, but she knew she would have to earn some money and soon. She also accepted that she had made a mess of things, selling the boarding house for less than its market value, then having to pay endless mounting bills for repairs she hadn't even known were necessary.

The cottage she'd bought so unthinkingly was sinking into the ground, she was sure, riddled with its own decay. Ill-fitting windows and doors, every corner of every wall festooned with creeping black fungus, bath water that was such a murky brown she was convinced her skin was changing colour. She looked through the window at a garden overgrown with weeds choking the life out of the decent plants. Trailing virile weeds they were too, absorbing every ounce of vitality from the soil.

For Joshua's sake she had wanted to make the garden a thing of beauty, the way he had planned it. She clenched both hands on the rim of the stone slopstone. But he had died and she had made the fatal error of coming to a snap decision while she was in a state of shock. She had thought she could do it all *alone*. She bowed her head low on to her chest, in that moment of self-awareness almost forgetting the man standing behind her.

Bill knew that if he didn't go away at once he would have her in his arms again. He no longer trusted himself. If he pulled her round to hold her tight she would push him away. His suspicion that Oliver was pulling a fast one had shocked her. She wanted him to be right, but yet in a perverse way she wanted to prove him wrong. She needed time to think, to be alone to ponder on what he'd said. So the kindest thing he could do for her was to go, right now, without as much as a whispered goodbye.

So he left her, an outspoken man, a flash-tongued man, made gentle and soft-spoken by his concern for her. Closing the door quietly behind him for once.

Oliver cried like a baby when Daisy suggested he climb the stairs to bed without help from her. She showed him how to cling to the banister, how to put the good foot up on each step then bring the bad one after it.

'I can't,' he sobbed. 'My leg won't do it. Why won't you carry me, Mummy? It hurts me . . .'

Almost crying herself, she crouched down for him to climb on her back. Up in the bedroom she tried again.

'Bring your pyjama jacket over here, love. It's there

warming by the fire.' She put urgency into her voice. 'Come on! Let's have it on you before it gets cold.'

For a moment she thought she had caught him out, but after an initial swift and automatic reaction he fell into the ugly limp, turning his ankle inwards and swaying from side to side.

'Let's have a cuddle, shall we?' He snuggled himself onto her knee. 'I like having my bed in your room. Sally can't, can she? Sally's not poorly like me.'

Daisy ruffled the wiry dark hair, holding him close. The next time she saw Bill she'd tell him how wrong he was. How cruelly, cruelly wrong.

Downstairs there were a million and one things to do, but the long letter she had decided to write to David couldn't be put off any longer. Soon there would be the Christmas post delays. She'd meant to ask Mrs Smith at the post office for last posting days ages ago. Meant to and done nothing. She sat down at the table and wrote quickly, her writing deteriorating as the words tumbled over each other.

At the end of the letter she wrote:

> So I hope you'll understand why I haven't written lately, and why I didn't write when Oliver first took ill. I was so frightened, David, and I wanted more than anything to tell you. But there was nothing you could do from so far away. The three thousand miles stretched to thirty thousand that awful week.
>
> I wasn't allowed to see him or touch him, only to look at him through a window.

For a moment she put down her pen, picturing the bleak hospital grounds with the wind howling round their grey stone walls. She saw herself standing on the

narrow gravel path with Bill Tattersall by her side, his
shoulders hunched, his hands deep in the pockets of his
battledress top. Did he never wear a coat? Did he even
own a coat? And gloves? Why did he never wear gloves
when he must know his hands turned purple in cold
weather? She sighed and picked up her pen.

Everyone round here has been unbelievably kind.
Oliver is staying away from school till after the
Christmas holidays, so I teach him reading and
spelling and the vicar's wife comes three afternoons
and gives him arithmetic lessons. My next-door
neighbour, the gossipy one, has almost adopted
Sally. She gives her thick slices of bread sprinkled
with sugar. Half her sugar ration by the look of it!
Did *you* ever have sugar butties when you were a
small boy?

Daisy stared at the far wall. David had probably never
heard of a sugar butty. They were the good old standby
of poorer families when the jam jar was empty and the
mother couldn't afford the twopence for the grocer at
the corner shop to fill it up for her again. Bill owed his
magnificent constitution and Tarzan-like torso to sugar
butties, he'd told her. 'I've got muscles on me like
grapefruits,' he'd sworn. Daisy smiled and sucked the
end of her pen. Bill had explained that the margarine
had to be spread thick so the sugar could stick. He'd
offered to make one for her and shaken his head sadly
when she'd refused, telling her she knew not what she
was missing.

Daisy went back to her letter.

I'm glad you've dropped work at times and had
some fun. The French restaurant you describe
sounds wonderful. All that food! Yes, I'd love an

341

American cookery book. Yes, *please*! Though I won't be able to make much use of it till this awful rationing comes to an end. I saw a woman coming out of the grocer's the other day with her cheese ration in her hand. She was eating it like it was a bar of chocolate. 'Not worth putting it in me basket, love,' she told me.

Daisy sat staring into space for a good five minutes. Trying to think of something scintillating to write. David had told her he sometimes read bits of her letters to the young dietician he was working with. The Jewish girl who had lost her family in the German concentration camps. Daisy read the letter over. Not a paragraph, as far as she could see, worth passing on. She decided to finish off, but added a postscript:

P.S. Nothing but postcards from Winnie. Rude ones with fat ladies and weedy men. Her baby should be due any time now. I wish she'd forgive me for moving out here. I miss her a lot.

Winnie had gone through a distressing pregnancy and a worse than terrible confinement. She screamed the house down, shrieking with her mouth wide open, her eyes starting from her head. She had pushed when she was told not to and she had held her breath when she was told to pant. In the end the midwife had been forced to slap her face in a desperate attempt to calm her.

Winnie had immediately sat up in bed and slapped her back.

Leonard had gone to work as usual, for which blessing Winnie loudly praised the Lord. He'd assured her that with his Red Cross knowledge he would be quite capable of delivering his son himself, but she didn't think she could stomach that.

His mother had stayed in her room, driving the midwife mad by shouting out for drinks when it wasn't convenient.

'Ignore her,' Winnie said. 'The old cow.'

At half-past three, the midwife had the doctor sent for. In her opinion the patient should have been booked into the hospital for a caesarian operation. The doctor at the ante-natal clinic should have spotted that the patient's pelvis was hardly big enough to accommodate the baby's head. The patient should have been X-rayed at least a month ago, then taken in for induction by breaking the waters when the baby's head was smaller.

She wiped the perspiration from Winnie's sweating face and tried not to think of the horrifying prospect of the baby being born with a grossly huge malformed head. She had seen only one case of encephalitis in her whole career, but she'd never forgotten it.

'We must try and relax between contractions,' she told Winnie. 'For the sake of our baby.'

'Why? Are *you* having one?' Winnie said in a tired whisper that sounded like walking on emery paper: 'You go ahead and relax. Don't mind me.'

An hour later the midwife did what she rarely needed to do. She sent for the doctor.

He came whistling up the stairs, but examined Winnie in a grim silence. An agonizing hour later he eased the baby out of Winnie's small frame, using forceps. Her screams, it was said afterwards, could be heard four streets away.

She was stitched without the benefit of chloroform, leaving the young doctor in no doubt at all of her opinion of him.

'You bloody butcher!' Her voice had almost gone but

she managed a fractured whisper. 'What do you take me for? A flamin' Christmas turkey?'

He fled the house, his ears burning, wishing not for the first time that he'd heeded his father's advice and gone in for accountancy.

But apart from a purple pressure mark on his nose and the forceps scars the baby was beautiful. A ten-pound boy. The midwife cleaned him up, dressed him in the little wrapover Chilprufe vest and the feather-stitched nightgown airing on the brass rim of the fireguard. And noted that he seemed to have grown out of them already. Then she swathed him in a cuddle-blanket so that all that showed was his round, puckered, boiled beetroot face. She laid him in his mother's arms.

'Who's a beauty then?' she said. 'He looks a bit bashed about, but he'll settle down all right.'

Winnie choked back the flip answer trembling on her tongue. For once in her life she was stuck for words. Tired and torn, she had already decided that she would top herself if ever she got pregnant again.

But the sight of her newborn son drained what little colour was left from her cheeks.

Her enormous bruiser of a son had corn-gold hair crowning a face as round as the fullest of moons, while a tiny fist, escaped from the blanket, looked as if it should have been wearing a boxing glove. But the most damning evidence of all in the middle of the jutting chin was a little holey dimple which Winnie could have sworn was winking up at her.

Leonard Smalley would never have believed he had it in him to father a strapping bouncer like his son. His pride knew no bounds. He even turned his back on his thrifty nature for once and went to the expense of having scalloped-edged cards printed. In silver lettering they announced the birth of Richard John, birth-weight ten pounds. Richard John was his father's name, and though his mother would have liked to be able to say the baby was his grandfather born all over again, she couldn't very well with her husband smiling at her from his photograph, a dapper little man with coal-black hair, small-boned and fine-featured in the way that all the Smalleys were.

Winnie had wanted the baby called Joshua after Daisy's husband, or Van after seeing Van Johnson in *Thirty Seconds over Tokyo*, but as in all matters when she tried to have her say she was quietly overruled.

'Naturally your mother's sided with you. The old cow,' she added underneath her breath. She was winding the baby after his second bottle of milk, one bottle merely serving to take the edge off his appetite.

'You've added his cod-liver oil and vitamin drops?' Leonard was an anxious, fussy father, furious with Winnie because her own milk had dried up straight away, sure in his own mind that somehow she had done it on purpose.

His mother wasn't at all surprised. She wouldn't have put it past her daughter-in-law to will her milk to dry up just out of spite. She would never on principle have given Winnie credit for anything, but she was secretly glad when she got up ten days after the birth to resume her duties round the house. The woman they'd had in temporarily had no idea how to make a bed up properly, or how to see to it that meals were always on time. Winnie did both superbly, but then she'd been trained to that kind of thing when she was maid-of-all-work at the boarding house up by North Pier.

Mrs Smalley's arthritis was worsening by the hour. The doctor told her to keep moving, to exercise her fingers instead of sitting with them folded in her lap all day long. He said he realized it would be a struggle for her, but if only she helped more with little jobs around

345

the house, especially now there was a baby there, he was sure she would feel better.

Mrs Smalley hadn't the slightest intention of taking the tiniest bit of notice of him. What did he know about a pain that never went away? It hurt her to move so she stayed still. It was agony to turn her head so she stopped trying to, sitting there as rigid as a plank, thin as a picked chicken, letting others do for her, growing steadily more and more incapable of doing anything for herself.

When Winnie told Leonard that running the house, looking after his mother, caring for the baby was more than flesh and blood could stand, he explained in his timid voice that surely she understood that his mother hated strangers in the house, creeping about and getting on her nerves.

'What about *my* nerves?'

Since the birth Winnie's nerves had been shot. They twanged like the elastic on a catapult, and her mother-in-law's whining voice sent daggers of pain shooting through her temples. Most days Leonard got his mother downstairs where she would sit by the living-room fire, calling out for cups of tea when Winnie was in the middle of doing something else. Sometimes Winnie hated her so much she fantasized about dashing at her with the rolling pin and bashing her brains out, or sticking a hatpin in her neck and watching her beady eyes glaze over as she passed away.

'Will you keep your eye on the baby for me?' she asked one day, wheeling his pram into the living room and parking it close to her mother-in-law's chair. 'If you jiggle the handle up and down a bit he might drop off to sleep.' She stared down in despair at the furious puckered face of her little son. His last feed was less than an hour ago, yet there he was smacking his lips and rolling his eyes in anticipation of the next one. 'I must get on,' she said, running towards the door because there was never time to walk anywhere. 'I haven't made the beds yet, and the breakfast pots are still on the table.'

Suddenly everything inside her welled up to a piercing scream, a terrible scream because it was soundless. Running upstairs she went into the room she shared with Leonard and closed the door.

Leaning against it she actually beat her chest with her fists. 'I hate him!' she yelled. 'I hate him, hate him, hate him.'

'An' I hate his bloody mother!' she shouted. 'I spit on her, the old bag.'

'Winnie!'

'Go away!'

'Winnie?' The old woman's voice rang out like a clarion call. 'The baby wants his bottle. Leave what you're doing and come down here. Winnie? He needs changing. *Winnie?*'

Winnie had always said that hysterical women needed their faces slapping, and serve them right too.

But there was no one in the house that morning capable of slapping Winnie's face, so she opened her mouth and screamed; tore at her hair and screamed some more. Looked wildly round the room for something to destroy, hurled her wedding-day photograph at the wall and rejoiced when she saw the way the glass splintered, totally obliterating Leonard's face.

Nora Jolly took her depression to the doctor.

Not to David's father. To unburden herself to him would have had the subtlety of a cut-throat razor. Besides, he probably knew all about her already and would realize she was talking of his son when she explained the reason for her low spirits.

She took great care with her outfit. Casual clothes

held no appeal for Nora. Sundresses she thought vulgar and had more than once sat on the sands attired as if she were on her way to a coffee morning. It looked as if it might rain, but Nora had yet to find a raincoat that was smart enough to satisfy her, so she decided to take a chance and zipped herself into a woollen dress the colour of dried sludge. It had a matching jacket with a neat piping of brown on the revers, and a small fur collar, and had been chosen carefully with due respect for the coupons involved and the amount of wear she would get out of it. All her clothes were bought with the same weighty deliberation, often after days of agonized thinking. She had only ever made one expensive mistake and that was in buying a tweed trouser-suit which she gave to her char when she realized it made her look like someone who bred pekes for a living.

When she was ready she studied her reflection in the long mirror. She looked slightly pale and definitely interesting with her hair caught up in an emerald-green snood. She left off her usual light dusting of powder-rouge on her high cheekbones. No point in going to see a doctor looking healthy.

The waiting room belonging to the new doctor was filled with coughing women, pea-green walls papered with framed certificates, and had a notice on the door which asked patients not to spit and to bring back their empty bottles. Nora's depression deepened. Looking round her she felt as out of place as an orchid growing from a muck midden.

A sad-eyed woman sitting next to Nora confided that she always came on a Saturday morning because she got Doctor Garland on that day.

'He's the only doctor I've ever been to who is in tune with my stomach. He doesn't send me away like all the others do, telling me it's wind, and to take bicarbonate of soda.' She patted her flat front. 'He *cares* about my stomach does Doctor Garland. What's your trouble, love?'

She was called in just then, and after less than five minutes came out again with a seraphic look on her face.

'He's a saint is Doctor Garland,' an elderly woman across from Nora said. 'What's your trouble, love?'

When it was Nora's turn she sat down in the chair indicated to her and waited for the doctor to finish the letter he was reading. He had smiled an apology and she accepted it gracefully, studying him from beneath the dark sweep of her dramatic eyebrows. The last woman to speak to Nora had told her that Doctor Garland's own troubles had made him into the understanding sympathetic man he was.

'His wife died in a terrible accident,' she'd explained. 'She was in a charabanc on a cripples' outing, taking them to Windermere for the day when the brakes failed and the coach rolled backwards down a hill. Some of the helpers got the cripples out while the others tried to drag big stones from the roadside and put them beneath the back wheels.' She nodded at the doctor's door. 'The coach was stopped from rolling slowly down the road into the lake at the bottom, but his wife fell and the coach ran over her.' Nora jumped as the woman clapped her hands loudly. 'Flat as a pancake,' she said.

The doctor would be, Nora guessed, about forty-five. He was wearing rimless spectacles on the end of his nose and his brown hair was receding back from a high anxious forehead, but when he put the letter down and looked straight at Nora she saw that his eyes were warm and kind. She also noticed that there was a pearl button missing from the front of his shirt where his tie had slipped sideways and that the sleeves of his jacket were just slightly frayed.

In the time it took him to take down her name and

349

address, Nora had discarded the prepared story of the sweetheart buried in a foreign field and her resultant sleepless nights and deep depression. Instead she thanked God she was wearing her oyster satin camiknickers trimmed with Brussels lace and smelled of her carefully hoarded Chanel Number Five scent.

'I have this little pain. Here, Doctor,' she said softly, smiling at him and pointing to a place due south of her midriff. She sighed and fluttered carefully curled black eyelashes. 'It feels a bit lumpy to me.'

The rain had come on properly when she left the surgery. It was the kind of rain used in films, a straight down sheet of water that soaked Nora's smart two-piece costume through before she'd even crossed the road to the bus stop.

The bus when it came was crowded with Saturday morning shoppers. It smelled of wet rubber, dead fish, and BO, and Nora couldn't find a seat. But she stood close to the boarding platform, smiling to herself, heedless of the strands of hair straggling down from the snood and the fact that the fur collar on her three-quarter jacket resembled a drowned ferret newly plucked from a watery grave.

The lovely Doctor Garland had said he would like to see her again in one week's time. He hadn't thought there was anything seriously wrong but Nora had told him about the stabbing pains in her head, and managed to make sure he noticed her ringless left hand and that he knew she lived all alone.

'Life can be very cruel,' she had told him before she left, holding out her right hand which he'd been forced to shake.

She got off the bus outside her block of flats and ran through the puddles like a young girl, not caring that her outfit would never come up the same after such a wetting.

Doctor Garland was such a lovely man. He had liked her, she could tell that, and when he discovered what an asset she could be to him he would bless the day she had walked into his consulting room. He was better looking than David too, more manly, more rugged.

Already she was beginning to wonder what she had seen in David . . .

Chapter Nine

In the weeks coming up to Christmas Daisy baked so many Christmas cakes her oven never got the chance to cool down. Because rationing was showing no sign of ending she made them from a Ministry of Food recipe which would have given her mother the palpitations.

Martha's cakes, made in October, could have stayed untouched in their air-tight tins till Easter and still come out as moist as wet sponges. Daisy could remember her mother's recipe off by heart, right down to the marmalade she always added at the last minute. Martha's ingredients included half a dozen eggs, a quarter of glacé cherries, a dessertspoonful of rose-water, blanched almonds, best butter, half a gill of sherry – not to mention the pound and a half of dried fruit and soft brown sugar. Each cake baked in a moderate-to-slow oven for four hours.

Daisy knew that *her* cakes that year were an insult, with their reconstituted dried egg, limited sugar and margarine instead of butter. Most of her customers provided their own ingredients, but as Bertha Tomlinson said:

'Them women queueing up for your cakes never knew there was a war on. Money talks louder than anything, and always will.'

She was sitting watching Daisy dip sprigs of holly into a strong solution of Epsom salts, to give them a Christmassy sparkle when they dried.

'Short of nowt,' Bertha continued. 'But then that's the

way of life, isn't it? Much always comes to more and always will. Where's your Oliver this morning?'

'With Bill Tattersall at the garage. He takes his collection of cars with him and sits in the little office there pretending to be servicing them.'

'Aye, well.' Both Bertha's wandering eyes were kind. 'Bill puts your little lad in the place of his own. It's only natural. But me and Mrs Smith think he did the right thing in letting his own lad stop with his grandparents.'

'How did you know . . .?' Daisy halted her holly-dipping for a minute 'I don't think he wanted it talked about.' She flushed. 'It's so *personal* and private.'

'There's nowt personal and private round here,' Bertha said cheerfully. 'It's all over the village that young Doctor Armitage is flying from America to pop the question on Christmas Day.'

'And what will my answer be?'

Bertha shrugged her shoulders clean up to her earlobes. 'Even betting, I'd say. Some say yes and some say no.'

'And what do *you* say?'

'*Me*? Ee, love. It's no business of mine. I'd be the last one to meddle in affairs that don't concern me. I leave all that to those gossips from the church.' She got up to go. 'I've seen Bill Tattersall out with a woman who looks old enough to be his mother. Divorced.' She mouthed the last word as if it was an obscenity. 'Mrs Smith saw them together in the pictures last week.'

'What was the film?' Daisy spoke quickly, well aware that her every expression was under close scrutiny.

'*Mildred Pierce*.'

'With Joan Crawford? Oh, I *do* admire her. She suffers so beautifully.'

'I should think so too, wearing a mink coat and diamonds as big as duck's eggs round her neck. I'd give suffering a chance any day with less than half what she's got.'

As soon as she'd gone Daisy ran upstairs, to have a good look and a bit of a think about the bedroom Auntie Edna and Uncle Arnold were going to sleep in over Christmas. She stood in the doorway muttering to herself.

She was downright glad Bill had found someone to go to the pictures with. She was. Honestly she was. He'd be more likely to fall for a divorcee than a young girl who might remind him of the girl during the war. He wasn't exactly a monk! Now he'd made the decision about his little boy he would want to make some sort of life for himself. Daisy was sure there would be plenty of women who would find him quite attractive. A tough guy with a soft centre would just about sum him up, she supposed. Quite attractive, if you looked hard enough.

She forced her mind back to the room. The walls would have to make do with a couple of coats of distemper, that's if she could find a colour deep enough to cover the cabbage roses and green trellises on the faded and dirty wallpaper. The ceiling with its damp patches and hanging cobwebs would have to make do with a quick brush over. She shivered. It was a cold little room, with the rain sliding down the window and the bare floorboards as cold to the feet as an ice-rink. Outside Pendle Hill was closed in with winter fog; the wind moaned and sighed, rattling the faulty catch on the sash-window. It was a lonely room, unused and unslept in for what Daisy guessed must be years. Jasper had followed her up, but after a quick sniff around went back to his basket by the fire. Daisy had a quick sniff herself, filling her nostrils with the all too familiar mushroom smell which seemed to be seeping in from the dripping fields outside.

Away from the kitchen, and the fire in the living

room, the cottage was colder than a tomb. Her auntie's little terraced house in Blackburn was as cosy as a hay-box compared to this. Daisy could only imagine Edna's caustic remarks about the black fungus on the walls and the sagging plaster on the ceiling. She rubbed her hands together to stop them going numb. How had she ever thought she could put guests in here?

Auntie Edna and Uncle Arnold would have *her* room. That was the solution. At least there'd be a strip of carpet on the floor and a mattress that didn't sag in the middle. Daisy stared at the double bed with its iron bedsteads painted a crude garden-fence green.

And saw that one leg seemed to be sinking into the floorboards.

'Dry rot,' Bill said at once, when Daisy mentioned it. He had carried Oliver on his back all the way from the garage, and the two of them were red-faced and watery-eyed from the wind. 'I'll go up and take a look.'

'I can put that right,' he said two minutes later, down on his knees in the chilly little room. He pushed the bed to one side. 'See here? There are about four or five boards affected, that's all. I can soon saw them out and replace them.' He crawled about, testing the floor with a screwdriver. 'I've got a few lengths of wood back at the workshop that would be just the job.'

'Do you make a habit of carrying a screwdriver about in your back pocket?' Daisy had wanted to say how kind he was, how good of him it was to help her out yet again. But for no good reason she found herself sniping at him like a peevish child.

He was busy taking a mental measurement of the rotted wood, the frown lines on his forehead deepening. Ignoring her. Infuriating her.

'I hope you enjoyed the picture last week,' she said loudly. 'Mrs Smith saw you there. With your *friend*.'

Finished at last, he sat back on his heels, pushed the beret off his forehead with a finger, replaced the screwdriver in his trouser pocket, dragged the bed back into position, and winked at Daisy. Pretending he hadn't heard what she said. Doing her a good turn. Driving her potty.

'Would you like a cup of cocoa and a piece of cake?' She flashed him her Betty Grable smile, all teeth and fluttering eyelashes.

The smile almost knocked him for six. What had he done now to get back into her good books? He could have sworn she was mad at him. *Seething* was the word that came readily to mind.

In the kitchen, filled with the warm spicy smell of Christmas, she kept her voice low. 'I don't think Oliver's limp is quite as pronounced these past few days. Miss Bates isn't coming any more and the doctor is pleased with his progress.'

Bill refused to be drawn. He had his own opinion about Oliver's limp, but he wasn't going to risk being sent away with a flea in his ear a second time.

Daisy cut a slice of cake and gave it to him. It was almost the last of a small one she'd tried out before she began her marathon bake. 'I'm sorry there's no almond paste or icing on it,' she said.

Bill stared down at it in amazement as it lay in the palm of his hand. 'Could I borrow your glasses, love? Or a magnifying glass? Sure you can spare it?'

He was beyond hope. He was rude, cheeky; he thought he could say exactly what he wanted and get away with it. He was an enigma, kind beyond reason one minute, sharp of tongue the next.

Yet she had seen him totally undone. And for that reason she could never feel indifference for him.

Before he went she invited him to dinner on Christmas

356

Day. 'I'm asking you now before you get swamped with invitations,' she said on a false laugh.

'But won't the good doctor be here?'

'And possibly his father. Along with my Auntie Edna and Uncle Arnold. Plus Mrs Tomlinson next door if her sister doesn't invite her. They had words last year.'

For a long moment he hesitated. For weeks now he'd been brushing the thought of Christmas firmly aside. Christmas was for children, a time of fingers fumbling with wrapping paper, eyes shining more brightly than the lights on the tree. His own little lad would be overwhelmed with presents, surrounded by love. Secure with his family. While he was no part of them, or ever could be. If he went back on his word and sent a present it would never be passed on. Besides which, he had promised. He had given his word. As a man of integrity.

He smiled at Daisy with a kind of liberation, as though she had unexpectedly released him from a temptation.

'I'll get a tree and fix it up with lights. I think I know where I can get some.'

'So you'll come?'

'If nothing better crops up.'

He looked so impudent grinning down at her, his eyes wicked slits of mockery, that she wanted to hit him, to take back her invitation and go inside and bang the door on him.

'I suppose you think you're funny,' she shouted after him, but he didn't turn round, just crossed the road with his hands thrust deep in his trouser pockets, the beret back on his head, whistling 'Jingle Bells'.

She banged the door anyway. Hoping he heard her doing it.

Winnie had banged more doors in the past few weeks than her mother-in-law had had hot dinners. And that was saying something! Old Mrs Smalley set great store

357

by her stomach. Whatever else her arthritis had seized up it hadn't been her digestive system. She expected three cooked meals a day, not to mention the snacks in between. The fact that Winnie had to queue for a lot of the food she lugged in carrier bags from the shops meant nothing to Mrs Smalley. Winnie did most of her shopping in the afternoons so that Leonard could see to the baby, but by then most of the best stuff had gone. When bread was rationed to nine ounces a week each, Winnie threatened to do away with herself.

Carrots became her standby. She used them in soups and stews, for sweetening puddings, and baking biscuits. She made carrot jam in desperation when all the points were used up, only to see Leonard's mother spit her first taste of it out into her hand.

Winnie tried. Oh, dear God, how she tried to manage. She bought a few tins of what the government called snoek, an unidentifiable fish, but was forced to hand it over the backyard wall for next door's cat. She wasn't like Daisy. She had never *aspired* to be like Daisy. They had been a good team, but Winnie had kept to her own jobs of cleaning and waiting at table. She only needed to *think* of Daisy these days for her eyes to fill with tears. She grew whiter and thinner than ever, but as she drooped and wilted the baby thrived, gaining at least a pound a week when the recommended weight at the clinic was no more than four ounces – six at the most.

The fact that Winnie had to leave him lying in his pram for hours at a time didn't appear to worry him at all. As long as there was something stuck in his mouth he was happy. Winnie dipped his dummies in condensed milk, jam, treacle, his bottled orange juice, anything that happened to be handy. She swore he smacked his lips in anticipation when he saw her making up the formula for his bottles. She started putting groats in one of them, thickening it, giving it more body. She enlarged the hole in the teats with a darning needle, and he slurped it down with a noise like water going down a plug-hole. If she laid him on his stomach, he reared his round head up, trying to see over the side of the pram. If she laid him on his back he kicked his way out of his nappy.

He would go to anybody, even perfect strangers, but he never took to Leonard's mother.

The feeling was mutual. There was something about this baby that puzzled Mrs Smalley. She preferred dainty babies. Leonard had been like a fairy in her arms, light as thistledown, and so quiet. At the rate this baby was growing he'd be sitting up at three months and walking at four.

'What are we going to do about Christmas?' Winnie wanted to know. 'The butcher says he'll save me a chicken, but I'll want some extra money.'

Leonard twitched as if she'd let a swear word slip. 'We don't bother with Christmas in this house.' He put a finger to his mouth. 'My father was killed coming up to Christmas. In Flanders Fields, so Mother likes to be quiet.'

'But that's thirty years ago!' Winnie forgot to keep her voice down. 'You mean you just carry on as if Christmas wasn't happening?'

'It's the kindest way. Mother can't even bear to hear a carol sung on the wireless. It destroys her.'

Winnie was flabbergasted. She hadn't really stopped bleeding ever since the birth, and there were days when she felt as if her life's blood was draining away from her. When she'd told Leonard, he'd looked her up in his Red Cross manual and said it was nothing to worry about. What was worrying him was his mother's arthritis which seemed to be getting worse.

'I'll go in to her now,' he said, having dispensed with

Christmas. 'Why don't you come with me? I'm reading *Silas Marner* to her. You might find it a change from those trashy magazines you seem to like.'

Winnie flung out a dramatic arm. 'Have you seen this kitchen? Do you ever bother to think how the work gets done? *You* did the washing-up before I came to live here so why can't you pick up a tea towel and help me now?' She was beginning to tremble. 'And while I'm at it, why do you have to read to your mother every night? She's not got arthritis in her eyes has she? The only place I suspect she's got it bad is in her backside. With sitting on it all day.'

Leonard backed away. Raised voices upset him. He was just like his mother for that. Wanting nothing else but peace, and things going nicely on day after day. Though Winnie was right. The kitchen was a mess. There were nappies on the table, more soaking in a bucket, bottles bubbling in a pan on the stove to sterilize them – he was insistent that Winnie did that each time they were used – and the tea things stacked any old how on the draining board. Winnie had no method. His mother was forever telling him that.

'Mother thinks,' he began unwisely, 'that if you let the baby wait for his bottle till you've washed the tea things and tidied away, you wouldn't get so tired. You're tired because you have no method,' he added. 'Mother says we ought to sit down and work out a plan for each day, so that you don't run round in circles. She's not as unfeeling as you think. She wants to help.'

In one bound Winnie was across the kitchen, gripping Leonard by the lapels of his jacket, her face an inch from his own, her teeth bared, her nostrils flaring.

'Help?' she screamed. 'Your flamin' mother? She wouldn't lift a finger to help me if I lay on the floor foaming at the mouth!'

Leonard tried to back away, but she had him pinned to the wall.

'Not unfeeling? Your mother?' She shook Leonard till her eyes bulged. Shook him with a glorious feeling of abandonment. 'Your mother is an unfeeling cow. Your mother is a lazy sod. Your mother is *evil*.'

Leonard recovered himself enough to grip her hands and thrust her from him. 'My mother is an angel,' he said, his voice breaking with emotion. 'I've told you. She brought me up all on her own when my father was killed in France. She kept this house like a little palace before her arthritis struck. Now that she's old and in constant pain I intend to see to it that as long as I'm alive she will never do a hand's turn again.'

'Even if it kills *me*?' Winnie's heart was so filled with black hate she had stopped thinking what she was saying. 'I'm not frightened of hard work. You know that. I've had to work hard all me life.' She twisted away from him. 'But I can't look after the house and the baby *and* be at her beck and call all day. She needs a part-time nurse. She *had* a part-time nurse before we got married. And a cleaning lady twice a week.'

Leonard thought he was winning, thought she was calming down. 'We're not made of money, Winnie. My grandfather on Mother's side left us a nice little legacy, but Mother won't have the capital touched, and the interest doesn't go half as far as it did. So we must all pull together.'

He was at the door congratulating himself that this time he'd sorted his wife out nicely, when she slipped round him and slammed the door shut, leaning against it with her arms outstretched in the form of a cross.

'It's your mother first, and me a poor second,' she said in a deceptively calm voice.

Leonard began to bluster. 'Come on, Winnie. Let's not make trouble. Why don't you try and be friends?

361

If you tried to get to know Mother better you'd realize she has a heart of gold.'

Winnie's eyes blazed into his. 'It's no good, Leonard. If you wanted a mealy-mouthed slave you've picked the wrong one. I *know* you can afford a bit of help for me and that's all I need. Just a morning or two with somebody to bottom the rooms and sweep the stairs down. Or help with the shopping. Or take the baby out in his pram. Or sit with your mother to keep her mind from addling as well as her legs.'

'Leonard!'

Winnie saw the way her husband almost stiffened to attention, watched him lift his head the way an animal does when given a command.

'Move out of my way,' he said. 'Mother's calling.'

'If you run to her now before promising me you'll think about what I've just said, I'll leave you,' Winnie said softly, giving no sign of the way her heart was thumping fit to choke her.

'Leonard! Can't you hear me? What are you *doing* in there?'

'I mean it,' Winnie whispered.

Leonard smiled an uneasy smile. 'For goodness sake, let me get at the door. Do you want me to force you?'

'If you put your hand across my mouth I'll bite your finger off,' she said clearly.

'Leonard?' Mrs Smalley's voice was growing weaker, more pathetic by the minute.

'She can shout like a fishwife when you're out of the house. I'm waiting, Leonard.'

Her eyes glittered as she stared at his weak little face, at his sparse little beard, his thread of a moustache. In her mind she was jumping up and down, sparring with her fists, daring him to start his nipping. In reality she was as still as if she had turned to stone.

'Tell her you're in here, talking to me. About something important.'

'Leonard . . . Leon . . . ard . . . ?'

His eyes were frightened. He lifted a hand and Winnie gripped his wrist so hard he winced.

She was almost crazy with a new-found power. He made a feeble attempt to push her aside and she laughed in his face.

'The baby is crying.' He was trembling now. 'If you won't let me go to Mother, at least come away from that door and let me see to my son.'

'He's not your son,' Winnie said.

And stepped aside.

In the middle of the night, lying awake in the spare room with the baby's cot pulled up to the side of the single bed, Winnie accepted that her marriage was over.

She could no longer stay here, but what was she going to do? In Winnie's world women never walked out on their husbands; they had more sense. Leaving your husband meant leaving your *home*, and what could a woman without a roof over her head hope to do?

She'd been forced to creep downstairs to mix the baby's bottles, and through the nick in the living-room door she had seen mother and son sitting there, by the only fire in the house, talking together in hushed voices. Unashamedly Winnie flattened herself against the wall and listened.

'My poor, poor boy,' Mrs Smalley was saying. 'The one thing we can be grateful for is that your father never lived to go through this. It would have broken his heart.'

'I wish I'd known him,' Leonard said, in the way he must have said the very same thing hundreds of times before. 'I wish I could remember him more clearly.'

In the cold light of morning, after staying awake all night, Winnie faced the truth. Living here with Leonard and his mother was impossible now. Walking away might not be the right thing to do, but she had to do it. She had nearly a hundred pounds in her post office savings book, not including the interest. She was far from destitute.

She wasn't going to be forced to leave. Nothing like that. Leonard would never throw her out bag and baggage into the street. His mother had often said he wouldn't hurt a fly.

If only she knew, Winnie thought.

Over in his cot the baby was champing on nothing, stuffing a fist into his mouth, sucking on it with loud slapping noises. Winnie took his dummy from the bed-side table, licked it clean because it had picked up a fluff of dust from the table, and wriggled it into his mouth.

For the last time she crept downstairs to the cold silent kitchen, still littered with last night's pots and pans and dirty nappies. She mixed her son two bottles of milk, adding groats and cod-liver oil drops to one of them as usual.

Chapter Ten

One morning the snow came. It fell in huge feathery flakes, dropping straight down from a leaden sky, to melt away almost as soon as it touched the ground.

On the twenty-first of December the schoolchildren, bundled in scarves, jumpers and woolly caps, jumped up and down in the playground, flapping their arms about to keep warm.

'St Thomas grey, St Thomas grey. The longest night and the shortest day,' they sang.

Daisy had been promised a cockerel from one of the hill farms. All above board, but *nothing to be said*, of course. In return the farmer's wife got a big Christmas cake, four dozen mince pies, and a massive dark pudding which Daisy had boiled for over four hours in Mrs Rothwell's old copper.

The farmer's wife was upset because one of the cockerels had died of a heart attack through being overfed all through its short life. 'Thirteen pounds was too much to gain as fast as that, but it roasted a treat all the same,' she said, waving Daisy off and watching her wobble on her bicycle all the way down the rough farm track.

'It's enough to make you want to turn vegetarian,' Daisy told the doctor on his next visit to Oliver. 'Force-feeding seems barbaric to me, but then I was brought up in a town where meat came in chops arranged in rows on a butcher's slab. We never thought of it as having walked on legs.'

The doctor, country-born and bred, had known for a while that the cost of his twice-weekly visits was an anxiety to the young woman watching him examine Oliver. He could see that she was overworked and desperately tired. In his opinion a reaction from her husband's death was long overdue. She seemed almost too calm, too serene, though the way she constantly tucked and re-tucked a strand of hair behind an ear gave her away.

Going over to Daisy he tilted her face and pulled down her lower eyelids. 'Good food,' he advised. '*Especially* anything that once looked over a gate. You look a bit anaemic to me.'

'I haven't *time* to be anaemic,' Daisy smiled. 'But I know what you mean. I'll just close my eyes and swallow, and won't dwell on how the meat's got on to my plate. The amount we're allowed won't make much difference anyway.'

The doctor left the cottage, got into his car and drove on to his next patient. He feared that little Mrs Penny could be working herself to a standstill. In spite of her apparent placidity, she had that pinched jumpy look about her, as if she were making tight balls of her fists, determined to keep going, without help, as far as he could see, from anyone. And that boy, Oliver, had him flummoxed. There was no muscle weakness as far as he could see. No reason to justify that sliding limp. Maybe the hospital would come up with something when they saw him early in the New Year, but he doubted it. If only he wasn't so damned busy. If only it wasn't the time of the year when every other patient had gone down with flu. Maybe he ought never to have gone in for medicine. He was too weary to show more than a superficial interest in any other manifestations than the purely physical.

Too disillusioned, he supposed.

Bertha Tomlinson had got proper fond of little Mrs Penny. After the two sweet sherries she allowed herself every Sunday dinner-time she would go as far as to wish that Daisy was the daughter she had never had. It was a pity she clammed up so much just when you thought she was going to tell you something really interesting, but Bertha hadn't been born yesterday. She'd formed her own conclusions on certain matters.

Little Mrs Penny hadn't had much joy from her marriage. From the two and two Bertha had put together she'd been more of a nurse than a wife.

Bertha moved her chair a little to get a better view of the road through her net curtains. She didn't mind helping out next door with the children. Sally was no trouble at all, but the lad was too canny for Bertha's liking. Oliver never missed a trick as far as she could see, sitting there with his ears flapping. He played on his mother too, letting her run about after him all day long.

She lifted a corner of the curtain. The vicar's wife was going up Daisy's path. To give Oliver his morning massage since Miss Bates stopped coming, and his arithmetic lesson. To be there while Mrs Penny went out delivering. Bertha nodded. Yes, there she went, wobbling past on her bicycle with her hair tied up in a bright red scarf, both baskets filled to their brims.

She hadn't been gone long when a taxi cruised slowly down the road. Bertha stood up to see better. It wasn't often a taxi came along the row of cottages. As long as the hourly bus ran, no one in their right mind considered taking a taxi. It was stopping next door. Was it? Yes. Definitely!

Forgetting to be circumspect, Bertha let the corner of the curtain drop and waddled as fast as she could to her front door, not even bothering to collect the sweeping brush kept handy for such occasions. She wrenched

the door open, cursing the damp that was making it
stick. If she didn't look sharp she was going to miss
young Doctor Armitage arriving earlier than he was
expected. Coming all the way from America to pop the
question and finding his beloved wasn't in. Oh, what a
crying shame. He'd have a pink fit when Minnie
Rostron answered the door in her bobbled jumper and
the purple toque from the last jumble sale.

Bertha dashed to the low dividing wall to tell Doctor
Armitage it would be a good hour before Mrs Penny
got back from doing her deliveries. She opened her
mouth, then closed it again.

Walking up next door's path was a young woman
with the reddest hair Bertha had ever seen. She was
staggering under the weight of a baby in a carry-cot,
followed by the taxi driver with a large suitcase and a
set of wheels to turn the cot into a pram.

'Mrs Penny's not in. She's gone off on her bike. She
won't be back for the best part of an hour,' Bertha
called out, determined to get her spoke in before Minnie
Rostron.

'There's *somebody* in, missus.' The driver humped the
big case on to the step. 'I can hear them coming.'

Bertha stood there, frantically trying to place the red-
haired young woman. She felt sure she wasn't expected.
Mrs Penny would have told her a thing like that.

'It's a bit parky this morning,' she said pleasantly,
talking to herself as it happened, because when the door
opened Oliver shot out like a bullet, almost making the
young woman drop the carry-cot.

'Winnie!' he shouted. 'Oh, Winnie . . . Mrs Rostron!
It's Winnie!'

When the door closed behind them and the taxi drove
away, there was nothing Bertha could do but go back
inside. So frustrated she felt physically ill. Ten minutes
later, having tidied herself up and taken off her hairnet,

she was on her way round to Daisy's back door, carrying an empty jug. Having run out of milk. Unexpectedly.

Mrs Birtwistle of Willow House was delighted with her Christmas order. Daisy explained that if she'd had more fat to put in it, she'd have made the pudding at least a month ago. She advised Mrs Birtwistle to be as lavish as possible with the brandy she put in the sauce.

'You can make the sauce with lemon-squash and arrowroot, as long as you cook it in the pan for five minutes.'

She was so serious, so dedicated, Mrs Birtwistle felt she could never thank Bill Tattersall enough for recommending her.

'If you're having trouble with your supplies from the wholesaler do let me know, Mrs Penny. They're as bound up with red tape as the retailer. Did I hear right that you are opening your shop again in the New Year?' Mrs Birtwistle tapped the side of her nose. 'My husband has fingers in a lot of pies. He knows that the Rothwells must have let the official side of things lapse. It must be very hard for you trying to unravel the mess they left for you.'

Which could be the understatement of the year, Daisy thought, free-wheeling down the hill. How could she run the shop *and* do the deliveries? And until she got established, how could she afford to pay an assistant? Where was the money going to come from for the leaking roof and the ominously bulging wall round the back of the cottage? How much would it cost to have the water supply up in the bathroom put right? Was there a dead bird in the tank, or was the tank rusting away? Would she wake up one morning to find water cascading down the stairs? And what was she going to do about Oliver and his worrying limp?

Thank God the snow had melted for the time being. She would be delivering every day from now on. Shirley had told her how it could be when the really bad weather came. For the next half-mile Daisy saw herself, loaded down with heavy baskets, head bent against driving snow, eyebrows frozen, icicles hanging from her nose and chin. Saw herself collapsing through sheer exhaustion, freezing solid where she dropped, her face stiffening into a hideous mask.

Where was Shirley now? Warm, Daisy hoped; warm and happy.

'Winnie?' she said, her voice cracking with disbelief. 'Winnie!'

They stared at each other without moving or speaking, then Daisy held out her arms.

There was so much to say, so much to tell, and most of it must wait, Winnie realized, till Daisy's next-door neighbour went reluctantly back to her own cottage. They did have a chance though to be alone for a few minutes. That was when the baby cried and they went upstairs together.

Winnie had put his carry-cot on Daisy's bed, and there he was making a noise that wasn't exactly crying, blowing bubbles, staring at his clasped hands in fascinated wonder.

'I've left Leonard,' Winnie whispered. 'For good.'

Daisy couldn't take her eyes off the baby. Compared to this bruiser her own two had been a couple of tadpoles.

She turned and looked Winnie full in the face, her expression an unasked question.

Winnie nodded. 'Yes. The Desert Rat. If the baby had come out of me wearing tattoos I couldn't be more sure.'

'Oh, dear God . . .' Daisy watched the tears gathering in Winnie's pale little eyes. They had begun to roll down Winnie's thin face before she could find her voice. 'Oh, love. You don't know how happy I am to see you. How much I've missed you.'

Clutching each other, they bent over the baby. Then Daisy began to laugh and even though it had more than a touch of hysteria in it, Winnie joined in and they rocked together, totally undone. Both of them.

They were a team again right from the start. They were drinking tea in the kitchen late at night, with the children in bed and Daisy busy on yet another batch of mince-pies. With Winnie folding nappies in between washing up the baking things. It was arranged that for the time being Winnie would sleep on a camp bed in Daisy's room, with the baby in his cot on top of the bedding box. When the spare room was finished she would move in there, apart from the two nights over Christmas when Daisy's auntie and uncle were there.

Swapping beds round, fitting people in. It was as natural and normal as if they had never left Shangri-La.

'I *had* to leave Leonard's house,' Winnie said.

'As bad as that?' Daisy thought it was time for another cup of tea. She went over to the sink and filled the kettle.

'Worse. Some day I'll tell you. I'd have topped meself if I'd stayed.'

'By what method?'

Daisy hadn't forgotten how to make Winnie laugh, and once she began she couldn't stop. The tinny sound that passed for mirth with Winnie filled the kitchen as she gave in at last to the tearing emotion buried deep inside her for so long.

Daisy got on with making the tea.

'You're balm to my soul,' Winnie said through her hiccoughs, surprising Daisy. 'They *trod* on my soul, those two in that dark gloomy house. They're *unnatural.* They'll be *glad* I've gone. When they get over the shock of having to put their hands in their pockets to pay somebody to do a quarter of what I was supposed to do.'

The tea was ready. 'So you told Leonard that he wasn't the father?'

'I got mad,' Winnie admitted. 'I was so mad I could have killed him. So I told him instead. But he'd have guessed. I think his mother knew already.'

'And he threw you out?'

'Leonard? He hadn't got the guts. No, I bided my time, cleaned the house from top to bottom, got the shopping in, left his mother a flask and some Spam sandwiches because her son won't let her lift a finger, ordered a taxi and walked out.' She sipped the hot tea. 'And here I am.'

'Here you are.'

They smiled at each other, well content. As if all that had happened in between had never been.

About half-past one, when the order was packed away and they were drinking what was left of a very inferior sherry and the last of Joshua's whisky out of cups, Daisy told Winnie that David was not only coming over from America for Christmas, but that he wanted to marry her.

'And take you back with him?' Winnie's voice was sharp with a terrible anxiety.

Daisy took a deep swig from her cup. 'No fear. I haven't said I'll marry him yet.' She looked at Winnie with bleary eyes. 'You should have sounded surprised when I told you that.'

'It was obvious, wasn't it?'

'What was obvious?'

'That he was in love with you. He fancied you long before Joshua died.' Winnie's pointed face looked furious. 'Are you in love with him?'

'No. Yes. I don't know. It's too soon.' Daisy found herself smirking. 'I'm flattered of course.'

'Why?'

'Why? On account of him being a doctor. And handsome. And fairly rich.' The whisky and sherry were warring in Daisy's head. 'I suppose I *do* love him really. Especially after all he's been through.' She slurped more sherry into her cup. 'Anyway, if I do marry him it won't be for ages. Not till a decent interval has elapsed.' She heard herself repeating it because it sounded so pompous. And so funny. 'Not till a decent interval has elapsed.'

Winnie knew that the drink had gone straight to Daisy's head because she was so tired, and so giddy with relief that she wasn't going to have to struggle on alone any more. To tell the truth, the cottage had been a real eye-opener for Winnie. Was this the place with roses round the door, set sweetly in a meadow, where Joshua was to have lived out the rest of his life in peace?

She had topped and tailed the baby in water so filthy-looking up there in the funny little bathroom she would have thought it was sewage if it hadn't crawled out of a tap. She had put him to bed in a room so damp she was sure he would wake with a bloom of mildew on him, and she had drawn the curtains against a distant snow-capped hill that looked like a crouching lion about to spring.

'Do you know, you've never said the baby's name yet,' Daisy said on the way upstairs.

'Gavin Joshua,' Winnie told her, making it up on the spot.

Winnie was scraping at the green fungus on the kitchen taps when Daisy got back from the morning delivery. The table was set for dinner-time and the soup Daisy had made the day before was simmering on the stove.

'There's a man upstairs putting new boards in the spare room floor. Oliver's up there handing nails and passing the hammer. I was just going to take tea up when I'd finished this little job.'

'Bill,' Daisy said, going red. 'Cocoa, not tea. He's a family friend.' Going even redder. Dashing about making the cocoa and rushing up with it still wearing her headscarf and coat.

Leaving Winnie gazing after her in some astonishment.

'She's nice is old copper-nob.' Bill wiped cocoa froth from his upper lip with the back of his hand. 'That baby of hers looks as if she's been at him with a bicycle pump.'

'His father was a big man,' Daisy said truthfully, then looked quickly at Oliver to see if his ears were flapping.

'Bill's brought us a banana,' Oliver said. 'It's on the mantelpiece where we can see it. But we haven't to touch it,' he added. 'Only look at it.'

'Oh, good! The trifle on Christmas Day.' Daisy had it spoken for already. 'If I cut it thin we might all get a slice.'

'You're excited, aren't you, Daisygirl?' Bill couldn't take his eyes off her. Winnie turning up like that out of the blue seemed to have given Daisy a new lease of life. Winnie coming meant she wasn't trying to do four things at once; that there was someone there for the children when she had to go out; that there was company for her in the long winter evenings. He didn't know how long Winnie was going to stay, but he hoped it would be for a long time. There was obviously a good

374

reason for her sudden appearance, and Mrs T next door would tell him all in good time, even if Daisy didn't.

'I'll put your tree up tomorrow,' he said. 'No chance of it drying out and shedding its needles if you want it put in the front room by the window.'

'More chance of it rotting in its pot,' Daisy said. 'But I'd like it there so that its lights can be seen from outside. I think I missed that as much as anything during the war. All those rows of dark windows without a welcoming light amongst them.'

For him to see, Bill thought. For the good doctor to see as he comes up the path.

David sent a telegram to Daisy. It said he wouldn't be arriving at the cottage until Christmas Day. That he was spending two days with his father who had suffered a mild heart attack.

'It's only natural,' Winnie said. 'And anyway it gives us a chance to get on.'

There had been a bit of a panic about the cockerels through the Food Inspector calling unexpectedly and getting wind of what was going on.

'Fair shares for all, my foot,' the farmer's wife told Daisy, offering her a goose instead on the understanding that nothing was said. 'The man's a right pillock. He's like a lot of small men. A bit of power and he thinks he's Hitler.'

'The grease will come in handy,' Daisy told Winnie. 'There's nothing like it for chests.'

Then thinking of chests she went quiet, remembering last Christmas when Joshua had been too ill to even look at his dinner, when he'd sent the children away from him because he couldn't bear their constant chatter.

'How can I tell David I don't want to marry him?' Daisy suddenly said in the middle of wrapping up a tiny doll for Sally. 'How can I hurt him when life has hurt him so much already?'

'Better to tell him now than let him go on hoping,' Winnie said, trying not to sound too chuffed.

'When he went away he looked like a man who couldn't take one more blow. Especially if his father dies.'

'He won't die,' Winnie said quickly, crossing her fingers.

'But if he does David will only have *me*.' Daisy picked up a small racing car and reached for the wrapping paper.

'But you can't *not* tell him, Daisy. Look what happened to me.' She shook her head violently as if to shake the memory away.

Daisy's auntie and uncle came on Christmas Eve. With the buses not running on Christmas Day, as Edna said.

'Two nights'll be enough,' Edna told Arnold, having a good look round Daisy's bedroom. 'I can smell damp.' She sniffed. 'And it smells like that dog has been doing his business in here.' She closed the door. 'What do you think to that Winnie living here? I thought our Edwin was a whopper when he was born, but that baby of hers has been here before. He'll be climbing trees before he's out of his nappies.'

'I don't like to see young Oliver limping like that.' Arnold's bald head shone like a billiard ball when he got round to removing his cap. 'He needs a man about the house, does that little chap. He needs *discipline*.'

'He needs his bottom smacking,' said Edna.

Daisy was in her element with the house full of people and the pantry full of food, even if most of it was mock this and mock that. The trifle sat on the slab, banana-less but beautiful, its topping of mock cream forked up into little peaks with hundreds and thousands scattered over it.

Because Christmas was, after all, for children she had divided the banana between Oliver and Sally, saving a bit for Winnie, who mashed it up on a saucer and dribbled it into the baby's ever-open mouth.

'Why not give him a chip butty and be done with it?' Edna said, not quite underneath her breath.

'He was born with two little milk teeth,' Winnie told her proudly.

'If you'd told me he'd come out smiling at you with a full set I wouldn't have batted an eyelid,' said Edna.

Bill came round for just a minute to check on the tree lights.

Daisy had taken Edna aside and told her briefly about his little son and surprising her, Edna had nodded, understanding at once.

'Best for the little lad to be with his grandparents. They've fetched him up from birth. It would be cruel to take him away now.' Her sharp monkey features softened. 'That young man has a sad look about him. It's a terrible price to pay for a moment's folly. I'm right glad you've asked him to his dinner tomorrow. That's what Christmas is supposed to be about.'

Just then, as if on cue, a group of carol singers from the church began to sing outside the door.

'In the bleak mid winter . . .'

Their voices rose clear and melodious into the cold night air.

'I'm *glad* you and Uncle Arnold are here.' Daisy put her arms round her auntie, who stiffened like a steel knitting needle. Not knowing how to cope with that kind of thing.

When Daisy opened the door to David's knock the next

morning it seemed as natural as breathing for her to go straight into his arms.

Her face was flushed, her eyes shone, and in honour of Christmas she was wearing a red jumper and a sprig of holly in her hair. David had forgotten how lovely she was, how warm her smile, how welcoming her manner. How low and husky her voice.

She thought he was fuller in the face, and told him so. He looked more in control of himself, less nervous. And she swore he'd developed an American twang in his voice.

There was no time to be alone, and no *room* to be alone in the cottage bulging with people, especially with the table fully extended with all its extra leaves slotted into place. Besides, the goose was due for another basting and the par-boiled potatoes needed putting round it to give them a crisp brown finish.

Winnie was given the job of introducing Bill to David, and they stood together on the rug, each holding a beer tankard and talking about cars. Daisy was in the middle of a last-minute crisis with the sprouts being ready before the carrots and the gravy coming to the boil before she'd had a chance to turn down the gas.

But at last they were all seated round the table that went back to Oliver Cromwell, with Daisy at the head passing round plates and keeping her eye on the children.

'Don't hold back. Help yourselves whilst it's hot,' she said, and watching her Bill knew that this was what she had been born for. Making people happy, keeping them warm and well fed. Giving of herself. Laughing, talking, her eyes bright as stars in her rosy animated face.

Daisy, sure at last that everyone was served, looked round the table, well content.

Sally was sitting in between Edna and Arnold, leaning first on one then on the other, flirting with them, knowing she was the favourite, accepting it as her right.

Oliver was in between Bill and Mrs Tomlinson, eating too quickly because he was hungry, holding his knife and fork wrongly, though Daisy had lost count of the times she'd showed him how. She saw him turn to Bill and whisper something, and the way Bill shook his head and put up an admonishing finger. Dear Bill. Daisy felt her heart constrict. How different he looked in his brown demob suit worn specially for the occasion. How *wrong* he looked in it.

David was listening to Winnie, who was obviously telling him about the baby. David listened carefully, his fair head inclined towards her – a doctor paying attention to what was said to him.

Later Daisy would ask him to examine Oliver's leg. She wouldn't let him see how worried she was, just put the facts and let him form his own conclusion. He would be frank and decisive, she knew that. This new David who had come back to her was not the broken diffident man who had gone away. He wouldn't be destroyed by what she had to tell him. He was his own man again.

When she brought in the pudding alight with a spoonful of brandy, everyone clapped. When she brought in the cheese and biscuits everyone groaned and said they couldn't manage another thing.

Then, as if at an unspoken command, everyone conspired to leave Daisy and David alone.

Winnie went upstairs to feed the baby, Edna and Arnold settled down on the settee with Sally snuggled between them, Mrs Tomlinson said she'd go back next door for a while to build her fire up, and put the cat out, and Jasper crawled into his basket, round-bellied from too much food.

Bill and Oliver disappeared on a mission of their own. Daisy watched them go, the small boy and the hunched-shouldered man, waited until she saw Bill crouch for Oliver to climb on his back, then went into the kitchen where David had already begun on the washing-up.

'David . . .' He had tied a tea towel round his middle and was swirling the glasses round in the hot water, as naturally and expertly as if he washed up for a living.

'David . . .?' Daisy tried again, but he was telling her about his father, explaining that he wished the old man would retire, but knew that he wouldn't, saying that he'd be glad to be back in England where he could keep an eye on him.

He was washing a plate with exaggerated care, scrubbing at it with the brush, doing it over and over again.

Suddenly they spoke together

'I can't marry you, David.'

'I've met someone else.'

In perfect unison, like choral speaking.

They were laughing when Bill burst into the kitchen, holding on to each other, weak with relief. Not seeing Bill standing there, his face a thunder-cloud.

Daisy lifted her head from David's shoulder to stare at him.

'Bill? What's wrong?' She went to him. 'Oliver's all right. Isn't he?'

From the depths of his misery Bill pushed her away, then caught her by the elbow and swung her round to face him.

'Oliver is a lot more than all right.'

'What are you trying to say, Bill Tattersall?'

'I'll tell you what I'm trying to say, Daisygirl. I tackled him head on about that limp of his. Set him down in the low field and told him the farmer would be letting the young bulls out. Told him he'd better look sharp, then ran on without looking back.'

'You *what*?' Daisy's voice rose to a shout. 'That's the cruellest thing I've heard in my whole life.' She made for the door, but Bill blocked her way.

'There were no young bulls. Haven't been for weeks since the farmer moved them on.'

'But for God's sake, Oliver didn't know that.' Daisy's eyes blazed into his.

'So what did he do? He *ran*. Ran like a small boy should run, lass, but stumbling a little because he's not used that leg properly for a long time. Running, love, then walking normally with me all the way back. He's upstairs now crying on Winnie's shoulder. Getting it out of his system, but he's okay. He'll be as right as rain tomorrow.'

Grim-faced and dignified in the terrible brown demob suit, he held out his hand to David.

'Congratulations. She'll boss you about and let fly at you now and again, but she's the best. I wish you luck. The both of you.'

He touched his forehead as if to push back the leather rim of his beret, and went out the back way. Turning at the door to thank Daisy for his dinner.

'I must go up to Oliver.'

Daisy was so upset she didn't know what she was doing. When Bill had put his hand to his forehead in that involuntary gesture she had wanted to take his hand and hold it to her cheek.

She snatched off her apron, plucked the sprig of holly from her hair, hardly knowing what she did. Accepting only that the sight of Bill walking away from her was breaking her heart.

'David . . .?'

Instantly he was at her side, turning her round and giving her a gentle push. 'Go to him, Daisy. Right now. You'll catch up with him if you hurry.'

He took her old coat from its peg on the wall and put it round her shoulders. Then he went to the door and held it wide.

Bill had walked so quickly he was back at the garage, sitting at his untidy desk in his little office.

'Yes?' He stared at her coldly. 'If you've come to apologize for what happened with Oliver, don't bother. I only did what anyone with an 'aporth of sense should have done long ago.'

Daisy stayed where she was by the door. 'I've not come about Oliver. I should be thanking you for what you did, and when I've calmed down a bit I will.'

'He had you over a barrel.'

'I accept that.'

Bill took a cigarette from the crumpled packet on his desk. 'And you've left the good doctor and your guests to tell me that?'

The elation that Daisy had felt as she ran from the cottage along the uneven pavement and across the road to the garage was fading away. Only the breathlessness remained. The man so calmly lighting a cigarette bore no resemblance to the man with the anguished eyes who had walked out on her not five minutes ago.

Now his eyes seemed to be mocking her. 'Doesn't he mind doing all that washing up on his own? Is he in training for when you're married?'

'We're not getting married,' Daisy said quietly.

Bill drew deeply on the cigarette, stared up at the ceiling and blew a perfect smoke ring. 'So that touching little scene I witnessed was your tender way of consoling him?'

'No it wasn't. He'd just told me that he had met someone else. He hasn't had time to say who she is yet, but I know.'

'You do?'

Daisy nodded, her eyes never leaving his face. 'It's a girl dietician from the hospital in Washington. David kept mentioning her in his letters.'

As she moved further into the room the coat slipped from her shoulders. 'David only *thought* he wanted to marry me. He'd got used to coming to the house when Joshua was alive. Joshua was very good for a man who looked and behaved as if he'd come back from the dead. He taught handicapped children for all his teaching life and David found in Joshua the understanding and comfort he needed. They were very close and when Joshua died I just happened to be there. I was the next best thing. I think I've understood that all along.'

'Are you trying to tell me you don't love David?' Bill looked straight at her.

Tears filled Daisy's eyes. 'Oh, yes, I love him. But not in the way you think. I'm *glad* for him. Happy that he's met someone. *Glad* that someone as nice as him is going to have a second chance.'

'Then why are you crying?'

Daisy choked on a sob. She was despairing, totally undone. This man didn't love her. He was stubbing out his cigarette in the revolting little tin lid, not even bothering to look up at her.

'I'm going. I'm flamin' going.'

The words burst from her in an angry wail. She turned, snatched up her coat from the floor and ran for the door.

'Daisygirl!'

Bill swung her round to face him, forcing her chin up with his hand. The twinkle was back in his eyes.

'Do you want me to tell you how much I love you? Is that what you came for? I'm not a man of poetry as you know, but if I was I would say that merely to look at you fills me with tenderness and the ache of wanting to make love with you. I *wish* I was able to speak of the way your smile warms my heart, and the way your laughter lingers in my head.'

His fingers traced the curve of her mouth, lingered as her lips parted. 'I would say all these things if only I knew how . . .'

His kiss left them both trembling, clinging together, swaying, until gradually they became peaceful again.

It was a long time before they walked back to the cottage and even then they stopped at least a dozen times to kiss and hold each other close.

'Happy, Daisygirl?' Bill asked her as they reached the cottage where the Christmas tree lights shone from the front window.

'More than I ever dreamed it was possible to be,' she whispered.